WINDFALL

WINDFALL

MAXINE PAETRO

PIATKUS

Designed by Laurie Jewell

First published in Great Britain in 1991 by
Judy Piatkus (Publishers) Ltd of
5 Windmill Street, London W1

**The moral right of the author
has been asserted**

*A catalogue record for this book is available
from the British Library*

ISBN 0 7499 0096 2

Printed and bound in Great Britain by
Biddles Ltd, Guildford and King's Lynn

*To my friends
at The Writers Room.*

ACKNOWLEDGMENTS

MY THANKS to these kind people who generously contributed their time and expertise:

Jim Calio, Gene Albert, Charles Lowrey, Lee Kovel, Janet Blackmore, Allison Adato, Fritz Yuvancic, Renata Rizzo-Harvi, Donna Brodie, Al Lane, Freema Gottlieb, Storm Field, Pat Fairris, and Jim Carr.

And special thanks to my brother Tony Paetro and my friend and broker, Lewis Robinson, who taught me about the stock market.

1

WHEN HARRIET BRAINTREE awoke, it was to the sound of sirens. Dean was still asleep, and judging from the narrow slash of light on the windowsill, it was not yet six o'clock. Harrie confirmed her guess by picking up the alarm clock and giving it a bleary glare. Then, since they didn't have to get up for another hour, Harrie prayed for the noise to stop so she could hook her knees behind Dean's and go back to sleep.

But silence would not return to the room. The siren grew louder and was joined by another, and in the way that New Yorkers can listen for danger with their subconscious minds, Harrie waited for the sirens to pass 111 Chester Street. But they did not. With a sharp and sudden stillness, the whining stopped, and then there were heavy footsteps in the hallway of the building. When they halted, the elevator groaned and rumbled.

□

Dean struggled up through the thick part of his slumber. He was aware of Harrie clambering over him, caught a flash of red as she got into his robe. There was a disturbance of some sort and he wished it away, wanting only to sink back into white sheets and darkness. But Harrie was pulling at his arm, shaking him. "What is it?" he asked, his mind stuck in the groove it had occupied when he'd been pitched into sleep last night. "Did you win?"

"What?" Harrie said. "What did you say?"

"Did you win the lottery?" Dean asked again. He opened his eyelids a crack and saw Harrie's face. It was drained of blood, and her hair, tousled from sleep, was squashed to one side, making Harrie seem unbalanced, about to tip over.

"The lottery? No. I didn't . . ."

"Harrie. What's the matter?"

"It's Mr. Tuckman," she said. "He's dead."

2

———◻———

*I*T WAS UNBELIEVABLE," Harrie said, fastening her seat belt furiously. She turned to Dean. "They stuffed him into that ambulance like he was a load of bricks. He was a person. He should be having his breakfast right now."

Dean checked his rearview mirror, then pulled the Saab out onto Chester Street. He glanced at Harrie. She'd dressed hastily in a T-shirt and jeans, hung the funny-looking off-the-shoulder gown on the hook in back, and slammed her door hard. She hadn't combed her hair and it didn't look as if she was going to.

"Do you think he felt it? . . . Of course he did," Harrie said, answering herself. She clutched her chest as though she might be feeling the fatal surge of pain herself. "I can't stand that he woke up alone to die."

Dean steered around a garbage truck that was taking up three quarters of the street. He reached out a hand blindly and touched Harrie's arm. "I'm sure it was over before he knew what was going on."

"I don't know. Anyone else, maybe, but there's no way death could have snuck up on Mr. Tuckman. He's as sharp as a knife."

"Was."

"Was. . . . Wonderful timing, you have to admit. I mean, it would have been nice if he'd given me some notice. Given me a chance to get used to the idea."

"That bum."

Harrie nodded. "What a pal." How was she supposed to believe that her friend was dead, that she couldn't call him later and tell him about the wedding? She'd just had dinner with him last week and he'd looked as fit as an athlete. They'd been sitting out on Mr. Tuck-

12

man's terrace, drinking wine, Sidney and Angel crab-walking up their arms . . . "Shit."

"What?" Dean accelerated past the garbage truck. He was no longer thinking about the old gentleman who had died. He wasn't even thinking about Harrie. He was thinking that he was driving the car in the wrong direction; he wanted to be going to Connecticut but, unfortunately, was going to Long Island. He was thinking about what he was giving up in order to go to this wedding that he didn't want to go to, and he was concluding that sometimes you got what you wanted, sometimes you got what you needed, and sometimes you got a sharp pain in the butt for no good reason whatsoever.

"Shit," Harrie said again. "The birds. Who's going to take care of his birds?"

"Haven't you got his keys?"

"Yeah. Okay. There's an idea. I'll take care of them until someone claims them."

"Good. That's very nice of you." Dean patted Harrie's knee and turned the car onto Seventh Avenue.

"But who's going to claim *him*?"

"Who?"

"Mr. Tuckman."

"Harrie, calm down. I'm sure someone will be notified."

"Oh, God. This isn't right. He's all *alone*."

"Har, it's an empty body. He's not aware of anything anymore."

"You're so sentimental, Dean."

"Yeah, well I'm sorry. I'm just trying to make you feel better."

"It's weird going to my sister's wedding with Mr. Tuckman lying in a stainless-steel drawer at St. Vincent's, don't you think?"

"There's nothing you can do right now, hon."

"I know."

"Do you want me to turn around? Do you want to forget the wedding?"

Harrie shook her head no.

"Are you sure?"

"My mom's counting on me. And Julie would go bug-nuts."

The plastic dry-cleaning bag over Harrie's dress flapped noisily in the breeze. "Get that, will you?" Dean said.

Harrie angled around and secured the flapping tail end of the plastic with the shoe box containing her green satin shoes. Then she turned back around and rolled down her window all the way. She sighed deeply, remembering the English sixpence Mr. Tuckman had given her to give Julie as a good-luck charm, and then she thought about how Julie, who'd said she was never getting married, was indeed getting married. Not that Alan was such a prize but still, Julie had fallen in love with him and, as these things sometimes went, Alan had asked Julie to marry him—and Julie had said yes. And from that thought it was a very small leap to wonder what it would take for the same, fairly ordinary series of events to happen to her.

Harrie turned her head to look at Dean and concluded for the thousandth time that Dean was born to be her husband. He loved her and she loved everything about him: the way he combed his fine, black hair straight back, the way his glasses sat on the bridge of his elegant nose, the way his fingers curved ever-so-slightly outward, the way his kisses on the back of her neck caused her knees to buckle, the way, when he was excited, the rims of his ears turned the color of a Betty Prior rose, and the way he loved her when she made him laugh. And all of these things were but the beginning of the way she felt about Dean.

She'd never loved anyone the way she loved Dean. It was as though she'd loved Dean before she met him, and having met him, having been with him for the last two years, Harrie felt there was nothing about him she didn't know. And knowing him so well was what made her feel that she would certainly know and love him for the rest of her life. So the big question was, would they get married?

Sometimes Harrie could not imagine anything else, it was just the when that seemed unclear. Other times Dean seemed to step away from her, hold himself back, and when he did that, Harrie's first thought was always that she'd said or done something that showed her up as the hick she sometimes felt herself to be. Other times, when she wasn't feeling paranoid, she thought it was getting married in and of itself that frightened Dean. Whenever she mentioned the word "marriage," he got quiet and vague, and seemed to fluff himself up and fold himself down, like a sparrow warding off the rain. "I'm just not ready yet," he'd say, and then he'd mumble about his job and how he didn't feel solid enough yet to take on the responsibility of a family. And that was understandable—wanting to feel secure in the world before making a commitment to another person. But couldn't he see that being married to her would be an asset, not a liability?

The thing was, she was so happy with Dean, she hated to push him where he wouldn't go. If he wasn't ready, she could wait. But the waiting would be easier if she knew what the outcome would be; or at least what the obstacles were to moving in together, making future plans. She knew Dean so well, there was just this one thing she didn't know. Why couldn't he make a commitment to her, to them? Sometimes it seemed to her that one small piece was missing— a task that would have to be done, a spell that would have to be worked, or a time that would have to come.

As they turned onto Houston Street, heading toward the place she still considered home, Harrie recalled the conversation she'd had with her mother just the week before. It had been a day so hot the air had shimmered and the plants had drooped, their leaves parched and hanging down like dogs' tongues. She'd been sitting in the kitchen of her parents' house in Spode, a dry speck of a town on Long Island's North Shore. She and her mother, their heads close together, had been checking off details in the elaborate plans for Julie's wedding, when her mother had reached out her hand. A coffee cup, suddenly jarred, had rattled in its saucer. A look of certainty had lit her mother's sun-lined face.

And Harrie remembered her mother's promise. . . .

3

---□---

CAKES!" Dottie Braintree had shrieked from the front porch of
the farmhouse, calling Harrie by the remnants of her baby name,
Babycakes; still calling her that twenty-seven years after an indignant
kindergartner had stamped her foot and declared, "I'm not a baby
anymore!" The older woman had gone to her daughter, embraced
her and at the same time scolded her for wearing white linen which
would have to be dry-cleaned when she could have worn any old
thing on the train.

Harrie had smiled and put her arm around her mother's narrow
waist. It had felt so good to be there. Two minutes in her driveway
and she had begun to feel that certain calm comfort of being safe and
at home. Together, Harrie and her mother had walked past the pansies
and geraniums planted in buckets and old crockery pots beside the
steps to the porch, and entered the coolness of the kitchen.

As it had always been, the kitchen was clearly Dottie Braintree's
domain. The room was dominated by a scarred oak farm table flanked
by a half dozen unmatched chairs, and in the center of the table,
surrounded by vegetables and reading matter and garden tools, was
Dottie's television which brought the world of daytime soap operas
to the hub of the Braintree Nursery. Harrie hung her handbag over
the arm of the chair that was "hers," and pushed the heap of snap
beans, the odd knobby squash, and the piles of catalogs until she
found room on the table for her book bag.

Dottie turned the volume of the television down, went to a cal-
endar hanging from the wall and made a note. Then, pointing to a
watercolor painting Harrie had made at a time in her life when the
best colors were black and red, she said, "Remember when you did
this?"

Harrie laughed. "I don't exactly remember, no. How can you keep this old stuff?"

"How could I throw it away, you mean." Dottie gazed fondly at "Red House with Black Tree," which hung as part of a collection of other baby Braintree memorabilia: finger paintings, construction-paper turkeys, dried wildflowers tied and hung up with string. A wall of glass-paned cupboards housed retired teddy bears, mixed sets of dinnerwear, a birdhouse, and several gallon jars of seashells which Harrie had collected as though each pearly piece were a precious stone. "It makes me feel like you're going to come barreling down the stairs any minute and ask for milk and cookies."

On this particular day, Ivy, the youngest Braintree, was at the beach. The second-oldest, Doug, who lived just down the road, was out working in the fields with his father. Julie, the oldest, was in her bedroom, stretched across her single bed, engaged in an intimate phone conversation with her childhood friend and bridesmaid-to-be Paula Devine. And Harrie, her book bag with its two unread manuscripts forgotten on the kitchen table, was stringing beans with her mother and catching up on the soaps just as she'd done during school vacations when she had lived at home.

"You're kidding," Harrie was saying, in mock horror. "She wouldn't do that. Marilyn is a snowflake."

"She did, though." Dottie went to the marred linoleum counter and returned with a pot of coffee. "I told you she couldn't be trusted."

"But her son! To leave him alone with Derek." Harrie shook her head, then grinned at her mother. "She has no shame. No shame at all. If you'd done that to Dougie, you'd have been hauled off and locked up for life."

"I know it."

"God," said Harrie. "Stop watching for a couple of years and the best person goes right to hell." Both women laughed.

"I wish I could get Julie to watch the stories with me," Dottie said wistfully. "It's more fun when there's someone around to talk to. Like now."

"Julie's been on the phone for an hour," Harrie said, ignoring the invitation to choose up sides. "I should go up and say hi."

"Oh, stay with me awhile. She'll come down when she's ready." Then Dottie pulled lists from her apron pocket and smoothed them out on the table. She took a pencil from a chipped blue creamer and shifted an errant butternut squash. "Move your chair closer and help me," she said. "Look here." And then she named the things that had been done: the champagne ordered, the names of her neighbors and what dishes they would bring to the reception, the alterations that had been completed on the dresses Harrie and Paula and Ivy would wear and the color of the ribbons to be tied in the branches of the tubbed little trees. "Have I forgotten anything? I don't want to find out I forgot something at the last minute."

Harrie pulled her camisole away from her skin. Air from the portable fan circulated faintly, barely touching her. Would it ever be cool again? she wondered. What was Dean doing? How had Julie figured out how to get married and she had not? "I think you've got it covered," she said. There was a long pause as Harrie watched her mother get ready to ask the burning question.

"So, how is everything?"

"How is everything with Dean, you mean?"

"Mmmm," Dottie responded noncommittally.

Harrie fanned herself with a lingerie catalog. "Oh, you know. I'm in total love with him."

"Has he said anything serious?"

"Mother!"

"Has he?"

"You've got wedding bells on the brain, you know that?"

"Don't be upset with me, honey. I was just asking."

"I'm not upset," she said. But as usual her mother had nailed her. Julie's impending marriage only made her more aware that she wasn't married. Not married, not engaged, and she was getting older by the minute. She glanced down at her stomach, which had recently taken to laying a fold of itself in her lap. She hadn't thought it would happen to her, but it was happening. She was losing her looks, and once you lost them, you never got them back again. And of course, just to add heat to the situation, there was the baby issue. Even if Dean were to be suddenly and critically struck with wedding fever, she'd be at least thirty-four before she'd have her first child—pretty late to start having the four kids she'd once dreamed of having. Time was slipping away so surely, she could almost hear it, and the sound was of rocks sliding downhill and becoming an avalanche.

"I'm so frustrated," she blurted without looking at her mother. "I know Dean loves me, but why should he get married? What does he need a wife for anyway? He knows I love him. He knows I'm all his. He can buy his own groceries, make his own bed, make his own pasta, for God's sake. Why should he give up his single life and marry me?"

"Is that what he says?"

"No. He doesn't say that. He just won't talk about marriage. You know how men can be. They like to be free for whatever reason, and if that should change, if he should decide to get married one day, there are women all over New York just dying for a terrific guy like Dean. They have radar. They have infrared blowguns. I've seen women climb all over him at parties, like he's sugar and they're ants, and he loves that. And I'm getting fat. Look at this," she said, standing, grabbing a handful of thigh and wiggling it. "Donkey kicks do *nothing* to this. And look at this." She pinched her cheeks hard. "Why am I getting these hamster pouches? What do I need them for?" She threw herself back into the chair.

"Now you stop that. Dean loves you. That's reason enough."

"I don't know. I mean, I know he loves me, but maybe that's not reason enough. I'm not getting any younger, you know."

"Cakes, you're still a young woman. Your sister is five years older than you and she's getting married."

"Terrific."

"I don't understand why you all are so hard on Alan. He's a very nice young man."

"He's fine." He's fine for a blah, boring, best-Julie-could-do-at-her-age-with-her-looks kind of guy, Harrie thought. "I like him," she lied. "My future bro-in-law."

Dottie laughed and hugged her daughter.

"What's so funny, if you don't mind my asking?" Harrie snapped, pulling away.

"Hey, hey, now. What is all this?"

How was she supposed to tell her mother that when she'd told Dean she loved him that morning, he'd just wrapped her in his arms and said, "I know, I know," instead of, "I love you too," as if her love for him made him *sad*.

"You didn't have a fight, did you?" Dottie asked.

"No. Sorry I'm being such a pill. I must have PMS or something."

"You want some Tylenol?"

"No, thanks."

"With Julie getting married, you're just feeling left behind."

"No I'm not."

"You could have been married. You could have married that hard-luck boyfriend of yours from high school, and instead of living a glamorous life in New York City, you'd be Mrs. Mark Weybourne, and you'd be standing on your feet all day and hauling feed sacks out to people's trucks and living right here in Spode. Not that I'd have minded sitting across the dinner table from that cross-eyed young man every Sunday for the rest of my life, but I don't think being Mrs. Seed and Feed would have fit you just right."

Harrie laughed, then wondered out loud, "You think if I'd married Mark, Jennifer Moffat would have moved to New York and become a literary agent?" Then she lost herself in the image her mother had painted. She was scooping grain into a burlap sack, when her mother reached across the table to take her hand and, in doing so, jarred her coffee cup almost out of its saucer.

Harrie looked up, startled by the sound. "What is it, Mom?"

Dottie steadied her cup and looked directly into her daughter's eyes. "It's going to be all right, honey. Everything's going to work out fine."

"What do you mean? With me and Dean?"

"Of course."

"I want to be with him always," Harrie said, her voice in a register reserved for the whole truth, nothing but the truth.

Dottie put her arm around her daughter and pulled her close. "You and Dean are going to have a beautiful wedding. We'll have white tulle everything and live doves in golden cages on the tables," she crooned.

"Really?" Harrie pulled back to look at her mother's face. And somehow she'd become twelve again. Food was not her enemy. The refrigerator was stocked with bologna and mayonnaise and chocolate layer cake, and she could eat anything she wanted and it wouldn't stick to her anywhere. Her small lavender bedroom upstairs was filled with romance novels and boxes with false bottoms, and rhinestone bracelets, and marionettes. And her mother had a way of knowing things. Her mother knew if baby birds were going to live or die. She knew if the milk was bad without having to smell it. She knew that Marilyn of *The Night and the Day* would abandon her adopted son. And she'd known that Alan Bieder would marry her sister Julie. "Promise?"

"Is the sky blue?" Dottie asked, setting her face into an expression of certainty. She leaned forward and kissed her daughter's cheek. "Now, go on," she said, rising, brushing her hands against her apron. "Go on up and see your sister while I make lunch."

"Okay." Her mother knew something and had made her a promise. She and Dean would have doves on the tables and white tulle everywhere. How would that go over at the Waldorf? "Thanks, Mom," she'd said, and then she'd bolted from the kitchen and run up the stairs.

⊡

"Whatcha thinking about, hon?" Dean asked.

Harrie started guiltily and dug around in her handbag. "Mr. Tuckman," she said.

"Yeah."

"I'm going to miss that guy."

"I know you are."

"Want some gum?"

"Sure."

Harrie handed Dean a stick and put her makeup bag on the seat beside her. Then she took out her hairbrush, bowed her head over her lap, and began to brush her hair.

⊡

Dean threw the car into neutral and waited for the light to change. As he waited, he watched Harrie run her brush up through her soft brown hair. He adored the shape of Harrie's head. When her hair was brushed off her face and neck, this extremely lovely and otherwise unseen line, which began below her nape and curved delightfully up to her crown, was revealed. He liked to think the back of Harrie's skull was his personal territory, that no one had seen it before, not even Harrie.

A horn honked behind them. Dean put the car into gear and

started forward. He must really love Harrie or he wouldn't be trekking out to Spode in the ninety-two-degree heat to watch Julie Braintree get married. He'd be out in Wilton, Connecticut, at Tyson Wales's annual male-bonding event, where he was supposed to be. And he'd be doing his best to grind Bob McCandless's ugly face into the mud.

As Dean accelerated the car into the lane farthest to the left on the Long Island Expressway he remembered the verbal pounding he'd taken from McCandless the night before. . . .

4

---□---

*D*EAN HAD LEFT WORK at a respectable eight o'clock. The day had been brutal, the market responding to the latest murmurings in the Gulf by dropping thirty points. It was astounding, Dean thought, how people expected their brokers to know things before the President of the United States knew them, and too many of his clients had called in with hysterical threats and accusations. The one client who hadn't called was his father—no surprise. Robertson Carrothers's portfolio represented more than half of Dean's total client holdings. But ironically, even though his father's portfolio had lost a half million bucks that day, his father hadn't seemed to mind. That was because his father kept his *real* portfolio at Morgan Stanley with his *real* broker, a man who could presumably predict the future.

Dean had stood under the building's massive overhang and breathed in the sharp night air. He'd shifted the focus of his eyes into infinite space—a great feeling after the hours of keeping his eyeballs glued to his computer screen. And it was good to stand under the moon and stars and get a little perspective on the stock market as compared with the universe.

After a few minutes of star basking, Dean's stomach growled and then he considered his options. One, go home. But he wasn't ready yet to be alone. Alone, he'd have to think about his father's love and his father's money, and he'd had enough of those thoughts that day. He considered option two, to buzz Harrie and go to her apartment, and that would be nice except for one thing. Harrie wouldn't let him get away with "I had a nice day, how was yours?" She would know that he'd been slam-dunked—just by looking at his face or by divining something from the way he hung up his tie—and then she'd tug his day out of him one word at a time until he'd given her everything including the skin and the bones. Then, when he was completely empty, she'd wrap him in angel wings, and if she did that, he would break down and *really* feel sorry for himself, and he currently felt sorry enough for twenty guys. So he wasn't going to go to Harrie's. Which meant the last alternative would be the best one. He'd go to Nelson's Bar and joke around with the guys and, while he was at it, sedate himself with beer. Laughter and beer were a formula guaranteed to sand down the memory of a bad day until it was too smooth to remember.

As Dean stood in the dark a mild rain, almost an atmospheric afterthought, began. He unfurled his umbrella. Then he stepped to the curb and cut through the long file of hired-by-the-hour blue sedans and smug black limousines. His glasses had fogged up, but he didn't need to see to find the way. He crossed against a light, turned a corner, and found himself thinking about his two older brothers: Rob junior, real estate entrepreneur and big-time shopping mall success story, and middle brother Henry, an artist whose canvases jumped from their easels into the eager arms of rock stars and CEOs. And Dean tried once again to understand how his own brothers could have outdistanced him so completely he could hardly be considered of the same caste. Where was his genius? Why wasn't he a Wall Street wizard? They'd all come from the same gene pool, hadn't they? Or had he been left in a basket at the front door with a note pinned to his diaper? "Pleeze TaKe gud cAre of my BaBy." Dean shook his head. He knew the truth.

Rob and Henry had made it because they were good at what they did. Simple as that. And they didn't have totally blissful lives. They had problems. Rob had a bum back and a shitty backhand, and Henry was depressed a lot; whereas he had a springy back and a first-class backhand, and was only depressed sporadically. Not more than once every twelve hours. Oh, and he had this small learning disability. Not much of a problem as long as you didn't have to read too much. Actually, his life didn't depress him. Why should it? Just because he had a secondhand car, a heavily mortgaged loft apartment in an iffy neighborhood, worked in a business that these days was a lot like betting on the horses and shoveling their manure at the same time? It occurred to him, not for the first time, that he'd get more enjoyment out of his job if only he didn't demand so much of himself. If only his father weren't so important to him. Hey, if only he'd taken up ballet, he'd be spending his days sweating, jumping around in a leotard, and hoisting lithe young lovelies into the air instead of draining his brain into a computer. If only.

Chip Martin—confidant, good guy extraordinaire—had advised, "Float, Dean-o. Float. Just use it and be used by it. Let it move around you. None of this is really about you anyway." Float. What a neat image. He imagined himself faceup on a raft drifting along on blue-green water off the coast of Antigua, the sun toasting his skin to a beautiful—and because this was a fantasy—nonhazardous brown. And then he found himself walking down the steps to Nelson's Bar.

⊡

The staircase opened down into the dark, smoky room. The bar itself was an island centered under a pressed-tin ceiling, surrounded by a tight circle of traders and clerks jammed from the bar all the way back to the door. A fog of smoke wafted toward the pin lights in the ceiling, eddying above the static crowd below. Stretching his neck, Dean scanned for Chip Martin's reddish hair, usually visible above head level like a buoy on a restless sea. Then Dean waded through the pinstripes and glen plaids, raising his arms at times, until the mob thinned and he stood at the far perimeter of the room where small tables were fixed, like islands. As close to Antigua as he was going to get that night.

"Dean-o," a voice called to his right.

"Hey," Dean responded, waving to Chip and three of their co-workers who were loosely gathered around the table, connected by the plate of pizza crusts at its center. Dean pulled up a chair and signaled the waiter for a drink. The three men and the woman had a vague look about them, Dean thought, as if they'd been drinking for a good long time. "Thank God. A transfusion," he said, lifting a bottle of beer and a glass from the waiter's tray. "Did you catch the closing price on Gramco?" he muttered to Chip.

Chip glanced at Dean warily, his expression that of a person waiting to hear bad news. "Not really. I was having my own problems. It went toes on you?"

Dean made the high-pitched sound of a bomb dropping, then exploding, before he chugged beer from the bottle.

"Uh-oh. You bought a few shares for Papa, did you not?"

"Sixty thousand, more or less."

"Holy cow."

"Yeah."

"Well, the bright side is, you have a client who buys sixty thousand shares."

"Some bright side."

"So, what did you tell the old man?"

"Buy, buy, buy, of course. The stock's getting cheaper by the minute."

Chip smiled and Dean smiled back, the perpetual optimism of the stockbroker. If it tanks, buy. Never admit a bad bet.

Dean said, "Funny thing is, I feel guilty and stupid, and my father doesn't give a damn. He told me to do whatever I want. He's not even going to miss the money. It kills me. If I were a different kind of guy, I could be hosing my biggest client and getting sleep all at the same time."

A waiter bearing a tray of pizza squares swept up an empty plate and replaced it with a full one. Instantly, four hands reached out and before Dean could snag a morsel, there was nothing left to snag. No one seemed to notice. "Hey," he said to the empty plate, "I'm starved."

"Did you hear? Laura's leaving us," Chip announced despondently. No one could look as despondent as Chip. His homely but lovable face was pleated with premature and hereditary folds of skin, giving him the look of a Chinese dog.

"She couldn't be," Dean said, unconsciously mimicking Chip's wrinkled look of disbelief. "What's happened?" He turned to the slender ash blonde in the white silk dress.

"She got bought," Bob McCandless offered before Laura could speak.

"Stolen," Ed Hanlon seconded.

"Where're you going?"

Laura Taft dropped a pizza crust in a plate, stretched lazily, and leaned back in her chair. As her breasts rose every man at the table watched, then looked guiltily down at his drink as her stretch ended and she folded her arms gracefully onto the table. "Prudential-Bache," she said with a smile. "I'll be just down the street. We can wave hello."

"I don't get it," Dean said. "What did they do to deserve you?"

Laura grinned. "Gonna miss me?" she blurted, then blushing, lowered her head, letting a sheet of oat-colored hair drop over her eyes like a curtain at the end of the first act.

Dean twisted in his seat. This was news. She liked him! Huh. Amazing thing about chemistry. First time he'd met Laura—and he still remembered the first time, a meeting in Wales's office—she'd been sitting directly opposite him at the blue-slate conference table, the shadows of her nipples staring holes right through her silk shirt and into his chest. He'd noticed the nipples, and her athletic conformation, and her pale skin so thin he could see the veins in her temples, and he'd thought, I wish I were attracted to this girl. What a couple they would make. Laura was the kind of woman who could make a difference to his career, elevate his profile, mark him a winner in the world of men. But wish all he wanted to, nothing about Laura moved him.

Conversely, frustratingly, the first time he'd met Harrie—and he remembered that time, too, in great detail—everything moved. There'd been a party, he'd been with someone, Barbara he thought, and Harrie was by the guacamole dip consuming taco chips with gusto. Her hair was falling out of her Gibson girl hairdo; an antique piano scarf was draped around her shoulders, the fringe falling all around her and about a hundred twinkly brooches skewering the cloth. He'd been moved, all right. He'd been pulled by an invisible cord at his midsection, right to her side.

Dean deliberately blinked away the vision of Harrie and filled his eyes with Laura. Still nothing. But anyhow, Laura was a good office buddy. She was a little younger and a bit more successful than he, and that should have made him feel competitive with her, but that wasn't how he felt. He liked her. She was open and not aggressive with him, and they'd shared information back and forth for a couple of years, very casually, no one keeping score. That was neat. Dean smiled at her. "Sure," he said. "I'm gonna miss you a lot."

"I told Laura she should have waited until after the 'Macho Olympics,' " McCandless said. "Her defection's a big loss for the blue team. Isn't that right, Carrothers?"

Dean's pleasurable thoughts evaporated. He stiffened his shoulders, then filled his glass. McCandless was like a rhinoceros, a big dumb rhino that charged anything. The difference between the two was that rhinos charged defensively while McCandless simply loved the sight of a crushed jeep. He was referring to the annual competition at the country estate of Tyson Wales, CEO of Hamilton, Warner, Pierson, and Wales, held for the purpose of sharpening the claws and fangs of the top moneymakers in the firm. Team Day was a day of recognition, celebration, bravado, and, in some cases, shame. In a single day a player's reputation could soar or it could plummet. Dean excelled at the silly games Wales created for this event, and it was here that he distinguished himself. Somehow, to Wales, the trophies Dean helped win for his team evened out his less spectacular performance with the bulls and the bears. It wouldn't be crazy to assume that the trophies and his father's account were what had kept him employed during the crash of '87. So you could say Team Day was important to him, but even failing at Team Day was preferable to not showing, which is what he'd have to do this year. Julie Braintree was getting married, don't you know? Management made note. McCandless knew this. Everyone did.

"Your tie's in your scotch, asshole," Dean said coldly.

"Thanks, buddy," McCandless replied. "Ahhh," he sighed in exaggerated relief as he mopped his brow with the damp silk, then flipped it over his shoulder. He resumed his sickening, sloppy attention to Laura. "You know my philosophy," he said. "Keep moving forward. Keep getting better things."

"The man's a product of generations of breeding," Chip said quietly, his voice tinged with wonder.

"Inbreeding, you mean," Dean muttered. He glared at the oblivious McCandless.

"Sometimes people just disappear," Chip said with a deranged look in his eye. He took on a Bela Lugosi vampire voice. "These things can be arranged."

"Uh-huh," Dean agreed. "You know, I was really looking forward to getting my fists into his guts in the lard wrestling."

"I was betting on you, Dean-o."

"I'd love to show you the view from my terrace," McCandless

growled, wolflike, while taking Laura's hand. "Maybe you'd like to come for a test drive in my new Supra."

Laura smiled wanly and pulled her hand away.

"Which team are you on, Dean?" Hanlon asked, his bland face innocent of motive. Hanlon was a newcomer. He was full weeks away from political sophistication.

"I can't make it this year," Dean replied. "I've got a wedding to attend." A few crummy days would have made a big difference, but as it happened, he'd already told Harrie he would go to the wedding before the Team Day date was announced. He'd known the wedding was a major deal to Harrie, but how major had not been clear until he tried to beg off. Actually, she'd been nice and understanding, but underneath that understanding was a very hurt and disappointed woman who wanted her boyfriend to spend time with her family and participate in an important family celebration. And since he loved her, he'd done the only thing he could reasonably do. He'd taken a ding to his career.

Dean swirled the beer in his glass and stared into its amber depths. He had an awful premonition that this wedding was going to push the two of them a little closer to the end. Women went gaga at weddings. He pictured Harrie sweeping his face with soft, moony glances and imagining the two of them joining hands, exchanging rings—and he was nowhere near doing that, no way, no how. He decided once again that he was going to have to be more explicit with Harrie, very soon. Tell her seriously that marriage was out for the two of them. The honorable thing would be to break up with her, but how could he do it? How could he explain to this utterly loving woman that although he loved her, marrying her would seal his fate, close off his options, and he wasn't ready to do that? Not with her.

The floor seemed to move beneath his chair as he thought of being without Harrie. He grabbed the table edge and glanced furtively at his companions. Damnit. He loved her. Why did he have to make a lifelong commitment? If only things could stay just as they were without hurting anyone: the kisses and homey nights of TV dinners, the two of them bundled in white cotton sheets and soft white blankets. The conflict was driving him nuts. And then, suddenly, Dean wanted to be with Harrie instead of pinned between his colleagues, all of them less fortunate souls with nowhere else to go.

Dean noticed that Laura had taken off her earrings, and the bow at her neck had become untied. She'd gotten looped. McCandless was florid. Chip was moribund. And Hanlon had slunk down so low in his seat he looked like a teenager. This after-work drink was becoming a slumber party, and he hadn't eaten as much as a sausage. He wondered if Harrie would still be awake.

"Stop," Laura said sharply as she pushed Bob McCandless away.

"Time to go," Dean said meaningfully to Chip.

Chip sucked in his cheeks. "I've been thinking about it," he said, his words coming one at a time, "and I honestly can't remember where I left the car."

"Try again."

"Okay." Chip stared off into smoky space.

After a silent minute or two, Dean probed, "Is it in the lot next to the office?"

"That lot was full, I do remember that."

"The one near the Korean restaurant?"

"I must have a ticket."

"Good thinking."

Chip patted his pockets, removed his wallet, painstakingly examined the contents: a driver's license; a photo of his cat; women's phone numbers, each neatly written on a separate slip of paper with a wide-nibbed fountain pen. "Is this it?" he asked, pushing the manila slip across the table to Dean.

Dean adjusted his glasses. The time and date were stamped in violet ink along the bottom of the parking stub. "You got it," he said. "I'm driving."

"I'll call a car," McCandless announced, pulling up his suspenders, picking up his jacket from the floor. "Don't worry about me and Laura. I'll give her a lift."

"We're taking Laura," Dean said. No way he was leaving Laura at McCandless's mercy.

"Right," Chip agreed. "Dean's our designated driver."

Laura flashed Dean an appreciative smile and stood up shakily. There was a thunderous sound as five chairs scraped the wooden floor. Then, like a herd of dazed buffalo, the five staggered purposefully out of Nelson's Bar.

◘

Dean remembered that he'd gone to Harrie's directly after dropping off his co-workers. Harrie had welcomed him with the angel wings he had foreseen, and then she'd made spaghetti and salad and given him a massage, and when the headache that had overtaken him in the car subsided, they'd made love like a pair of soft old bears. He'd fallen asleep as Harrie waited for the lottery drawing in the totally expectant way she had of believing anything was possible, even winning millions of dollars when the odds were four hundred million to one. And as he drifted off to sleep, nestled against her body, he'd found himself wondering what it was about this wonderful woman that made him fight so hard against her.

◘

"It's the next exit," Harrie said now from the seat beside him.

"I see it," Dean said, flicking on the directional signal.

Moments later Dean dropped Harrie at the Calvary Church and drove off to park his car in the heart of downtown Spode.

5

———□———

JULIE STARED at the face in the mirror. She hated the way she looked. Her face was blotchy, her chest was blotchy, even the mirror giving her this less-than-passing grade was blotchy. She dabbed concealer on a welt on her chin, rubbed off the excess, dampened a tissue, rubbed some more, dabbed again, then threw the tube of cosmetic across the Formica counter and wailed. "Mother, *do* something."

"Honey. You've got hives, that's all. You're just nervous. Lie down for a few minutes. Lie down and let me put a cool washcloth on your forehead."

"Hives!" Julie shook off her mother's soothing hand. "Make them wait," she said urgently. "Make them wait. I'm not going out there like this. I look like a waffle. I look like the bottom of a running shoe. I look like a tire tread. I'm a mess. This was all your idea. I'm not going out there, I don't care what anyone says, I will not be embarrassed this way." She threw down her glasses and cried into her cupped hands.

"Julie." Harrie put an arm around her sister. "Get a grip. What do you think, there's a firing squad out there? This is your wedding day."

"I know, I know," Julie wept.

"It's the heat," Dottie said, wringing out a washcloth.

"You're scared," Paula offered. "I was scared too when I married Lane. I think even when I married Ronnie. It'll be over soon, and you'll be fine, and later, much later, you'll get bored and you'll wonder why you ever—"

"She's scared 'cause Alan's a wienie."

"Ivy, gag yourself," Harrie said to her younger sister, who was now leaning nonchalantly against the bathroom wall, flower-topped

32

hairpiece clinging to the side of her head by the strength of a single hairpin. Most of the time Ivy was so quiet, so self-contained, you really had to work to get her to say anything. Then once in a while she'd utter a few words, and they were the exact words you wished she'd kept to herself.

"Julie dear, let's go over there." Dottie pointed to the cracked Leatherette chaise longue. The ocher paint in this underground room just sucked all the color out of people and turned their skin to mud. No wonder Julie thought she looked bad in here.

Dottie eased Julie into a prone position and carefully arranged the satiny folds of her daughter's gown so it wouldn't crease. She admired the blizzard of seed pearls stitched onto the bodice and fingered the lace trim edging the bell-shaped sleeves. What she wouldn't have done to have a dress like this when she got married! Three hundred and twenty-eight dollars. Bill had just looked at her when she told him and, without saying a word, had turned and walked out of the house. Remembering, Dottie swallowed. The wedding cost as much as a down payment on a new pickup truck which they sorely needed, but Bill had understood. Julie had never really had anything special before this, and here was her big day and she couldn't even enjoy it. Dottie went to the sink, dampened the cloth, and returned to the chaise. Julie had a way of huffing and puffing, then going completely frail sometimes, just collapsing under the weight of her own bones. Dottie stroked the arm of her thirty-seven-year-old child, who at this moment resembled nothing so much as a broken snowy egret lying alongside the road. "Let's just be quiet now," she said, putting the cloth over her daughter's eyes.

"This is crazy, crazy," Julie muttered. "This is someone else's life. I have a different life. I have a life that I'm in charge of."

"I just don't understand, honey," Dottie said helplessly. "She looks beautiful, doesn't she, girls?"

"Of course. Beautiful," the two sisters responded in unison.

"That's not the point," Julie said loudly. She tore the cloth from her face and struggled to sit up. "You just don't understand and I can't explain it to you."

Dottie shook her head and stood, and as she did so the thousands of pink bugle beads attached to her dress shimmered in the fluorescent light.

"You girls make her just sit for a minute," she said, her face crinkled in agitation. "And Cakes, you help Julie with her makeup. You're so good at that. I've got to go upstairs. People will be wondering . . . Honey." She tilted up her daughter's chin. "Juliana Moonflower. You look beautiful. Your dress looks like it was made for you. You could be a royal princess, you really could."

"I don't feel like I know him. It feels crazy to get married to someone I don't even—"

"The way I remember it, you've known Alan Bieder since you were in the second grade," Dottie said.

"I don't think he even likes me, but why should he? I look like a bunch of ants made a picnic out of my face."

"Oh, you do not, you nut case," said Harrie. "Go on up," she said to her mother, pushing her gently toward the door. "We've got it under control."

Dottie shot a last bewildered look around the ladies' room. "Everything's going to be just fine," she mumbled to herself. Then, beads swinging with her jerky steps, she wobbled on unaccustomed high heels toward the stairs.

⊡

"Honestly, I don't get it," Harrie said to Julie. "You're getting *married*. All you've talked about for the last year is Alan, Alan, Alan."

"I never told this to anyone."

The sister and the best friend paused in their ministrations, fastened their gaze on Julie's face.

Julie looked around, thought about speaking and changed her mind. "I can't tell you." She covered her face and eased herself prone. "I should relax. I'm getting married in a few minutes."

"Julie, what is it?" Ideas flashed through Harrie's mind, all of them having to do with sex—something she could hardly imagine Julie doing with anyone. Sex seemed like too much fun for Julie. And too messy. "What were you going to say?"

Julie sighed. Eventually her voice, muffled by the cloth, emerged. "He spits," she said.

"At what?" Harrie asked.

"When he talks. He spits when he talks."

Harrie looked blankly at Julie, then at Paula, then back to Julie. Ivy, having gagged herself, grunted in the corner.

"You mean like—" Harrie couldn't finish the sentence. How embarrassing, if not exactly a surprise. Her fastidious sister. What if Dean were a spitter?

"I shouldn't have told you."

"Everybody's got some little flaw. Nobody's perfect, you know," Paula said from her perch on the dressing table ledge. She half turned to the mirror as if summoned by her own flaws: a space between her front teeth, and a nose that looked as though her Maker had pressed it with His finger and said, "You, girl. I'm giving you wavy hair and big brown eyes. So now you also get a flat nose." She turned back to Julie. "What's the big deal?"

"It's not just spitting. He pushes food with his thumb. Don't tell me you've never noticed," Julie said indignantly. "And he never reads anything but the sports section and it's forever, that's what. Spitting and pushing forever. For better or for worse."

"God, Jules," said Harrie. "D'you want to live at home until you die? D'you want to be a pruny old maid watching TV with Mom and peeling potatoes until you're ninety-four? I can't even believe we're talking about this at the eleventh hour plus, for God's sake."

"Right," said Paula. "Try marriage a couple of years and if you don't like it, get a divorce."

"I'm not you," Julie retorted fiercely. "You can have as many divorces as you want, but that doesn't make it right."

"Hold it," Harrie said firmly. "Just hold it, right now." The room was starting to reverberate from the argument, and nothing about this earthquake felt real. Julie loved Alan, and he loved her, and personally, she was not going to let this love match fall apart in the basement of the Calvary Church. "Julie, you've got ten minutes to get ready. Paula, I'd love a Coke. Wouldn't you like one too?" she asked her sister. "I think there's a machine down the hall."

"Okay. I give up." Paula shrugged, found some change in her handbag, and left the room.

"Ivy, go upstairs and see what's happening. And come right back."

"Please," Ivy said petulantly.

"Please," Harrie agreed. She waited until she and Julie were alone and then put a hand to her sister's hair and stroked it. Julie hadn't gotten the good hair in the family. Even Ivy's unrelentingly straight hair had sheen. Julie had inherited some ancestor's frizz which was now curling madly in the humid air. "Your face is much better. Take a peek. You look like Mary Steenburgen."

Julie sighed. She got up from the chaise longue and, as though she were a woman twice her age, moved overcarefully to the mirror and peered at her image. Then she went to the sink, gingerly placed a towel over the front of her dress, and washed her face.

Harrie stood beside her. "Okay, sister dear. Time to get real. Spitting and pushing?"

Julie dried her face, sat down once again in front of the mirror. She appraised her visage mournfully, then applied cover-up lavishly under her eyes. "He's acting weird," she said. "He doesn't say anything unless it's an answer to a direct question."

"He's just having the last-minute jitters. Grooms are supposed to get them. It's practically part of the ceremony."

"Then he's been getting the last-minute jitters for the whole past month. And now I'm getting them. I don't know. I don't think either of us thought we were really getting married. It was a game, sort of. Mom saying, 'Alan is such a nice boy. Why not have him over for supper?' and across the street Mrs. Beider doing the same thing, and the two of us playing along—and who wanted to be alone, really? And then one day, instead of 'Invite Julie over to the barbeque,' it was 'Ask Julie to get married'—"

"You're crazy."

Julie shook her head sadly.

"Look at your ring," Harrie said in a tone bordering on reverence.

Julie held up the white gold band with a diamond at the center and a cluster of little emeralds at the sides. In the silence, the two breathed as one.

"That ring is a promise," Harrie said at last. "It says he loves you, that he wants to live and die with you."

"I guess," Julie admitted.

"It cost Alan a lot of money."

"No. It was his grandmother's, remember?"

"Same thing. It was his *grandmother's*. God, I'm so jealous really," Harrie said, admitting the truth and then pushing on. "In a few minutes you're going to be walking down that aisle with Dad and everybody's going to be beaming all these happy wishes at you and then the man you love is going to put a wedding band on your finger—"

"I *do* love him," Julie interjected, suddenly remembering. "I do. He's my childhood sweetheart. He's my chipmunk."

"There you go," Harrie said. "Let me finish your face," she added, shaking a bottle. She touched on makeup base, smoothed cream rouge onto Julie's cheeks, verbalizing the rosy pictures as she did so. "And then you guys are going to kiss in front of everyone, and every unmarried woman in the place is going to burst into tears."

"Not you."

"Oh, really? I'm going to be the hankie queen."

Julie laughed and touched her sister's hand. Harrie sucked in her lower lip. She imagined herself and Dean standing before the altar. He would be wearing a gray morning suit and she would have on an achingly exquisite gown, traditional of course, but with a low-cut back and a generous bow at the base of her spine and a train that would stretch halfway down the aisle . . . Dean was sitting upstairs in the church somewhere. She hoped no one on her side of the family had gone up to him and said, "So when are you and Harriet tying the knot?" Yecchh. She could imagine Dean just *shriveling*. "And then you're going to get on a plane and go to Bermuda! The pink sand. The sky-blue water."

"Mmmmm," Julie sighed softly. They'd picked out a little white bungalow at one of the nicest hotels. She'd bought a tiny suit of white Lycra cut high, exposing her hipbones. She really felt sexy in that suit. And not every thirty-seven-year-old could wear it, either. "It's funny about knowing Alan in the second grade," she said. "Sometimes I think about that. If someone had come up to me in the playground and told me that one day I was going to marry Alan Bieder, I would have just sat down on the blacktop and screamed my head off."

The two women laughed.

"Remember when Alan took you to the senior prom?"

"I remember trying to get dressed and you sitting on my bed making fun of me."

"I didn't."

"You *did*."

"Well, you were wearing a pink ruffled thing Mom made for you that made you look like Miss Piggy."

Julie snorted with laughter. "I guess you're right."

"Hold still now," Harrie said. "I don't want to get mascara all over your nose."

"We signed the lease on the apartment. The one with the swimming pool."

"You told me," Harrie said. She fluffed Julie's bangs. "I don't think you need your glasses, do you? I'll bring them out to you when you get into the car."

"Okay," said Julie. "We're going to buy new living room furniture right after we get back. We saw two suites at Seaman's that are real possibilities. Alan likes this one with a striped couch the best. I was leaning toward . . . Well, anyway, the striped is more practical and Alan likes it."

"Now you're talking," Harrie said, taking her sister's hand.

"I'm sorry I said that stuff about Alan."

"It's okay."

"I don't know why I said it."

"Don't worry about it. Let me look at you." Harrie took a cotton swab and gently smudged the eyeliner under Julie's eyes. She set the headpiece on Julie's hair and folded back the veil.

"Wow," said Paula from the door. She placed three cold, sweating cans down on the countertop. "You look like a different woman."

Julie smiled shyly. "I don't know what was wrong with me."

"Here's your bouquet," Harrie said. She buried her nose in the ribbon-tied bunch of late-summer flowers. "Make sure you throw it straight at me. Mom said I'm next."

"Okay."

"Have you got something old?"

"Mom's pearls," Julie said, lifting them from her neck.

"Something new?"

Julie lifted her skirt, displayed her garter.

"Good," said Harrie. "Something borrowed?"

"Can the pearls count twice?"

"Sure. And something blue?"

"Cornflowers," Julie said, and touched one in her bouquet.

"Excellent. And here's a sixpence for your shoe," Harrie said, hiding the rush of sadness she felt as she thought of Mr. Tuckman. "That's for a little extra luck."

Julie slipped the coin beneath her arch, then stood. She posed before the mirror, then turned left, right. "I do look pretty, don't I? You can't even see these horrible welts unless you stand right on top of me." And then, excitedly, "What time is it anyway? We have to go. Where's Ivy?"

As if her entrance had been cued, Ivy came in through the door.

"Good. We're ready," Julie announced. She fluffed a sleeve, tugged her neckline up over her small bosom.

Ivy looked pale, and her expression was typically flat as slate. "Well, you may be, but Alan isn't," she said. "He's not here."

⊡

Dean looked around the small wood-frame church. He was an alien surrounded by aliens. He knew no one. No one knew him. He could be in a foreign land, or on another planet. He crossed his arms and smiled at the elderly man sitting beside him. The man was carving some sort of quadruped from a bar of soap, the shavings falling silently onto a piece of paper in his lap. "Is it a dog?" Dean asked the old gentleman, who nodded and continued carving. "It's very nice," Dean said, and then he turned his attention to the neck of the woman in front of him. Her short blond hair was cut into a sharp V in back, which pointed to the knobby line of her vertebrae, which disappeared down the back of her dress. Dean followed the line, imagined a fatty pinch of flesh at the base of her spine, a pair of tight buttocks, and there his thoughts ran out of fuel. He used to be turned on by all kinds of women. He remembered when the cleavage formed by the juncture of toes in a scooped-front shoe would get him excited. But no more. Was he getting old? Or was he chemically locked into Harrie? Harrie had looked cute in that green bridesmaid's dress. There was something pleasing about the frothy green skirt swirling around her calves, and the off-the-shoulders top which set off her glossy hair and peachy complexion. He had to admit it, Harrie's looks stirred him as no bony blonde's could.

Dean shook his head and leaned back in his seat. He wished he had the magazine section. He'd left last week's unfinished puzzle wedged between the front seats of his Saab. The car was a hundred miles from here. Actually, it was six or seven blocks away in a small shopping center in front of a bakery, which was the only parking spot he could find on this Saturday in Spode. His shirt was getting damp. He wanted desperately to take off his jacket. How could this minuscule church hold so many people, so little air?

In the aisle, the procession of aliens dressed in brightly colored false silks and satins continued, accompanied by the sound of the old organ which was pumping out watered-down songs from the seventies. The aroma of roses, sudden and strong, washed over him as an abundantly made-up matron lurched and bumped into the pew behind him. To Dean's left was the hard arm of the pew. To his right, the recluse carved. In front of him, the blonde with the pointed haircut bobbed and gossiped with her neighbors, three Long Island twangs of different pitch weaving a cacophonous chord. And planted behind him, the empress Josephine's entire rose garden. Dean felt pinned. He wanted to escape.

Magazine, magazine. If only he had his crossword puzzle, a thing he could lose himself in, a thing he could solve. It was late. Shouldn't the service have started? Yes, there was Dottie coming up the aisle on the arm of Harrie's hulking brother. Dean smiled at Dottie and she gave him a wink. Uh-oh. He knew what that meant. Dottie envisioned another wedding like this one, the next time starring Harrie and himself. Dean squirmed in his seat. He ran a finger under his collar. No way, he told himself angrily, no way. Anyone who thought so had just better forget about it. Why were women so eager to get married? Faces of women who'd tried to nail him flashed through his mind: Barbara, Sandy, Nadine. He reached for a hymnbook and flipped it viciously, the blocks of words as obscure as runes.

Dean burned, then tried to calm himself. Getting steamed about the inconvenience, the imposition, the implications, the heat, was a waste of time. What was the matter with him? All this was was a wedding! A little exposure to a wedding and he was getting all bent out of shape. He should flow with it, find some little thing to enjoy: the shape of the windows, the—the what? He was stymied. Suddenly, all he could think of was that the weather would be perfect in Wilton, Connecticut. Dean grabbed his conscious mind and flew.

⊡

Dean remembered Tyson Wales's farm in vivid detail. As if he were an invisible spectator with an aerial view, he called up a vision of the stately colonial home, a star in its constellation of cottages and out-buildings. He saw the series of ponds connected by a brook that dropped down a gorge into a wide, crashing stream. And he saw the polo field, a closely cropped meadow of green velvet bordered by stone walls and hedgerows, peopled by his co-workers, tiny stick figures in red or blue T-shirts. Sounds wafted up to him—shouts, laughter, the raucous, combative noise of office warriors fighting to prove who could hurl a ladder the farthest, which team could catch and bag the largest number of flapping chickens, who could bowl the highest number of points underwater. But he was above all of it. The politicking, the camaraderie, the chance to score.

Dean thought about the way the conversations would go on Monday—the gleeful replays, the pointed teasing—the way he'd sense the new bonds that had formed in the polo field, on the veranda over g and t's. He couldn't lie to himself. The ding hurt. Maybe he'd lost the plus from his C+ rating at the firm today by saying no to Tyson Wales. It was so easy these days to imagine being on the street. Whole brokerage houses were going bust. Former stockbrokers were getting jobs in restaurants and department stores. If he lost his job, what would he do? Get a job selling advertising space for the *Atlantic Monthly?* Or maybe he'd be selling cars at the Mercedes showroom in Darien. . . . Dean was standing in what seemed to be an actual car showroom, next to a neat blue convertible, when the sound of swarm-ing bees—or was it shocked voices?—brought him back to the pres-ent.

"Folks," Bill Braintree was saying. He was standing in front of the altar, arms crossed, eyes focused on the floor. "Folks, we've got a missing bridegroom. We haven't heard from Alan. We hope he's all right. I think the best thing we can do for now, as there's another wedding party backed up behind us, is leave here, and go back to our place as planned. There's food. And a band. And you all know the way. Thank you very much."

The voice of the crowd was an ocean's roar.

⊡

"I've got to go with Julie," Harrie said to Dean. She was holding his arm against the tide of people flowing out of the church. She lowered her reddened eyes. Her whole face was furiously pink. "It's a good thing I don't own a weapon," she spat. "It's a good thing none of us do."

"Maybe Alan's been in an accident."

"One can only hope. That slime. Can you find your way?" she asked.

A new flock of wedding guests was arriving, clustering on the lawn in small, fluttering groups. The most prevalent color was flamingo. In another minute, Dean knew, he would be alone amid a new set of aliens. "No problem," he said.

"You go down this road, turn right at the Carousel Restaurant. Well, first there's a blinking yellow light, then there's the restaurant."

"Uh-huh."

"Stay on Fishtail Road until you come to this bald intersection."

"Bald?"

"There're no buildings or anything. Fishtail just runs into the highway. Then go east."

"I know the way, hon."

"There are signs. And then you'll see the trees."

"I'll see you in a little while."

"I can't wait to look up my horoscope and Julie's. This has been a day from hell, all right. This day will live in infamy as long as there's a Braintree alive on the planet Earth. And I'm sorry you missed your sports day for this debacle."

"Don't worry about it."

"I can't help it. You made a big sacrifice. But honestly, I'm glad you're here. I think I can bear up for Julie because you're here."

Dean put his arms around Harrie and hugged her. He kissed the top of her head. I love you, he thought, but didn't say. A wave of guilt swept over him.

Harrie squeezed Dean hard. "Julie didn't deserve this," she said into his shirt. "Nothing could be more humiliating. Nothing. And this is partially my fault."

"What?"

"No, really. There was a moment before the organ started playing when if I'd kept my mouth shut, *Julie* would have called off the wedding. I talked her into seeing it through. I practically set her up for that bastard to . . . I hate him for this. I hate him." A car honked behind them.

"Go on." He patted her back. "Your family's waiting for you."

Harrie signaled to her brother, then turned back to Dean. "He'd better be at least in the emergency room," she said darkly. "Or Doug's gonna put him there."

Then, back straight, chin high, Harrie marched to the car, leaving a trail of round holes punched into the asphalt by the furious assault of her high-heeled shoes.

6

---□---

DEAN STOOD at the corner and watched cars pull out of the parking lot. The car marked "Just Married" in shoe polish—the one packed with angry Braintrees—squealed and left rubber on the road. When the car turned the corner, he started the walk to the shopping center.

As he walked Dean found he was shaken by what had just happened. It was as though he'd been listening quietly to music, when without warning someone had blasted up the volume. What was the story behind this fiasco? Could this guy Alan really be such a dog that he would dump the woman he loved on their wedding day? If so, he was capable of anything and Julie was lucky she didn't marry him. Although . . . give the guy the benefit of the doubt for a minute. Assume he's sick or dead or has amnesia. Or if none of that was true, maybe he'd found out something terrible about Julie at the last minute. Like she was pregnant with someone else's child. Or they were second cousins.

Dean had a dark thought, a familiar thought. What if Alan loved her and Julie was the wrong girl? What if Julie was pretty enough for Alan, and interesting enough, and good in bed, and *everything*, but she still wasn't right? Love wasn't enough. Even right wasn't enough. You had to have both. If Julie wasn't the right girl, no matter how much he loved her she wouldn't become the right girl—and if that was the case, how could Alan marry her? Sometimes it all seemed so clear. Love and right weren't on the same track. He could never understand why women didn't get that. Of course, the flaw in his otherwise flawless logic was that love was so hard to find. If you found it, how could you walk away from it?

Dean crossed the street, then went into the shopping center parking lot. He took the keys out of his pocket and opened his car door. It was then that he noticed the beat-up body of the blue Camaro parked in the spot beside his. There was a guy in the car dressed in a tuxedo, staring off into space. Dean took a wild guess.

"Alan?" he asked.

"Hi," said the nowhere man.

Dean walked around his Saab toward the Camaro and appraised what looked like recent damage to the Camaro's driver-side fender. Was Alan injured? Worried and at the same time relieved, Dean leaned inside the window. There were fumes in the car, warm beery fumes. He gently shook Alan's arm. "Alan," he repeated. "I'm Dean Carrothers. Harrie's friend. Are you okay?"

Alan turned to Dean and after a while seemed to focus his eyes. "Nice ta meetcha," he said, a broad smile illuminating his face. "What are you doing here?"

"Are you okay?" Dean asked again.

"Sure. I'm okay. How are you?"

Alan was drunk. Maybe he was in shock. He should be checked out by a doctor. Definitely. "Hey, Alan. You don't look too good."

"I don't think I can get out of here." Alan pulled up the handle and shoved against the door. The door creaked, but it did not give. "I'm stuck," he said, shrugging his shoulders.

Dean pulled at the handle, also without luck. The jamb was bent. Even the roof of the car was dented. "Have you tried the other door?" Dean asked.

"Can't reach it," Alan said. He lunged toward the passenger's side of the car and was pulled short against the straps of his seat belt.

"Let me." Dean reached inside the car and undid the seat belt catch.

"Oh, yeah." Alan regarded his apparent freedom with distrust, then slid over and opened the door. He disembarked shakily.

Alan looked pale, his blondish hair was disheveled, his face shone with sweat, but he seemed otherwise intact. Still, he could have internal injuries. How could you know?

"A great day for sailing," Alan said conversationally, squinting into the sun.

"Great day for getting married, I would have thought," Dean returned. He guided Alan to his own car and helped him inside. "Wait here," Dean said, closing the door. "I want to make a phone call."

"Sure," Alan replied nonchalantly.

·

Dean listened as the coin dropped down the chute; then he dialed. Bill Braintree answered the phone, and in a few spare sentences, Dean informed him of Alan's status and their immediate plans. Then he bought a container of coffee and brought it out to the car.

"Thanks,"Alan said. He leaned back in the seat, seemingly content to be a passenger. "I wonder where we're going."

"The hospital over in Smithtown." Dean pulled out of the lot and, silently repeating the directions Bill had given him, pointed the car west.

"Is something wrong? Are you sick or something?" Alan asked.

"Not me. You."

"Me? I'm okay."

Dean shot a glance at his passenger. He and Alan were about the same age, that is to say, mid-thirty-something, but Alan was like a kid. "Alan. You've been in an accident. Something happened to your car."

"Oh, that. I ran it into a telephone pole. I must not have been going fast enough," he added sorrowfully. He looked down at his tuxedo, opened the jacket and ogled the front of his pleated shirt. "Not a scratch on me."

"You mean you *tried* to wreck your car?"

"I was hoping I would die," Alan said matter-of-factly. Then he laughed. "I'm really a fuckup. Aren't I?"

"You said it." Dean shook his head. How was he supposed to go now? Straight to the highway. Then was he supposed to turn left? He braked at a yellow light and swiveled to stare at the man beside him. Alan's jacket flapped open like an unzipped banana peel. The wind had blown his thin hair into spikes, brought color to his cheeks, and molded his expression so that he seemed to possess the insouciance of a fashion model. All he needed was a day-old beard for the look to be complete. This was not, Dean thought, the way a man should look who had just jilted his bride and purposely wrecked his car. It was irritating. "Listen, I don't know how to break this to you, but you missed your wedding."

"I did?"

"You did. Right now Julie's having a breakdown and the Braintree clan is on the warpath. I don't think your life is worth a cent in this town."

Alan gazed out the window. He ripped an opening in the coffee container lid and cautiously sipped. "Where'd you say we're going?"

"The hospital, Alan, the hospital. I want to make sure you didn't rupture your spleen or something." Dean shook his head again with exasperation and accelerated the car with a lurch.

"My spleen's okay."

"You don't know that."

"I could use a beer."

"Too bad." What was wrong with this guy? Didn't he give a damn about anything? He hadn't even mentioned Julie. There were a bunch of nice people who would never be the same because of Alan's irresponsibility. What was he, a sociopath? Dean turned onto the highway. "Drink your coffee," he snarled.

"Hey." Alan turned to Dean with a scowl. "Don't talk to me like that. I may be drunk, but I'm not an asshole. I didn't do anything to you."

Dean clenched his jaw. After today, he'd never have to see this creep again. He noted the sign indicating the hospital's location and exited the highway. "Fine," he said. "Forget I said anything."

⊡

The waiting room at the Smithtown General Hospital was filled with people. Dull green paint coated the walls, and the floors were beige linoleum tiles with green squiggles—like cabbage worms on sand. Seated together again, Dean and Alan waited in silence uncomfortably pressed between strangers. A woman dressed in a tennis skirt and a man's jacket cradled a young girl with a bandage around her head. A blue-jeaned teenage boy whose chest was tattooed with a crucifix plucked at the cast on his arm and allowed his worshipful girlfriend to twirl his hair. An old man stared accusingly at his bloodied toes protruding from a cut-off shoe. Dean didn't know where to look. He rummaged on a table which held a tattered assortment of unreadable literature: *Modern Agriculture, The Watchtower*, Park's Seed Catalog, *Baby's First Month*. For the second time that day, Dean felt like an alien. "I'll be back in a minute," he said to Alan.

"We should get out of here," Alan replied. "There's nothing wrong with me."

"Soon," Dean replied. "Somebody will examine you soon. I'm just going to get the magazine section out of the Saab."

"I want to go to sleep."

"Close your eyes. I'll be right back."

"I'm worried about Julie."

Dean sighed and sat again. "Yeah," he said. "After the doctor looks at you, we should call in." He leaned forward and rested his elbows on his knees. "Would you mind telling me what the hell happened?" he asked, turning his head to look Alan in the eyes. "I mean, forgive my curiosity, but what the hell happened to you?"

"About the wedding?"

"About the wedding."

"I don't know, I don't know," Alan said tonelessly. "I guess I panicked."

"But why?"

"I don't know." Alan heaved a great sigh. "Everyone was on me. I had to get out."

That wasn't an answer. That was an excuse. "What was it?" Dean asked. "Did Julie say something? Do something? Is there some other woman?"

Alan sighed again and ran both hands through his hair. "No, no. Nothing like that. It was the pressure, I guess. Something was building up inside me for weeks, and I couldn't put my finger on it until last night. I just kept trying to hold myself together because I knew I was supposed to. And the whole time I kept thinking, I don't know if I really love her. Do you know what I mean?" Alan appealed to Dean. "Really love her, enough to never want to be with someone else."

Dean nodded. A cloud of something dense and dark descended and surrounded him. He could see the cords standing out in Alan's neck and little bubbles of saliva which had gathered at the corners of his mouth. He could see Alan all right. And he could hear him, but his sense of touch had been turned to another channel. All he could feel was a familiar aching throb.

"Christ," Alan continued. "The whole wedding machine for the last six months. Her mother. My mother. Apartments and furniture and all those little intimate talks with the Reverend Farley about sex . . . I don't know. You ever been married?" he asked Dean suddenly.

Dean shook his head.

"You would have if you'd found the right person, right? I mean, you want to be married, don't you?"

"Sure," Dean agreed dully. Was this what he expected to hear? Alan was relating to him. Alan was finding kinship.

Alan nodded, his hypothesis confirmed. He ran a hand across his mouth. "My father took me aside last night. For a talk, you know? Said he hoped I'd be as happy in forty years with my life as he was with his."

Dean grunted affirmatively.

"Yeah, well, what's he got to be so happy about?"

Dean shrugged. "I guess he loves your mother and his kids and he's happy. What's the matter with that?"

"My mother's a size twenty. She's two hundred and fifty-five pounds of woman. My father runs a gas station. He makes eighteen grand a year if he's lucky. The Braintrees don't exactly have the lifestyle of the rich and famous. And there's everyone saying how *happy* they are. It kills me. Just kills me. And so Julie and I get married and rent this little apartment in North Spode and I keep my job at Allstate and she has a kid and stops working, and then what?"

Dean shook his head again. His thoughts were unfolding and he was helpless to stop them. If I marry Harrie, he thought, I will have a life of Sunday dinners in Spode and my downhill career as a stockbroker. Harriet Braintree is the wrong girl. Wrong girl. And he had *known* Harrie was the wrong girl when he met her, and still he fell in love with her. What kind of self-destructive act was that? He'd never thought their relationship would go this far. He'd never dreamed there would ever be talk of marriage. He'd thought they would have fun and then, sometime later, it would be painlessly over. Somehow the in-love part had snuck up on him.

"D'you understand?" Alan asked. "Can't you hear the doors slamming shut?"

Dean focused his eyes on Alan, stretched his memory to recapture the sense of Alan's words. "You wouldn't have to stay here," he said. "You could move. You could get a different job."

"If I marry Julie, this is my life," Alan said, disregarding Dean. "This is my life. And I don't even know if I really love her."

But I love Harrie, Dean reasoned, relieved to identify the difference between himself and Alan, the slob. The relief lasted a second and then the gloom descended again. That he loved Harrie, of course, was the problem. He loved her—her spirit, her loving nature, her warm acceptance of him with all his faults. This last was priceless and he knew it. No one had loved him this way before. Would anyone love him this way again? It was diabolical to love and be loved and know that to marry the source of the love was to be doomed to a diminished life. Alan, the goon, was lucky. Not loving Julie was Alan's escape hatch. He was out. Dean worried his lip with his teeth. What was he to do? It wasn't fair to stay with Harrie when he knew she wanted to marry him. But how could he walk away? If he told her the truth, she would leave him. And he wasn't sure he could bear the loss.

The two men sat in silence, although the still air seemed to throb with passion. At last, Dean spoke. "I don't know what to say. It's a shame it had to go this far, that's all. A shame you couldn't have known sooner."

"I know. How do you think I feel? Why do you think I tried to cream myself?"

"Couldn't you have just called? You could have called Julie even last night and said, 'I'm sorry I can't go through with it.' And then she could have made up something. Made up a story."

"Dean, the car wreck was an impulse. You know what I mean? I was going to the wedding. I didn't plan to fuck the telephone pole. I was drunk. A crash seemed like a good idea at the time."

"Oh, man," Dean said, imagining an impulsive turn of the steering wheel, the sound and feel of the impact. He would never do such a thing. He would never let things get so out of control. "You were lucky. You could have bashed your brains out."

"I guess," Alan said sadly. " 'Buckle up for safety.' That's my motto."

A small joke provoked grins, then laughter, then tearful whoops as the two men seized the chance to dispel their mutual misery. But when the laughter subsided, they were still in the dismal waiting room with a number that might never be called. "How do you feel?" Dean asked. "Physically, I mean."

"I told you, I'm okay. I think I'm getting sober, though."

"You're sure you don't hurt anywhere?"

"Yeah, I'm sure. I wouldn't mind if something was wrong with me. I might get a little sympathy from the families. But this sitting around is going to make everything worse. I've got to face the music, whatever that means. What do you think it means?" Alan asked, standing up, straightening his clothes.

"Got me," Dean said, sympathetically. Poor guy. The music was going to be a full hundred-and-thirty-seven-piece symphony orchestra. He went ahead of Alan and opened the door for him. They walked in step toward the car. Alan's means of breaking off his engagement lacked brains and subtlety, but the guy was working with what he had, Dean decided. All things considered, Alan had made the right decision. Marriage was forever. Or at least it should be. "Hey, Al," Dean said, fumbling with his car keys. "Better to find out now than years from now."

"What do you mean?" Alan asked.

The two paused on either side of the car. "If you don't think you love her, you can't marry her. You just can't do it." Then car doors opened and closed, seat belts were locked.

"I wish we were driving to Alaska," Alan said.

"I know what you mean," Dean said. "I know what you mean." He started the car and headed out to the highway.

7

—————◻—————

*H*ARRIE LAY on her back and stared at the ceiling of her old bedroom. The luminescent stars she'd pasted up there when she was eleven years old still remained after twenty years, as did the unicorn lamp and all of her dolls, which now sat in a neat row on her dresser. Harrie had no feeling whatsoever in her legs. Julie had ripped off and balled up her wedding dress, then fallen into sleep on her lap as though she'd been felled by a mattock, the weight of her head cutting off Harrie's circulation below the knees. Harrie could hear the sounds of guests leaving downstairs. She could hear her father's voice, hoarse and fractured from unaccustomed use, and she heard her mother trying to be chipper in the wake of the disaster that had struck that day.

There was no separating oneself from the stunning pain that had been visited upon them all, thought Harrie. It wasn't just that Julie had been publicly rejected, and so every feeling person hurt for her; it was that they all felt so *responsible*. Either for actually pushing Alan and Julie together or for simply wishing that Julie would finally get married, to whomever, just so the thirty-seven-year-old spinster would stop living at home with her parents.

Harrie was also angry at herself for feeling embarrassed in front of Dean. And yet she *was* embarrassed. It was not that she was ashamed of her family. To the contrary, she thought them courageous and strong. It was the fact that this public humiliation could have happened that shamed Harrie, and she was sure such a thing would not have happened to a member of Dean's family.

As Harrie lay pinned to the narrow bed by her sister's sorrow she remembered the thousands of hours she'd spent in this room dreaming of a grander way of life. She'd done her dreaming under the light of her unicorn lamp—a glitter-dusted Do Not Disturb sign hanging from the doorknob—dressed in her mother's castoffs or in a fantastic costume of her own design. Books fed these dreams: love stories about castles shrouded in mists, women shrouded in cloaks, and men shrouded in mystery. And anything could happpen in the stories as long as the endings were happy.

When Harrie moved to her studio apartment in New York City, she'd made the most of her resources, both the creative and monetary kinds. She'd fashioned her own brand of chic from stores that sold recycled clothes from earlier decades. She'd bought end tables and an armoire from bargain antique shops in Brooklyn. She'd gotten dishware in the Bowery, found remnants of fancy English fabrics uptown and covered the cushions of her thrift shop chairs. Her apartment was small, but she was pleased with the way she'd managed to convert a ground-floor cell into a girl's heart of a nest. When Harrie was by herself, her apartment, with its working fireplace and French windows opening onto a courtyard garden, perfectly reflected her taste and romantic nature. But when Dean was there, the same place seemed miniature and fussy and unsuitable.

Harrie worried because Dean's background was so different from hers. He had grown up in his father's grand, white-pillared mansion in Litchfield, Connecticut, quite unlike her family's run-down old farmhouse on the Island. Dean and his brothers had private school educations. She and her sibs had gone to public school all the way—but never mind the past. Dean lived now in a loft in lower Manhattan: a vast expanse of stained-oak floors tastefully furnished with heirloom antiques and modern appliances. Sometimes leaving his place, going to hers, scared the charm right out of her apartment, reducing it in her eyes to a jammed, crammed, chintz-lined shoe box stuffed with kitsch.

Harrie often wondered what it would be like to have rooms, multiple rooms of her own. Her collection of *Architectural Digest, House and Garden, World of Interiors,* crowded her bookshelves, which went to the ceiling beside her bed and around both sides of her fireplace. And the magazines, like the romance novels she'd consumed in her small bedroom in Spode, inspired her fantasies.

Although Harrie had lived at 111 Chester Street for ten years, she knew this address was only temporary. At thirty-two years of age, she was more than ready to make a real home. She had only to let her eyes go out of focus and she could imagine pushing open a heavy, hand-carved door onto a splendid marbled foyer, and from there the rooms beyond shifted and changed daily, giving way to new pictures, new ideas.

Sometimes the marbled foyer would lead to a paneled sitting room where deep velvet armchairs faced the fireplace and tea would be served on mahogany trays. She could see a music room glowing with light filtered through sheer curtains, illuminating the grand piano which she would learn to play. Sometimes she envisioned a conservatory filled with towering palms and orchid plants blooming in a never-ending display of mauve, purple, and bronze. On other days Harrie saw modern spaces: bedrooms opening onto terraces and tiled bathing rooms with sauna and steam, roof gardens with European statuary. And although the furnishings and the settings would change with each browse through the slick house-and-garden books, each smudgy shopping trip through the Sunday classifieds, one aspect of the dream was fixed. This future place was where she belonged with her family, and with Dean.

But Harrie was realistic about the spending power of her income from her job as a literary agent. A third of her salary paid her taxes, another third paid her rent, and once the other necessities of life were paid for, she had worn dollar bills in her wallet for luxuries—hard Italian sausages, goose down pillows, an antique bedspread, a lottery ticket once a week, inviting fate to lend a hand. Harrie could afford these tempting bits and she could look to more in the future. She was doing well. She had sold three dozen books so far this year, and several of her authors were catching on. The hard work she had done earlier in her career was beginning to pay off with new clients and easy relationships with important editors. It seemed reasonable to hope one of her authors would write a future blockbuster, the prayed-for "runaway best-seller." It could happen. And if you wanted a happy life, you had to picture it so you could take steps to make the fantasy come true.

Julie stirred in Harrie's lap. For the last half hour, Harrie had been aware of the crunching noise of tires moving across the peastone parking area beside the greenhouse, out to the service road alongside the highway. How Julie could, in her sleep, distinguish between the sound of cars departing and that of one arriving was a mystery, but she did discern the difference and she woke up.

"He's here," she said. "Alan's here." Julie unfolded herself and went to the window. Harrie shook out her pins and needles and, limping, followed. The two stuck their heads out of the dormer window and watched as Dean got out on the driver's side of the car and Alan disembarked on the other. The men walked slowly across the gravel and clomped up the porch steps. Julie gave Harrie an intense, hysterical look. "I never want to see him again!" she said.

There was a knock on the screen door, a squeal as it was opened, a muffled "Get out of here" in Doug's voice, a protest in Alan's. And then there was the crack of a punch to bone, followed by the soft thump of a body hitting a wooden deck. In sympathy perhaps, Julie's knees buckled and she dropped in a heap to the bedroom floor.

⊡

"Blue Team won," Dean said, putting down the receiver. "Chip left me a message on my machine."

They were in Harrie's apartment. It was late, close to midnight, and after the three-hour drive, they'd at last arrived at a full stop. Dean lay barefoot but fully clothed on Harrie's bed and watched as Harrie covered the birdcage containing Mr. Tuckman's cockatoos. The cage now occupied the place once claimed by the TV set, which had been summarily relegated to the floor.

"You don't sound too happy about it," Harrie said. "I thought blue was your team."

"It was." And they'd won without him. Dean threw a long sigh. From his prone position, he took in the whole of Harrie's studio apartment, which at most totaled four hundred square feet. Everything in the room was in plain sight and everything was in its place. Dishes were neatly aligned in the wooden rack beside the little sink in the kitchen alcove. A bistro table and two chairs posed before the fireplace. Hatboxes were stacked on top of the armoire, their floral paper concealing their utilitarian purposes. A wooden trunk served as a coffee table in front of the love seat and stored Harrie's sweaters as well. Chintz tiebacks cheerfully adorned the windows, and sheer voile panels fluttered in the slight breeze. Beside the bed, on a tabletop the size of a serving dish, were a Bakelite radio from the forties, a small alarm clock, and a candle in a silver holder. A toasty glow came from the beaded boudoir lamp that was balanced atop the radio. Cozy, Dean thought, the kind of place a man could never make for himself, but could thoroughly enjoy when created by a woman. He was about to tell Harrie how comfortable he was in this room, but when he looked up at her, she seemed to be in a standing trance.

"Har? You awake?" Dean asked.

Harrie turned. "I was trying to remember if I've ever had a worse day."

"And what did you decide?"

"I think today's the top of the pops." Harrie stepped out of her shoes, walked to the armoire, which served as a room divider of sorts, and put the shoes inside. "I got caught cheating on a math test once in the fifth grade—and that was the worst day for a long time. Then there was the time my wraparound skirt fell off in the parking lot in front of our entire varsity basketball team. I think that was the worst day for about ten years. But for pure, wretched misery, I'm gonna give today the blue ribbon."

Dean stretched out his hand. "Why don't you come to bed?"

"I hope the birds will be okay here. They can't be in a draft, you know." She held out a hand in front of the air conditioner to make sure no air was blowing on the cage; then she pulled the green dress from her shoulders, unzipped it, and watched it drop to the floor.

"I fantasized today about taking that dress off you," Dean said sleepily. "But that was a long time ago. I don't think I can do anything anymore."

"Julie's wedding night and she's still at home. In her single bed. Alone." Harrie sat on the bed and pulled down her pantyhose.

"And I fantasized about doing that."

"Taking off my pantyhose? How kinky," Harrie said with a smile. She unhooked her strapless bra.

"And I thought about doing that a whole lot of times."

"Oh, really?" Harrie turned and put a hand through Dean's hair.

She unloosened, then took off his tie, unbuttoned his shirt, removed his glasses and put them on the night table.

"Yes," he said. "I'm sure of it." He lifted a hand and touched her breast lightly as Harrie leaned across him.

"Mmmm," she said as he caressed her. He reached around her and brought her down to his bare chest.

"You have the greatest skin," he said. "I've never touched skin like yours."

Harrie kissed his neck in answer. All of her thoughts and sensations were suddenly and exclusively concentrated on the points of her body in contact with Dean. Dean ran his hand down her back, stopping at the place he liked, right at the base of her spine.

"And I thought about doing this," he said, gently pinching the flesh there.

"Did you think about this?" Harrie asked, wriggling against him. She fiddled with the hook on his pants, tugged on the zipper, then pulled down his pants until they were a pile of cloth on the floor. And then she was lying again beside her lover, feeling his hands moving over her, reminding her of times they'd made love in the past, promising her tenderness to come. Harrie's hand floated across Dean's chest, remembering the textures of his hair and skin, finding landmarks she'd memorized before. She touched him gently but purposefully. "Too bad you're so tired," she said, sliding her hand down his belly, coming to rest at a part of Dean that seemed not to be tired at all.

"It's a shame," he said. He kissed her then, a languid kiss, and Harrie reached out for the lamp and turned off the light. Sheets rustled. The air conditioner purred. Fingers touched ridges and hollows and secret places. Then Dean tucked Harrie's body beneath his and found his way inside her. "Because," he said, "I love . . . to do . . . this . . . to you."

Harrie felt so at one with the rhythm of Dean's body, she could swear the rhythm was her own. She felt no inhibitions, no consciousness. She felt surrounded by Dean, connected to him in every way, so it was no surprise that she easily, inexorably came with him.

The surprise was that she cried, the tears streaming from her eyes onto her cheeks and his shoulder.

"Hon? Are you okay?" Dean asked, already half in sleep.

"I'm fine," she whispered, but Dean had slipped over the edge of consciousness. And Harrie, having been released by passion from the restraint of her emotions, quietly cried out her grief and her anger, and her relief at being in the arms of the man she loved. Then she followed him into sleep.

8

---□---

THE SUN, unhindered by the large office buildings far to the north and east, threw its rays full force upon the pavement. Harrie pressed the buzzer, then pushed the door open and locked it behind her. She adjusted her eyes to the dim light in the foyer of the old brick townhouse in Chelsea that housed the office of the Luna Casey Literary Agency. Raoul—the receptionist, general assistant, and literary agent in training—greeted Harrie, who returned the greeting and went into the room beyond.

"Harriet darling, is that you?" Luna Casey called out, her voice lightly colored by the English accent she was accorded at birth.

"It's me," Harrie replied.

"Because there's a messenger coming for Ballantine's damned contract in a minute and I want you to take a fast look before— Harrie dear, forgive me. I almost forgot. How did everything go this weekend?"

The office was the parlor room of the old townhouse. At the far end of the room, facing out to the back garden, a wide and multipaned window stretched its arched frame to the top of the eleven-foot ceiling. Luna's desk sat before it so that she looked into the room, the light behind her softening her features. A fireplace, its mantel stacked with manuscript boxes, was centered on the longest wall. Harrie's desk faced Luna's, a beach of worn and overlapping Oriental rugs between them. Three claw-footed, oak chairs hedged in a coffee table that was piled high with magazines and manuscripts. Swaybacked bookcases lined the room.

Harrie dropped her handbag into a file drawer and placed her book bag beside her chair. "Well, for starters, Mr. Tuckman died on

Saturday morning, then my sister got stood up at the altar, and I went to a funeral yesterday—and how was your weekend?"

"Oh, *no*, Harrie. Not that dear old man."

"Heart attack," Harrie said quietly. "Coffee, Luna?"

"Please."

Harrie went to the coffee maker and prepared mugs for them both, then returned to her desk. "I never expected Mr. Tuckman to die," she said. "He was so different from the rest of us. You know what I mean? Somehow above the ugliness of life. Like when he took the subway, all he'd notice was that there was an absolutely wonderful string quartet playing for spare change. Or he'd walk down Forty-second Street, and while the rest of us just set our eyes straight ahead and hope not to get mugged, he'd take note of the moldings on the buildings or the gargoyles—and the funny thing is, no one ever harmed him, Luna. It was like he had a magic shield or something."

"Well, dear, he lived a good life then."

"Until his heart got him . . ."

"He was in his seventies?"

"Seventy-five."

"I think seventy-five good years is damned good luck, Harrie."

"It is. I know."

"Well, I'm very sorry."

"Thank you."

"So now tell me about your poor sister. Tell me about the wedding."

"The un-wedding, you mean." Harrie sipped coffee that was still too hot to drink. "The un-groom chickened out at the last minute and ran his car into a telephone pole."

"He didn't! Was he badly hurt?"

"Not a scratch on him. Unfortunately. God. And over a hundred people came to our house for the reception—couldn't let all that food go to waste, of course. And we had a band!" Harrie put her hands over her face and screamed into them.

"It sounds like an Irish wake."

"Exactly!" Harrie said, clapping her hands. "Booze and dancing, and upstairs, my sister the corpse, lying in my lap." The two women laughed.

Luna, who had a long-held and glittering reputation, was Harrie's boss, but as Harrie was paid mainly through commissions on the books she sold, she was in effect in business for herself. In the ten years Harrie had been with Luna, they'd worked together in the same room, their phone conversations mingling in the open air, and they'd become friends as two women of any age, any position can become when they have mutual respect and very little privacy.

"The good news is that it felt great to be part of the family gathered around Julie," Harrie said, shaking a fist. She told Luna about her brother bringing Alan down at the front door, and how her mother, who'd always been right, was wrong for once, and how miserable she'd been. "She has this kind of love-hate thing with Julie. They've been hissing at each other for thirty-seven years, and with Julie getting married, I think they were about to make peace at last . . ." Harrie gazed into her coffee. "Mom is starting to plan my wedding," she said. "Although I think she ought to consult with Dean before she books the church. Alan's bailing out on Julie wasn't exactly reassuring to a guy who's—how shall I put this?—a little squeamish about marriage."

"No, I don't suppose it would be."

"Jan Nugent on eight for you, Harrie," said the voice of Raoul on the intercom. "She says it can't wait." And then other buttons on the phone began to blink. Harrie took her first call of the day from an author who'd had an anxious weekend over an impending offer for her first novel. Harrie soothed the author, made a call, left word for a senior editor, then, switching to a different channel of thought, picked up a call from an agent she worked with overseas.

While other agents had business relationships with their clients—the content of their conversations dealing mostly with the terms and conditions of a contract, the success or failure of a sale, the couched bad news of another rejection—Harrie's clients, all of them romance fiction writers, were also her friends. "Mollie," she said, taking another call. "Is it a boy or a girl?"—a question that might have referred to a real birth or that of a character. And so the day progressed. An editor on the line, a contract spread before her on the venerable oak desk, dust motes hanging in the air between the two women like magic dust. And before half the day was done, a heartbroken author's heart was on the mend, a contract had been checked over and sealed in an envelope, editors and clients had been spoken with, and coffee cups had been refilled again and again.

At just past noon, the gourmet delicatessen was called and in minutes lunch was delivered. On this day, Luna and Harrie rearranged the contents of the take-out containers on fine white china and transferred their iced tea from the waxed paper cups to lead crystal glasses. Linen napkins were taken from the sideboard, as was the heavy sterling flatware. Then Luna and Harrie brought their now elegant meal out to the cast-iron furniture that was grouped beneath the ancient pear tree in the garden.

"The heat, my God," Luna said, lifting the collar of her starched shirt away from her neck. Renegade wisps of hennaed hair which had escaped from tortoiseshell combs fanned around and flattered Luna's no-longer-youthful face. Bees drugged by the heat were buzzing the potted lilies along the fence. Harrie watched as one entered a blossom and emerged pollen-coated and drunken, flying so slowly she could have picked it easily out of the air. She sipped her iced tea, taking care not to drink it all too fast. The sugary taste made her feel for a moment—beelike, and she followed the insect with her eyes as it wobbled purposefully to the next white flower. And then she envisioned baskets of flowers and white tulle and doves on a long table. She felt a familiar tug; again a wandering thought had found its way home to Dean.

"Luna," Harrie said casually.

"Here it comes. Dear Aunt Fiona . . ." Luna said dryly, referring to an advice columnist for a London tabloid. She speared a lettuce leaf and folded it into her mouth.

"I was thinking about taking a course in economics at night," Harrie declared. "Half the time I don't know what Dean is talking about."

"Women," Luna muttered. "Three steps forward, two steps back."

"Or maybe I should just take one of those quickie courses in understanding the stock market."

"Harrie."

"Hmmmm?"

"Perhaps you could simply ask Dean how you should look, act, and dress, and adjust yourself accordingly." A pause. "I'm sorry, dear. I didn't mean to—"

"Bitch," Harrie said sweetly. "It's easy for you to say. You know how to get married, having done it four times."

"I suppose you think that proves something," Luna replied, returning the volley, not liking to dwell on even one of the marital disasters she'd been party to. "Listen, Harriet darling. The world has changed a lot for women in the last twenty years. We've made some progress with the law and perhaps in business. But when it comes to marriage, men make the decisions. Women have only the right to say no."

"Someone's lecturing."

"Sorry again. You're right, of course. Frankly, my back was up from this damned novel before you uttered a word about Dean."

"Which novel?"

"*Saigon Warrior*," Luna said disdainfully. "Not the worst of its kind by any means. Guns, drugs, aircraft. Someone will buy it for a tidy sum. It just worries me how, after all these years, women are being portrayed in this type of mainstream fiction."

"Give me a for-instance."

"The main female character is described as having a Ph.D. in economics. As far as I can tell, she only uses this degree to help the hero figure out how to launder his money in foreign markets. She's gorgeous, of course, can't get enough sex with our hero, does the cooking and the washing up, disappears from the room happily when he tells her to leave, and—here's the part that set me off—after being with him for a year, she knows not one thing about him and is happy not to know. She's like a geisha girl in Lycra pants and scuba gear. Tell me. Does that sound like any woman you know?"

"Well," said Harrie, "the sex part sounds familiar."

"You. You make me laugh," said Luna, proving her statement with a throaty chortle.

"You know, I did know someone like that Ph.D. character once."

"Really? A contemporary of yours?"

"Mmm," Harrie affirmed. "Lisa, my roommate at school. She

came to the party with a few theories, but when she got out of school, she honed this geisha thing to a fine art. All the nuances, like you said. Stretch pants, lacy underwear, steak on the grill and beer in the fridge. *Sports Illustrated* on the coffee table. The appearance of utter compliance and availability equipped with a high IQ and this stunning bod. And the text was: 'You are my everything.' But it was a trick!" Harrie concluded smugly.

"Do tell," Luna replied, her attention captured.

"The trick was this. Lisa always had at least two boyfriends at a time. When she was with one, she was all his. But she always let him know in the most subtle way—like putting on fresh lipstick, or fresh panties—that when she left her apartment or his, she was going to be with someone else."

"What a wicked girl," Luna said. She opened her handbag, took out a mirror, and applied fresh lipstick herself. "And what did this behavior achieve, exactly? Brawls under her window at night?"

"That, and a rich husband who dotes on her."

Luna blotted her lipstick, inspected her teeth. "So why haven't you taken a leaf out of your friend's book, Harrie? As I get the story, Dean knows he's got you when and where he wants you."

"The two of us were so different. My friend enjoyed the game, the war between the boys and the girls. I suppose she was more sophisticated than I was. Am. Even flirting with another man when I feel committed to Dean would make me feel . . . dishonest."

"Too bad, I say. Having dates with other men could move things into your court. Have lunches anyway. Like with that young Simon Wickham I keep trying to set you up with."

Harrie shook her head.

"For heaven's sake, there is nothing in the world wrong with having lunch with someone. As regards this exclusive arrangement with Dean, you're working without a contract, if you don't mind my saying. And Simon is quite pleasant company."

"Thanks anyway, Luna," Harrie said, thinking of the nasal young Englishman with the old man's clothes who was one of Luna's favorite clients. How could Luna imagine her with that stodge?

"All right," Luna said, exhaling her exasperation. She flicked at her mascaraed lashes, then closed her compact with a snap.

"Who's the special guy?" Harrie asked.

"What special guy?"

"The special guy for whom you bought the new duds. And the new ear bobs."

"Don't wink at me, you naughty girl."

"Well?"

"Lovely gentleman I met last week at Sotheby's. He's taking me to dinner at Lutece."

"You look beautiful."

"Thank you. I think I'll give that *Saigon Warrior* to Raoul to read," Luna said thoughtfully. "Get a man's opinion. To be fair."

"Good idea. . . . Honestly, Luna." Harrie's voice was impatient. "Men are falling around you in waves and you just wade through them. All I want is this one man. I think if our positions were reversed, I'd be willing to share a secret or two."

"I would share my little heart out, but I don't think you're ready to hear the truth."

"I'll bet I can take it."

"No, you can't. You'll just get your knickers in a knot and then you'll disregard what I've said."

"Go ahead. Try me."

"The secret, my dear, is to decide to marry a man who wants to be married."

"How do you know if a guy wants to be married?" Harrie asked, the picture of nonchalance.

"You'll know"—Luna arched her eyebrows dramatically—"because he will tell you so."

"Come on. That's so simplistic. Surely it takes time for some men to decide to marry a person they're with." Harrie stared at Luna, who hadn't moved an eyelash. "Dean loves me," she said through gritted teeth. "I know he does. He couldn't be without me."

Luna leaned forward and whispered conspiratorially. "As I was saying, darling. A Gypsy once told me if you love a man and want to marry him, take three hairs from his head, wrap them in a handkerchief that has been worn for three days next to your heart, then place it under your mattress. Oh, and light a candle, a white one, for three nights. Results are guaranteed."

"That's better," Harrie said, grinning, falling back into her chair with relief. "I knew you'd tell me."

"Whatever are we going to do with you, Harrie-girl?" Luna asked affectionately.

Harrie smiled. "Lend me a hankie," she said.

9

---□---

*I*T WAS SEVEN O'CLOCK in the morning, and the line at the Park Row Gourmet coffee shop take-out station was three people deep by eight people long. Dean was feeling great. His head was clear and his blood felt clean, the way it always did after his morning jog. He hummed as he anticipated his fried egg sandwich and contemplated the wonderful body encased in a tight brown skirt and tiger-skin-print blouse on the woman to the front and left of him. Then the tiger-woman turned and Dean forgot about his sandwich. She impatiently shoved back a sheet of oat-colored hair from her face revealing her profile. The woman was Laura Taft, and she saw him too.

"Dean," she said, her face flushing with pleasure.

"Hello, Laura," Dean replied, glad to see her too. He stepped toward her and they kissed cheeks. The tight ranks of hungry people seemed to close in rather than part for the two friends, so their embrace was more physical than either had planned. "How's your new job?" Dean asked, stepping back, hoping to cover his feeling of awkwardness.

"Only great. I'm crazy about it."

"No kidding?"

"It's the real thing." The block of people moved forward en masse. "Let me come back there with you," Laura said, vacating her space, earning a disgruntled look from the person behind Dean. "Nice jacket," she said, and touched Dean's sleeve.

"Thanks." Dean put an unconscious hand to the knot of his tie. Laura was glowing. And she seemed to be moving at a slightly faster speed than he was, even with all his clean-blooded vigor.

"I've never felt so alive in a job before. It could be the famous honeymoon period, but it's hard to believe this won't go on forever. I like my clients. I like my accounts. I like my secretary. I even like the boss." Laura shrugged, displaying her palms and a warm grin.

"Well, that's great, Laura, that's really great." Dean took her arm and moved her forward as the line moved.

"And you?" Laura asked, rat-tat-tat. "What's the latest? Tell me all the gossip."

As the lines inched closer to the take-out counter Dean told Laura about the small doings in the office. Then they collected their breakfasts in brown paper bags and, as it was still so early, decided to eat together in City Hall Park, across the street.

The small triangular park was nearly empty, and Dean and Laura had their choice of benches, finally choosing one near the huge disk-shaped fountain which was sending up a pleasant spray. The two stirred and sipped their coffee, delighting in the specialness of the island of park caught between rushing streams of early-morning traffic, and the unexpected pleasure of one another's company.

"What do you think of the rumors about Cyclops going private?" Laura asked, a look of glee lighting her smooth face.

"I don't know," Dean said.

"I know what you mean. Half the time you don't know whether to believe the gossip or not, but when the gossip is reported in the *Journal* . . ."

"I mean I must have missed it. I didn't know they were buying themselves back. Doesn't Armstrong International hold a majority share?"

"About thirty percent, but they've given their blessings. With luck they could grab around eighteen a share."

"Huh," said Dean. "It was in the paper this morning?"

"Yup."

"Did they happen to mention Friday's close?"

"Twelve and a half, off an eighth."

"Well. I wondered what I was going to be doing this morning." Laura smiled.

"Thanks for the tip."

"*De nada,*" she said. She glanced at Dean shyly, then sipped her coffee.

Dean easily interpreted Laura's look and her silence. "How did I miss that story, you're dying to know," Dean said, bunching up a piece of waxed paper, balling it in his fist.

"What?" Laura said. "I didn't say anything."

"Don't get coy with me," Dean responded playfully, sinking the "ball" into a trash bin. "You were wondering what kind of boob I am, that I didn't read the *Wall Street Journal*."

"Huh," Laura grunted, not quite conceding, but not denying either.

A white pigeon with a brown ring around one of its eyes waddled over toward Dean, bobbing its head and making hopeful cooing sounds. Dean tossed a crust of roll to the bird, which was joined by another bird, then by hundreds of birds falling from the sky in a whirring, blinding storm of food lust.

Laura squealed in mock horror and shielded her face.

"Oh, no. Alfred Hitchcock strikes again," Dean said, shooing birds that were levitating at bench level. "What do you say, Laura. Let's blow this joint." He rose from the bench and stood in the pool of pigeons. "I'll walk you a few blocks."

They gathered up their trash, dropped it into the bin; then Dean grabbed his briefcase and put a hand under Laura's elbow. Wading through the flurry of birds, they approached the curb, waited for the light, and crossed the street.

"So how come?" Laura asked, looking at the traffic, not at Dean. "How come you missed the Cyclops story?"

"I guess the old pigeon ruse didn't work," Dean said, and grinned sheepishly.

"It was quite impressive, actually," Laura replied, grinning back.

They reached the curb and Dean maneuvered Laura so he would walk on the street side of the sidewalk; he used the moment to order his thoughts. He knew it was dumb to be embarrassed, but he was always anxious before he told someone, especially when it was someone he'd known for a long time. He didn't want Laura to think he was excusing himself, but it would be better if she knew, rather than assumed he was lazy or stupid. "It happens all the time," Dean said. "I'm dyslexic."

"Really?" Laura said, and then, as she imagined what life as a stockbroker might be like for a person with a reading disability, she repeated, "Really? You're dyslexic and you're in this business? How in the world do you do it?"

"With my winning personality?" Dean cracked. Laura's mouth was open in dismay. She looked so young, Dean thought. She could be twenty-one, not thirty-one. He smiled. "It's a challenging kind of disability," he said. "Keeps you on your toes."

"I should think so. Don't letters transpose themselves? And numbers?"

"Yes, but not all the time. If I'm rested, if I'm concentrating, I can read pretty well. Under stress, I have to work much harder and it's almost guaranteed I'll make mistakes."

"So what do you do? How do you absorb enough to get by?"

"God. I haven't told anybody about this in so long."

"I'm sorry."

"Hey, I brought the subject up. It's just every time I tell someone for the first time, I realize how weird it seems to other people. Like an acrobat with vertigo. Or a deaf harpist."

"But it also says you're a real fighter," Laura said, hoisting her shoulder bag into a better position, marching in step with Dean's stride. "I know you didn't get by on your winning personality, as you call it. I mean, it helps, but it's not enough. You wouldn't have survived on the Street this long with just your charm. As considerable as it is."

"Well, thank *you*," Dean said. "But anyway, I don't want to make this sound worse than it is. I don't have any trouble with graph-type information, or ticker tape. And information that's broken into lots of subsections. Annual reports. Newsletters. And I *can* read, you know. It's the big blocks that give me trouble—"

"Like newspapers."

"Like newspapers. But listen. Dyslexia has its compensations. When you can't depend on reading and writing, you get good with your mouth. You know? I'm a pretty good salesman. And I'm a total crossword puzzle addict."

"Really? You're good at crossword puzzles?"

"Pretty fascinating, isn't it?"

"Dean, you don't have to mock yourself. It must have been tough when you were growing up."

"Yeah. You could say team sports were a problem. Couldn't keep which goal was which straight in my head. Choosing up sides was always fun for the kid who couldn't tell left from right."

"Poor Dean."

"I hate to hear myself talk about this. It's so boring."

"Hardly," said Laura. There was very little about Dean that bored her. He was as compact and as graceful as a jaguar—the cat *and* the car. She adored the way he kept steering her around, just a light hand under her elbow cuing her when to walk, when to stay. He made her feel so precious, so feminine. It was a very nice feeling, and then this. His dyslexia. She could see why he hadn't told her when they were working together. One didn't offer up one's vulner-abilities in the jungle. She lifted her hair away from her face and held it there, giving Dean a look that was almost bold. He smiled at her, then averted his eyes. Did he like her? He certainly seemed to, con-cluded Laura. Before, when they were at the same firm, neither could have afforded a messy office romance, but now? She wished she knew if Dean was still involved with that woman he'd been seeing. Harrie. She could call Chip Martin. No. Chip would tell Dean she'd asked about him. Maybe Dean would make an overture, suggest a future meeting, and then she could find out more. And if he didn't, she could always invite him out for one innocent lunch.

While Laura was tentatively forecasting the future, Dean was rooting around in his past. It made good storytelling to talk about his kid days—shooting the ball into the wrong net, the nightmare spelling bees—but the actual memories of the humiliation and self-loathing were still raw. Of course, they didn't know he had dyslexia when he was growing up. His mother had protected him and given him her unconditional comfort because she just loved him. And then she'd died. His father had decided early on that something was wrong with his youngest son, that Dean was dumb, or at least not as smart as Rob and Henry in the important ways—an idea Dean found very easy to believe. When a perceptive teacher in his eleventh-grade En-glish class caught the symptoms and had him tested, he was vindicated and with the vindication came tangible help. But a learning disorder did nothing to improve his status in his father's eyes. Robertson Car-rothers had been as unmoved as before. Instead of persuading him that Dean had done well for a person with a handicap, the diagnosis confirmed his father's belief that he was substandard. How could he ever forgive his father for this? And how could he ever make it right with himself? There was something about the way Laura reacted that reminded him of his mother: sticking up for the little boy he'd been. And he appreciated her tip this morning about the Cyclops deal.

"Wow, it's late," said Laura, looking at her watch. "Almost eight-thirty."

Dean smiled. "Well, I'd better get to it if I want to make some money on this Cyclops thing."

"Me too," Laura said. Her heartbeat accelerated. It had been so long since she'd felt this way. That was worth something even if nothing else happened, she thought, protecting herself against the real possibility that Dean would simply turn now and say goodbye.

"Say. Want to get together for lunch sometime?" Dean asked, shifting his weight, glancing at the traffic light.

"Love to," Laura said. Had she seemed casual enough? Sincere enough?

"Good. Let's do it," Dean said. The light changed. "I'll call you."

"Okay," said Laura, aware that in seconds Dean would be part of the crowd and the moment would be lost. She followed her instinct to close the sale. "Listen, I can do it next Wednesday, if you can."

"Sure. I'm free on Wednesday."

Laura nodded.

"I'll call you Wednesday morning," Dean said with a wave. Then he crossed the street.

10

---□---

*D*ESIREE BELINKY burst into the diner like a flower shot from a cannon, her long black curls blowing back from her face, a scarf like a flame streaming behind her, her small skirt hiking up her thighs as if it were afraid of her knees. She paused in the entranceway and, turning her face in a hundred-and-eighty-degree arc, swept the room for Harrie.

Desiree was late. She was always late, but she never expected to be. Today was no exception. She had been out the door and on time, in the lobby in fact, when the sight of her reflection in the long mirror beside the elevator made her scoot back upstairs to change her top, change her skirt, then put them both back on again. Then down once more to the lobby, and while some people might ask themselves if they'd remembered to turn off the stove, Des wasn't sure if she'd reset the answering machine after snatching the phone off the hook on the third ring to find it was her neighbor wanting to borrow her champagne glasses. And so she'd gone up to her apartment again. She had checked the machine, which was on—she'd obviously turned it on automatically because, after all, the machine was to her social life what a pacemaker is to a faulty heart—and had at last departed her apartment building on the Upper East Side to cab it down to the coffee shop two blocks from where Harrie lived in Greenwich Village. And so she was late.

Harrie looked up sharply from the Sunday *Times,* almost as if her name had been called. Desiree's presence in a room seemed to change the makeup of the air somehow, seemed to energize it or make it nervous. Harrie waved to Desiree, rose from her seat and met her with an embrace.

"Hey, Har," Desiree said.

"Hey, Des," Harrie replied. They kissed cheeks, hugged each other, ruffled one another's hair.

"You look great," squealed Des.

"You too. There was sort of this stun-gun effect when you walked in just now," Harrie said, indicating the stares in the restaurant and sliding back into her seat.

Desiree laughed self-consciously, sat down. "I was wondering about this skirt . . . Sorry I'm late, by the way."

"I hadn't even noticed." Harrie glanced at her watch. "We've got plenty of time." She bundled the newspaper and put it on the seat beside her.

"I can't believe we've got the whole day to shop. Just the idea of it makes me drunk with happiness."

"I thought you just wanted to buy shoes."

"You know me. It's the small things that make me happy. Shoes and eggs Benedict."

"God. I haven't eaten eggs Benedict in years."

"And sausage in maple syrup."

"You can eat these things? How do you get away with it, exactly?"

"Every now and then you have to make nice on yourself, and today's the day," Desiree said, lifting a manicured hand to signal a waiter. "I'm famished. Do you know what you're having?"

"I was going to have two soft-boiled eggs and dry toast."

"Ah," Desiree said to the waiter who had responded to her request for service and was leering at her, pad in hand. "Eggs Benedict for me, sausage, and please bring some syrup. Also orange juice and coffee. My friend will have . . ."

"The same," Harrie said with resignation. She glanced surreptitiously at her lap to see if her tummy was pushing out her denim skirt, adjusted her blouse a bit, then returned her attention to the waiter, who repeated the order with a thick Greek accent. Des thanked him and he pushed off from the table, shouting the order to the kitchen as he went.

"Why are we being so good to ourselves, I'd like to know?" Harrie asked. "Why am I breaking my three-year-long hollandaise sauce fast?"

"Because I got crapped on by a Neanderthal." Desiree leaned

into the table, the lower half of her heart-shaped face narrowing as her smile disappeared.

"No. Don't tell me. What happened?" Concerned, Harrie examined Desiree's expression. What had only moments before been radiance had reversed itself into sadness of the same intensity. What kind of horror story would Des tell? A one-night stand? A broken date? Des had had more than her share of these disappointments, Harrie thought. And yet she was so pretty, so full of life, so in charge of herself. It was amazing to them both that she couldn't make her social circumstances work as well as the rest of her life.

"He seemed okay to me, he really did," Des was saying. She twisted a clump of wild, black hair around a finger and released it, found another clump and did the same again. "Not perfect by any means, but a nice Jewish boy. An art director, or so he said. I met him in the Hamptons a couple of weeks ago. I told you about him, didn't I?"

Harrie nodded. The story had been light on facts, but bright with hope. Des, always on the lookout for her version of Mr. Right, the long-sought-after "Dr. Applestein," had accepted an invitation from a friend to spend a weekend in Southampton. She had met the art director at a cocktail party, had had an electrifying conversation over Bloody Marys, and had, from that moment, developed a relationship-to-be in her mind.

"I mean, there was no clue that he was a bum. He was so normal, so average. But cute. And funny." The waiter inelegantly plopped platters of steaming food on the table, then sauntered away, snapping a dish towel against his leg and whistling tunelessly. Desiree sighed, put a paper napkin under her coffee cup to soak up the spill in the saucer, took another and tucked it into the waistband of her small black skirt. "He was also balding and chunky and not exactly a brain surgeon. . . . I don't know what gives him the right," she said angrily. "Even if he was a brain surgeon, he had no right."

"This doesn't sound like a story with a funny punch line, Des. What happened?"

"To make a long story short?"

"No, you don't have to."

"I want to."

"Okay."

"So, where was I? Oh. So Dr. Applecreep calls a few times. I'm great, he tells me. I'm the most fabulous. Can't wait to see me. He's going on a shoot. He'll be back and then we have to get together. All these hour-long schmoozes on the phone, you know? I'm starting to get quite gooey over the guy."

"I know," Harrie said, nodding sympathetically. "I know."

"So. He calls me at the office on Thursday at about a quarter to five. He's at the airport. He just got in and he wants to take me to dinner. Special place he knows in Brooklyn. He wants to pick me up at work and drive right to the restaurant. I'm a mess, Harrie," Des said, slicing off a bit of eggy muffin, chewing it. "I've been on the phone the whole day rerouting a tour group that decided it didn't want to go to New Zealand after all, but wanted to spend two extra days in Fiji and two days in Tahiti, plus the usual mayhem. So there's Stanley at a pay phone. Shrimp fra diavolo, he says. The best clams posillipo in New York, he says. Plus I want to see him. I tell him I want to go home and change. I was wearing this schmatte I haven't worn in two years, giving it a last chance, you know? But no. He's at the airport, he's getting the car now, he can't wait. So okay. I make up my face and decide true love will prevail.

"So Stanley shows up at the office. Not as cute as the one time I saw him, but he's been on a plane all day and who cares anyway? It's who they are that counts, not what they look like, right?"

"Sure, but it's so generous of you, Des. You don't hear men saying things like that."

"Right," said Desiree. "Damned right." She paused for a while as she thought about this. "You're so lucky. Dean is so great."

"Go on," Harrie said—silently, guiltily agreeing. "Go on with your story."

"Okay. So we go out to Brooklyn in this rent-a-Lincoln. The restaurant is one of those old places where the waiters have stars on their jackets to tell how many decades they've been working there and they're snotty to the patrons and the patrons eat it up and the food is ninety percent olive oil and ten percent garlic and it just slides down your throat, you don't even have to chew."

Harrie laughed appreciatively. "I know that place. Portofino."

"So you know," Des said. "It's like in this warehouse district, a million miles from nowhere. So there we are. Me and Dr. Appleslime.

We've had the eleven courses and a lot of vino and we're having a pretty good time, to be honest, and we're drinking our espresso and he says to me, 'So where do you want to go to fuck?' "

"No!" said Harrie, dropping her fork into her plate.

"I swear, not even 'Wanna go back to my place and watch *Wiseguy?*' "

"What a—"

"What a shithead. 'Where do you want to go to fuck?' And he's not kidding! In this day and age! I was furious, and devastated of course—I mean, where did my future husband go? What just happened? But what could I do?" Desiree asked rhetorically. Harrie just shook her head, mesmerized.

"I couldn't slap him in the face and walk out," Desiree continued. "I was trapped. There I am in Brooklyn. I've got about five dollars in my wallet. I say, very nicely, 'Not tonight, Stanley, some other time maybe. I'm really tired, yada yada,' and he says okay, he gets the message, and then he says, 'Excuse me for a minute,' like he's going to the john." Desiree paused to sip her juice. She patted her lips with her napkin.

"So, go on," Harrie said, breaking into Des's thoughts.

"So anyway, I'm crushed really, but the anger is taking over and I'm actually feeling relieved, you know, that I acted like a lady and I'm going to be home soon alone in my bed, and I drink my espresso, and I wait. And I wait. And pretty soon the waiters are clumping up behind the potted palms . . ."

"Oh, Des," Harrie said, reaching out and taking Desiree's hand in hers.

". . . and I can just feel them talking about me and all of a sudden I think Stanley's not coming back."

"What?"

"Well, it's been so long. What can he be doing? Reading John le Carré? No, he must have left. So I start to think about my options. Five dollars. A credit card, but of course they don't take Amex at Portofino. If he's stuck me with the bill, will they take a personal check? They'll have to. And how will I get home? And I'm going on and on like this in my head. Am I going to have to call my father and ask him to drive in from Riverdale to pick me up, God forbid, at half past ten, or borrow money from the waiter—when Stanley comes out and says, 'So are you ready to go?' pissed-like. And he flips his Visa at the waiter. So where was he all that time?"

Harrie shrugged.

"Well, here's what I think. I think he's phoned someone else and made a late date. I've had sleazeball blind dates before who've done that, although where they find action at the last minute is beyond me."

"Probably the person they live with, who thought they were out of town," Harrie interjected.

"Yeah. That sounds right. Hmmm. You mean like their wife."

Harrie nodded.

"Yecchh." Desiree shook her head. "Horribler and horribler."

"And so?"

"And so we go out to the car—he says not another word—and he puts a tape into the deck and blasts the sound track of *Les Misérables* all the way to Sixty-fifth Street."

"Oh, God," Harrie said, laughing. "He's been to the theater, so that means he's not a slime?"

"I know. And besides, I hate the music from that damned show," Desiree said, laughing now with Harrie. "How did he know?"

"Maybe it was just your lucky night."

"So it would seem."

"I guess it could have been worse. You didn't have to call your father."

"True. At least he was taking me home. But still, as I'm riding in this stupid Lincoln, Harrie, I'm doing such a job on myself. Like, how did I make this guy up? What's the matter with me? And the whole going back to square one, all alone, no boyfriend on the horizon. The nice warm feeling I had turning into dog-do. Har? Do you think I'm coming across as desperate?"

"Don't," said Harrie firmly. "Don't dump on yourself."

Des looked down at her eggs, moved the cold remains around with her fork. "I can just hear my friend Patti, my *married* friend Patti, saying that I'm trying too hard and if I just stop looking, Dr. Applestein will show up all by himself. . . ."

"Des, this couldn't have been a clearer case of it was him, not you. Don't turn it around on yourself. What did you do? You liked him. You went on a date. He turned out to be a shithead. That's all.

You're not trying to pretend he's not a shithead. You don't want to see him again. *That* would be desperate." Harrie paused to see if she was having an effect. Des looked so wilted. Harrie continued. "And as for Patti, I admire you so much for going after what you want instead of just passively waiting—"

"It's just, I want to learn something from this," Desiree broke in, "like only go out with old friends of the family. Or never go to Brooklyn for dinner. Something I can do something about, not that men are animals or that I'm defective somehow and I'll never get married, so I might as well just hang up my ovaries and forget the whole thing."

"I know what you mean. I feel that way with Dean sometimes. That if I want to get married, it's up to me to *do* something."

Both women sighed.

"There are plenty of good men out there," Harrie said, she hoped convincingly.

Desiree nodded distractedly. "I hate being single, I really do. If I were married, I could be spending all this energy on something really important, like taking care of my family. Or my painting. It just seems so stupid and so wasteful. And so endless. No wonder I think every man I go out with could be *him*. No wonder I'm such an optimist. I want to stop dating. I want to wear skirts that cover my knees and I want to break out the dishes I've been saving up for my future life."

Harrie had her second guilty thought, which was very much like her first. Dean was attractive and decent and they loved each other. She didn't have to go out on blind dates anymore. She might not be married but she wasn't single either, or not really. If she were dating, she'd be having the same kind of experiences Des was having; she'd had them. Good guys who were interesting, but not interested in her. Terrible guys who wanted her, but whom she couldn't like in a million years. But mostly, predominantly, guys who were fine and thought she was fine, and between them there wasn't enough chemistry to ignite a match.

"It's going to make quite a masterpiece," Des said with an ironic laugh, referring to the mural she was working on in her spare time. "If I can finish it and hold on to my sanity. I've got a new name for it. Wanna hear?"

"Sure."

" 'Aging Beauties of the Western World.' Like it?"

"Um. I think you can do better."

"Okay. But it fits. Fits the piece and fits my life. I think of you, me, about a dozen of my other friends. All we want is to obey the law of nature—mate, reproduce—and all these men who don't want what we want . . . Of course," she said, brightening slightly, "there's some hope for us all. There's Julie."

"Guess again," Harrie said miserably; miserable for Julie, miserable at being included in Desiree's roundup. Des obviously felt that single was single, and that made Harrie's already profound desire to marry Dean double on the spot.

"Uh-oh," Desiree said, her coffee cup halted halfway to her mouth.

"Uh-oh to the millionth power," said Harrie, a surge of anger charging through her. "I don't want to play 'Can you top this?' but Des, this was your worst nightmare in broad daylight." Over warmed-up coffee, with Desiree gasping and sputtering across the table from her, Harrie told her friend about the wedding disaster. They were still puffing indignantly when they took the subway to Grand Street.

·

The Lower East Side was like a pushcart bazaar brought into the 1990s. On this as on every Sunday, Delancey Street was closed to traffic and swarming with keen-eyed shoppers magnetically drawn to the open stores which sold all kinds of merchandise at sharply discounted prices. Harrie and Desiree had found their way around the steaming asphalt streets, stopping briefly here and there, perusing a rack of garments, a shop full of bed linens, until they reached the object of their quest, El-Ray's Designer Shoes. Desiree pushed open the door.

The shoe store was so dark it seemed subterranean. Women of every age dressed in Anne Klein, Calvin Klein, Adrienne Vittadini—their tans gleaming, jewels glimmering, hair sprayed into place—claimed the vinyl banquette along one wall. The opposite wall was a floor-to-ceiling rack of single shoes of every description. The narrow space between the walls was filled with an undulating mass of shifting females. Dark-haired young men passed shoes overhead, shouted numbers down to the basement, wriggled their way through the crowd, which was alive with a kind of hunger. Desiree had the hunger. She was wallowing in it. But today Harrie was exempt.

Harrie stood at the front of the store, apart from the melee. An air conditioner whirred overhead; a cash register beside her banged and clanged as a middle-aged woman rang up sales and conversed with her customers. Desiree seemed to have shrugged off her sadness and was flirting with a shoe salesman, but Harrie found she had no interest in shoes. Desiree's story, coupled with Julie's disaster, had shaken her all over again, made her wonder what was going to happen with her and Dean. She was picking through these thoughts, trying to make some order from them, when a voice interrupted her.

"I beg your pardon?" Harrie said, struggling out of her mood. She turned to the woman at the cash register, who was beaming a beneficent smile. She appeared to be in her late fifties. Her hair was white, worn in a long braid down her back, and dark-framed glasses hung from her neck on a silver chain. She was holding a thin, black cigarillo, its smoke a fine blue ribbon that dissolved in the refrigerated air.

"I said," the woman said, "whatever you're worried about, forget it."

"Oh, I was just thinking . . ."

"Worrying is more like it, but you're the one person in the world doesn't have to worry. That's some aura you got on you, sweetheart."

"I beg your pardon?" Harrie said for the second time.

"Hang on a minute." The woman rang up a cash sale, handed a shoe box in a plain plastic bag to a customer, then turned back to Harrie. She tapped the ash off her cigarillo, took a drag, exhaled pleasurably. "I said that's some aura you got. You hardly ever see one like that."

Harrie failed to repress a dubious smile. What was this? Shoes and aura readings? One-stop shopping? The woman looked the psychic type, sort of. Eccentric, but at the same time very down-to-earth, like someone's wacky aunt. As she watched, the woman rang up another sale, then continued what she'd been saying.

"It's violet. Very rare. And you got a rainbow."

"Is that good?" Hell, she could play along. A violet rainbow. No. Violet *and* a rainbow.

"The best. Let me see your palm."

"Come on," Harrie said, grinning shyly. "Do you do horoscopes or something?"

"I do a little of this, a little of that. I've got a small gift." She paused to inhale, blew the smoke out in a long stream. "My name's Ceil, by the way," the woman added, and stuck out her hand.

"Harrie." She reached out to accept the handshake.

Ceil took Harrie's hand, turned it over, stretched out the fingers, and bent them back slightly. She put her glasses on her nose, peered intently. "I knew there was an *H*," she said. "I thought it was 'Heather.' I keep getting 'heather,' a lot of it." She took Harrie's other hand.

"We grow heather," Harrie said, staring at her own palm as if she had never seen it before. "My father has a nursery." And Harrie envisioned the field behind the greenhouse as it was in late summer, as it was last weekend, a sheet of violet haze. She could almost smell the perfume of the blossoms, and see the fireflies flickering in the twilight.

"You were born when?" Ceil asked. She patted Harrie's hand between her two, then released it.

"March. March thirty-first."

"Aries. I should have known. Aries has the dream and the drive. My sister's an Aries. She sells condos in Sarasota, Florida. Give me a minute, doll," Ceil said, swiveling to answer a question from one of the swarthy young shoe salesmen. "We're getting in the new Joan and Davids next week." The man turned and was swallowed up by the crowd. A pale girl in a fuchsia tank top and matching jeans, a baby on her hip, stepped up to the counter and awkwardly pulled out her wallet. Ceil examined the girl's check, her identification, clanged open the cash register. Harrie stood on her toes. Where was Desiree? She should hear this. This was good.

"And the boyfriend?" Ceil asked, banging the cash drawer closed, picking up where she had left off.

"What about him? What did you see?" Ceil hadn't asked if she had a boyfriend. She had stated it. Well, that could be a fifty-fifty guess. If she said she didn't have a boyfriend, Ceil would have a stock response to that, Harrie supposed.

"When was he born?"

"Oh. In October. He's a Libra."

The woman took Harrie's hand again, ran her thumb across it; then she released it and crossed her arms over her bosom. She gave Harrie a wide and very satisfied grin.

"What? What is it, Ceil?"

"Harrie, you got a charmed life, that's all you've got to know. You don't have to do a thing. The gun is loaded and it's going to go off."

"Gun, what gun?"

"It's a figure of speech, doll."

"Oh, okay," Harrie said.

"No, this you should understand. Listen. The mumbo jumbo goes like this. There's a silver cord entwined with the gold," Ceil intoned in a dramatic voice. "Within a fortnight all your visualizations will start realizing themselves . . ." She peered at Harrie over the rim of her glasses. "You want the fat trimmed off the flanken? Here it is. You're one lucky girl. You got so much good fortune coming, you couldn't believe it."

A bovine woman with neat little feet elbowed her way to the checkout counter and demanded Ceil's absolute attention. "Those are mine," she said, pointing to the shoe box on the counter. "And these and these." The woman opened her wallet, peeled a credit card out of a plastic pouch.

"No, we don't take cards, doll. Good checks only. And cash." Crisp bills crossed the counter, and the woman carried her bags to the door.

Harrie couldn't bear the suspense. Would she have been so interested had Ceil clucked her tongue and uttered a dark prophecy? Probably not. But how could she resist "You're one lucky girl"? Silver cord entwined with the gold. It was an analogy; her skin tones were warm, Dean's were cool. So poetic, really. Harrie crossed her fingers. What if this woman really knew things? The interruptions were driving her crazy.

"So. Heather, sweetheart."

"Harrie. Are we getting married? Can you tell if we're getting married?"

"Harrie. Like I said, this is all you gotta know. You got a helluva time coming up. There will be tests, but I'm not wrong. I've never seen such an aura." She put her hand on Harrie's cheek, looked kindly into her eyes. "Your sister," she said. "She's a seven and a half?"

"Julie?" Harrie tried to get oriented. She wished she could see her aura.

"The skinny one with the hair." Ceil made a circular motion above her own head.

Harrie nodded dumbly.

"I've been saving these for someone needs cheering up. Charles Jourdan, one of a kind sample." Ceil reached below the counter and thrust a shoe box into Harrie's hands. "On the house," she said. "And your friend over there?" Ceil nodded toward Desiree, who was steaming over to the counter, laden with shoe boxes. "There's a blue coat over at Shapiro's. Fifty percent cashmere. It was made for her. Take it from me."

"I will. Thanks for the shoes," Harrie said, reluctant to leave. Why couldn't Ceil tell her more? Was that fortnight part true? Visualizations would what? Would start realizing themselves. What did that mean? "Thanks for everything."

"You're welcome," Ceil said. "Don't mention it." Then she rang up Desiree's purchases.

·

"She knew Julie wears a seven and a half. I can't believe it," Harrie said to Desiree as they made their way across Grand Street.

"Uh-huh."

"She saw a silver cord entwined with a gold. That's me and Dean. I think it means we're getting married."

"Uh-huh."

"You don't believe any of this."

"I'll let you know after I see the coat at Shapiro's."

·

"I don't know how I resisted, but I spent the whole day with Desiree 'Supershopper' Belinky and I didn't buy a thing," Harrie said to Dean as she put milk in his refrigerator. She unwrapped a roll of paper towels, poured fresh sugar into the sugar bowl.

Dean was slicing carrots for a salad. "I hope we timed dinner right. I hate it when we miss the beginning of *Sixty Minutes*."

"There was this interesting woman. I think she owns the shoe store we were in today. She's a psychic. She said I have an amazing aura." Harrie opened a package of potato chips and nibbled a few. "Dean? Wouldn't it be great if we lived together? We're together all the time anyway."

"We'll see," Dean said, then quickly turned to the stove. He pulled down the door, poked at the chicken with a fork, scowled, and closed the door with a bang.

Harrie was eating potato chips, looking at him.

Dean grimaced. He reached out a hand and pinched a fatty fold at Harrie's waist. "Do you really think you should be eating those?" he asked.

II

------□------

*H*ARRIE THOUGHT the guests at Chip's birthday party could have been professional models; they were that well put together. The men wore boxy jackets and short, fat ties. The women wore black: short black skirts, black chiffon blouses, black blazers, flat black shoes or short black boots. Both sexes had sleek hair, geometrically shaped or slicked back with gels, and collagen-puffed laugh lines under pale nectarine-colored tans. They were scented with sandalwood and myrrh and lavender and stood with postures at once relaxed and correct. Overall, Harrie saw a kind of perfection of appearance that blunted her natural tendency to say, "Hi, I'm Harrie," and so for most of the evening she had stood shyly at Dean's side and had only now, on her way to the bar, met a woman toward whom she felt an affinity.

"She said a violet aura with a rainbow?" the woman asked Harrie. Her name was Riva Perez, and she was an intense brunette in a stretch velvet dress of a style that had hardly seen Paris, let alone New York. Around her neck was a long gold chain and hanging from it was a crystal pendant. Harrie's admiration of that smoky quartz finger had provoked a conversation about psychic energy and auras.

"It's been a week, but I'm sure that's what she said," Harrie answered. "She made it sound like violet is fairly unusual."

"Yes. Well," the brunette said pensively. "Violet. From what I remember from the course I took, violet is a combination of red and blue." Then the woman laughed, *har har HAR,* the sound of a sea gull circling a fishing boat. "I mean, obviously violet is red and blue but what I mean is, violet is a combination of the two colors of auras. Think, think," Riva exhorted herself. "Try to remember." She fingered her crystal agitatedly and looked toward the ceiling. "Blue for the sky. That's spiritual. Right. Right. And red is emotional." She lifted her hands, flames leaping into the air.

"What was the course you took?" Harrie asked. It was hard to imagine this colorful woman in the workaday pin-striped suit of a senior v.p. in a pharmaceutical company.

"Psychology, second year. Jung was very big on auras, did you know that?"

"Carl Jung?"

"The same. He was into a lot of weird stuff. Collective unconscious. Scintillae. Luminosities. Yes," Riva said emphatically, as though Harrie had doubted her word, "he was. I wish I could remember more, but you never think you're going to have to remember most of what you learn in college, do you? I actually did a paper once on parapsychic luminosities . . . Why can't I remember more? Oh, wait. Seems to me violet had its own meaning apart from red and blue. Some sort of dynamism. What was it? I don't know. Sorry. I've scraped bottom."

"Sorry. Really, I am."

A waitress bearing a tray of snail-like objects approached the two women. "Yum," Harrie said dubiously.

"This is spicy squid," said the waitress, indicating a wet circlet in a doughy boat, "and this is sea urchin roe, and those," pointing to what seemed to be Ping-Pong balls in parchment wrappers, "are paper shrimp."

"No, thanks," said Harrie. "I'm saving myself for the mocha mousse."

The brunette woman popped a squiggle into her mouth, chewed for a long time, then cleared her throat. "Errmm," she said as she stared past Harrie's shoulder, "I think I can almost see it. Just a glow. A little shimmer. Or is that from the clock?"

A piece of music ended and another began. A swirl of women brushed past Harrie and Riva and went through an arched doorway to a connecting room. Light came from two main sources: Small floor fixtures sent beams toward objects of interest—plants, paintings and carvings, an oval pool of inky glass that was the dining table. The other source of light was the face of the Met Life clock which was so close to Chip's apartment, it seemed to be peering into the windows. The face was as bright as the full moon, its tower a neon jewel.

Riva tapped her teeth gently with the crystal. "I have a thought. Maybe a rainbow means material wealth. Did she give you any numbers?"

"No. She did use the word 'fortune' though . . . You swear you can see my aura?"

"You have to look off-center. Like this." Riva demonstrated. "See if you can see mine."

Harrie looked past Riva's modern cut with the notch in the bangs, a haircut that must have cost over a hundred dollars. She squinted her eyes.

"Anything?" Riva asked.

"Afraid not. Maybe it's time to change your batteries."

They were laughing when Chip appeared, resplendent in his tuxedo. "What are you two up to?" he said, putting his arms around them both.

"Riva's checking out my aura. It's violet, you know."

"I know that," Chip said. "And a very pretty color it is, too. But what color's mine, Riva? Should I turn off the lights?"

"I'm not going to play with you, Chipper," Riva said coyly. "You'll make fun."

"I will not."

Harrie discreetly ignored the sparks flashing between the two and, smarting slightly from the loss of Riva's complete attention, turned into the room. Groups of people were seated at the bar, huddled in an alcove, sprawled in front of a television large enough to be used at an outdoor drive-in theater that was broadcasting a music video.

There was something about these gatherings of Dean's friends that made her feel as if she were watching a film made in the 1930s where the characters were spoiled and wealthy and lived silly, celluloid lives. These people were so smooth, so self-assured, and, in many ways, identical. It wasn't that Harrie felt inferior to Dean's friends exactly, it was just that she didn't feel *like* them. Her friends tended to be more varied. More odd. More inclined to be antisocial. Very inclined to be intellectual. But then writers prided themselves on their eccentricities, and that was as pretentious, Harrie had to admit to herself, as the smug clubbiness she sensed in this room. And were these people actually pretentious? Or was it just that she didn't belong here?

Harrie fingered the collar of the antique cream-colored blouse she was wearing, a blouse Dean had said warmed her complexion and made her look as sweet as marzipan. The blouse was belted over a mauve silk skirt and the two extra pounds she'd added in the last month. She wore lace stockings and satin shoes someone had worn to a wedding in the 1950s and she'd snapped up for twenty dollars at Secondhand Rose.

When Harrie had looked in the mirror before they left for the party—her hair loosely knotted at the back of her head, pearls lying against a satin sheen—she'd thought she looked romantic, almost edible, as Dean had implied, in the nicest way. But her distinct style was too distinct in this environment. It was singular, completely original. And probably wrong. Why hadn't Dean told her? Or hadn't he thought so? And why was it so important suddenly for her to be like everyone else?

Harrie lifted a glass of champagne from a tray and sought Dean out with her eyes. He was across the room by the window, standing with other handsome men and women, fitting as surely with the group as one of many beads on a string. And yet Dean was a man she knew to be both kind and selfish, sensitive and tactless, perceptive and as thick as a block of stone. In fact, imperfect. In fact, unique. So, how could she clump him up with a group of strangers she thought of as black-and-white characters in a movie half a century old? How could she assume that because these people seemed privileged and hip, they were also shallow and vain?

Was she feeling inferior, after all?

Impossible. She dealt with senior editors, famous authors, foreign publishers, all as equals. Then why the need to run down Dean's friends? Because she was afraid, that was why. When she saw how well Dean fit in, it made her sure she didn't fit in at all. And that made her ask if this "not fitting in" was the problem between them, the wall, the elusive condition that kept Dean from making her his wife.

"But it's my birthday," Harrie heard Chip say.

"Well, I know that, dear one. Happy birthday," Riva said, giving

Chip a kiss on his cheek. "But I want to mingle." She turned to Harrie. "You should buy a lottery ticket," she said. "The mysterious rainbow. You never know. Just in case."

"Nice meeting you," Harrie said, waggling her fingers. And to Chip, "She's very nice."

"And that's just for starters." Chip looked around his apartment as though he were a maître d' surveying the premises.

"You look sad."

"I do?"

Harrie nodded.

"Yeah. I know."

"You still love her, don't you?"

"For my sins," Chip said, jutting out his chin in the direction of Riva's departure. "It's been three years and I still miss her."

Harrie took Chip's arm and squeezed it. She liked him so much, and she wasn't alone. She could count at least four of Chip's former girlfriends right here in the room, but for some reason, Chip was stuck in the state of bachelorhood. She'd fixed him up with Desiree once but they hadn't clicked. Too straight, Des had said. Wrong type, Chip had said. Now, having met the one who got away, Harrie thought Riva was the reason Chip couldn't find someone to love. "Have you asked her out recently?" Harrie asked, her eyes on Riva, who was now chatting with a man in a gray jacket and a streaked-blond "fade." "She seems to have come to the party by herself."

Chip sighed, the folds in his face seeming to deepen by the minute. "Sure. Every couple of months, when I've forgotten what it feels like when she turns me down, I ask her out. I just asked her if she'd stay until the end of the party. Maybe we could, you know, talk . . . But she said no." Chip took a long drink of champagne. "This is what slays me about you and Dean. The chance he's taking on losing you."

"He is?"

"Well, isn't he?"

Harrie shrugged. There was an unwritten rule these days followed by marriage-minded women who'd reached a certain age—say thirty. To wit, they gave a man six months to a year to get real or get out. Desiree considered this more than a guideline. It was a law. Yet here she was, two years into the relationship and thirty-two, and she couldn't imagine breaking up with Dean. "I love him," Harrie said simply.

"Riva loved me too," Chip said. "At the time, I just couldn't—I don't know why I valued my damned freedom so much."

"Can't you work on her? Can't you just woo her to death?"

"I've tried, Harrie. She said she could never trust me again. She said she was so mad at me when I broke up with her the last time, she just poisoned me in her head."

"That's a quote?"

Chip nodded.

"I'm sorry," Harrie said. "I really am."

⬚

Dean excused himself from the group. He was feeling off somehow. Was he being affected by the shattering noise of the TV? Or the tedious conversation? He chose not to examine the flash of bitterness he felt at his peers' obvious competence in their careers, in finding mates, raising kids, buying homes. Instead, he asked himself why it was that these people could only talk about business or their mortgages and babies. Didn't anyone read the newspaper besides the business section, or read a book, or have an original, nonmercenary thought? Harrie seemed to be having a good time, Dean noticed. Maybe she'd found the party so exotic she hadn't noticed the quality of the conversation. Although one never knew with Harrie. She could be converting lead into gold.

Dean stood alone. He pushed back his hair, adjusted his glasses. He could use a couple of aspirin about now. He made his way through the gloom, edging past a clutch of women jammed into the juncture of two walls. "She's a little downtown for him, don't you think?" he heard one of the women say. The shot creased his forehead. The bitch could only be talking about Harrie. He snapped his head around to see who had spoken, and saw a round little person whom he recognized as an account executive from his firm's advertising agency, speaking to a woman he didn't recognize and to Laura Taft.

Dean opened his mouth, then shut it as he created, then rejected hypothetical retorts. What did it matter what they thought? Harrie was more woman than any one of them could ever hope to be. But he knew what the remark meant. Wrong family. Wrong schools. Wrong clubs. *Wrong girl.* There was a jolt to his temple and a smell of garbage spoiling. Dean went to the kitchen, spotted the open garbage bin, found the lid and capped the can. A waitress returned to replenish her tray. "Can I git you somethin'?" she asked, her southern drawl a cushion of warmth in the cold tile room.

"Just a glass of water, thanks," Dean said, opening a cabinet, retrieving a pint-size jar of aspirin Chip kept next to the Worcestershire sauce. He took the glass of water from the young woman, gulped his pills, and knew he'd had enough of this evening. He put the empty glass in the sink, then went to find Harrie so he could get the hell out of Yup World.

⊡

The driver was a two-pedal man. The taxi lurched its way down Seventh Avenue toward Harrie's apartment, stopping, starting, swerving suddenly, causing Dean's jaw to lock down hard enough to bite through steel, and causing Harrie to clutch her armrest so that her silk-and-satin-clad body didn't slide around the backseat. Harrie was aware that Dean had slipped into a bad mood, and when that happened, he was prone to snapping, and she was feeling too vulnerable tonight to have a fight. So she held on to the armrest, and when they stopped at a red light a block from her apartment, she touched Dean's arm and said, "Let's get out here."

The newspaper stand was a small sliver of store wedged between a boutique and an artists' supply shop. Gregory, the owner, was a swarthy, fiftyish man who seemed to own one pair of baggy trousers and a T-shirt. His beige hair was shoulder length and his mustache covered the whole of his mouth. Muscles bulging, he was collating the bulky sections of the next day's Sunday *Times.* He exchanged greetings with Harrie and Dean, bundled up a complete newspaper and took it to the counter.

Harrie longed for a candy bar. The mocha mousse she'd been waiting for had never materialized. More than once, she'd eyed the wine goblets filled with the stuff, but Dean had seemed so impatient they'd left the party before she'd had a chance to indulge herself. And now she faced a tempting display of candy inches away from the cash register. What she wouldn't do for a peanut butter cup! She patted her stomach surreptitiously and called up her willpower. She thought of Dean shaming her out of potato chips, and of Lycra-wrapped sylphs with Ph.D.s.

"You should get a lottery ticket before I have to close down the computer," Gregory was saying. He stroked his mustache, parting it neatly, twirling the ends. "It's some kind of special deal tonight."

"How so?" Harrie asked, running a wistful finger across an orange wrapper.

"They call it a Bonus Jackpot Explosion. They're going to pay out the whole ten million all at once, not the way they usually do it where they take twenty years to pay, so you hardly notice the money."

"I've bought a lot of tickets from you, Gregory, and I've never won a thing," Harrie said, Riva's advice sounding loud and clear in her mind. She cast a glance at Dean, who was standing restlessly at the door, newspaper under his arm, brow crinkled, foot tapping a silent command. "But okay," she said, pushing past her candy lust. She took a card, filled in little boxes with a pencil, paid Gregory for the newspaper and the slip of paper with a rainbow on its face. "Well, hell. What's another buck. I might get lucky. You never know."

"You've got to be in it, to win it," Gregory said, quoting the current advertising slogan.

⊡

Dean shed his clothes, relieved to be undressed, relieved to be in a place he thought of as safe harbor. Just the act of hanging his clothes on Harrie's hangers, all threaded through crocheted tubes or padded with quilted fabric, calmed him. The armoire smelled of potpourri, and the bathrobe Harrie had given him last Christmas carried a trace of the scent. He glanced at Harrie, who was undressing in the middle of the room. She had a classic body, Dean thought, the kind you saw carved from marble, standing at the tops of imposing staircases, ensconced in the Met or the Louvre. He could easily imagine an urn under Harrie's arm and a transparent drape over her shoulder and across her thigh. Underwear fell to the floor, a cloud of white nightgown drifted down over her head and shoulders, stopping above her ankles. And Harrie, chattering happily about her lottery ticket, parceled out the sections of the paper each would read—the book review section for her, the magazine section for him, the rest in a pile beside the bed. Then the two got under the covers.

⊡

"Fourteen minutes and counting," Harrie said. She thumbed the re-mote-control channel changer, found the station, then sat back and observed the picture tube. Satisfied with the reception, she turned to Dean, who had begun his attack on the crossword puzzle. "How's it going?" she asked.

Dean removed his glasses, closed his eyes, and massaged the bridge of his nose. "I haven't got the attitude for this tonight," he said. He flipped the magazine to the floor. "I'm going to take a bath."

"Don't you want to see what I look like when I win ten million dollars?" Harrie asked. She wanted to engage with Dean right now, wanted to dispel her lingering, unpleasant mood. On the walk home, she'd reminded him of the shoe store lady's prophecy and told him of her conversation with Riva, and he'd actually snorted in response. Would it kill him to play along with her, be a kid for a little while?

"Yeah, well, I have a feeling you'll call me if you win." Dean cinched the sash of the robe, stuck his feet into his scuffs, and heaved himself out of the brass bed. "Keep me company, why don't you? Doesn't a bath sound nice?"

"I guess I could at least brush my teeth." Harrie stood up on the bed, walked springily across the mattress, and from there stepped awkwardly to the floor. She said, "You know, the trouble is, you have no faith."

"I don't, huh? You don't really believe this psychic crap, do you?" Dean put out a steadying arm to Harrie.

"What if I do?" she said. As a matter of fact, she was on the fence. She wouldn't go so far as to give money to palm readers, but she also wouldn't say that just because you couldn't prove something, it was crap. Besides, whether she believed or didn't believe wasn't the point. The point was, the words "Let me see your palm" were an invitation to venture for a short while into the fascinating world of "What if" and Dean just couldn't tolerate the prospect. No wonder his job had him so strung out. "What if" was the beginning and the end of the stock market. "Maybe I do," she continued. "I think it's possible that some people have an extrasensory gift. A little clairvoyance."

Dean groaned. "Please. A woman who works in a shoe store is clairvoyant?"

"Maybe. Maybe. You haven't yet come up with an explanation for how she knew Julie's shoe size. Or how she knew I had a sister at all, for that matter."

Dean laughed. It was a maniacal, frustrated laugh. He shot out a hand to tickle her.

Harrie sidestepped him, pushed away his hand. "Fine. Laugh. How did she know?"

"Honey, please come take a bath with me. I'll give you a toe massage that'll send you to the moon."

"No."

"Please."

"Maybe."

Dean gave Harrie a kiss on the side of her neck, then shuffled into the bathroom. There he dropped the stopper into the bathtub drain, turned on the water, and watched as the stream poured into the tub. As he watched the sound seemed to increase, as though the tub were a radio being turned ever louder. The water pounded. It thundered. He remembered the warning at Chip's. That foul odor. That jolt he'd ignored. Now the sound of running water was as loud as the Hoover Dam. Let me be imagining it, he prayed. His vision was fine. He was just feeling stress, that was all. He had to relax. Let his muscles uncoil. What he needed now was a nice warm bath and a good night's sleep. But would he sleep? Or would he have a *Nightmare on Elm Street* kind of night: running legs, floors dropping beneath him, twisted sheets—and pain.

Harrie piled the towels on the hamper. She said to Dean, "Someone's going to win. Why not me?" She bent her head and gathered her soft, light brown curls together at the top, twisting them, then securing them with a lacquered chopstick. Straightening, she squeezed toothpaste onto her toothbrush and, with the water gushing into the sink, scrubbed her teeth vigorously.

"Why not, Beauty," Dean said automatically, trailing his fingers in the bathwater. Why tell a butterfly about the existence of winter? He sat on the chipped rim of the claw-footed tub and, moving his head only slightly, watched Harrie brush her teeth. It sounded to him as if she were using an electric sander.

"Ten million dollars," Harrie said. She adjusted the temperature of the water and lathered up her washcloth with rose-scented soap. "God, I could have fun with that. Even after taxes, I could have fun with that." She applied the warm cloth to her face and inhaled the floral aroma.

"Don't you ever worry about being disappointed?" Dean asked. Harrie worked herself up. She crashed. She worked herself up. Crashed again. And not just with lottery tickets. She had a kind of house-of-cards deal with the whole world.

"What, honey?" Harrie said, lifting her head away from the streaming water.

"Nothing, Har. I was just talking to myself." He rotated his fingers gently at his temples.

"Okay," Harrie said. She turned off the water. She dried her face, creamed it, unpinned her hair. She stretched out her hand. "Oh, come on. Humor me. Let's just go watch together for a couple of minutes."

"My bath will get cold."

"Come on. You're such a stick. I used our birth dates."

As Dean stood looking at Harrie his vision flickered. A blank circle appeared before his right eye, and as he stared, hoping the blank was an illusion, not a symptom, a hole in Harrie's image dropped out. "Okay," he said softly. "I give up."

Pleased, Harrie led Dean out of the bathroom, pulled him into the bed behind her, fluffed pillows around them both; then, clutching the scrap of colored paper, she stared at the television screen.

Dean twitched his eyes from side to side. He'd lost all but about thirty degrees. His peripheral vision was gone and the pounding had started. It wasn't his imagination. This headache was going to be a killer. The kind that made him want to blow his head off with a gun. And it was almost upon him: the black, the bad, the death of all other things. Were there pills in his shaving kit? In a moment, moving would be unthinkable. "Harrie," he whispered.

"Hmmm?" she replied distractedly.

"My pills. In the bathroom."

"You're not getting a migraine?"

Dean nodded his head once—nearly imperceptibly as far as she could see, an excruciating arc of pain to him. The sound of television voices passed over him, vibrating his bones. A wave of nausea rolled up from his belly. He clamped his jaw and screwed his eyes tightly closed. The noise! The light! He lifted his hand, pointed toward the TV. The sound vanished. He felt a cold glass against his lips. He opened his mouth, accepted a tablet, swallowed. He mumbled thanks, then placed a pillow over his head. Could he cut himself off from all light and sound? Would the pill work, or was it already too late?

Harrie crawled back into bed, carefully, carefully. She reached out a hand to touch Dean's arm but withdrew it, knowing that any sensation would be agony. Dean seemed so far away. He was hurting and she couldn't do anything for him, and that made her feel powerless. Helplessly, Harrie turned to the now muted television screen. A sitcom was in its final moments. Soon the drawing would begin and if she won, her world would unfold like a flower: a golden peony shot with light and filled with honey.

Aware of Dean breathing beside her, Harrie closed and rested her eyes. Images flickered, cords entwined. She saw fields of heather, a violet haze. And these images spun and pushed at the walls of her studio, a space too small to contain her imagination. She envisioned rooms, spacious and filled with beautiful things, and she clutched the scrap of colored paper that might be a ticket to those rooms and a happier life with Dean.

When she opened her eyes, the reverie shattered and her vision was filled by a drum of whirling Ping-Pong balls. One by one, balls flew down a chute. Harrie tried to make the numbers on the balls match those on the two-by-three-inch piece of paper in her hand.

But she could not.

Before three balls had dropped, she knew she had lost. Had she expected to win? She sighed deeply as her fantasy withered and folded, enclosing, perhaps, the green bud of another fantasy she would have tomorrow. Then Harrie pressed the button that turned off the television. She looked at Dean, huddled as far from her as possible. And she switched off the light.

12

---□---

*P*UCK. PUCK-PUCK.

The secretary-receptionist tapped on the keys of the antique Smith-Corona. Harrie was deep in the heart of the Empire State Building, in the waiting room of the law offices of Schoonmaker and Schoonmaker, Attorneys-at-Law.

The room looked to Harrie like a color plate from a pre-Depression interior design book. There were dark Victorian lamp tables and men's club couches and chairs whose heavy feet rested on ancient Persian carpets. There were hunting prints on all of the walls but one, and on that wall was an ornate gilt-framed mirror. Below the mirror, seated at a desk so large it made the woman seem even tinier and more shriveled, was the receptionist, who was addressing envelopes with her manual typewriter. She squinted through the thick eyeglasses on her wrinkled-up nose and plucked from time to time at the blue Orlon cardigan that was connected by a chain across her collarbone. Occasionally, she barked into the receiver of an old-fashioned, rotary-dial phone. Harrie wondered if anything in the room had changed since the building was erected. It was funny, but after an idle hour of watching dust motes, she'd taken on an old feeling herself—as if she might be a doll with a porcelain face and layers of poufy clothes which had been propped in a chair one day around 1931 and forgotten.

Mr. Schoonmaker's letter, now folded in her pocket, had been very brief. It had stated simply that as attorney for the estate, he had some things to discuss with her regarding Mr. Tuckman's will, and had asked Harrie to please phone for an appointment at her convenience. The letter seemed so calm, so devoid of emotion. Mr. Tuckman was dead and this letter had all the passion of a phone bill. Harrie had made the appointment immediately, and now she sat in the old chair waiting, wondering why she was there.

Across from Harrie sat three men who had all entered the room after her. They'd given their names to the receptionist, and after each had done so, the gnarled old woman had sighed, painfully straightened up from her chair, and walked down a corridor toward the offices in a gait that suggested she was moving against a gale-force wind. Harrie had smiled at each of the men as he entered, uttered a soft "Hello," then stared out the window or glanced at a magazine, which was, to her surprise, a current issue. But Harrie saw nothing through the window, and she wasn't reading.

She was thinking about Mr. Tuckman.

Harrie remembered when she'd first moved to New York after graduation. The small apartment was dark, and the air was so still she'd gone to the windows at the rear of her studio and pulled up the shades. Next, she'd unlocked the security gates, opened the lead-framed panes, and peered out into the garden.

It was a garden in the sense that it supported plant life, but it was nothing like the kind of garden she'd known in Spode—no rows of dahlias interspersed with tomatoes, no sweet peas growing up the corn stalks with pumpkin vines filling in between. This garden was a square of shade-loving ground cover, stretched like a carpet around the trunks of five dauntless ailanthus trees. There were two concrete benches at the end of the flagstone path, and the place was bounded by the sides of neighboring buildings and a rickety wooden stockade fence at the back.

Intrigued, Harrie had climbed out of a window. She'd picked her way down the path, plopped onto a bench, and was inhaling her first breaths of dank air, when she heard an awful screech followed by a "Hel-looo dowwnn therrrre," which arched and flew and dipped from far above down onto the curly greensward. A shouted-down invitation followed this greeting, and Harrie found herself, not long after, stepping out of an elevator car into a tropical island of Mr. Tuckman's creation: a many-windowed penthouse room filled with jungle plants and shrieking cockatoos, worn velvet furniture and hundreds of framed photographs. The sound of Broadway show tunes from the thirties and forties snaked sinuously through the room. And there was Mr. Tuckman himself. He was in his mid-sixties at least, Harrie had decided, but he was so limber, so animated, and his hair so thick, he could almost be mistaken for a man in his fifties. And the stories he told . . .

After that meeting, Harrie had gone upstairs to the penthouse once a week, where she and Mr. Tuckman would share a meal and enjoy one another's company. Harrie would tell of her authors and the novels they wrote, of her friendships with men, her hopes and fantasies, and, years later, of her love for Dean. And Mr. Tuckman, a childless widower, would tell of the days when he and his late wife, Jasmine Defoe, were on the stage. "Jazz and I, we did have fun," Mr. Tuckman would nearly sing, and then he would recount a tale of an opening night, a fire backstage, a forgotten cue, a chance opportunity. He told of sharp-edged city days, and long weekends at the Tuckmans' country home reading and rehearsing in front of the fireplace, entertaining their now deceased theatrical friends. And he reviewed new plays for Harrie.

On summer evenings, like the last evening she'd shared with her friend, Harrie would bring the wine, and Mr. Tuckman would cook their dinner, and then they'd sit out on the roof terrace surrounding his living space and, with a cockatoo or two perched on the railing, watch the sun set.

Harrie remembered the last time she'd rung Mr. Tuckman's bell.

·

"Come in-n-n," Mr. Tuckman had said. He'd kissed Harrie's cheek and accepted the bottle of wine she brought. He was wearing a white shirt, khaki walking shorts, and canvas shoes.

"Hey, we're twins," Harrie said, pointing out their nearly identical apparel.

"What do you know?" Mr. Tuckman grinned. He combed his hair back with his fingers while pushing a bird beak away from his scalp. "Sid, give Harrie a kiss," he said to the peaches-and-cream-colored bird on his shoulder.

"There ain't nothin' like a dame. Whee hoo," the bird whistled, its crest unfurling, its irises dilating and contracting.

"Show-off," Mr. Tuckman said fondly, and put the cockatoo on a stand in the vestibule.

"Do you think they mind when you have quail for dinner?" Harrie asked, lifting her nostrils to the piquant scent of broiling bird.

"Aw. It keeps 'em in line, doesn't it, Sidney," Mr. Tuckman said, scratching a feathered chin. "Grab some glasses, honey, and let's get some air."

The art deco vitrine held wineglasses of varied shapes and patterns. Harrie chose two iridescent tulips that made her think of soap bubbles. Above the case were photos of Mr. Tuckman with his beloved Jazz and fellow cast members, all long gone.

"I can never get over how happy she looks in those pictures," Harrie said. She joined Mr. Tuckman on the terrace, adjusted a chair and sat next to her friend. "Did she always look like a bride?"

"Jazz? She was a lot like you," Mr. Tuckman said. "I don't mean she looked like you, although you are both beauties in your own ways. I mean she had a beguiling nature. And she embraced life every minute she was on earth. Just like you do."

"Beguiling nature?"

"She was enchanting, my dear. Jazz was a bit of an enchantress, and a bit of a dreamer." Angel, Sidney's mate, flew out the open terrace door and Mr. Tuckman stretched out his arm to her.

Harrie uncorked the wine and poured. " 'If you don't have a dream . . .' "

"So true. And what are optimists if not dreamers? Jazz had dreams of stardom. She worked at it, so you couldn't say it was all wishing and hoping."

"Was she disappointed? That she never got to the top?"

"Oh, I don't know, honey. She was a happy woman. We had enough. We had each other."

Harrie sipped her wine and thought that Mr. Tuckman didn't seem to miss his old life. Rather, he seemed happy for the past, pleased in the present. "That's a lot," she said.

"Angel and Sidney are having an anniversary."

"They are?"

"They are. I got these two old birds thirty years ago today."

Angel crab-walked along the back of Mr. Tuckman's chair to Harrie's arm, then down her arm with her pinchy little walk, and up her hand until she could bite Harrie's glass with her sharp black beak.

"Well, maybe just a sip," Harrie crooned to Angel. "Seeing as it's your thirtieth. What is that, by the way?" She tickled the bird's cheek. "Your mango anniversary?"

"Pretty girl. Pretty girl," said the bird.

"Yes, you are," Harrie answered. Thirty years was a long time to be with a person, she thought. And she wondered, would she and Dean celebrate a thirtieth anniversary? Would they have sweet lives of the Tuckman kind? "How long do cockatoos live?"

"I don't know for sure. Some kinds of parrots live over eighty years. Low-fat diets, you know. Seeds, fruit, chili peppers, and exercise. We could all live so long."

"Is that your secret then?"

"I just have good genes."

"To your genes," Harrie had said, touching her glass to Mr. Tuckman's.

"To your dreams," Mr. Tuckman had replied.

□

Harrie blinked her eyes and brought herself into the present. She was starting to worry about how her seizing those birds might look. Her intentions had been honorable, but the birds were worth a couple thousand dollars each, and they weren't hers. Dean's assurances that she'd done the only reasonable thing had not completely set her mind at ease. Would Mr. Schoonmaker believe that she'd just taken the birds for safekeeping? She'd almost asked him at the funeral, but stopped herself from making what might have seemed a very inappropriate request. Now she had a terrible feeling that the birds would be just property to the lawyer and would have to be sold to settle the estate. God, that would be awful. She wouldn't be able to buy them, and they meant so much to her. They were more than valuable property, more even than pets. They were part of Mr. Tuckman's life with Jazz and they'd taken on almost symbolic meaning to her. Mr. Tuckman and Jazz. Sidney and Angel. Happy couplehood.

Although Dean hadn't seen it exactly that way.

At first, he had been willing to agree that the birds were cute. He'd given Sidney a peanut and scratched Angel's head. He'd been polite about the bird dander in the air and the screeching at first light of day. He'd been less polite at Harrie's refusal to spend the night with him in his apartment because she didn't want to leave the birds alone. There'd been a spat over that. "I didn't say a thing," Dean had snapped as he banged his loafers on the trash can, emptying them of sunflower hulls. The bits of peach-colored down floating in his cereal seemed to be the limit, however, and he'd left for work this morning without saying goodbye.

Was it too much to hope that Dean would say, "Bring the birds. Come live with me"? His apartment was huge compared with hers; bright, draft-free, perfect for the birds. If the birds were hers. And if he wanted to live with her.

Harrie pushed her hair back and turned a page. She patted the pocket with Mr. Schoonmaker's letter in it and she looked at her watch. This had been the longest hour of her life. Didn't Mr. Schoonmaker feel the slightest bit urgent about this matter? Didn't he think anyone else had schedules to keep? Apparently not.

These last thoughts had begun to take on volume and intensity, when the elderly secretary called the room to attention. Her back to the corridor, her legs braced two feet apart, she announced, "Miss Brain Tree. Mr. Schoonmaker is available to see you now. Second room on your right. God be praised."

And then she leaned into the invisible hurricane and tottered very slowly back to her desk.

13

———□———

*M*R. EUGENE SCHOONMAKER rose from his chair and walked around his desk to shake Harrie's hand. Here was the man she remembered from the funeral. He was tall, at least six two Harrie figured, and except for his eyebrows, which were so full and long they seemed like small wings, Mr. Schoonmaker had not a hair on his head.

"Hello, hello, howaya," he said, shaking her hand briefly, then indicating the chair he wanted her to take, one of the set from the reception area. He returned to his desk, the surface of which was nearly obscured by teetering stacks of papers, lawbooks, and paper coffee cups. "I didn't mean to keep you, Miss Braintree, but I was having a telephone conversation that just wouldn't quit."

"You were on the phone?" Harrie was pricked with the kind of perturbation she used to feel waiting for her mother to pick her up from school. First, the long stone-kicking wait until she was sure her dizzy mother had been in a horrible crack-up, then relief when the rusty old Ford turned the corner and her mother was waving her hand and pushing open the door for Harrie, then fury when the reason for the delay turned out to be that her mother had gotten absorbed in a game show. Her irritation must have shown, because Mr. Schoonmaker said, "Hey. What's the matter? You got another appointment, or what? I said I'm sorry, Miss, uh, Braintree."

Mr. Schoonmaker's voice was as warm and as rough as a cat's tongue. Harrie sputtered indignantly, "My appointment was for *noon*. It's after *one*. Don't you think other people have things to do?"

"Go ahead. Yell all you want. We got good acoustics back here."

"Well, that's the weirdest apology I ever heard."

Mr. Schoonmaker pawed at a stack of files, found the one he was looking for, then lit a cigarette. "Do you mind?" he asked.

"No, go ahead," Harrie said stiffly.

"Oh, for God's sake. What do you think I am? A monster? I know you're upset. I saw you at the service. Crying behind the mausoleum."

"But, I'm not—"

"Want some coffee?"

"No, thanks."

"All right now. Before we proceed to the business at hand, I want to get this appointment thing straight. I've got you down for one. Not twelve, when I always eat my lunch, but one."

Harrie shook her head vigorously. "I have the letter right here." She unfolded it, and mysteriously the figures that had so clearly spelled out twelve now clearly spelled out one. "Omigod."

"Does it say one?"

"I don't understand it. I was so sure . . ."

"Well, that's a relief. I'd hate to think the old babe is losing her marbles. I have lunch every day at noon."

"Please accept my apology. I shouldn't have blasted you. I was entirely wrong."

"Listen. I understand how upset you must be. And all's well that ends well. Now," he said, tipping back his chair, rocking it a little. "I want to tell you about David's will."

"There's something I have to know," Harrie said.

"I'll read the will in its entirety if you want me to. Actually, it's customary."

"No, I mean, I have to know this one thing right now. You knew Mr. Tuckman had a pair of cockatoos? Well, I took them to my apartment because I didn't want anything to happen to them, and I know them, of course. I wanted them to be safe. I wasn't just taking them, you understand?"

"Sure," Mr. Schoonmaker said, rocking in his chair. "You wanted to protect them."

"Right."

"And so?"

"And so I wouldn't want anyone to think I had simply appropriated them. Although I have been secretly hoping Mr. Tuckman wanted me to have them. That is, of course, unless he wanted someone else to have them." Harrie gave Mr. Schoonmaker a guilty look, then folded her hands in her lap and looked at them.

"Well, well," the lawyer said, one corner of his mouth curling up: a semismile. He inhaled tobacco smoke, then blew it out pleasurably. "You want the birds."

Harrie stared. She could feel her heart beating against her blouse. Had she been inexcusably gauche? Was there any way of disgracing herself that she hadn't yet tried?

"So you shouldn't suffer unduly, Miss Braintree, David left you the birds," Mr. Schoonmaker said, tapping off his ash.

"He did? Oh, good," Harrie said, grinning with relief. "I was starting to dream of being sent away for five years to life . . ."

"He also left you his piano and a few other little things."

"Well. The piano," Harrie said. Where would she put the piano? She took a quick mental tour of her apartment. It would have to be the piano or the bed. One or the other. Both were out of the question.

"Why don't I read the will? Do you have time?"

Harrie nodded.

Mr. Schoonmaker reached for the file he had uncovered earlier and lifted out a document bound in blue paper. He took his reading glasses out of a small case and centered them on his nose, then took another drag of his cigarette. He leaned back in his chair. He spoke. " 'I, David Solomon Tuckman, of the cities of New York and Cold Spring Harbor, actor (retired), do make, publish, and declare this my last will and testament, hereby revoking all previous wills heretofore made by me, intending hereby to dispose of all property of whatever kind and wherever situated which I possess at my death and to exercise my power of disposition. I hereby give and bequeath—' "

The receptionist appeared in the doorway. "I'm going now," she said, without preamble. She pushed at her glasses with a knobby hand.

"This is David's friend, Miss Braintree," Mr. Schoonmaker shouted.

"Hello, dear."

Mr. Schoonmaker addressed Harrie. "You've met Becky?"

Harrie nodded. "Nice to meet you," she said.

"Becky's going out for a while," the lawyer continued. "She's going to stop at the deli. Have you eaten? May I treat you to a pastrami sandwich?"

"No, thanks. But would a Diet Pepsi be too much trouble?"

"One Diet Pepsi," said the woman in a raspy voice. "That's with caffeine or without?"

"Without, I guess," said Harrie.

"Good," she said. "It's better for you. Although the saccharine is another story." She made a note on a little pad. "And you, Eugene? Chocolate malted?" Receiving a nod, she muttered, "One day your arteries . . ." then turned on her orthopedic shoes and hobbled out of view.

"Don'tcha wonder what she means by one day? I'm seventy-six. How much longer am I going to need my arteries?"

"Why doesn't she phone the deli?" Harrie asked. "It hurts to watch her walk."

"She wants to get some air."

"What?"

"How long can you fight the same fight with a person? She wants to get air. So let her. I'm lucky the crazy old dame will still get into an elevator."

"Oh," said Harrie. "She's been with you for a long time?"

"She's my sister. Wacky old babe." Mr. Schoonmaker's thoughts seemed to trail off. Ashes fell on the jacket of his bright summer-weight plaid suit. He brushed at them absently, then said, "She was best friends with Jazz Defoe, you know. They were in the chorus together in *Anything Goes* back in 'thirty-four. Fifty, sixty years ago, Becky was quite a looker. You shoulda seen her in a bathing suit."

Harrie tried to imagine the elderly woman as a "looker," but failed. Too much flesh had shifted, and arthritis had warped her bones. But then the woman had to be close to eighty years old.

"You said Becky was a dancer?"

"Danced and sang. Always a chorus girl, though. Jazz got speaking parts. She did okay. Did David tell you he was the male lead in a Broadway show? *The Fifty-Cent Fantasy,* 1939. The story was, he was the owner of a movie house and he was in love with a movie star. Pixie Romaine played the lead. She must be dead now thirty years. Died in Atlantic City. Drinking problem, you know." Mr. Schoonmaker sighed. "I had a little thing for Pixie."

"I saw some pictures of the cast," Harrie said. "Mr. Tuckman wore baggy pants and suspenders—"

"And a bow tie. That's right. And Pixie wore this gold dress, wrapped tight right around here," the lawyer said, sweeping a hand across his hips. "Anyway, the show closed after ten months, but for a little while David Tuckman was a star. David was a little younger than Jazz. About thirteen years, to be exact. Quite the scandal back then." He drained the remains of a cold coffee container with as much pleasure as if it were chilled champagne. "Boy, those were the days. We felt like we owned New York. Like we were going to live forever. Me and my sweetheart of the moment, Becky and her *beau du jour,* and Jazz and Tookie. Sardi's. Toots Shor. 'Twenty-one.' Out on the town. Jazz called David Tookie, did you know that?"

"No, I didn't."

"You still hear the songs from that show I was telling you about. The one with Ethel Merman. 'I Get a Kick Out of You.' You heard that one?" Mr. Schoonmaker sang a few lines.

Harrie had to smile. The man was a character. A sweet character. "Were you in the theater too, Mr. Schoonmaker?" she asked. Mentally, she put hair on his head, spring in his step. She could imagine it.

"Naw. I was in law school when Becky and Jazz were on the stage. Columbia. And when I passed the bar, the Tuckmans were my first clients. Contracts and the like. Yes," he said, tipping back his chair, "New York was our oyster, all right. Me in business with my brother. My big sister on the stage. I dated the most beautiful girls . . . Oh, my. Those long weekends at Blackfern. Did David ever tell you about Blackfern?" The attorney cocked a winglike eyebrow.

"No, I don't think so."

"Hard to believe," Mr. Schoonmaker said. "Blackfern was the

love of their life. It was a castle, you know. A quasi-castle, really, right on Long Island Sound. They spent every weekend there."

"Oh," said Harrie. "Blackfern was their country house?"

The attorney nodded.

"Well then, he did sort of mention it. He never said it was a castle. I remember him describing a fireplace. A stone one that you could walk into. And I've got pictures in my mind of some cocktail parties. And I'm not sure . . . maybe he said something about a swimming pool. He didn't talk about it much."

"No. After Jazz passed away, he sort of bricked Blackfern up, figuratively of course. Too many memories, I suppose. Too many memories of glorious times. And it was Jasmine's house, after all. Left to her by her father. So even though she left it to him, he just walked away."

"How sad."

"Well. Did David seem sad to you?"

"No, and that's the damnedest thing," Harrie replied. She crossed one arm under the other, brought her hand to her cheek and drummed her fingers there. "He had such a happy disposition. I wonder if I would have recovered from the loss of a person I loved so much. Somehow I don't think I would have."

"You can't be like that, sweetheart. Sadness is okay. Like you being sad that David is gone. But things change and you gotta change. Every time a door closes, another one opens. Yesterday you worried you were a parrot thief. Now you got birds to call your very own." He gave her a mischievous and very toothy grin.

Harrie laughed. "What is that thing they say about being careful what you wish for? You might get it? Two big birds take up a lot of room in a small apartment."

Mr. Schoonmaker chuckled to himself.

"What's so funny?" Harrie asked.

"Nothing. Just wondering if you've got any more wishes."

"Wish I had my Diet Pepsi."

"Hold on to that thought. Becky will be here sometime this century. Shall I continue with David's will in the meantime? I sorta got off the track."

"Oh. Go right ahead."

"All right. Let me sum up the bequests. David gave his books to the Lincoln Center theater library. He gave his plays and photo collection to the Yiddish Theatrical Alliance. There were some cash gifts to a half dozen repertory companies, the Retired Actors Fund, the Art Deco Society, the American Cancer Society, and to some of his other friends, namely Becky and myself. I guess we're the closest he had to family." The attorney ran his finger down the page, turned to the next. "Some clothes and furnishings to the Salvation Army . . . Let's see. Here you are, Miss Braintree. 'I leave the property known as Blackfern, which consists of a main house, a cottage, stables, and three outbuildings on three and a half acres in the town of Cold Spring Harbor, the bonds in my accounts at Salomon Brothers, listed separately, my two Moluccan cockatoos known as Sidney and Angel, my baby grand piano, and the rest, residue and remainder of my estate to my incomparable friend Harriet Periwinkle Braintree, with whom I shared countless happy times. I make these bequests because of Harrie's many kindnesses to me—' Oh, Becky. Your timing is impeccable."

"Blackfern?" Harrie said to Mr. Schoonmaker. "Did you say he left Blackfern to me? I didn't know he still— Are you sure this isn't some kind of mistake?"

"Oh, it's not a mistake, Miss Braintree."

Harrie felt a flush, then light-headedness, then a ringing in her ears. Could she have heard what she thought she heard? Was it a joke? Or a mistake? "Thank you very much," she said in a whisper as Becky put a cold can and a straw in front of her, but it was David Tuckman she was thanking.

"Thank you, dear," Mr. Schoonmaker said to his sister, who was laboriously making her way out of the room. "Will you go back down and get me some ice?"

Becky waved her hand dismissively as she exited.

"Damned malted is warm. Twenty minutes it took her to go to the corner and back. Can ya beat it?"

Harrie gripped the arms of the old leather chair, a chair that now seemed to be slipping and sliding between her conscious and subconscious worlds. Was Blackfern really hers? Could this be true? Gratitude to Mr. Tuckman washed over her, and then elation nearly carried her away. How incredibly generous of Mr. Tuckman! Blackfern! It was the gift of a lifetime and it would change her life.

And now she wanted information. Where exactly in Cold Spring Harbor was the house? What did the house look like? How many rooms? Three and a half acres! She retrieved images Mr. Tuckman had placed in her mind, and then she added to those images, enhanced them with the sounds of laughter in front of a stone fireplace—the Tuckmans at home entertaining their friends from the big Broadway musicals: Judy Holliday, Ethel Merman, Ray Bolger, sipping martinis, singing. She imagined Mr. Tuckman wearing a cravat and a smoking jacket, Jazz in a satin sheath, an ostrich-feather boa. Oh, God. Those movies from the thirties. But now she would be in one. Soon she and Dean would be tossing logs into the flames, having Chip and Riva over for dinner. Harrie knew now where the baby grand would go; there would be a music room, and a conservatory where the cockatoos could screech their hearts out. She would get a carpenter. Her brother had a friend who did carpentry, and of course, everything looked better after it was painted . . .

Mr. Schoonmaker's voice interrupted her thoughts. " 'Rest, residue and remainder' means everything not specifically bequeathed. That means it all belongs to you. Why don't I finish? Where was I? Here you go. 'I make these bequests because of Harrie's many kindnesses to me, and because it makes me happy to close my eyes dreaming of what she will do with it all. Good luck, Harrie dear. I wish you much happiness in all you do.' And that's the end," Mr. Schoonmaker concluded. " 'In testimony whereof I have hereunto set my hand this nineteenth day of April in the year 1990,' and it's duly witnessed, of course." He closed the blue folder and slipped the will into an envelope. He handed it to Harrie. "This copy of the will is for you."

"I'm in shock," Harrie said, staring at the envelope in her hand. "To say the least."

Mr. Schoonmaker chuckled. "Forgive me for laughing. I could have prepared you, I suppose, but my love of the dramatic got the best of me. I wanted to see your face when I told you that David Tuckman left you the house. But my dear. The house is not a house you can live in. It's a pile of junk. The land is a different story."

"I never had a house of my own," Harrie said dreamily. "Is there a floor plan anywhere, by chance?"

"You'll want to bulldoze the house, of course. I was out there last week, and the place has fallen into quite a state of disrepair."

"I can't believe Mr. Tuckman left me his house. He never told me he still had it. He hardly ever talked about it. Just once in a while. 'Out to the house,' he might say. 'After the show on Friday night, we'd drive out to the house.' He made it sound like a very little house. With roses on it."

"Yes. Well, they might have had some roses, but if they did, the roses were the least of it. Oh, Blackfern was really something once upon a time," Mr. Schoonmaker said. "Old Sanford Defoe made so much money in steel, he didn't know what in the world to do with it all. So he had part of this stone castle—a minor castle, you should know, but a castle anyway—brought over from Scotland by ship. Then he added on to the thing, blended in a little Tudor style here, a little Italian villa there. You have any idea what all that would have cost? Well, there wasn't any income tax to speak of back then, so what was five or ten million for a house?"

"Five or ten *million?*"

"What do you think it would have cost to take the castle apart in Scotland, ship it over block by block, then put it back together? It was insane, but those people back then didn't care. If they had it, it was coming in faster than they could spend it. The only kind of millionaire we've got today like those old millionaires is Donald Trump, I guess. And you see where that's gotten him."

"You're boggling my mind. I'm going to faint."

"Here. Sip some of your soda." He pushed the can toward Harrie. "Now, listen to me. That house is just a pile of junk, Miss Braintree, not worth restoring. It has no architectural value. Except maybe to salvagers, it isn't worth a thing anymore. When Defoe died during the war, he left the house to Jasmine. When Jazz died in 1963, she in turn left her estate to David, but the house has been virtually abandoned by him since her death. You understand? To David the house *was* Jasmine, and he loved it too much to live there and too much to sell it," Mr. Schoonmaker explained. "So he paid the taxes every year, but he never went back. That's why the house is a ruin. But the land is worth a few million. I was thinking if you don't want to sell the land, you might want to tear the house down and build something modern. Something you could heat."

"I can't believe he left it like that. All alone."

"Oh, there's been a watchman to protect the place from the worst vandalism, but there's been some stone throwing. Lotta windows got smashed, and there's been some graffiti. The whole interior is in absolute shambles. I mean the plumbing, the wiring, the whole bit. Now, as I said, the land is worth quite a bit. And of course, as his heir, you'll be taxed on the dollar value of all David has left to you. The taxes on the property shouldn't run more than a few hundred thousand, so if you sell, you'll have made quite a profit. And then there's Jasmine's trust."

"Sell the property? I couldn't do that." Mr. Tuckman had closed his eyes dreaming of what she would do with it all. Harrie's mind spun with possibilities. She wanted a map, right this minute, and a floor plan and keys! But hundreds of thousands in taxes? "Do I have to pay taxes even if I don't sell the house?"

"You certainly do. Its appraised value is something over four million and the state wants its fair share."

"But that's terrible news. I couldn't raise that kind of money in a lifetime. And I can't sell the house. I feel like I live there already. And Mr. Tuckman knew I wouldn't sell it. He knew I'd want to live at Blackfern."

Mr. Schoonmaker groaned. "Well, you may be right. David was very fond of you and I can see why. Said you reminded him of Jazz."

Harrie smiled. "He told me that too."

"I suppose he knew what you'd want to do when he left you the money from Jasmine's trust. And believe me, if you want to live in that place, you're going to need it."

Harrie looked up.

"Yes," Mr. Schoonmaker said, lighting his fifth cigarette of the hour. "Jasmine's father had set up a trust fund for her before he died. When Jasmine died, the trust was dispersed and David put the money into bonds. Since then and until he passed on, David lived on the interest, paid the taxes on Blackfern and the rent on Chester Street. I, uh, took the liberty of doing some numbers for you, Miss Braintree.

After you've paid taxes on the estate, you'll still have a nice little bundle."

"Enough to fix up the house?" Harrie asked, holding her breath.

"I suppose so," Mr. Schoonmaker said. "I suppose you'll be able to make do on just over seven million dollars."

14

————□————

$\mathcal{D}$EAN CLICKED ON his directional signal and slowed the Saab for the exit. Then he shunted the car off the Long Island Expressway and coasted down the off-ramp toward Cold Spring Harbor. It was just past lunchtime on a Tuesday, and he had dropped, at Harrie's strong request, millions of things he should be doing at the office. Most of the things had to do with Harrie's money, but Harrie wanted to see her castle now, not this coming weekend, and she would not see it without him.

At this moment, Harrie was sitting beside him, her lap filled with reference books and copies of newspaper articles from the twenties, thirties, and forties—clippings from the *Huntington News*, the *Oyster Bay Beacon*, and the *Cold Spring Harbor Star*. With her ankle-length brown wool skirt, her lace-up boots and chamois-colored cardigan, his girlfriend had taken on sepia tones appropriate, Dean thought, to photographs of the times of which she had recently become enamored. The traffic sounds blew in through the cracked-open windows, the radio brought in an erratic signal from New York City, and above it all, Harrie quoted little bursts of old news.

"Dean. Get this. 'This past Sunday, Mrs. Ethel Kensing-Smythe held an Easter lunch at Windward, her home on Green's Point, situated on the Sound. Her two hundred guests and their children enjoyed a splendid buffet beneath pink-striped tents on the east lawn while the Laurel Park string quartet played from the gazebo. The children, over eighty festively clad young of the Smythe and Kensing clans, scrambled for sterling-silver eggs filled with chocolates hidden amongst tulips and narcissi at the feet of the flowering forsythia hedges.' Dean! Sterling silver eggs."

"Mmmm," said Dean. "Could you unfold the map, Har? Could you navigate, please?"

"Oh. Okay." Harrie bunched papers and books together, set them in a stack by her feet. She took a map from the door pocket and straightened it on her lap. "Turn right at the light," she said, "then left on Mill Road." She stared out the window. "It's hard to believe, isn't it? The opulence. Mrs. Fergusen and her gymnasium, her launches and Hupmobiles. The Kensing-Smythes and their movie theater, their private planes, their zillion-dollar art collection. The Paynes, the Whitneys, the Roosevelts. Can you imagine what this area was like when there were five hundred of these mansions all clustered from here"—she stabbed the map—"to here?" She stabbed another point an inch away. "What a place this must have been. What parties they must have had. I just wish there was more to read on Blackfern. Just this one little article." Harrie reached again into the side pocket of the car door and retrieved a photocopied page that she had folded and refolded to the point of disintegration. " 'Blackfern Castle, built in 1345 in Dunwoodie, Scotland, was—' "

" '—taken down and reassembled on Long Island's North Shore in 1915 by steel baron Sanford Defoe . . .' " Dean cut in.

"Killjoy," Harrie muttered.

"Am not," Dean said.

"Are too. Turn right at the corner," Harrie directed. "We go straight out on this road for three miles." She jabbed the button on the console that controlled the window, and took a deep breath of the air. "We're getting closer. Can you smell the water?"

"No, and neither can you smell the water three miles away. What is this?" Dean asked, indicating the community they had entered. "A housing development?"

"I don't know. We're on Kings' Road. That's where we're supposed to be."

"Wow," Dean said a minute later. "Forgive me for noticing, but this place is one step above a trailer park."

Dean was right. The road they were on was straight as a ruled line and it was intersected by other straight roads. To the left and to the right were block after block of tract houses laid out in neat rows like a formation of cards in a gigantic game of solitaire. "I didn't imagine it would be like this," she said softly. "This looks like Spode."

Dean reached over and patted Harrie's knee. "Well, let's not get crazy yet, sweetface. Schoonmaker told you the land was spectacular . . ."

"I know. I mean, look what it says here." Harrie smoothed out the article. " 'Perched on a cliff, the noble lines of the battlements outlined against a dawn sky, one can easily imagine this castle the seat of the lord of the County Perth . . .' "

"Is that our turn?" Dean asked, indicating a road to the right that cut through an unexpected patch of fir trees.

"Let me see. I don't see a sign." Harrie fetched the map once again from the floor. "Do you see anything that says Little Cove Road?"

"Nope. And I believe you're the navigator." Dean slowed the car and pulled into the road. "We've gone three miles exactly. Want to try it?" With Harrie's consent, he headed the car onto the thin line of dirt road parting the woods.

Instantly, the climate changed. The sky darkened. "I'm getting kind of a chill," Harrie said as the evergreens cast a flickering green shade over the silvery skin of the Saab. "My scalp just lifted. This has got to be right."

"What a road," said Dean, swerving to miss a hole. "My tires."

"It's got that magic-kingdom feeling already, hasn't it?" Harrie asked. She buzzed down the window again. "Oh. Dean. Smell." And she hit the button that controlled Dean's window, took the window all the way down.

"Goon," he said with a laugh.

"Smell," she commanded.

Dean complied. "Smell. Drive. What a guy I am."

"There," Harrie said, taking in a breath. "There's a gate. My God. Look at those." She undid her seat belt and grabbed at the door handle.

"Harrie, damnit. Let me stop the car."

"They're centaurs. They're guarding the entrance. Oh, God. I can't believe them. Where's my key?" Harrie patted her pockets, skirt, sweater, until she found the padlock key on a scrap of string in the glove compartment where she had placed it. She pushed open the car door and nearly ran toward the iron gate. The air was moist and cool, and somewhere in the underbrush a stream declared itself with a delicious shushing sound. Harrie stood at the gate and tipped her head back to admire the marble statues which stared down imperiously from their positions atop the gateposts. "Just look at you guys," she said out loud. She touched the stone wall with her fingertips, saluting the wall, claiming it. Then she followed its path with a proprietor's eye as it ran from each post through the woods, where it was quickly consumed by a tangle of mountain laurel and native azaleas. Harrie fitted the key into a heavy padlock, turned it with a trembling hand, and swung open the iron gate.

The driveway, flanked with towering rhododendron, curved out of view, seeming to drop below the horizon. Dean's soft beep on the car horn called her. She secured the gate in an open position with a stone, then jogged back to the car.

"My hands are shaking," Harrie said, tucking them under her armpits.

"It *is* unbelievably thrilling, isn't it?" Dean said with a grin. "Like discovering the *Titanic*."

"Just like that," she agreed. "You know, I kind of want to walk down the driveway very quietly. Sort of sneak up on the house and catch it in repose, but at the same time, I can't wait to see it." Harrie stared at her centaurs. "Look how fierce they are."

"I wonder how far in the house is from here. Couldn't be too far. I don't mind walking."

"No. Let's drive. I can't bear the suspense. If it's a palace, I can't wait to wallow in the glory of it. If it's a dump, like Mr. Schoonmaker says it is—No, it doesn't matter what he says. I'm going to love it."

Dean put the car into gear. "What if I just drive real slowly?"

"Yeah. Good compromise. Don't go more than five miles an hour. That's the new speed limit at Blackfern," Harrie said, her eyes fixed straight ahead. "My first decree." She reached across the seat and put her hand on Dean's thigh and held it there.

"Yes, ma'am," Dean said. He covered her hand with his and gave her a sidelong glance. Harrie looked terrified, he thought. But that was okay. That made two of them. Although he was terrified for completely different reasons. Harrie was having a good kind of terror. Unexpected bounty. Seven million dollars and a dream house. She was afraid of being rich and happy, or to be fair, Harrie was having your basic fear of the unknown.

He was having an entirely different fear, or maybe bunch of fears. Like, what would people think about her seven million in his hands? He was managing her money, right? So he was making money from her. She was in effect paying him. What did that make him? A gigolo? A mooch? An opportunist? He clamped his jaws tightly closed. No matter how honestly he managed her account, people would always be looking at him a little funny. Human smarmy nature.

Of course, Harrie had insisted he be her broker. "So what?" she'd said in answer to his expressed discomfort. "Someone's got to make the commissions. I'd rather it be you. I trust you." So there was another portion of his terror. She trusted him. Trust was fine, and he could understand why she wouldn't want to give her account to a different broker. But Harrie had this ridiculous goal for the money. She wanted to spend it on the castle. And if she didn't want to be standing in her stocking feet with no money in the bank in about a year's time, he was going to have to make the money grow like weeds. And there was no good way to do that without risk. "Do whatever you think best, Dean," Harrie had said blithely and, he thought, unfairly. Harrie had simply closed her eyes and put him in charge, and now he was going to have to be brilliant so that, one, she could refurbish what was described as an uninhabitable mutt of a millionaire's castle; two, she would have money left when this craziness was over; and three, he could hope to carry off a plan that was just bristling with risk in a way that didn't make him look like he was churning her account for commissions.

And of course, if he lost her money for her, his name would be Asshole forever at Hamilton, Warner, Pierson, and Wales. Dean stifled a groan. If only Harrie would consider selling the house. If only he could tuck the money away for her future. He would stash it in zeros and thirty-year notes, put some in CDs so she could treat herself to a richer lifestyle; he would build her a solid base of blue chips for her future heirs. But this wouldn't do at all for Harrie Dreamcakes. And just thinking about the frothy cocktail of B-rated funds, bonds, and stocks he would have to buy for her made him feel as if he were standing at the rail of a sailboat in a choppy sea.

Dean clenched his hands on the steering wheel. He guessed all this worry meant he was a decent guy. He had to give himself that. He cared about the girl, he really did. Any number of other men he knew would be delighted with what he was viewing as a problem. When he looked for the bright side, all he could see was that Harrie's millions dwarfed his father's portfolio. There was some pleasure to be had there: not being chained to his father's metallic will. But there was a clanking going on anyway. Just a different kind of chain. Dean turned to look at Harrie, who had the window down again and was leaning out.

"We're coming to a clearing," she said.

"You're going to get your face whacked by a branch."

"Look. There's someone there. Behind that little house. I saw someone move."

Dean slowed the car once again in the dirt road which had turned into a pair of parallel ruts. "That's got to be the gardener's house." He put on the brakes.

"I bet that's the watchman," Harrie said, unsnapping her seat belt. She stepped out of the car. "Hello!" she shouted. She waved her hands.

A muscular, bejeaned young man with short red hair shaved closely around the ears, sleeves rolled up on his denim jacket, and a tattoo on one forearm walked in long strides toward the car. As he came closer the jingling of keys hanging from a belt loop became audible, and light bounced from a silver chain around his wrist.

"You must be Mrs. Braintree," he said with an unexpectedly sweet voice. He stretched out a hand to be shaken. "I'm Georgia Newell. I've been watching the place for Mr. Tuckman."

Georgia? He was a woman! Harrie blinked, dropped a disbelieving and investigative look to the speaker's bustline, then returned it to her face. "Nice to meet you," she sputtered at last. Georgia's hand was small but strong. Too strong. "This is my friend, Dean Carrothers," Harrie said, discreetly massaging her fingers.

The two shook hands, Dean with a wary look on his face, Georgia with a neutral look on hers.

"Did you know Mr. Tuckman?" Harrie asked, linking her arm through Dean's, standing half behind him.

"I only met him the one time when he hired me," Georgia said, "and then I just got paid by his bank. He was a relation of yours?"

"Good friend."

"Oh," said Georgia, looking past Harrie and Dean. "Well, he was very nice to me. I'm sorry he's gone."

"I am too," Harrie said. "I miss him a lot. I can hardly wait to see where he spent all those glamorous weekends," she added; then she turned and looked at the cottage. "What a sweet little house."

"I'm not much of a housekeeper," Georgia said, "but I try not to be too much of a pig. I sudsed everything down pretty good before you got here. The tub and all."

"Oh, you didn't have to do that," Harrie remonstrated. Georgia's voice was tinged with a soft southern undertone. If you didn't look at her, Harrie thought, but just heard her, you'd expect her to be wearing a baby-blue shirtwaist dress with an eyelet collar. "Was this the gardener's cottage?" Harrie asked while staring at the tiny dwelling before her. The proportions of the roof and building were pleasing to her eyes. The tile roof arched over a single eye of a dormer, and a trellised entranceway bearing the thorny skeleton of a rose framed the front door. There were two multipaned windows on each side of the door, and in front of the house was a tangle of garden, bisected by a crumbling brick walkway and decorated with a black motorcycle. Harrie stared for a moment at the vehicle, then lifted her eyes. "There's a chimney," she said. "Does the fireplace work?"

"Sure does. I'll show you around," the young woman answered, brushing past Harrie and Dean.

"That won't be necessary . . ." Dean said.

"No, we don't want to inconvenience you," Harrie added.

"No problem," said Georgia, turning the doorknob with a firm twist. "I'm all packed and ready to move out."

"But . . . not because of me?" Harrie ventured.

"No. I was going to leave this month anyway. There's a rally next week starting in Maine and ending down in Baja."

"What kind of car do you have?" Dean asked, following behind Harrie into the little house.

"No, not a car. My chopper," she said, indicating it with a backward thumbing motion.

"You're going three thousand miles on a motorcycle?"

"Four thousand five. We do it every year. Our club. Now," she said, "let me show you where the hot water heater is." The kitchen was small, lined with cabinets, floored with linoleum. The water heater stood on one side of the porcelain sink, and a butcher's block table stood on the other side. The windowsill was deep, and piles of unmatched dishes and motorcycle magazines were stacked there.

While Dean questioned Georgia with great interest about her bike Harrie looked around the room. In less than thirty seconds, she had painted the room white, stripped the cabinets to their natural pine, taken up the linoleum and stripped the floor as well. She'd cleaned the sills of rubbish, filled them back up with a collection of bottles and jars and filled these containers with rose hips and faded hydrangea blossoms and silky heads of the clematis vine that clung to the outer wall. "I love this room," she said, but Dean was squatting before the water heater, talking with Georgia who was showing him the pilot light, and they never heard her.

"Now, this is the flue," Georgia said, standing in front of the small fireplace in the living room, wiggling a piece of metal. "Cranky old thing, but it works. In here's the one bedroom." She led the way.

A box spring and mattress were shoved tight into one corner. Beside the bed was a trunk which was also a night table. A small lamp, an ashtray, a cigar box, books and more magazines were stacked on it. By the door was a hat rack, a suitcase, and an assortment of dumbbells. Against the opposite wall was an old pine wardrobe that was not very different from the one Harrie had back home on Chester Street.

"There's another little room upstairs for a short person that doesn't have to use the bathroom in the middle of the night," Georgia said with a chuckle, "and the bathroom's in here."

Harrie examined the interior of the bedroom. She mentally stripped off the old wallpaper, which was predominantly green and brown, substituted something with a white ground; a nice blue stripe, she decided, and flowered curtains, and a sleigh bed. She would hang a collection of framed, pressed flowers beside the bed, put down some white carpet on the floor.

"It all works," Georgia said to Dean as they exited the bathroom and bedroom, Harrie trailing behind. "The septic system was just overhauled last year, and as long as you don't run too many appliances at the same time . . ."

"Well, I don't think we'll be staying here, but thanks anyway," Dean said.

"Oh, and you better keep setting mousetraps after I'm gone. Damned creatures move into the stove insulation, and the next thing you know, you've got to get a new stove."

Dean nodded absently. He could believe there were mice here. The whole place was like a big mouse nest. He followed Harrie and the strangest-looking woman he had ever met out the front door. Her shoulders were broader than his. And she had a grip that could dent steel. Dean loosened his shirt collar.

"I don't know what any of these plants are," Georgia was saying to Harrie. "Well, this one's a rose. I know that. And that climbing thing that grows over the bedroom window has a purple flower."

"Clematis."

"Yeah, well. And that tree has little apples on it that taste terrible. But it looks very nice for a couple of weeks in May."

The two stood silently in the garden looking at the tree.

"If I'd known you liked gardens, I would have cleaned it up a little for you. I could have mowed, I guess," Georgia said in her disconcertingly sweet voice.

"Please don't worry. It'll be fun for me to restore the garden. I've been gardening since I was old enough to walk." Harrie touched the small tree, which was laden with hundreds of small red fruit she knew to be crab apples, and marveled at the way her skin was tingling. It was as though all of her senses had been abraded with something fine, like diamond dust, so she could absorb *everything:* the feeling of the slow, flickering drive through the black-green woods, and the aroma of the evergreens, and the shushing sound of the brook, and the roughness of the stone wall and of the crab apple tree, and the warmth of the cottage which was like the home of a rabbit in a fairy tale. She could feel something growing inside her too—a new feeling, that her back was straighter, and that she had more blood in her veins, that her chest had expanded, that her hair had grown. And she had a suspicion that these new feelings were but the opening notes in a burgeoning symphony of sensation, and while the feelings were extraordinary, she was almost afraid that she would take in too much, too fast. And so Harrie was glad for the small talk, the weeds, the motorcycle. These mundane things were a line to the earth and without them, she thought, her euphoria would simply float her away.

"Now, you want to be out of that house by dark, Mrs. Braintree—"

"Please call me Harrie."

"Well, okay, Harrie. Anyway, if you don't know where you're going in that house, you could step through a floor or something. Wait just a minute so I can get my flashlight."

What did Georgia do for company out here anyway? Harrie wondered. She'd seen a telephone in the living room, but no trace of another person. There hadn't even been a television set. Maybe Georgia didn't want company.

Harrie tried to imagine being out in the little cottage alone and the thought seemed appealing. Her life in the city was so packed with events and projects. Every morning started with a rush, a list of things to be done. There would be a hundred calls, a lunch appointment, a crisis, a meeting, a decision, a sale or the development of another plan, drinks with an author or editor. If the day could be summarized with a single sound, it would be the exaggerated, agitated, electronic ring of the telephone. If it could be described in a single word, it would be "NOW." Work time was quick time, hyper time, and it left no tracks. If you wanted to stay with it, Harrie had often thought, you had to ride it, strap yourself in, hold on, try to get ahead of it if you could.

And then as suddenly as the day started, it would abruptly brake. The phones would stop or the check would be paid, and Harrie's workday would shudder, then crash into silence. Papers and possessions would be wearily gathered. Then there might be a television meal with Dean, both of them fatigued beyond conversation. Or she would cook a condensed but nutritious one-pot meal for herself and eat it in bed, the pile of manuscripts that could never be read during the day stacked on the night table beside her. But in minutes, sleep would simply cancel her consciousness, and, in so doing, toss her unread pages into untidy sheaves on the floor.

The life she lived now, Harrie thought, was lived for the weekends. But surely she could alter that. Would Luna say no to a four-day week? Why not a three-day week? As long as she had a phone, why wouldn't it be possible to work from here? If she could do that, she could have a life with weekdays, full days that she could own entirely. Real time. The gardener's cottage, snatched probably in a piece from some little village somewhere in the British Isles and dropped here on Long Island, could serve as her home base while she prepared to make Blackfern her true home. . . .

"You don't have to take us," Dean said to Georgia. "We have the layout of the house and grounds in the car."

"Got to. I really couldn't let you go up without me the first time. Just give me a minute."

Dean and Harrie shrugged at each other. Harrie buttoned her sweater and pushed down her sleeves. She gave Dean an irrepressible grin. "My house," she said. "We're going to see it now."

"Let's get in the car, goony bird," Dean said.

"That's Lady Harriet to you," she retorted, allowing Dean to open her door. Georgia joined them minutes later, and in the fading light of an October afternoon, the small party of three entered a woods that ended at Blackfern Castle.

▣

Of course, Harrie had the door open before the car stopped in the circle of gravel at a level above the house. Then, with Dean and Georgia trailing, she headed down toward the massive building whose turrets and parapets blended with the tops of the surrounding trees. Wide curved steps, weedy and broken in places, led downward to circular landings, which in turn led to other steps and at last to a forecourt of cobblestones and the full view of the magnificent structure. The castle itself was forty feet tall, massive, yet happily accessible; this accessibility having to do with a seamless marriage between the original fortress and its human-scaled additions: two wings with window frames and doorways and open sitting areas beneath stone porticoes. The castle had been breached by time and crime. Trees broke through a conservatory ceiling, one of the wings had a sadly swaybacked roof, rubble and trash were strewn around. But Harrie saw only the castle's majesty.

"I'm fainting," she said to Dean in a whisper. "She's beautiful. And it is a 'she,' isn't it, honey? She's like a beautiful matron, with her corsets undone, a little bit tipsy, just coming back from a party with her husband, the archduke of something-bury."

Dean laughed. "You're sure?"

Harrie nodded an emphatic yes and squeezed Dean's hand.

"Beautiful lines, that's for sure," Dean said. "This part looks like it's original," he added, waving a hand toward the central body of the structure. "Imagine building something like that without modern machinery. Without cranes."

"There's another road to the front," Georgia said, "but a couple of big old trees fell across it in a hurricane a few years ago, and since no one was using the house anyway, they just lay there." Georgia led Harrie and Dean to the doorway. She took the ring of keys into her hand. "Front door key," she said, holding it up. She inserted it into the lock and turned it. "You'll be able to see for about forty-five minutes or so."

Harrie took in a deep breath. Georgia stood aside as Harrie gingerly pushed open the door and stepped inside the dim, high-ceilinged room that served as a foyer. It was twice the size of her studio apartment in New York! A crystal chandelier, fractured and lopsided, dangled above their heads. Corridors branched from this entranceway to their left, to their right, and straight ahead. Harrie walked with Dean into the next room before her, a room whose grand dimensions and walls of stone gave off an almost cathedral-like feeling. There were tall, narrow windows along one wall, glass-paned doors opening to opalescent sky at the far end. On the wall to Harrie's left was a fireplace large enough to walk around in. "That's the fireplace," she said to Dean, "the one Mr. Tuckman used to tell me about." Harrie stood where the sofa would have been. "I wonder what became of the sofa they used to have in this room. Judy Holliday sat on that thing."

"They call this the Great Hall," Georgia said. "This room and the room we came through and the dining room are really the only three rooms that came intact from the original castle, the way I heard it. The architect did his own thing with the rest of the rooms. Why don't I take you all through the north wing first."

Then Georgia gave a dazzled Harrie and a reluctantly impressed Dean a tour of the house. The north wing, the living quarters, contained a shabby paneled library, a tiled kitchen, pantries, a long dining hall with another huge fireplace, and, upstairs, a string of little servants' rooms. The south wing held the bedrooms and baths, a room with a domed and frescoed ceiling that Harrie thought had been a music room, two sitting rooms, and a ruined conservatory, its blue and white harlequin-tiled floor winking with shattered glass. As the three entered each space, Georgia neutrally pointed out the pitfalls, telling what she knew. Harrie, gasping and exclaiming, lifted dust cloths from odd remains—ancient upholstered furniture, sealed cartons—and Dean mentally recorded the sprung pipes, the broken walls, the corroded wiring exposed beneath.

And then they stood once again in the Great Hall, Harrie panting a bit from exertion but glowing all over.

"Now, out there," Georgia said, pointing beyond the vast chamber, "is what they call the loggia. I don't think there were any castles from Scotland that had loggias."

"Mediterranean," Dean said.

"What, honey?"

"I think loggias originated in the Mediterranean countries. Wow, did you see this? We're standing on someone's grave."

"Just a gravestone, I think. The old lady, the one whose husband built this place, had a weird liking for gravestones. There are a few in this floor, and a couple in the walls, back thataway, and she's got a bunch of them in the garden."

"I wonder why," Harrie said, already moving through the hall toward the light beyond, a light so pure and translucent gray that it turned the interior of the room to black. "Are there any ghosts?" she asked.

"No more than one or two," Georgia replied with a laugh. "Now, there are some boards out of the flooring and the railing is very unreliable . . . I want to check something upstairs and I'll be back in a minute."

But Harrie was already outside. They could call it a loggia if they wanted to, but it was a porch really, wide as a house and splendid with its columns and iron scrollwork, but still it was a porch. And the porch did not look out on the branch road to the Long Island Expressway as did her parents' porch in Spode. It looked out on the branch of the Atlantic Ocean known as Long Island Sound, which was even now shifting below the seawall, sending the finest spray into the air. The sky was salmon and plum, and those colors were reflected in the gray-green waters, and then Dean was behind her, his arm around her shoulders, his cheek in her hair. She was afraid to speak.

"That lawyer was right about this setting," he said.

"Uh-huh," said Harrie. She covered Dean's hand with hers, squeezed it.

"It's spectacular."

"I thought I would feel out of place here," Harrie said softly. "I thought it would seem too grand for me. But standing here, looking out at that . . ." She turned and put her arms around Dean's waist, her head on his shoulder. "I feel like I live here. I feel like I want to live here."

"Honey. Be serious," Dean said, trying to mask his irritation with a gentle tone. "This place isn't livable. Didn't you see the shape it's in? The ceiling is caving into the whole north wing. Did you see how the walls are coming apart from water damage? The pipes? They're broken everywhere and the wiring is corroded, which means every inch of it has to be replaced. This house is a ruin."

"I don't care," Harrie said, pushing away from Dean, turning back to face the reflection of the setting sun. "I don't care how long it takes or how much it costs. That's what the money is for, isn't it?" she asked rhetorically. "And what's the matter with you anyway? Why are you being so . . . I don't know. Such a drag?"

"What? I don't know what you're talking about," Dean retorted angrily. He was here, wasn't he? He'd driven her here and spent the last two hours breathing mold and plaster dust, leaping over broken floorboards in the dark, and he hadn't complained once.

"I don't know, exactly. You're not excited. I can tell. You're not happy for me."

"I *am* happy for you. I'm fucking thrilled for you. What do you want me to do, dance a jig in the Great fucking Hall?"

"I rest my case," Harrie said. She crossed her arms.

"You do that," Dean muttered. "Look. I drove you here. I did the tour. I don't know what else you want from me."

"I want to know what's going on. We've been on two different wavelengths the whole day. I've been doing cartwheels and you've been grinding about something. Why don't you be honest and tell me what it is? Don't you like this place? Is it because it's my place? Is that it?"

"Don't be silly. That's not it," Dean grumbled. "I'm worried, that's all." He walked to the railing and leaned on it cautiously. "This whole thing is making me nervous. All the money. How to do what you want without gambling. I mean, in order to keep this bankroll of yours liquid and growing, we're going to be shooting craps half the time. And you're making me responsible."

"Aw, Dean," Harrie said, crossing to him. "That part will be all right. At least, how can we worry about it? You'll do a great job and if we lose some, we lose some. I know there's risk involved in being in the market."

"But *I* care, Harrie. I don't want to 'lose some.' You can't go into a situation like this thinking you're going to lose some. That strategy is fine over a twenty-year period. Win some, lose some. The ebb and flow of the marketplace. You want the money now. I still remember October 'eighty-seven. And July 'eighty-nine. And the recession. I know what can happen."

"Okay, Dean. But I think this worrying about the money is part of the process of making a plan. You're working on the problem, that's all." A wave of water hit the wall hard and sent a mist into the air. Harrie moved in closer to Dean and put an arm around his waist. He was worried about her, that was what this was all about. He was trying to protect her, and she could see why he was worried. Investing everything in a house wasn't everyone's idea of a sound financial plan.

"And I'm worried about you falling in love with this house," Dean said quietly. "It feels like a real genie out of the bottle to me. Three wishes, and the first one is 'I wish I could spend seven million dollars on wallpaper.' "

Harrie laughed. He knew her. That was love. "And what's the second wish?"

"You want us to live here."

"Oh. I guess so. Can't you see it?" Harrie looked up at Dean's face. His lips were pulled into a tight line, and he was staring down at the breaking waves.

"Not really. No. This isn't my fantasy. It's yours."

Harrie ran her hands lovingly over the railing and shook her hair in the soft breeze. Dean was right. It was her fantasy and he couldn't see it yet, but he would. Blackfern deserved to be restored, and when it was finished, Dean would see what she could see so plainly—San

Simeon, Pickfair, Blackfern: a grand and generous house in which to have a family. Dean, their children-to-be, and she mustn't forget her parents. Her father would flip when he saw the conservatory, and her mother would fall in love with the house as she had. But in the meantime, Dean was staring at her like she was a crazy person and she knew why. She had a little more imagination than most people.

She said, "I think you're right. About whose fantasy this is. But you haven't had a chance to even think about it. What if we lived in the cottage for a while, Dean? So that we can get a feeling for the place. I can fix up that cottage in about a minute. I'll call Laura Ashley, Country Floors, Pierre Deux. Get a contractor through the newspapers. In two weeks you won't believe it's the same house." Empowered by her new feelings of growth, Harrie pushed on. "You have to try to visualize more, Dean. Try to imagine it. Dinners in front of that fireplace. Music in the conservatory. A sailboat. Our children playing on the lawn. Our friends coming out to spend long weekends with us . . ."

Harrie blinked away the sight of dismay on Dean's face. She could still hear her words, "our children playing on the lawn" reverberating, and that she had said those words frightened her. Some sort of taboo had been broken; she'd skipped right over the proposal of marriage and flown on to children! Is that why Dean looked thunderstruck? Or was it only a reaction to the notion of living here? Whichever. She was *right* to declare herself. Two years was a long time to be dating without making plans for the future. She was a woman of means now. And she was going to be thirty-three in six months. She had a right to know if Dean was with her or if he was just a bystander. She walked to a pillar and plucked at a honeysuckle vine that embraced it. "What do you expect me to do? Just walk away from all this? Is that what you'd do if this had happened to you?"

"I don't know," Dean replied. His throat had tightened and his words came out in a strained croak. "I don't know," he said again. "I don't know what I'd do."

"So can't you play along with me? Dean?" she asked, moved by Dean's suddenly vulnerable stance. "Can't you just live my fantasy for a while. See how it goes?"

"Har . . ."

"The commute's not such a big deal. It's less than an hour into the city by train. That's practically nothing."

"I don't want to commute. I like living five minutes from work. I like to run in the morning. You know that."

Harrie gulped. Georgia would show up in a minute, and she didn't want Dean to use the interruption as a way of avoiding the issue. In fact, Harrie felt him weakening. "Can we talk about it some more? Can we talk about it on the way home?"

"Sure we can." Dean put his hands in his pocket. The house faced east and so the setting sun was not visible, only its effects upon the sky above the water. And as he watched the sky the salmon was turning purple and the purple was turning black, and the air was getting colder, and he longed to be in the car heading home. And yet even if he pried Harrie away from here tonight, she had, in her mind, already taken up residence in this place and he could not imagine how in the world he was to fit into this picture. Still, she was right about one thing. He could hardly blame her for wanting to enjoy this magnificent gift. "I guess I'm afraid," he said quietly. "I'm afraid this house is going to change our life together, parts that I liked a lot."

Harrie swallowed. "Say what you mean."

What he meant was, he saw a fork in the road and they were upon it, and although he had had months to prepare for this moment, examine it, twist it, control it, he had ignored it, and now it was here. He would have to walk one of the roads with Harrie, or he would have to let go of her hand and walk away. How could he do that? He started to speak. Cleared his throat. Words came out. "Maybe we can come out for weekends once the weather gets better," Dean offered. "Like in the spring." Hoping to send a subliminal suggestion, he jingled the car keys in his pocket. Would this offering suffice? Would Harrie be appeased? Could they go now?

"Say. That's a good idea," Harrie said, taking Dean's arm and snuggling in close to his lean body. "When the cottage is fixed up, I can live out here. Maybe three or four days a week. And I can get a station car and come in to the city by train. I don't mind the train. I'm used to it. And you can drive out on the weekends." She shot him a joyous look. "That way you don't have to commute and I can supervise the renovation." Harrie gave Dean's arm a little shake. This was good. A compromise they could both live with. And she felt something big had happened; Dean's offer to spend weekends was a step forward in their relationship, and it illuminated the step away that he hadn't taken. Her lungs filled with the sweet air. "And we don't have to wait for spring, Dean. It will be beautiful out here in the wintertime," she continued. "We'll get the *Times* delivered. We'll have big toasty fires and walks in the woods."

Dean sighed and wrapped his arms around Harrie. Something about Harrie made him feel years older than she. That quality of hers. That enthusiasm which brushed away pipes sticking out from the walls like broken bones, walls that looked as if they had danced with a wrecking ball, and his reticence that felt bitter to his own tongue. "Maybe that could work," he said, giving her a hug. "It might be good to get away to the country on the weekends."

"Yea, Dean! Good. That's great!" She reached her arms around his neck and kissed him jubilantly. "I love you," she said.

"I love you too," he answered. "Now can we go? I'm hungry and cold."

"Me too," Harrie agreed. "Let's find Georgia." The two walked briskly through the empty doorframes from the loggia to the Great Hall. "Dean. We should get a new car for you. Like a Mercedes. To make the drive out more pleasant. And I want to have a party. A big one, right away, like on a Saturday during the day, before it gets cold. I want to invite Luna and Desiree, and my folks, and your family and Chip and just everyone. To celebrate. And to show everyone the before. And then I'll have another party when it's finished."

"Uh-huh," Dean said.

"I'll get tents," she continued happily, "like Mrs. Kensing-Smythe. Pink-striped ones . . ."

And as Dean listened to Harrie's plans he could not ignore the sudden constriction of his heart. He'd felt warm, now he felt cold. He'd reached out a finger and Harrie had firmly grasped his whole arm. And how had that happened in such a slender portion of a minute? Was it the Mercedes? The pink tents? He tried to find balance but it was lost to him. This was all too weird. Hadn't he been thinking recently that the limits to their relationship had nearly been reached? Hadn't he concluded that Harrie was the wrong girl? And now he had committed to weekends of living together in the gardener's cottage, and Harrie wanted to get all their friends together in something that would clearly resemble an engagement party. And wouldn't it be natural for people to assume such a thing?

Dean rubbed his hand across his chest and watched, dazed, as Harrie went down the corridor to the south wing, calling out to Georgia. Did Harrie think they would be getting married? It wasn't his imagination. He could feel it. The damned genie. Her third wish. Christ. If he hadn't been able to imagine marrying Harrie before, marriage to her was even more unimaginable now. She was a multimillionaire, for God's sake, and he was earning barely a hundred K. And she wanted to buy him a car! Before, he could have maybe walked away from the relationship. "I love you but it's not going to work." Well, maybe he could have done it. But how could he do it now? What would he say to her? "I'm sorry, but now that you're rich, and have this house, this relationship has just crossed the too weird threshold and I have to split."

Dean shuffled to the fireplace and, there, stirred ancient charcoal with his shoe. How could he leave her? How could he stay? He heard Harrie calling out his name and he answered, the echoes bouncing from the stone walls. "I'm here, here, here, here."

And he felt whatever control he had of the relationship slip stealthily away.

15

———□———

*T*HE DAY was everything Harrie had wished for and more. She'd hoped for good weather, but hadn't dared to expect clotted-cream clouds in a pearl-blue sky. A mild breeze stirred up fallen leaves like a tattler with a good bit of gossip, and light pranced on the tide below the seawall.

There were no pink tents to be had in Cold Spring Harbor and environs, but Harrie's hundred guests found the feast no less sumptuous under a regal white one which had been set up on the lawn (recently and mercilessly mown) above the water. There were a half dozen tables in the tent laden with delicacies: smoked salmon, caviar, lobster tails, pâtés, accompanied by all kinds of breads and garnishes. There were chafing dishes brimming with creamy oyster stews and lobster Newburg and au gratin potatoes. There were roasted meats and salads of wild greens, and platters of crisp vegetables and fruits. The dessert table held bowls of mousse, whole poached pears in raspberry sauce, air-spun soufflés, rich cakes and tortes and chocolate confections dusted in sugar. The last long table served as a bar, and the drinks were poured and the food carved and dished up by handsome young waiters and waitresses in uniform.

From the tent the guests brought their plates to the loggia, which was adjacent to the lawn. Tables were set in a double row, one row nestled against the warm stucco wall of the castle, the other against the railing just overlooking the bay. Over the gentle clatter of silver against china, over the sighing of the water caressing the seawall, Harrie heard laughter. And the feeling she had was a sweet mix of well-being and pride that she'd done well, provided the means for a good time for her friends.

After lunch, the tables were taken away and there was dancing in the shade of Harrie's "porch" and out onto the lawn, the music by a band from a famous late-night television show. And while people danced Harrie and Dean took turns giving the guests mini-excursions around the estate.

⊡

"They called this the Druid Garden," Harrie said, standing in the semicircular patch of mown weeds hedged in by massive evergreen shrubs.

"Uh-huh," Desiree said. "I mean, why?"

"Well, apparently these"—Harrie touched one of the well-worn stones respectfully with the toe of her leather pump—"are druid stones. They came from England, around that area where Stonehenge is located. Apparently, Mrs. Defoe used to see druids dancing here in the garden on nights when there was a full moon."

"No kidding," said Des dryly.

"Come this way, Des. There's a secret courtyard I want to show you. It has a fountain they used to fill with champagne."

"Har, this place is gorgeous, I mean it, but my heels weren't made for this National Geographic trek. Why don't you show me the inside of the house?"

"Oh, all *right*."

"I'll wear my Reeboks next time, okay?"

"Okay. It's a deal." Harrie gripped Desiree's arm and steered her to a gravelly ridge of a path. "I just get chills all over," Harrie rhapsodized blissfully. "Everywhere I look, I see something I'm in love with. The way the sun hits that tree and breaks up into those shafts of light. It's almost biblical. And the way the loggia faces the Sound. The way it looks so totally different back here in the garden. Like it's a family house, not like a castle, but the castle part is fortress enough to warn away intruders."

"Oh, shit," Desiree said. She wobbled on a mossy step cut into the hillside. Leaning against Harrie, she took off her shoe with the detached heel. "You got anything in a size six? Black preferred?"

Harrie took the pieces from her friend and banged the heel onto the shoe with a stone. "Here," she said. "This should hold temporarily, but I want to get you new shoes."

"What?"

"Just tell me where you got those and I'll have a new pair sent."

"Don't be ridiculous, Har. You don't have to buy me any shoes. I've got thousands of shoes and I can always use an excuse to buy a new pair."

"I'd like to buy you a present, Des. I've got a whole new feeling about money these days. I've got bags of it and I'd like to share it around a little."

"Then fuck the shoes. Buy me a house in Amagansett," Desiree said with a laugh. "Kidding," she amended. "I'm kidding. That was tasteless."

"Oh, please. It's just me." Harrie paused, then said, "This party cost thirty thousand dollars."

"You're joking."

"Well, it wasn't just for the food and all. There was some airfare and some hotels in town and some emergency carpentry so my guests didn't fall through the deck. But still. That's almost a year's salary. Used to be. It feels wonderful to spend money like this."

"My God. It must feel amazing. It must feel insane."

"So what do you say to this idea? Why don't we go shopping?"

"Whoa, Nellie. I'm not in your league."

"We're going to do the ultimate shopping orgy," Harrie said, her eyes half closed. "I'll have a limo, a stretch, pick us up and take us anywhere we want to go. And wait for us. And the driver will handle our packages. No subway. No Loehmann's. The whole day for shopping in the best stores. And everything we get is my treat."

Desiree put both hands into her hair. "Supermarket sweepstakes? Are you sure?"

"Uh-huh. Shoes, lingerie, gaudy things, whatever we want. Diamonds for our ears."

"Diamonds?"

"Yes. Matching pairs."

"I might be dreaming."

"You're not."

"If you're not going to change your mind, I'm going to get excited now."

"Change my mind? I'm not going to sleep until we do this. It wouldn't even be any fun without you. And I want you to help me shop for birthday presents for Dean."

"Sure. Presents for Dean. Of course."

"I have no idea what to get him. I wanted to get him a car and he about took my head off."

"Well. A car."

"Well, what? He's my lover. What am I supposed to get him? A tie tack?"

"I see the problem," Des said, casting a nervous look at her friend. "How's he taking all this?"

"Like a man," Harrie said; then she laughed. "Just like a man. I've got more money than he has and I think it's unsettling to his self-image."

"Is that what he said?"

"No, but the whole car fracas. And he's nervous about being my broker now that I've got some money. And I suggested that we live here and . . ."

"And what?"

"He got nervous. But you know, Des. He can't see it. He can't see what I see. He's not like me. He doesn't have my imagination. But it's enough that I see it. I'm going to get the cottage fixed up immediately. And we're going to spend weekends out here, together, and then I just know Blackfern's going to cast its spell on him."

"Mmm-hmm," Des said noncommittally.

"But first," Harrie said triumphantly, "presents."

"Next Saturday," Des said quietly. "Okay?"

"Saturday it is."

"Eeeeeeeeee!" Desiree let out a delighted scream and wrapped her arms around Harrie.

Harrie laughed, then turned her friend around and headed down the steps they had so laboriously climbed. "I'm going to have to show you the house some other time," she said. "We've been gone too long."

"Okay. You'll invite me out another time."

"And listen, don't mention the shopping orgy to Dean, okay? He's already bitching about how I'm spending the money."

"I won't say a word."

·

"Ex-straw'd-nry," Luna said, staring down at the tombstone. " 'Moira Beckett, aged four years, safe now in the arms of the Lord.' What was this woman about, collecting these things?"

"She was the mother of the showgirl who married David Tuckman," said Dean. "She may have been eccentric."

"May have been, indeed. Fabulous mantelpiece," Luna added, "and the size of this room is really quite, quite. And the view from here out to the water is divine."

"It really is. The living quarters are this way. The kitchen, especially, is magnificent . . ." Dean heard himself say with pride. What was this? Proprietorship? Or had he just been infected with Harrie's madness?

"Lovely," Luna agreed, stepping over the threshold to the tiled space beyond. She started to speak, cleared her throat as if unsure she should give voice to her thoughts, then overrode her caution. "Dean, if I may be candid. I'm a bit worried about Harrie's decision to work part-time. Not that I object, you understand, to her using her time as she wishes. It's only, her clients are bound to resent her absence, if you know what I mean. She's more than just an agent to them. She's sort of a confidant and unofficial editor as well. I would hate to see her fall back after all the years she's put in on her career."

"I understand," Dean said thoughtfully. "But you could look at it another way. It's kind of interesting she wants to keep working at all."

"Mmmm." Luna pulled at her hair, which was clasped in a large bow at her nape. "Yes. One could see it that way."

"Don't get me wrong. I wouldn't want to see her stop working. It's just, whenever you see those lottery winners on television, and they've just won twenty million dollars and they say they're going to buy a new house but other than that, they don't want their lives to change—it seems strange, doesn't it? Twenty million and still working in a factory, making lawn furniture, or whatever."

"It might seem like lawn furniture, I suppose, but agenting has its exciting moments."

Dean grinned self-consciously. "I know that. I didn't mean— You know what I meant, Luna. She's rich. She doesn't have to work."

They stopped in the center of the room that would be the kitchen again one day. The woodwork was water-stained and warped, and animals had been nesting behind several sprung cabinet doors.

"I wonder if this lovely old stove can be restored," Luna said, touching the surface of an enormous enamel-trimmed, cast-iron appliance with her manicured hand. Blue crepe de chine rustled as she stretched out her arm.

"Did I offend you? I didn't mean to."

"Oh, don't be silly. Of course you didn't. I had been thinking the same thing and you named it, that's all. And it wasn't just Harrie I was thinking of, to be perfectly honest. I am afraid I'm going to lose her, and that would be more than a loss for the business. I'm quite attached to having the dear girl about."

Dean stifled an urge to put his arm around Luna. She looked so genuinely sad. "Well, she's not going to leave," he said. "She seems quite sure about this part-time thing. Don't you think she can keep up if she works on the phone a couple of days along with the three days she spends in the city?"

"Yes, yes. I'm a bit embarrassed I brought it up, Dean. Of course Harrie can manage if anyone can. I was just sensing the future, and thinking how much I would miss her if she were gone."

"I wouldn't worry about it anymore, Luna. Her plans are to work."

"I won't think about it again," Luna replied, giving Dean a reassuring smile. "And what about you, Dean? How are you? You're looking very well, I must say, and you seem to be quite enjoying yourself."

"I'm having a good time. I really am." And with a little shock, Dean realized he was.

⊡

"Incredible. Smashing. Truly," Riva said, her shiny hair swinging in slow motion as she turned her head to take in the entire panoramic view from the tower of the castle proper.

"It is pretty nice, isn't it?" Harrie replied modestly. "From here, you can really see how the grounds were laid out. Like that garden and that one leading to the walk through the pergola that leads to the bay. I can't wait until I can get a landscape crew in here to cut the hedges into shape and trim the walks. Just that, and the lawns and this place will look a hundred times better."

"Harrie. It will be heaven. You must feel like a goddess. And that woman was a true seer. She knew."

"Woman?"

"The woman who saw your aura. And what did I say about that rainbow? Didn't I say money?"

"Can you believe it? I forgot all about that shoe store woman. What have I been thinking about?"

"You must tell me where that shoe store is. I'll go down this Sunday. Although with my luck, she'll tell me something boring. Like what I'm having for dinner."

"I feel so guilty. I should give her something."

"Flowers are always good. I have a wonderful florist on Seventy-second and Lex."

"I don't know if flowers are enough . . ."

"Well, send a nice note, too. I'm sure she wouldn't expect more. Now," Riva said, dusting off her hands, switching to a businesslike voice, "you are going to need an architect, and sooner would be better than later. You'll want to do the plans through the winter so you can start construction in the spring."

"Uh-huh." Harrie nodded. "I've collected the names of some architects whose work I've seen in the magazines. I'm about to start setting up meetings next week."

"Harrie, I have just the man. Roger Mayhew is his name and he has his own firm. Graduated from Yale in 'eighty-three. Yes, he's only about our age, but he's already won several important design awards and his work was featured in *Metropolitan Home* last May. I believe he studied in Italy for a term or two. Yes. I believe he did."

"He's a friend of yours?" Harrie asked.

"He lives in my building. He's a baby superstar, Harrie, truly. In another year you won't be able to get him, but right now, well, this could be quite a project for him. For his portfolio, you know. If this were my place, I'd hire him and in about a year I'd be looking for the pictorial in *Interiors*."

"Well, how can I say no? Give me his number and I'll call him on Monday."

"Nothing could be easier." The two women turned and found

the stairway that led into the building. Gripping the handrail, they took small, shaky steps down the circular stone staircase. "God, I envy you. If you get bored with all this happiness, call me, why don't you? I'll take your place for as long as you like."

Harrie laughed. "I'm not bored yet."

The two reached the foot of the staircase and walked through an arched doorway toward another staircase which would take them down to the Great Hall. "Don't let me forget to get that number from you, all right?" Harrie said. "Maybe Roger can help me with the cottage right away."

"I can't wait to tell him," Riva said. "This is going to be just great."

·

"Wow," said Chip quietly as he surveyed the scene from the tower.

"Yup," Dean answered, just as quietly.

"Wow," Chip repeated.

To which Dean could only reply "Yup" once more.

"W—" Chip began.

"That's enough," Dean said, putting out a hand.

"—what a view," Chip finished.

"Yup," said Dean.

The two slugged down their glasses of champagne, then descended the stone staircase.

·

"Harrie, I know this is no time," Jan began tentatively, eyes squinted in her small face, as though she might be slapped if she got out of line.

"No problem," Harrie said, opening the stable door. "Solid oak." She patted it, then hooked the door to the wall with a piece of wire and entered the building, which still smelled of hay and manure after standing empty for almost thirty years.

"It's very nice," Jan said. She followed Harrie, picking her way daintily over odd bits of lumber. "Are you going to get horses?"

"I don't know yet. Could be fun to have a big old horse." For the kids, she thought. "What were you going to ask me?"

Jan trailed Harrie through the barn. "I'm worried about Lois's motivation," she said. "If she doesn't really love Rory, then why is she willing to stay with him? She doesn't need the money."

"Well, I thought she felt insecure without him," Harrie replied, trying to separate the characters in Jan's thinly disguised story of her marriage from the actual events in Jan's life. She opened the double doors at the far end of the barn. "The paddock's through here," she said. "We can sit on the fence for a few minutes."

Jan obediently followed. "Well, okay," she said, wrinkling her face. "If you're sure we won't ruin our clothes."

Harrie sighed. She was wearing pale peach and Jan was wearing navy blue. If one of them could get dirty, it would be Harrie, not Jan. She put both hands behind her on the top of the fence and hoisted herself up. She hooked her shoes onto the lower rail. "See?"

"Okay," Jan said. She struggled, mimicked Harrie's movements, and was at last seated beside her agent. "Okay," she said again, "but will we like her? Will we think she's a wimp if she's just staying with Rory because she's insecure? Wouldn't we like her better if she just got her things together, called Urich on the phone, and moved in with him? I know it puts the custody issue in jeopardy, but what's more important to my reader, that Lois be a strong person or that she be a self-sacrificing wimp mother? Harrie. Harrie?"

Harrie was gazing off into the distance, thinking how happy she was to be sitting on a rail, not worried about her guests because every time she returned to the party she found the food abundant, the wine flowing, the band playing, and her friends laughing and dancing. She was reveling in these feelings when she was pulled to attention by the nagging sound of her own name.

"What?" she said sharply. Jan winced. "I'm sorry," Harrie said. "I must have zoned out. What were you saying?"

"Oh," Jan said, looking down at her shoes. "I was wondering which is more important, that my heroine be true to herself or that she sacrifice herself for her child?"

Jan, please shut up, Harrie begged silently. Canceling her wish, Harrie went over the story with the author. Then, with Jan tripping along beside her, they headed back to the party.

⸱

Bill Braintree walked the length of the ruined conservatory. Dean thought Bill walked as though he was uncomfortable in his suit. He had a ranging gait and his feet rolled to their outsides as if he were straddling rows of cauliflower. Every now and then he raised his head to look at the ceiling, such as it was, or bent it to examine a drain or a louver, and when he made such a movement, his thatch of oiled hair lifted away from his neck like a bad toupee. "Does she know how much it will cost to replace the glass in this thing?" Bill called out from across the room.

"I don't think so," Dean replied. He suddenly felt as uncomfortable as Bill looked. What had happened? He had finally found himself going with the flow, as silly as the flow was, and now, in the presence of a realist, he was the one trying to justify Harrie's folly.

"Harrie called this a greenhouse, but this is what they call an arboretum. They kept the heat high and grew palms and such in here. Camellias and orange trees. A real rich man's toy. Nothing practical about it at all." Bill shook his head and walked over to a rusted machine in one corner. "Humidifier," he said. "The heaters must have been over there. And the fans were over there." He pointed to several locations and Dean nodded. "Every pane of glass is a different size," Bill continued, and then he laughed. "Let's see. Fifty thousand panes of glass at about eight dollars a pane plus labor. What's that, Dean? You're the finance guy."

"Something like over four hundred thousand. I know. You don't have to tell me. I'm on the team that wants Harrie to sell the house."

"Don't waste your breath. Once she gets a notion . . ." The two men grinned at each other. "Is she gonna blow the whole thing on this house?" Bill asked.

"I'm afraid so. I'm doing the best I can to protect her money, Bill, but Harrie's tough. I socked a few hundred thousand into long-term notes so she won't be a poor old lady someday, but that was her limit. She likes to throw the money up in the air and dance in it. Not really, of course, but you get my meaning."

" 'Fraid I do."

Dean nodded. "Her plan is to spend it—make the house what Mr. Tuckman would have wanted—but I'm trying to make the money go as far and last as long 'as possible." He jammed his hands in his pockets and looked straight into the weather-worn face before him. "Do you play the market?"

"Nope. The stock market scares the hell out of me."

"Yeah. Well, I don't know how reassured you're going to feel about my plan. I've got a lot of Harrie's cash in stock because that's where I can get the quickest growth and sufficient liquidity to satisfy her. But basically, by diversifying her account into funds, bonds, and the market, I'm hedging against disaster in any particular arena."

"I see. She bought me a truck, you know?"

"Yeah, I went shopping with her. Do you like it?"

Bill sighed deeply and looked up through the twisted metal frame that was all that remained of the arboretum's dome. "I like the truck. I needed a Chevy. I didn't need a damned custom BMW. No one needs a BMW truck."

"I tried to tell her, but she saw it in one of those places that sell exotic cars. Listen, I'm starting to feel like a real pill. I'm always saying 'Don't' these days."

"I getcha, Dean," Bill said, putting his arm around Dean's shoulder, steering him out of the conservatory and into the relative coolness of the house. "Harrie's got to be responsible for herself. Uh. She said she wants us to come and live here after the place is finished. I suppose she told you that."

Dean nodded. The two stopped and stood in the wrecked music room. "What did you tell her?"

"I told her we'd talk about it some other time. What else could I do? You can't rain on someone's parade, not when it's already rolling down Main Street with a dozen baton twirlers, and floats, and the entire high school marching band."

Dean smiled. "That's about where I came out, Bill."

"What a girl."

"You said it," Dean replied.

·

"Now why is it again that Dean's family didn't come?" Dottie asked Harrie.

Harrie frowned. How had her mother found the flaw in the otherwise perfect everything? "I told you," she said, opening a closet door, then pushing it closed against its warped frame. "His father had to be in Honolulu, and one of his brothers lives in Massachusetts, and the other one was just too busy. I don't think you should take it to mean anything." But it did mean something. Dean had offered up reasons for their absence before he'd hardly time to ask them.

"I see," Dottie said in the same words, the same tone of voice Bill Braintree used when he didn't understand at all. She paused, then shook the wrinkles out of her voice and started again. "Well, Harrie, your house is just gorgeous. It's like one of Victoria Holt's castles come to life."

"Mom, look out this window. Can't you just imagine a king-size poster bed right here with a canopy? You could lie in bed and read the paper and look out at the water."

"Like a queen." Dottie stared around her. It was hard to see what Harrie saw, make pretty pictures around the heaps of plaster and mice droppings, but if anyone could do it, it would be Harrie. "I wish Julie would tear herself away from the party and come see your place."

"No, it's okay. Blackfern will be here for a long time. I'm glad she's having some fun for a change." Harrie dusted off the window ledge with a shred of old curtain and sat on the sill. The tent looked so pretty from here. The wind, playing with the pennant that topped the tent, flicked bits of music up to Harrie's perch. The day couldn't be more perfect. What better time to propose to her family? "So, what do you think of my idea?" she asked her mother without turning to face her. "What would you think about moving here when the house is all done?"

"Oh, I don't know, Cakes. It certainly is grand, but your dad and I are kind of used to our little place. We like it there."

"But Mom. Don't you think you could like it here, too? Think of how nice it would be to be on the water. We could get a sailboat next summer. I think Doug already knows how to sail."

"Sail? He worked with his friend Kip on a boat one summer, but I don't know if he was doing the actual sailing," Dottie said doubtfully.

"Well, anyway, he could learn. And Dad could make the green-house operational, or if he really wanted to, he could still drive to Spode every day. It's only forty-five minutes. Or we could put up some new greenhouses. There's one very sunny spot by the stables . . ."

"I don't know, dear. I don't know if he'd like to drive to Spode. He gets up so early. And what would happen to our business if we moved?"

"Mom, can't you try to imagine? Julie could have her own suite of rooms, and so could you and Dad. This bedroom, for instance, would be perfect, wouldn't it? And if Doug didn't want to live here, we could at least put him up easily and regularly. And I think it would be very good for Julie and Ivy to be closer to New York. Can't you see us all going in to the city, our long, black car pulling up to the theater, dinner after that at some great Italian place like Joe and Rose? The car taking us home to our castle on the bay? You know, you don't go out enough, Mom. You never leave Spode."

"Well, Harrie, there's always so much to do." Dottie cast her eyes around the bedroom—a space ten times the size of the room where she laid down her head every night. It was so empty in this big place. All of these rooms with just the six of them rattling aound. Seven when you counted Dean. But still too many rooms per person. And such big rooms. How would you ever feel comfortable here? "I hope Ivy hasn't gotten lost," Dottie said, half believing it was possible to lose a person in this imaginary world of Harrie's.

"She'll be back. She wanted to check out the gardener's cottage." Harrie felt the subject change. She would have to try not to feel injured. As with Dean, it was a lot to expect other people to see what she saw. Once the place was heated and the walls were straightened and painted and the floors were polished—once the house started to take on its former grandeur—they would all be able to put themselves in the picture.

"I think we should go find her, Harrie. It's not too far?"

"Not at all. Ten minutes at the most." Harrie walked behind her mother and turned around at the door. She looked back at the room and deliberately separated her overlapping visions. In the first she saw the warped floorboards, the decayed walls of muddy yellow, the cracked glass in the leaded windows, the ceiling that had crumbled, exposing damp and moldering ribs of lathing. Then Harrie applied her opalescent overlay: sea-green walls, sharp white ceilings and trim, thick carpeting, a four-poster bed, a window seat the length of the room, a doorway cut through the wall into the room beyond that could become a sitting room or a most generous bath. And then she thought of the architect Riva had recommended. What would his vision be? Her ideas were probably dull compared with those of a professional, especially a "baby superstar." "You know, Mom," Harrie said carefully, walking beside her mother down the long corridor that led to the central staircase, "I'm going to hire an architect. Next week, I hope. He comes very highly recommended by a friend and he's sure to have some wonderful ideas."

"Well, that should be fun," Dottie said brightly. "Oh, look." She pointed down. "Ivy," she called out. "We're up here."

"Harrie. Mom," Ivy responded, gripping a banister and leaping up the stairs two at a time. She met them at a landing. Her hair was lying in damp strands against her forehead, her thin face glowing with excitement. "Harrie," she said again. "I love it. It's like a gingerbread house."

"Harrie's little cottage?" Dottie asked.

Ivy nodded her head vigorously. "I don't know whether to live in it or eat it."

"Live in it?" Harrie repeated. Ivy hardly looked like herself. She was wearing the ever-present black stretch pants and matching sweatshirt. Her hairstyle still looked as if she cut it herself without using a mirror. She still wore no makeup under her deeply shadowed eyes, no color on her cheeks, just her signature blur of red lipstick. All that was as it always was. What was different was Ivy's expression. She was happy! More than that—she was enthusiastic. Harrie could not remember when Ivy had last showed enthusiasm.

"I climbed up to that attic," she said, pushing hair away from her eyes. "There's a pull-down ladder in the closet?"

Harrie nodded.

"That attic could be a little bedroom, couldn't it?"

"I guess so," Harrie said, staring at her sister. "It could be a bedroom." For a short person who didn't have to go to the bathroom in the middle of the night, Harrie remembered Georgia saying.

"Well, then I don't want to wait. I don't want to wait for the main house to be finished. I want to live here now. Can I?"

"But Ivy, I won't be living out here full-time. Just a few days a week, and then Dean and I had planned to spend weekends . . ."

"Oh," Ivy said, her excitement withering, then dropping away, her more customary frown returning. "Oh, I get it."

"No, wait," Harrie said, reaching out and taking hold of her sister's hand. Ivy wanted to be here! Harrie, finally feeling what her sister was saying, saw a way to fix the relationship that had been broken when she went off to college, then to New York, never to live at home again.

Harrie thought Ivy must have felt her leaving as abandonment, and if so, she'd been right in a way. She'd been in the seventh grade when her mother brought Ivy home from the hospital. Being in junior high had made Harrie feel quite the grown-up, and having a new baby in the family also felt like a promotion. She wasn't the youngest anymore, and more than that, she'd been deputy mother to her little sister. Having just put away her own dolls, it was miraculous to have this new living, breathing doll! It had all been delicious: feeding the baby, bathing the baby, carrying the baby strapped to her stomach while her mother caught an afternoon nap. And when Ivy started to talk, Harrie had entertained her in her room for long afternoons. So for five years the sisters had been close, but then Harrie had suddenly gone. And much later, it had been hard to find a way to relate to a sister thirteen years younger than she, whom she hardly saw and barely knew. Here was a chance to put some of the love back, get closer to Ivy. And since she wanted her family at Blackfern, perhaps if Ivy came first, it would be the beginning of what she hoped the future would be.

"I'd love to have you," Harrie said. "If it's okay with Mom, it's great with me."

"Mom?" Ivy asked, trying unsuccessfully to contain the hopefulness she'd already expressed.

"Ivy, I'm sorry, but no, and that's final. It could be dangerous. What if something happened to you? What if some bad kids from town came out here to do mischief?"

"But Harrie is going to be out here all alone."

"She has a point," Harrie said.

"It would be better if the two of us were here, wouldn't it be, Harrie?"

"You bet," Harrie said, almost to herself. She saw both sides—serene solitude, the birds for company, books to be read at her leisure, and the jangled reverse: fidgety impatience while she waited for Dean to arrive for the weekend. Would she truly enjoy the green silence of the woods, the absence of another voice? It could be wonderful to be sharing all this beauty with Ivy.

"I'll go home on the weekends. How's that? So you and Dean can be alone."

"Mom?"

"You girls alone here in the woods. I won't stop worrying for a minute. I've just gotten used to you living in New York."

"I'll get an alarm system, the kind that's wired to call the police."

"And you get some good locks. Even in poor old Spode, there've been robberies and lootings and I don't like to think what else."

"So if Harrie gets all that stuff, well, is it okay?"

"We'll talk about it with your father. Speaking of your father, let's collect him and Julie. We should be getting home now."

Dottie put her hand on the banister and, fastening her gaze on the littered steps, began a tentative descent. Ivy hung back. She whispered to Harrie. "Har. I really want to be here."

Harrie put her arm around her sister. She said, "Let's both work on Mom a little bit."

"Yeah?" Ivy said hopefully.

"Yeah," said Harrie. "She's not gonna keep two sisters apart."

16

———⬚———

HARRIE SAT across from Roger Mayhew in a coffee shop in Oyster Bay. Roger was a titan: six foot three, blond hair hanging loose to his shoulders, and his clothes—all rayon and raw silk—seemed to blow around him like tatters clinging to the muscled form of a romance novel sea captain.

Roger's coffee, cold in its cup at the edge of the table, was surrounded by small sheets of graph paper covered with hastily inked sketches. Some sheets were crumpled, some marked over, some sandwiched between Polaroid photos taken that morning. There were sketches of the vestibule and of the Great Hall, and other sketches of the north and south wings with their roofs removed, revealing the naked layout of the rooms below.

And Roger had made a detailed drawing of the portico at the end of the north wing, and a view from the portico with convergent lines disappearing into a point in the distance. He narrated as he sketched, punctuating his speech with the ripping of pages from a small leather book, and pushing them toward Harrie. "Like this, don't you think?" he'd say, always including her as if he was giving voice to their joint vision.

Harrie thought Roger's voice was like the color sky blue—warm, open, capable of filling with sun or storm clouds. He was testy, ebullient, passionate, self-assured. And the object of his attention was her house. And, although she was uncertain of his gender preference, her.

"I love the way the land lies here," Roger said, placing a Polaroid snapshot on the table beside the graph paper. "Here," and he drew a sketch indicating a terrace below the house. "Here is an opportunity. The portico just sits there, so. What if"—he chewed his lip, drew a rectangle with sure strokes of his pen—"we put a reflecting pool here:

We add to the stone wall here. Two urns, or spheres—I'll design something—placed here and here to create symmetry, and look what we have. Can you tell from this, Harrie? The eye would go left, right, the vista enclosed. In the foreground, the reflecting pool. Black to the bottom. The sky brought down to the earth. Maybe a plume of water rises from here. Then, in the midground, the terrace. Some soft bushes planted in a line above the stones, backing the hard edge of the new wall. Then, the eye goes here, into the distance. Knock down this little clump of trees," he said, flipping another photo onto the table, stabbing the doomed clump with his finger, "and we're done. A million-dollar view for almost nothing."

"How fast you are. I can't believe you just created that out of thin air."

"Well, to be honest, I did something like this once before. On paper anyway. In Italy. I studied for a few terms in Milan."

"Riva told me."

"The design was for a beautiful villa in the countryside. A restoration. Anyway, the project was terminated."

"Oh. That's too bad. How much is almost nothing?" Harrie asked, her gaze darting from Roger's aquamarine stare to the safer resting place of the drawing.

Two lines created a fold between his eyes. Roger opened the leather book to a calculator. He poked at the calculator as he talked. "Oh, probably fifteen for the pool. Three for the wall and the landscaping. My fee. Twenty percent for contingencies. Call it twenty-five thousand."

"Oh," said Harrie brightly. Twenty-five thousand did sound like almost nothing, after having had a party that lasted a day and cost more. "That sounds like a bargain."

"Exactly," Roger said, closing the book with a soft leather thump. "But this idea is the easiest kind. It's a beautiful detail. *Un dettaglio meraviglioso.* But the real work, and in some ways not the part you really notice, is where the bulk of your budget must go. We've got to make the house sound, safe to live in."

He had taken the job, Harrie decided. So she had him, but she hadn't offered the job. Not that it mattered. She would offer it to him. "What do you think this will cost? I know you can't be definite at this stage, but what's your guess?"

"I can't say. I'll have to bring in my contractor and my engineer and have a thorough look at what we have to work with."

"Just a guesstimate. You must have an idea."

Roger sighed. Ran his fingers through his hair. There, Harrie thought, that gesture. Feminine, or dramatic? She didn't know. She wished suddenly for Desiree. Des should meet him. This man shouldn't go to waste.

"Well, the roof has to be replaced completely. What I'm most afraid of is that the timbers are gone. One small leak and rot sets in. Carpenter ants arrive for dinner. And then you might as well have Styrofoam holding up your roof. Replacing the timbers is going to be a big, expensive job, but if we don't take care of the roof, you might as well have the bulldozers in and start over." Roger paused. He straightened out one of the drawings, crumpled another. He seemed to Harrie uncomfortable—a doctor telling a patient she would be on medication for a long time.

"Look, I hate to give you bad news, but you have to know this. The fellow who put up this house wanted to be closer to the water than was good for the house. He would've been better off putting it up on the hill where the cottage is, but I suppose he wanted the water view and he didn't want to cut down the woods. At any rate, here the house is. The walls have just about disintegrated from the moisture. You can almost push them down with your hand. On a positive note, and this is the good news, we would've had to take the walls down anyway to replace the plumbing and the wiring. And of course, the heating system is a disaster. The furnace is nearly as old as . . . I don't know what. It went in before we were born, that's for sure. Before our parents were born."

"Yeah," Harrie said, toying with the spoon in her saucer. Should she have listened to Mr. Schoonmaker? Was it too late? Stop. She had more courage than that. "I don't know much about furnaces, but I know mine looks like scrap metal."

"Don't look so sad, Harrie. We can get a new one." Roger gave her a radiant smile.

For a moment Harrie got lost in the smile, and the moment seemed to last almost to the edge of embarrassment. "Back to the estimate," she said with a shake of her head. "I don't mean to be dogged but I'm going to worry about this if I don't have a number in my head. What if I can't afford to have you do this?"

The twin lines appeared again between the aquamarine eyes, and the fold they made was met this time by horizontal lines in Roger's forehead. Then he hunched his shoulders and made two walls on the table with his forearms. Between the walls lay the leather book. Out of a loop at the edge of the book came the fountain pen, which Roger uncapped with flawless teeth. He found a ruled page, made a column of neat notations. Opposite the column appeared numbers with many zeros after them. Roger took a subtotal. Made more notes. Totaled again. Slammed the book shut and put the flat of his hand down on the cover, hard.

"Look," he said earnestly. "I want this job. I can give you almost any number you want, depending on what you want to do. Do you want to make the house sound, then take a break? We can do that. I'll give you a blind rough estimate of three million, depending on the roof supports being okay. It'll be more like five million if they're shot. What you'll get for that is a house that's straight and true, and all the mechanicals will be in working order. Then the rest will be up to you.

"Do you want to restore the house to its original condition? Hand-painting, gilding, restoring the frescoes, resetting the tiles. That's one kind of price. If we want to open up the house, modernize it—I have an idea for fronting all the guest rooms onto the Sound, for instance—that's a different kind of price. What about the interior design? Do we want tinted plaster or paint? New cabinetry or old? Do we go with antiques, or do we call Conran's, or do you want to use what you have? There's another kind of price. May I make a suggestion?"

Harrie nodded dumbly.

"Give me the job. I'll bring my people out. We'll give the place a thorough physical. Then we'll make a shopping list. I'll give you a breakdown of what it will cost for everything down to the baseboards. Instead of hiring a contractor, I'll do the job. Whatever the estimate, that'll save you ten percent. We'll talk after the inspection and then we'll make decisions. Okay?"

"Okay," Harrie said with a smile.

"Good," said Roger heartily. He put his hand over hers and squeezed it. "Blackfern is going to be a very good house again."

Harrie blushed, took back her hand, and Roger, seeming not to notice either of these things, called for the check.

⊡

"It's driving me crazy," Dean said to Laura. The salad bar restaurant had not been set up with intimate conversations in mind, and Dean was doing everything he could to block out the clatter of dishes being thrown carelessly into tubs by busboys, the din of voices ricocheting around the high-ceilinged room, the presence of the two people beside them deep in talk and their vegetable lasagna. "I've got all these millions stashed in corporate paper and B-type stocks. I feel like I'm looking over my shoulder all the time. Is the market going to fall apart? It's happened before."

"Dean. Talk to my brother. Please. His tour company's ripe to go public. He and his partner have been talking about nothing but expansion for over a year, and they're solid. They practically own the hotel-booking end of the Caribbean vacation business. SouthEast Airlines books all of their promotional tours through my brother . . ."

"I don't know, Laura. Anyway, if it's so hot, *you* should do it."

"He's my *brother*," Laura chided him. "Doing this deal would be a big conflict of interest."

Dean exhaled loudly.

"I can't believe I'm trying to sell you on this. Every one of twenty guys I know would lick my shoes for an opportunity like this."

Dean pushed a radish around his plate. He gave it a little putt with his fork-iron and it caromed off a cherry tomato before hitting the rim of the bowl and coming to rest. This deal of Laura's seemed risky. A travel-agenting business, for God's sake. Bringing it public. He'd have to go to Wales, and if it was a dumb idea . . . But if it was a good idea . . . Would Laura know? Could she be objective about her brother's company? Would her brother tell her the truth about how his business was going, or was he a puffer and a strutter like Dean's own brother Rob? "Of course I'll talk to him," Dean said with a hint of bluster.

"Good move," Laura said, tucking back the hair that perpetually slid forward over her left eye. Dean had no experience bringing a company public, but he was bright enough to handle the deal, she thought. She wouldn't sell out her baby brother just to get somewhere with Dean, she knew that for sure. And besides, if he needed help, she could give it to him. Unlike Harrie. Harrie offered the most feeble kind of support, that old-fashioned "Anything you do is wonderful" stuff that women used to give in the 1950s. If Dean got into Isletrek with Scott, he could succeed in a way that he had never succeeded before. It would be an ego boost that would last for ages. And when he looked around to see how he'd pulled it off, he wouldn't have to look farther than the building down the block where she worked. Even Harrie would profit from this deal, and if she did, it would all be to the good. Then no one would have to feel guilty. "Got something to write with?" she asked.

What was that? A little tremor in her voice? Dean asked himself. "Sure do," he said, taking a pen from his pocket. Then he acknowledged a twinge from his conscience. The woman liked him. And she was right; there were lots of brokers who would be grateful for an opportunity to launch a successful public offering. But even if this Isletrek deal wasn't viable, Laura was offering up what she had, and no one made gifts of that size in this business. Trade maybe, but give? So, Laura liked him and not just as a friend. The body language was so loud anyone who bothered to look would notice. The squirming in the seat. The constant pushing back of the hair that made a man want to push it back for her. The little jiggle of the breasts when she took his pen. The lace bra you could see through her shirt. The quiver in her voice.

"He works out of his Westport office," Laura said, scratching out a name and number. "Make sure to remind him that we're friends."

Friends. "Okay," Dean said, exhaling mentally. She'd said it. They were friends. Nothing else had passed between them, so what did he have to feel guilty about? "Thanks," he said.

"Keep me posted." She capped the pen and handed it back to Dean. She raisesd her hand to signal the waiter, and the check was brought to the table.

"What are you doing?" Dean asked as she turned the check over with one hand, reached for her handbag with the other.

"It's my turn. You paid last time."

"Come on," Dean said, wiggling his upturned fingers, then taking the check from Laura. "You can leave the tip if you like."

"Fine," said Laura. She tossed three singles onto the table. "A tip for him. And one for you."

"What?"

"AC Industries," she said, standing. She brushed nonexistent wrinkles from her narrow lap. "We think it's going to split."

Dean stared at Laura openmouthed. What? Say again. ACI was going to split? He would have to check this out, and immediately. If Laura was right, he would have to get Harrie in and do the same for his father, double quick. "Thanks, Laura," he said. But he wondered. If he should be grateful, why did he feel weird? Damn. It was awkward taking help from Laura. He was older. And he was a man. He should be helping her. Nothing was normal anymore. He was surrounded by women who were trying to give him things. Had he, without knowing it, taken a wrong step into a parallel dimension?

Dean stood abruptly, straightened his jacket. Bullshit. He just didn't want to be manipulated. If Laura was going to help him, he might as well take the help. If she expected something in return, well, it would have to be repayment in kind. If that wasn't okay, too bad. Sex and love were not up for trade as far as he was concerned. Cute as she was.

Dean looked up. Laura had begun to make her way out of the restaurant, and he started after her. As if a switch had been thrown, his unspoken angry thoughts were gone. And he found himself hypnotized by Laura's twitching behind as he followed her out the door.

⊡

"Sure, I think she's cute," Chip said to Dean. They were sitting side by side on a bench in the locker room of the squash club. Chip unbuttoned his shirt. "I asked her out once but she gave me the usual crap about not dating within the company."

"Hmmm." Dean stuffed his socks into his shoes, stood and put the shoes in his locker. He took his athletic shoes and sweat socks out of a duffel. He sat back down. "I think she likes me."

"Oh yeah?" Chip queried, with not a little interest. "What makes you think so?"

"Instinct."

"Huh!"

"Really. She's sending signals. I got a boner walking out of the restaurant behind her, and I swear I had nothing on my mind. Or if I did, it was the opposite of being turned on."

"You got a boner, and she did it to you from in front of you? Don't you know rear-end collisions are always the fault of the car behind?"

The two men pulled off their street shirts simultaneously and put polo shirts on.

"Trust me on this, Chip. She was blinking her taillights."

"Okay. So what are you going to do about it?"

"I don't know. Nothing, I guess." Dean put a sweatband over his head, picked his racket up from the floor and banged the strings against the palm of his hand. "She's been helping me, giving me tips on the market."

"That's friendly. I mean, like what?"

"Like ACI's going to split."

"Could be, could be," Chip said reflectively. He bent to tie his laces. "I can see that. Not the stupidest thing I ever heard. Thanks for telling me."

"So what does she want in return, Chip?"

"I see where you're going. But don't do it, buddy."

"I keep thinking, since lunch that is, maybe Laura knows something I don't know. Like maybe I haven't been paying the right kind of attention to her. She's the right type, you know what I mean? The bones, the breeding, the business brain." Everything Harrie was lacking.

"Don't do it, buddy," Chip said again. "You do it and you're going to live to regret it."

"C'mon, Chip," Dean said with irritation. "I didn't say I was going to do anything."

"I wish I had what you have with Harrie." Chip looked earnestly at the side of Dean's face. Dean, looking down at the floor, tapped the side of his racket rhythmically against his thigh. Chip said, "I guess I have to count your blessings for you. Harrie is beautiful, she loves you, and she's rich. And you love her."

"I do love her," said Dean, somewhat reluctantly. "But maybe love's not enough."

"Well, if it isn't, I don't know what is."

"Something's wrong. Ending up with Harrie is just not what I planned for myself. A lot of things about our relationship are great, but there's an important piece that just won't work for me. And this stupid house of hers is making the wrong part feel like all of the parts. You've got to admit, our relationship is getting pretty bizarre."

Chip stood up suddenly, jammed his clothes into his locker and banged the door shut, hard. Three years and he still woke up in the morning thinking about Riva. "I'm getting this very bad feeling, Dean-o. Like you're about to do something stupid and I can't stop you."

Dean hefted his duffel into his own locker, shut the door, locked it. His sense that he was onto a new piece of self-knowledge was evaporating. Chip just didn't get it. He didn't understand. Why couldn't he just listen? Why did he have to argue with him? He wanted to tell Chip about his mother—what he could remember of her— about her cool sweetness, like a peach sorbet. The image he had in his mind was lifted from a photograph he kept in his desk drawer at home.

There were the five of them, on Cape Cod for a holiday weekend. His father was at the rear of the posed grouping, his mother in the center. Rob junior and Henry flanked their mother, but he, Dean, stood in front of her, coming up to about her waist. And his mother, thin-boned and lean (almost too much so—had the cancer already bitten into her?), had bent slightly from her waist and crossed both arms over his chest, and he could tell from her expression that she loved him the most, that the other men in her family didn't exist at all. He almost remembered that moment and he did remember the cleanliness, the ethereal whiteness of her skin and her clothes, and a faint scent of lilac. And hadn't that ethereal beauty lifted his father, calmed him, refined him by its very presence, added a standard to be met? And meeting that standard had been a necessary ingredient without which Robertson Carrothers would be selling office equipment for a living instead of having become a takeover tycoon. In hundreds of ways Sarajane Winston Carrothers had made a crucial difference. The right woman could do that. But how could he tell Chip about his mother? If he told Chip he had always thought he would marry someone like his mother, Chip would think he was a pervert. Or a nut. "For Christ's sake," Dean said, "I'm just thinking out loud. I'm just talking. Remind me not to do it ever again."

"You want my advice—"

"No."

"—you should marry Harrie, have a couple of kids, kick back. Take up polo or something. You have a rare opportunity here and—"

"Chip?"

"Yeah?"

"Let's go out on the court so I can kill you."

17

————□————

*I*N THE THREE MONTHS since David Tuckman's death, Harrie's life had shifted to a plane as full of promise and revelation as the onset of puberty. She'd cut back the number of days she went in to the office to two, more or less, and she'd moved some things from Chester Street—pots, linens, warm clothes—and set up a quasi-permanent residence in the gardener's cottage. And she'd bought a car, a sturdy Volvo sedan.

Ivy had also set up a quasi-permanent residence in the cottage. She'd dropped off a canvas bag of black things, two pairs of cowboy boots, and a futon and stowed them in the small upstairs room. On some afternoons, without warning, Ivy would drive up in an old blue Rabbit, greet Harrie with varying degrees of enthusiasm, then sprawl in the chair in front of the television. She would eat the dinner Harrie prepared, or she would go out, sometimes not returning until long after the fast-food restaurants and movie houses had closed. And she looked terrible in the mornings. Harrie worried. Was Ivy sleeping with the electrician (a brooding young man who had once come looking for Ivy at the cottage)? Was she doing drugs? When asked, Ivy gave monosyllabic non-answers, leaving Harrie with a feeling that she'd failed Ivy. She *was* having a new relationship with her youngest sister, but what was it? Girlfriend, foster mother, innkeeper? Whatever the label, she was surely responsible for the nineteen-year-old.

Meanwhile, down the path toward the water, Roger and his crew had taken Blackfern over in force. A quarter of a mile from the house, Harrie could hear the sounds of demolition, and since the house was a construction site, she tended to stay around the cottage. The days were short, but Harrie, still operating in a businesslike fashion, had segmented them into parts.

First, in the mornings, she did her household chores. She fed the cockatoos, made breakfast for herself, and Ivy when she was there: steel-cut Scottish oatmeal or soft-cooked scrambled eggs and muffins with jam—a new kind of breakfast for living in the country. Then she straightened up the three rooms and bath, and after that, she'd go to her table by the window across from the fireplace and, with Sidney and Angel chattering contentedly beside her, she'd apply herself to the business of being a literary agent. By noon Ivy would be gone. She would have driven off to spend the day with a friend or gone to Spode. Then Harrie would prepare for lunch with Roger.

By one o'clock Roger would appear, blocking all the light from the doorway, then stooping and entering the small living room. At the beginning, Roger's dazzling presence intimidated Harrie, but quickly tiring of the self-induced pressure to seem a certain sophisticated way, Harrie forced herself into normalcy by deliberately dressing down. No makeup for Roger, and no romantic clothing either. She wore baggy jeans and Dean's sweaters, and the trick on herself worked. No longer self-conscious, Harrie asked layman's questions over soup and cheese sandwiches. Equally comfortable, Roger gave her his daily progress reports, elicited her opinions, made recommendations.

On Fridays, the days that by evening became the beginning of weekends with Dean, Harrie found it harder to work. Fridays were slow days. The workmen left early; Roger, who lived in an apartment in Oyster Bay during the week, went back to New York; and with Ivy gone as well, Harrie found herself thinking about how long it would be before Dean's car pulled into the drive.

Things had gotten better with Dean, Harrie felt. They saw each other less during the week, and that made the weekends so much more special. She had time now to take a leisurely bath before he arrived, and put candles on the mantelpiece, and bake a pie. Dean said he thought the absence of city noise was having a beneficial effect on his sleep, and he hadn't been moody since their cottage weekends began. And Dean was doing better at work. The market was healthier for the moment and he was making money for his clients. Even his father's account had prospered, and, perhaps because of this, Dean's father had had a burst of goodwill. Harrie had been invited with Dean to the Carrotherses' house for Christmas dinner! Last week she'd shopped feverishly for gifts and for the outfit she would wear. But Christmas was weeks off. And today wasn't a Friday, it was a Thursday. Thursday morning was a phone morning, and Harrie was in a brusque but ruminative mood.

Standing at the table, which was littered with engaging sketches and pieces of moldings and color chips on one side, manuscripts, typewriter, and fax machine on the other, Harrie glared at the telephone. Then she snatched the receiver from its base and made a call. Raoul gave her five messages, but told her, with some kind of edge in his voice, that he had no time to chat.

Harrie hadn't wanted to chat. She shrugged off the unexplained slight and tapped out a number. She spoke with Jan, who wanted a critique of a chapter, and Harrie, having read the chapter and been unmoved by it, told Jan what she thought. Then, in quick succession, she talked to an editor about a change she'd made in a contract. She called a potential client with regrets; she wouldn't be able to take her on. She spoke with a foreign-rights director about a sale in Germany. She spoke with another agent who wanted a reference on an assistant who'd applied for a job. And if she made these calls more with a sense of duty than with passionate interest, she hadn't yet allowed this fact past her subconscious.

As Harrie talked she walked around her cottage. She poked her fingernail at the new grouting between the bathroom tiles. It was hard. She ran a hand over the new wallpaper in the bedroom; she hadn't gotten a stripe after all but a print of a twining vine, sweet peas climbing up her walls forever. She straightened a dust ruffle, tugged on a curtain, frowned at the bed frame which was a painted iron one instead of the sleigh bed she had envisioned.

Gripping the cellular phone and talking all the while, Harrie went to the kitchen, and as she'd done in the other rooms, she admired her work: the butcher block table, the stripped-down cabinets, a wonderful enamel sink with a marble backsplash that Roger had found for her in an architectural salvage yard.

Harrie paused between phone calls, opened the front door, and walked out into the garden. Autumn was gone, winter was beginning to assert itself, and the summer holiday feeling she'd experienced in mid-October was leaving her. As the air cooled and the planet turned on its axis she became aware of a palpable change in herself, and this

change was expressing itself as a pull away from the city and toward
the sea. At this moment, for instance, she wanted to set the phone
on the little brick path of her bare front garden and go down to the
seawall to watch the tide. She was sure something about the weather
had promoted this fisherman's wife outlook, and it was so silly. There
was no one to wait for at the seawall, and if she wanted to stay
attached to her business, and she did, she must make her calls. And
read. And stay interested. Even if she was changing. Was this "change"
an excuse for truancy? Was it *I don't have to go to school anymore
and I don't want to*? Or was it an actual, physical metamorphosis—
a city person transformed to a water person? This could be. She'd
heard of stranger things. She put the phone down on the path, went
back into the house for her favorite blue quilted jacket, then started
down the grassy rut of a driveway toward the castle.

In a way, she thought, as she meandered down the path whose
every bump and stone and root she was committing to memory, she
was becoming a snail. The house she carried on her back was invisible,
but it was real. Last week she'd unpacked one of the boxes that
contained some of the "rest, residue and remainder" of Mr. Tuckman's estate. Des had been sitting in the armchair in Harrie's Chester
Street studio, keeping her company, while she sat on the floor and
dug in the box. Inside the carton was a half set of the complete works
of Shakespeare, an old Osterizer mixer-blender, the gray cashmere pull-
over that had belonged to Mr. Tuckman, which she was wearing now,
and three photograph albums.

The album that fascinated Harrie was fat and heavy and loaded
with treasure. The covers were made of tooled burgundy leather with
a mirror set in the front face and a spray of carnations carved into
the back, and there were several dozen heavy black pages between
the covers. Each of the pages contained six to eight deckle-edged
snapshots, all black-and-whites that had turned brown and yellow.
The photos were of the Defoes from around the time of World War
I until, judging by the clothing the family wore, the 1930s. And the
setting for this silent staging of the Defoe family saga was Blackfern.

The early photos were group portraits in front of the castle. Later
there were pictures of Jazz Defoe on horseback, young men at the
wheel of their new cars (sometimes Jazz would be sitting on the car's
bonnet, or posed with a foot on the running board). There were

photographs of babies and groups at an outdoor party, with lanterns strung from the trees. But of all the pictures, the ones that interested Harrie the most were the ones of the interior of the house. And if she worried that she might be somewhat overfocused on furnishing the house as it once was, she had only to show the photos to Roger, who was as excited as she about her find.

Before seeing the photographs, she had read about houses that required two servants for each room. She'd tried to imagine what it must have been like to have the morning paper ironed into crisp, uncreased sheets; to have flowers in all of the rooms, not to mention the linens, changed daily; to think nothing of having twenty or sixty people for dinner, because all one had to do really was make decisions about the menu, and get dressed. Now she had pictures of the people who lived such a life in her actual house. And with her desire to replicate that environment and the money to do it—it could be done. What could be more unlike the life she had led during her thirty-two years?

Had it been only three months since Mr. Tuckman died? Had it been only three months since the beginning of her change from a woman in a box to a woman of the sea? Harrie smiled at her new description of herself. Being virtually alone out here four or five days a week was giving her more time to think, to reinvent herself as a mermaid or a fisherman's wife or, giving new meaning to the word, a housewife.

She hugged herself and looked up at the sky. It was going to be yet another beautiful day, a day she would have missed entirely had she gone in to the city to work. And the weather had been unbelievable of late. Dark clouds and crystalline dusting of frost on the grass. Or, suddenly, a clear day as hard and as blue as sapphires.

Last Saturday had been a dream. The sky had been bright; the air had been cool and sweet, smelling of vanilla and maple leaves and sea spray. Julie had come out for the day and, of course, Dean was there, and the three of them had scrambled down the bluff to Black-fern's little beach on the Sound and there they'd had a picnic—a feast of quail's eggs and caviar and smoked trout and tiny melons the size of tennis balls. Clad in sweaters and jackets and laced-up shoes, they had gotten only pink noses in the sun. It was a day that made it hard to believe winter could be cruel, and Harrie had felt the time to be a magic time.

They'd been talking about the recent Thanksgiving dinner at her parents' house in Spode. Harrie lay down on the blanket and closed her eyes—not to sleep, just to enjoy the soft sun and recall the warmth of her mother's kitchen, and to invent a future Thanksgiving meal at her own table. She picked out the table in her mind. It would be Queen Anne: a mile-long stretch of mahogany dressed in white linen and set before the dining room fireplace. There would be twenty chairs and a breakfront full of crystal and bone china with a gold rim.

All of the people who had reveled in turkey and trimmings at her mother's kitchen table were transported to her table, and there were new faces. There was a little boy and a little girl, and their features were Dean's and hers respectively, and since this was her fantasy, what the heck, Julie was there with her husband and children, and Doug with his. And Ivy would have a fiancé, a distinguished man in his mid-thirties. And Dean's father would be there with the Carrothers brothers. The Carrothers brothers. How funny. Had they been called that?

Harrie had dozed. When she next became aware of sound, it was Dean's voice she heard. He was telling Julie about his dyslexia—he didn't tell many people—and Julie was commiserating. Harrie heard him say how stupid he'd felt as a child, and then, to her surprise, she heard Julie declare how ugly she'd felt while growing up and how it affected her image of herself to this day. Remembering now the thrill she felt overhearing this connection being forged between her lover and her sister, Harrie marveled all over again. It was working. Step by step, her family was coming together at Blackfern.

Reaching the end of the path, Harrie pushed through a little copse of saplings and found herself standing on the edge of the grass. Off to her right and below was the castle, looking grand on its seat above the water. Before her, the lawn sloped down to the seawall. The water was the color of marble today: dark green veined with white foam. The sea gulls swooped and called out their salutations as Harrie walked down the gentle slope. And as the water drew her closer she wondered how she was going to motivate herself to go back to the telephone. She would just do it, that was all. She was still an agent. It was what she did. And she did it well. So, she would walk to the seawall and she would think about the calls she had to make. Then she would go to the castle and collect Roger. She had a lovely pâté she'd bought in town that Roger particularly liked, and she would heat up her mother's soup. Then after lunch with Roger, she would work. She really would.

So deciding, Harrie set off on her rounds.

18

—▫—

*H*ELLO, HELLO," Luna said, with a cocked eyebrow. "Harriet Braintree, I presume."

"Sorry, Luna," said Harrie, brushing her gaze over Luna, then dropping her handbag into a drawer. It was Tuesday morning, almost eleven o'clock, and she hadn't seen her office in a week. "I know it's been a while. You just can't imagine what's been going on at the house."

"Do tell."

"It's too boring. Suffice it to say, I've had to be there or I would have been sorry. Yesterday the carpenters dismantled half the paneling in the library and were about to throw it onto the dump."

"Really," Luna commented with no inflection.

"It would have been a tragedy. Sanford Defoe had those panels custom made. He used to hang out with Roosevelt in that library. You don't just throw things like that out. They tried to tell me how warped the boards were, but some of them could be saved, for God's sake. They could be planed."

"You've got a mountain of mail on your desk."

Harrie looked down at the several small heaps on her desk that was not her desk. Her table in the cottage seemed like her desk now. This one, the one buried under the unopened mail, was like a piece of furniture from an earlier time in her life. Like her unicorn lamp in her old bedroom in Spode.

"We didn't want to open anything that might be personal. And since you did say you were coming in . . ."

"Can I get you some coffee?"

"Thanks, no." Luna's line flashed and she picked up the telephone.

Harrie made a cup of coffee for herself, then returned to her desk to sort out her mail. Somehow word of her inheritance had leaked out. Possibly the transfer of the title to Blackfern had appeared somewhere. Or maybe one of Mr. Tuckman's other heirs had told someone in the press. However it had happened, there'd been a mention in *USA Today*, that a young literary agent named Harriet Braintree of New York had inherited a fortune and a falling-down castle as well. One little squib in the Lifestyles section, and she was getting "mountains" of mail.

She slit open the first envelope. A piece of lined paper and a photograph of a mother and child standing in front of a trailer fell into her hand.

"Dear Miss Harriet—Lucky you. Somebody is looking out for you. I'm not so lucky. My little boy Robert was born with a bad heart. He needs an operation really bad but I didn't have any insurance when he was born and now I can't get any . . ."

Harrie sighed and put the letter to one side. How much should she send? A thousand? Two? Ten? Was she being conned, or was this little boy truly sick? How could she know? She opened the next envelope.

"Dear Harriet Braintree," was typed with a manual typewriter on white bond. "You don't know me and you have no reason to trust me but I have an idea I think you'd like to know about. Enclosed is a picture of an office building in downtown Tuscaloosa. It is going very cheap, only a half a million. Now, my idea is this. If you buy this building and let me manage it, we can be partners . . ."

"Dear Ms. Braintree. People always tell me I got a gift I can see things. I can see that your money is cursed unless you clean it by giving it to people what hasn't got any money. If you don't and spend it on yourself you will bring only unhappiness down on yourself . . ."

"Jeez," said Harrie, crumpling the letter and throwing it into the trash basket.

"More save the seals?" Luna asked from across the room.

"No. I already gave to save the seals. And the elephants. And the fruit bat society."

"Lady Frances of Assisi."

"And MADD, and leukemia." She thought for a minute. "And muscular dystrophy."

"Have you given a lot?"

"Yeah. But I get the feeling it's never enough. The thank-you notes always leave an opening to ask for more. But the foundations and charities are a piece of cake compared to these." She waved a hand over the letters. "These 'Send me money and I'll light a candle for you' letters are horrible."

"Wretched article. You can't save the whole world, you know."

Harrie nodded. Beneath the mail from supplicants was a stack of business mail, and there were phone messages from last week that she hadn't returned. She felt as if she were lying on the desk and the mail were lying on her. "I don't know what to do about these manuscripts, Luna." She put her hand on a stack of fat envelopes. "I can't take on any more clients. I can't take care of the ones I have."

"I know. I've been waiting for you to say something. Harrie dear, I think it's time we talked." Luna spoke into the receiver, asking Raoul to handle their calls. "I think I will take that coffee now." She got up from behind the desk, went to their little kitchen alcove, and returned with a fat, steaming mug. She closed the door. Instead of going back behind her desk, she sat in one of the lovely carved chairs and invited Harrie to take one of the others. Thus seated in the center of the room, they put business aside.

Harrie looked at Luna's face. Luna was a big one for eye contact. She had stared down many an editor, Harrie knew, but now she seemed to have her gaze everywhere but on Harrie's face. "This isn't working for you, is it?" Harrie said.

"No, Harrie dear. It's not."

"Oh, boy," Harrie said sadly. She put her mug of lukewarm coffee down on a manuscript and twisted her fingers together. Her stomach tumbled at the certainty that in moments, without warning, her life at the Luna Casey Literary Agency would end. But then, she'd been kidding herself thinking it could continue. "I guess you're firing me," she said.

Luna lunged forward and took one of Harrie's wrists in her hand and shook it. "Nonsense. I'm not firing you."

"You're not?"

"How could I fire you? It's not that at all." Luna released Harrie's wrist and sat back in her seat. She went on. "I do think you should take a leave of absence. For a while. Until you've gotten things together at the house, or until you want to spend the kind of time one must spend doing this job."

Harrie nodded. "I haven't been fair," she said. "I've been letting a lot of people down."

Luna demurred. "Now, Harrie. Everyone who knows you understands. It's just that those of us who are working for a living have to get on with things . . ."

"And I'm slowing things down." Harrie exhaled loudly. "What are you going to do?"

"Raoul's been looking for a chance. I guess I'll give it to him."

"Sure," Harrie said, understanding Raoul's distance now.

"He's been taking your calls. Making some suggestions. He's always been a good reader."

"He'll be good. He's got good judgment. People like him."

"Harrie, this doesn't have to be permanent, do you understand? I'm going to be a complete mess without you." And as Luna said this her voice quivered and she pressed her lips together tightly. Tears filled her eyes.

"Oh, Luna," Harrie said, getting up from the chair and putting her arms awkwardly around her mentor. "I'm sorry."

Luna patted Harrie's arm and collected her emotions. "Please forgive me," she said, then stood, plucked a tissue from a box on her desk, and dabbed gently at her eyes. "I'm being quite silly."

"No."

"Will you be all right?"

"You mean without my job?"

Luna nodded.

"Sure. I'll be okay. I guess. I need a little while to get used to this idea."

"Well, look, Harrie. You don't have to leave this minute. I'm not booting you out. What would you like to do?"

"Come in for the rest of the week, I guess. Call some people and clean up some things."

Luna nodded.

"Maybe I'll take Raoul out to lunch."

"That would be very generous." Luna paused. "You've got some commissions due. And of course, we'll send your mail on to you.

Listen, Harrie. We're acting like someone died. We're both being quite maudlin."

"Well, it's sad."

"It's nothing of the kind. You're moving on, that's all. You have a new life and new prospects. We should celebrate, not mourn."

Harrie perched on the edge of her desk and looked across at Luna, who was forcing herself to look happy. Luna had behaved absolutely properly, Harrie thought. For the last three months she had been treating her job as something she had to do, the office as someplace to pick up her phone calls. And now she would just have to wrench herself from this false sense of security and, as Luna said, move on. What would she do with herself now? Would there be any reason to come in to the city at all?

"I'm taking you out to lunch this very week," Luna said. "Someplace really special."

"My farewell lunch," Harrie said.

"Now listen. One more time. Any time you decide to come back for good, let me know. Your job will be waiting for you."

"Thanks," Harrie said with a smile. "I will."

□

Dean loosened his scarf and opened the buttons of his overcoat as he entered the ground floor of the Griffin Club. He looked around the vast, high-ceilinged room, which was divided into sections and purposes. To his left was a large semicircular receiving desk, topped with marble, attended by men in blue uniforms. To his right was an elevator bank and a large coatroom and, oddly Dean thought, a gift shop selling mugs and ties and other fraternal paraphernalia.

Directly before him was an open waiting area filled with worn modern furniture, and behind that floated an imposing staircase. To the side of the staircase, under a coat of arms dominated by two gilded griffins, was the entrance to the bar. Seeing that the waiting area was empty, Dean wondered if Scott Taft, Laura's younger brother, was waiting for him there. It had taken quite a while to put together this meeting. Taft had been away, and following his return, Dean had had to break the first lunch date they arranged. Taft had broken the second. But at last, today, they were meeting. Dean checked his coat, decided to try the bar first, and was about to enter its dim recesses, when a stocky man in a charcoal-gray suit, pink shirt, and black and white paisley tie came up behind him.

"Dean Carrothers?" The man stuck out a plump, pink hand. "I'm Scott Taft."

The two shook hands, and in those small seconds silently appraised each other according to height, girth, and age. Each having found in the other at least one flaw that would permit friendship, they walked to the room where they would have lunch.

The dining room was in a well of sorts, centered under the mezzanine floor above it. The furnishings were plain, almost drab compared with the entrance room. The floor was vinyl tile, the tables plain, uncovered wood, and a row of steam tables bordered one of the long walls. The waiter took their drink orders (mineral water for them both), and over these drinks, the two men exchanged pregame conversation about Laura, the schools each had attended, and the fact that they'd grown up in neighboring towns in Connecticut. Again, each having passed some test of kinship, they collected their buffet luncheon and began to talk about the business at hand.

"It works like this," Scott said, putting half of a buttered roll in his mouth.

Dean sipped his Perrier and waited while Scott chewed. Unlike his sister, Scott seemed to have his hair under control. And where Laura was slim, Scott was almost stout—made of softer, yet sturdier stuff.

"Our function is to package vacation programs. In a way, we're like the in-house hotel-booking agent for SouthEast Airlines. Our deal with SouthEast is really something, Dean, and it's been in constant operation for the last ten years. See. SouthEast runs a promotion. Six days, five nights in Bermuda, X dollars per person per night, double occupancy, round-trip air fare included."

Dean nodded. "Sure. I see those ads all the time."

"Good, good." Scott bobbed his head. "Well, SouthEast doesn't book the rooms. We do. About fifteen hundred rooms daily on average, throughout the year. That's roughly half a million rooms annually—that's just through SouthEast—and we make a markup of twenty percent per room."

Dean whistled. "What's the average price per room?"

"One fifty," Scott said, blotting his lips with a napkin. "And of course, we book the flights and make our markup on that. So, we're grossing about eighteen million, just from this one account. Our overhead is low—personnel, computers and fax machines—but we've got minimal office space requirements. It's a good little business. We've netted about three million annually for the last five years."

"Not bad," Dean said, impressed. He wondered how much Scott Taft was earning.

"And I guess we're at a point where we don't want it to be a good *little* business anymore. Another major carrier has approached us about booking their European tours. In order to take them on, we'd need to expand our base of operations. And there's a hotel in Guadeloupe we've been wanting to buy. We've been booking into that hotel for a decade, but believe me, getting the whole one twenty per night added to the twenty percent would give a real lift to our bottom line. But," Scott Taft said, spreading his hands, "we don't have the capital we need to expand. We're extended out as far as we can go now."

"So that's why you want to go public."

"Right. Down payment on the Hotel St. George will run us fifteen million after we've talked them down. We'll need another five million to open a European base of operations. Do you think we could raise twenty million bucks? What's your honest opinion?"

"I think it's something to talk about." Dean said. He felt a surge of excitement that he was afraid to trust. Was Scott Taft's company for real? Would the analysts think so? Was a twenty-million-dollar offering feasible? The broker's commission on a deal like this, if he remembered correctly, was twenty percent of the brokerage house commission. What would that be on twenty million dollars? Half of one percent? "I wish we could just shake hands and it's done," he said. "But there are a few things standing between you, me, and twenty million dollars."

"Too bad," Taft said ruefully.

"You said it."

"So, give me the bad news. I must seem pretty naive to you, but I'm a salesman. That's what I know."

"No, listen. You've got to start somewhere. And the place to start is by getting together your financial statement."

"Done," said Taft. "I'll have it to you by messenger this afternoon."

Dean allowed himself a smile. "And we'll want to see your contract with SouthEast. If there are any restrictions, if the contract can be canceled . . ."

"No, no. The contract is engraved in gold. Then what?"

"I'll take your financials. I'll want a kit of all the materials describing your operation. Then I'll do a report and take all this information to our investment-banking division. Then it's in their laps for a while. They've got to check you out. 'Due diligence'—that's what it's called."

"Coffee, Dean?"

A waiter cleared dishes from the table. Dean knew he must have eaten something, but he couldn't imagine what. "Yes, thanks," he said. He watched the waiter pour. He added milk and sugar mechanically. "This is pretty exciting, Scott."

"I'll say. So don't stop. What next? We're checked out, let's say."

"Then a lot of work goes on in our offices. The legal types get into the act, then the SEC, then NASDAQ. If the numbers are right, and the documents are right, we could go public—"

"When?"

"In sixty to ninety days."

"Wow," Scott said.

"Wow," Dean echoed, as pleased and anticipatory as the young man sitting across from him. If he'd first thought Scott Taft was just an average-to-bright yuppie who had stepped into a good thing, he was beginning to see him as an adventurous businessman who'd made a brilliant career out of the tour business. Oh, God, he thought, let this be for real. If he could be the point man, there was an opportunity here for glory. Glory and money. And an answer to the nagging, constantly badgering problem of where to put Harrie's wealth. He would get her into Isletrek in a big way and on the ground floor.

The meeting concluded with a very sincere handshake in front of Grand Central Station, and a promise of another meeting within the week.

Dean took a subway train to his office, never noticing that he was underground at all. When he arrived at his desk, still flushed with excitement, he made a call.

There was a stock he had liked for the last couple of weeks. It was a restaurant chain that he'd seen written up in a travel magazine. No notice of this stock had been taken by the financial wizards, but Dean had a gut feeling that the company was undervalued, that it had been quiescent for a long while, and that soon it was going to move. He picked up the phone and placed an order—a small one, five hundred shares each for Harrie, for his father, and for himself.

By the time the market closed that day, the stock had gone up a point.

19

————□————

I'M SEEING Anthony tonight," Desiree announced.

"Tell me," said Harrie.

They were in the cottage. Desiree had appropriated the easy chair, thrown both legs over one of its arms, and Harrie was at her all-purpose table collecting photographs and blueprints so she could give Des an orderly and documented tour of the house.

"We're having dinner at eight tonight, so I gotta get home at a decent hour and do the routine. Maybe we could catch the three-something train. Is that okay?"

Harrie nodded. She knew the routine. An hour of emergency aerobics at the health club in Des's building, followed by a sauna bath and a cool shower. Then, with the prep work out of the way, Desiree's beauty regimen would begin in earnest with masks, oils, powders, and meditation in a darkened room. The routine was reserved for what Des called a Special Night. But how had it gotten to be a Special Night so fast? She thought Des's relationship with Anthony was only three weeks old. Had she missed a chapter? "But I thought you just met Anthony. Isn't he Madrid?" Harrie asked, referring to the destination this latest of Desiree's targets had booked through the travel agency where she worked.

"I think An-tho-ny could be he," Des sang. "The long-awaited Dr. Applestein. He's cute, he's nice to me, and his mother lives in Santa Fe, far, far away. And he's Jewish. I asked." Desiree threw a long, soulful sigh. She looked past Harrie into the fire that was sputtering fitfully in the fireplace. "He's short, Harrie. And a little older than I ever thought I'd like, but fifty is supposed to be a very good time for people. The well-adjusted ones, I mean. I think at fifty you're past the strivings of the thirties, past the desperation and the misgivings of the forties, and you come to terms with yourself."

"I haven't dipped into *Passages* in a long time, but I think that's right."

"Anthony's kind of like Stuart in *L.A. Law*. He's thinner than Stuart, and not as gray . . . Anyway, I like him a lot. A lot, a lot."

"I kind of got that feeling."

"Vish me luck, dahlink. I'm shivering in my Susan Bennis–Warren Edwardses," she said, looking down at her two-hundred-dollar designer shoes. Somehow she hadn't worn the athletic shoes she'd promised to wear on her last visit to the house. "You remember that little blue dress you got me on the spree of a lifetime?" Desiree let her sentence trail off as she savored the memory of that day. She could remember every part of every minute. Up at dawn. Well, up at nine, which was the same thing on a Saturday. She'd gulped down juice and coffee, eaten a slice of toast over the kitchen sink, then put on a full-length body stocking under a beltless, zipperless tunic dress. This way of dressing was a trick she'd learned from her days as a fitting model. The dress could be shucked in a flash, and the body stocking was smooth and invisible under everything she would put on from evening gowns to trousers. She'd worn comfortable flat shoes, tucked a pair of heels into her bag, and put her makeup on in the elevator.

The limousine, a black Caddy, had glided to the curb outside her apartment building and her doorman had handed her off to the chauffeur (a very cute guy, too bad about the mustache) and she'd climbed into the back of the car and thrown her arms around Harrie. "I think we should work from uptown to downtown," Harrie had suggested. "James," Harrie had said—and the driver's name *was* James— "Bloomingdale's, please."

And so had begun a day so perfect that not even the passage of time and the repeated telling of it to her awestruck friends and relatives had dimmed her euphoric memory. And the way she remembered it, the doors to the department stores had blown open at their approach: Saks, Lord and Taylor, Henri Bendel. Personal shoppers had appeared carrying armloads of clothing in the right sizes and colors, accessories had materialized without their asking, discarded garments had been whisked away. They had shrugged sweaters over their heads, squeezed into leather pants, stepped in and out of countless skirts. And when their selections were made, Harrie had slapped down her gold card, and then they'd simply carried their booty out to the waiting car.

In a word, the day had been blissful. Eight hours after it all began, Desiree had disembarked from the limo sated and fatigued, the possessor of forty parcels of loot up to and including diamond studs and the full-length Blackglama mink which she could hardly bear to be separated from, even when it was only hanging a few feet away, as it was now.

"Which one was that?" Harrie asked.

Desiree returned to the real world. "What? Oh. The dress. It's the one with the wide belt and the black piping? I'm wearing that and my mink and very little else. I want to give Anthony something to remember when he's all alone in Madrid."

"Des, don't you worry that you might get something?"

"Oh, Harrie." Desiree unswung her legs, dropped them to the floor, then bent her head between her thighs and ruffled her hair. "I take precautions."

"He'll only be away for two weeks, right? Don't you think if he's Dr. Applestein he can wait till then?"

"I'd rather get something started now if it's going to happen. I want him thinking about me all the time until he sees me again. What are you doing over there?"

"I know what the next two weeks are going to be like. You're going to be gooey and running all over everything."

"Worry, worry."

"I remember the last Dr. A. A Special Night, then *nada*. I think you ought to have a little consideration for your best friend."

"Har. You've got to trust me. This one's different. This one's a mensch. Do you want to take me on the tour or what?"

"Yeah, I want to take you on the tour. And I thought I had a surprise for you," she said, thinking about Roger. She wished Des wasn't in such a rush. "You know, I think you approach this whole dating thing like it's a game show."

"What do you mean?"

"Like the little hurdles and milestones. The three-date decision. The Special Night. The six-month cutoff. It's like you're constantly doubling all the money on the next question, and if you're right you win the championship and an all-expense-paid trip to Paris . . ."

"And if I'm wrong? . . ."

"You win fifty pounds of cheese."

"You're a scream, Har," Desiree said with a laugh.

"I know."

"Don't worry about me. I'm good at this. I'm very good at being single. And I can't afford to waste any time. The clock is ticking, you know."

"That's it. That's what made me think of—" The game show, she finished silently. *Beat the Clock* and *The Gong Show* and *Love Connection* all rolled into one. And yet they'd had this conversation a hundred and twelve times, and things never seemed to advance for Des. It was amazing, when she thought about it, how much had changed for her in the last three months and how little had changed for her friend. Desiree's voice broke into her thoughts.

"So, Har. You gonna show me the house or what?"

"Okay, okay." Harrie laughed. "I want to start at the beginning this time. I want to show you what the house looked like in 1915 and work forward."

"Okay."

"Let me show you these pictures," Harrie said. She secured a perch on the armchair and put the photo album in Desiree's hands. "No, wait," she said, leaping up again, grabbing a rolled paper from her table. "Let me show you the aerial photograph first." She unfurled the sheet. "See, we're here."

"Uh-huh."

"This is the drive we took to the cottage. It's a service entrance, really. This is the main entrance to the house."

"Uh-huh."

"This is the gatehouse. Remains of, anyway. And these are the old stables."

"Uh-huh."

"So now I'll show you the old pictures."

"Okay." Then, "Har?"

"Hmmm?"

"What was the surprise you mentioned?"

"Never mind. I don't think you'd be interested. Now pay attention. See how the conservatory looked when it was built? You've got to keep this picture in your mind, because it's hard to imagine anything this splendid from the wreck that's left."

"Well, what was it, anyway? The surprise."

"Can't you pretend to be interested in my house? Just for me?"

"I *am* interested. I took a day off from work, didn't I? Let's go."

Harrie sighed. She closed the album and put it on the table. "There's a man I thought you'd like."

"Oh yeah? Who is it?"

"My architect. Roger Mayhew."

"So tell me."

"Wait a minute. I thought tonight was a Special Night."

"So. I can still hear about this Roger, can't I? It doesn't hurt to have a backup plan."

"Okay, okay. I'll tell you about Roger. I thought we'd have lunch with him."

"What do you mean? He's here?"

"Sure. He's working down at the house. He does a lot of the work himself."

"Oh. Well, what's he like?"

"He's a creative person. Very intense."

"How old?"

"About our age."

"Nunh-uh. What's he look like?"

"Gorgeous. Blond." Harrie indicated shoulder-length hair. "Broad." She stretched out her hands. "And too tall to get through that door without stooping."

"Good God. Is he seeing anyone? He'd have to be."

"Don't know."

"Is he straight?"

"Don't know."

"Well, what do you think?"

"I like him."

"Huh. So what are we waiting for? Let's go."

"I don't think he's Jewish."

"So, he's not perfect. Who is?"

Harrie laughed. "Stand up," she said.

Desiree obeyed. Harrie went to the hook behind the door, got

Des's coat, which she stroked and handed to Desiree, and her own jacket. She put on her jacket and opened the door. She was reminding herself what she planned to make for lunch, when she became aware that Desiree was just staring at her, that she hadn't moved.

"Aren't you going to change?" Des asked.

Harrie looked down. She was wearing her jeans, her work shoes. Dean's argyle sweater under her jacket. "What do you mean?"

"Harrie. You go out like that? You're not wearing any makeup. Have you combed your hair?"

"Come on, Des," Harrie said patiently. "You're letting the heat out." She shooed her friend out the door and closed it.

"Have you?"

"I combed it. Look. This isn't Fifth Avenue. It's a construction site."

The two women started down the path.

"But you used to love to dress. As much as I do."

Harrie laughed. "That was before I became a woman of the sea."

"What the hell is that supposed to mean?"

"I don't know. Things are different out here. Things are more basic somehow," she said, becoming aware of her feelings of change again. Des seemed so silly suddenly. So frilly. Mascara seemed out of place at Blackfern. And a short skirt in this weather? "Now that I've stopped working for Luna—"

"You what?" Desiree asked in alarm.

"I thought I told you."

"You did *not* tell me. When did this happen? And why?"

Harrie stooped to pick up an empty beer can. She crushed it and put it in her pocket for disposal later. When did it happen? It had happened so gradually over the past three months that her meeting last week with Luna seemed almost a formality. "Last week, I guess. But I haven't been coming in regularly for so long . . ."

"My God!" Des exclaimed. "Let me get this straight. You quit your job and you are living out here alone?"

"Not alone exactly. Ivy drops in and spends a night or two a week. Julie's been by. And Dean comes out on the weekends."

"Huh," Des grunted meaningfully.

"Huh, what? What's that 'huh' supposed to mean?"

Desiree shrugged prettily. She dug her hands into the velvet-lined pockets of her coat. "I just never thought you were that close to Ivy, that's all. I never thought you got along with her particularly well."

"She can be a little impossible," Harrie said vaguely.

"Why isn't she in college? Why isn't she going to Europe or something, like all the kids do?"

"She's quite contrary about all the things we thought we should do when we were growing up. Like college. Like marriage. 'Who needs it?' is her attitude. And my folks are just letting her kick around until she decides what kind of work she wants to do." The little cleared area around the cottage was ringed with trees, and as they entered the thicket and followed the path the trees became closer and taller. Harrie loved these trees, felt loved by them. "But we're getting to know each other better," she said hopefully.

"I'll bet you are."

"It's just temporary. The cottage is kind of close right now, but later, when the house is finished—"

"And when's that going to be?"

"Roger thinks a year, maybe. God, Des. I can hardly think about anything but the house. A year. By next Christmas. Wait till you see the dining room. I want to start family traditions. Thanksgiving. Christmas. You know. Stockings for the mantel and a tree with ornaments I've collected. Those handmade, one-of-a-kind ones you sometimes see in antique shops. And I think about this long mahogany table and my family there, and Dean's. And you of course. By then you'll be Mrs. Dr. Applestein."

"Awwwright," Des said with an optimistic lift of her thumb.

"It's so nice out here," Harrie said. "Look around. Look at how beautiful everything is. These trees and the rhododendron stay green all winter."

"I just wonder . . . First, you quit your job. Now you're talking about Christmas a year from now."

"So what's wrong with that? I'm making plans."

"I've just never seen you looking so . . ."

"Happy?"

"So schlumpy."

"Thank you very much."

"Why'd you quit? I thought you wanted to keep working. I

remember asking you about this, clearly, when we went shopping that time. So, by the way, where are you going to wear the tons of clothes you just bought?"

Harrie shrugged. "To be honest, I didn't quit exactly."

"Oh, no. Did Luna fire you exactly?"

"I'm taking a leave of absence."

"Oh, that's different. That makes sense." The two walked in silence for a moment. "I just hope you make an effort on the weekends, that's all. You could comb your hair at least. File your nails."

"Des . . ."

"I just don't want you to become some kind of suburban cow who doesn't get out of her housedress all day. Although you're starting to become an interesting character, Har."

"I take milk baths now on Friday nights. And I have someone come in from the city to give me pedicures."

"Really?" Des asked.

"No." Harrie laughed. "Plain old bubble bath. But I do comb my hair."

"And I hope you read the newspaper at least," Des continued seriously. "Even if this is only temporary. I don't like the idea of Dean surrounded by all those Wall Street females all week and coming out here and finding you lying around in a nest of I don't know what. Paint chips."

"You know, I don't know whether to be flattered that you're worried, or insulted that you don't take me more seriously."

"I take you seriously. That's why I'm worried."

"No, Des. I mean, I don't feel like you believe in me in this place. It's like you think that this is a dream I'm going to wake up from."

"I do not."

"Yes you do. I think Dean is hoping it too." Harrie plucked a twig from a cherry birch. She peeled back the bark and handed the twig to Desiree. "Chew that."

"Why?"

"Because you trust me."

Desiree chewed tentatively. "Tastes like wintergreen."

Harrie nodded.

"Okay, now tell me a druid told you about this," Desiree jeered.

"You laugh. You all laugh. Ivy takes me seriously."

"Ivy!" Desiree cried in disbelief. "Since when do we cite Ivy as an authority on anything?"

"I think Dean wants me to get tired of all this, come to my senses and sell the house."

"Huh."

"It's not going to happen, Des. If I pray at all, it's that he will fall in love with this place as I have. We're so happy here. Happier than we ever were. I keep counting how many socks and pairs of underwear he's left out here, and every time it's more than the last time . . . He left two sweaters here last weekend." Harrie gave Des a blushing smile.

"Oh, I see. Once he's got all his Calvins in your drawer, it's common law."

"You think I'm nuts?"

"I'd give more weight to a diamond ring—"

Harrie didn't give her friend a chance to finish. The path ended abruptly and Harrie pulled Des's arm to halt her. "Just look." They stood at the edge of the clearing and looked down at the castle, at the water, at the low-lying clouds that seemed to touch the waves. "There's all kinds of boat traffic out there. Tankers. And there are freighters, and at night you can hear the foghorns. And there are so many birds here. I've counted three different kinds of sea gulls. I'm supposed to be here, Des. This is my home now."

Desiree swallowed. Harrie was looking out at the water like it was a lover. It was hard to know what to make of all this. Harrie's leaving her job, cutting herself off from the city the way she had, seemed crazy. Literally. Any other person in Harrie's position would buy a fantastic apartment in New York and one in London as well, take a few months off to travel, start a business. But Harrie had become a recluse. A confident recluse. It was just amazing how she had changed. For God's sake, it hadn't even been a month ago the two of them had gone from store to store to store joking and falling on the floor from laughter, doing the thing that used to, anyway, make them the happiest—shopping. Now Harrie was in a trance over three kinds of sea gulls. Not that that was wrong. It was just strange. And it made her feel uneasy. As if someone new was inhabiting Harrie's body. A space alien. Maybe Harrie knew what she was doing. What was so great about working in New York anyway? "It *is* gorgeous," Des conceded. "It's really a pretty view."

"At last you're going to see the inside," Harrie said enthusiastically. She was practically carrying Desiree on her back as they descended the sloping lawn to the castle.

·

In a way, Harrie had to block her ears. Every time she said "Look at this, Des," Des grunted "Huh" and asked her another question. "Don't you get lonely, Har?" "Why don't you take a few trips, go to the Galapagos, Machu Picchu, Ko Samui?" "Are you sure you should be leaving Dean alone so much?" "Where is this Roger, anyway?" And so at last, in desperation, Harrie gave up and went on a search to find Roger, with Desiree following close behind.

They had accepted various suggestions as to Roger's whereabouts from the carpenter, an electrician, and a carpenter's assistant, when Harrie decided to try the top floor of the north wing. There, in a former maid's room where she and Roger had talked about putting in an entertainment room, they at last found Roger.

He was with Ivy and she was with him. They were nude, limbs interlocked, lying on a canvas drop cloth, and they had a fuzzy look on their faces: a blend of spent passion and the high that was connected to the smell of marijuana in the air.

"This is *disgusting,*" Harrie said to the startled couple on the floor, whereupon Ivy jumped up and tried to cover herself with her hands, whereupon Roger stood up too and, exposing himself with cool deliberation, gallantly draped the tarpaulin around Harrie's little sister. The sight of Roger's skin, as white and luminous as alabaster, burned out Harrie's vision, so that she was forced to wheel around blindly and stumble out of the room.

"Well, at least we know he's straight," Desiree said with aplomb.

·

Bob McCandless was digging into his ear with the little finger of his right hand, controlling the direction of his urine stream with his left. Dean watched the reflection of this revolting scene in the mirror over the sink, then took off his glasses and splashed water on his face.

"Hear Lady Luck's been giving you big sloppy wet ones," said McCandless.

Dean ripped off a paper towel and dried his face. He took another towel and cleaned his glasses.

"I'm going to start taking notes when I'm around you," Mc-Candless went on. He flicked. He zipped. He lumbered over to the sink and put his unwashed hand on Dean's back. "Like what's your secret for finding rich women? You can tell me."

"What do you want, McCandless?" Dean said, rippling his back muscles like a horse trying to dislodge a fly. He stepped away from the man, adjusted his glasses, combed his hair with his fingers.

"Yep. It's pretty fucking fantastic. First your old man. Then your old lady. Life's tough here on the Street, ain't it, Dean-o? No cold calls for you. You just roll out of bed in the morning and you've stepped in it."

Isletrek, Dean wanted to say. He wanted to hold the word in front of him like a crucifix to ward off a vampire. "You're a jerk, you know that, McCandless?" Dean said. It was a weak retort, he thought, but the best he could do on short notice. He shot out an arm and pushed open the men's room door. Isletrek was his own thing. When Isletrek was out, he was going to make McCandless eat shit.

If it occurred to Dean that Isletrek was another gift, he blocked the thought and made it disappear.

⊡

One entire wall of Dean's loft was glass. The lamps inside the large and open space were turned down very low, so that the dazzling lights of the World Trade Center piercing the black night made Dean's windowed wall simply disappear.

Harrie wasn't looking at the view. She was lying on a long leather couch and she was talking to the ceiling. Actually, she was talking to Dean, but Dean was across the room sorting out his bills and writing checks at a small desk, only occasionally looking at her reclining form.

"It was hateful," Harrie said to the ceiling. "It was vile."

"I think it was only sex between consenting adults," Dean said. He addressed an envelope. He shouldn't have called McCandless a jerk, he thought. Shouldn't have let on that he'd been gotten to. He should have laughed at him. He pictured that now. Yeah. Laughing would have been cool. Even blowing a raspberry would have been cool.

"Come *on*, Dean. Ivy's nineteen."

"An adult, as I was saying." Still, calling him a jerk was a safe midpoint between laughing at him and popping him one on the nose. But he'd learn from this. Next time, he'd laugh at him.

"It was so embarrassing. God. You really think it's okay for a *professional* person to be screwing his client's sister during working hours?" Harrie demanded shrilly. "And what about the dope they were smoking?"

"Not dope!" Dean replied in a mock shocked tone. "I've never smoked a joint, have you?"

"I don't know why you have to make me feel like a little old spinster who sleeps with her cats. It was my sister. Naked with a man. People have had nervous breakdowns over less than that."

Dean laughed. He took a sheet of stamps out of a drawer and folded a strip into pleats. Then he started tearing off the stamps and sticking them onto the envelopes. "Not jealous, are you?"

"What!"

"I dunno-oh. Good-looking guy having lunch with you every day, only today he gets it on with your sister."

"You're making me mad all over again," Harrie said, sitting up, kicking out her legs and planting them hard on the coffee table.

"Okay. I'm sorry."

"What are you sorry about?"

"That I've been giving you a hard time." Dean shut off the desk light and went over to the couch. He sat down next to Harrie and put his arms around her.

"That's better," she said, resting her head on his shoulder.

"So, then what did you do?"

"What do you think? Marched out of there with my fur flying."

"I'll bet."

"And then I couldn't start my car."

"No? What was wrong with it?"

"The engine was cold, I guess. So Des went and asked Roger for a lift, and he apologized and drove us to the train."

"He apologized?"

"Sort of. He said he was sorry I was so upset."

"Oh."

"He wasn't sorry he *did* it. Don't let me give you that impression. Boy. 'How to Get Feet of Clay in One Easy Lesson,' by Roger Mayhew."

Dean laughed again. Thoughts of Bob McCandless shriveled and shot into a corner like a deflated balloon.

"What's funny?"

"Nothing. The whole thing. It's a funny story. What happened to Ivy? Did you lock her in the dungeon?"

"I told her I was really pissed off at her and she looked at me like I beamed in from Mars. "

"I think you're right. It was pretty hostile."

Harrie nodded. "I told her I was leaving, so she had to go. Wanna bet she's in the cottage right now with Roger, doing it in the bed?"

"Ivy's not as tough as you think she is. She's probably curled up in her bedroom in Spode, afraid you're going to tell your mother."

"I *should* tell my mom. I should tell her about that and the late nights and the money Ivy borrows but never pays back. She got acceptable scores on her SATs. Des is right. Why won't she apply to college? Why do we all accept her just loafing around? You know what she had the nerve to say to me?"

Dean shook his head.

" 'I don't get it. Isn't this the place where all your fantasies come true?' " Harrie folded her arms in front of her. "I wanted to slap her little face." She thought for a while, reviewing the pictures of herself sitting between Des and Roger in the truck, fuming, no way on earth to make light conversation. Des had finally turned on the radio and sung all the way to the train station. "And Des is another one," Harrie said into the silence. "Nothing about the house excited her. I mean, you can't expect people to embrace your passions to the same degree you do—"

Dean lifted an eyebrow, which went unacknowledged by Harrie.

"But *something*. Some little enthusiasm. I just feel like I'm leaving Des behind or something. Like this house is making me outgrow her somehow."

"You're starting to have very different interests."

"I wonder if she's jealous. All the way back on the train, she hammered at me about why I should go to Machu Picchu and how I'm starting to look like a bag lady."

"Not a good day, huh?"

"Bummer. How was yours?"

"Well, apart from the fact that Bob McCandless called me a gigolo—"

"He what? How did he dare? What did he say exactly?"

"It doesn't matter."

"It does too."

"I can't remember. Something about my rich girlfriend. It goes with the territory. At least he says it to my face. God knows what the civilized people are thinking."

"I can't believe you're the only broker at your firm who's handling a big portfolio for a friend."

"I know. Anyway, I kind of lost it. I called him a jerk."

"Good. I'm glad."

"It wasn't cool but at least I didn't let it pass."

"Right. I hope I never run into the guy."

"The important thing is Isletrek is checking out so far. If it flies, we're all going to do okay."

"Of course it will."

"And I won't feel so anxious about the size of the checks you're writing to your sister's new boyfriend."

"New boyfriend—? Dean!" She slapped his leg. "That's not funny."

Dean grabbed Harrie's wrists in one hand and pulled her to him. "No fighting," he said, hugging her. "I picked up your Christmas present today."

Harrie relaxed against Dean's body. She freed her hands and slipped one between the buttons of his shirt. "You did? What is it?"

"I'm not telling."

"Give me a hint. Bigger than a breadbox?" She listened to Dean's heartbeat as if for clues.

"No, and I'm not giving you any more hints."

"Smaller, huh? Animal, vegetable, or mineral?"

"Mineral. And that's positively all I'm telling you."

"Mineral. Oh, good. Will I love it?"

"You'll love it."

Harrie beamed.

"Ready for bed?" Dean asked. "I've got a big day tomorrow."

Harrie nodded. "Love you," she said, giving Dean a gentle kiss on the mouth.

"Love you too."

·

But it turned out that Dean did not get quite the early start on the night's sleep he had planned. He carried Harrie into his bedroom and laid her down on the bed. The kiss he gave her was followed by a deeper kiss. Harrie threw her arms over her head and murmured sleepily, "Are we in bed yet?" and Dean said, "Yup," and pulled off his tie, and after two or three unbuttoned buttons, the shirt went off over his head, and then all the clothes of both parties (except for one rolled-up cotton camisole) went on the floor.

"How'd you get so sexy?" Dean growled in her ear, and Harrie laughed softly and ran her nails over his back and up through his hair and she wriggled as Dean's body ground against hers. She purred as his hands gathered her and parted her and slowly separated her from herself. "You make me this way," she said, touching him. Surrounding him. And then she gasped as he pierced her. Eyes closed, she saw a flash of alabaster, so she opened her eyes. "Dean," she said. "Uh," he said, and she saw the drop cloth fall away and she saw parts of Roger she had not dared to imagine, and she saw him flick the canvas as one would a cape to a bull. "Oh," she said.

"Yes," said Dean.

"Kiss me."

Dean complied, swallowing her, inhaling the scent of hot skin burning together.

"I want you to—" *Hurt me. Brand me. Marry me.* "I want you to—"

"Stop?"

"No. Don't stop."

"Does this feel good?"

"Oh, yes," she said, squeezing her eyes so tightly that sparks, like hot diamonds, were ignited behind her eyelids. And she followed the pull of the heat.

"God," he said, "I'm coming."

"Me too," she sighed, a pale thing beating her wings against the star-filled night. Suspended, she fluttered, she fought, she caught . . . the ring. Then she dissolved and plummeted, cradling Dean safely as she fell to the sea.

Then the tide swept them home to rest.

Mineral, Harrie thought, over the echo of the waves. Diamonds were mineral.

20

————◦————

HARRIE WAS SITTING in the passenger seat of the Saab and Dean was driving.

"Explain it one more time," Harrie said. "This stuff is a little arcane to the mere mortals among us."

"If you'd just concentrate," Dean said. "It only seems technical because the terms are foreign to you. It's just buying and selling, which you certainly know plenty about." He flashed his lights at the car in front of him, and the elderly Chevy Nova obliged him by moving out of the passing lane.

Dean depressed the accelerator. Harrie had taken so long to dress, they were now good and late. She'd wavered and debated with herself and tossed apparel around until the bedroom at the cottage looked as though it had been vandalized, and he hadn't been able to help her much in choosing what to wear, because, basically, her wardrobe was so idiosyncratic that nothing she owned would be right for Christmas at the Carrotherses'. He wouldn't have been able to explain to Harrie why it was that his family and their kind wore the same styles from generation to generation, because the dress code was just the pointed tip of the iceberg, and copying it badly was somehow worse than ignoring it. So when Harrie had selected the boxy yellow suit jacket she liked so much, to wear over a vividly floral dress, he'd kissed her and said she looked fine. Now they were late. He visualized their tardy entrance set to the tune of Handel's *Messiah* with a chorus of snide remarks.

"I'll try to keep it simple," he said, forcing his voice to sound calm, even though he felt like pushing a button in his Batmobile and jettisoning everything: the girl, the job, and the dinner with his family. Especially the dinner with his family. That would be like a scene in a horror movie when the music has turned heavy and you know the guy with the knife is going to plunge it into his intended victim— only in the case of his family the knife would be a little sterling-silver penknife, the kind you could hardly believe could kill a person. But it could. And just like in a horror movie, you knew the victim was going to get stabbed but there was nothing you could do about it. Better to focus on the things he could do something about. Such as handling Harrie's money. "It's like this," he said. "Isletrek needs money for expansion. Their company is worth X. Let's say it's worth thirty million."

"How do you get thirty million?"

"You look at their assets and their profit statements for the past few years. Their contracts with their clients are assets, and in this case SouthEast Airlines has a huge contract with them. And Isletrek's got a sterling financial history. That's basically how you figure their net worth."

"So let's say SouthEast drops them."

"Let's not say that, Harrie. Let's not muddy the picture here. Isletrek has had a long-standing contract with SouthEast and their contract is good for three years, so SouthEast isn't going to drop them."

"Oh." She was already drifting. She knew she should be interested in what Dean was telling her, but she was feeling so much anxiety about what was ahead, she found it hard to focus. Here she was about to meet the famous Robertson Carrothers and the rest of the family, and all she wanted to do was get relaxed so she wouldn't come across as nervous or addled, and Dean had picked this moment to teach Public Offering 101. And he was getting irritated with her. Which was making her feel nervous and addled.

"Now you've derailed me," he complained. "What was I saying?"

"Isletrek is worth thirty million."

"Right."

"So why don't they borrow it? Why do they want to sell the company?"

"God."

"God, what? That's a good question."

"It's shares in the company we're talking about, you understand that? Isletrek needs capital for expansion, and they want to stay out of debt so they can keep that pretty profit picture I was telling you about."

"Okay. I get it. And you're being a toad." Harrie shot Dean a look, then stared out the window. Was she dressed okay? She had on the yellow wool jacket she'd bought for the occasion. She looked lovely in yellow, she thought, and this particular outfit was demure without being stodgy. She'd pinned a small Christmas corsage to her bust—a few holly leaves and three little red ornaments—so if the outfit didn't seem formal enough, this touch of Christmas spirit would dress it up. She hoped Dean had been telling the truth when he said she looked great, because she was a little worried that she looked a bit broad from behind—but worrying about that now was stupid. What she should do is forget about her outfit and focus on what was actually worrying her. For instance, why had Dean waited two years to introduce her to his family? Would Dean's father like her? Would she like him? Would she survive Christmas in Litchfield, or would she say and do enough idiotic things to keep her awake at night for months?

"Sorry. I'm nervous," Dean apologized.

"*You're* nervous? Because of me?"

"No, of course not. These clan gatherings always make me edgy," Dean said, steadfastly keeping his eyes off Harrie's corsage. It wouldn't have done any good to tell her about the corsage, because if it weren't that, it would be something else—the dress, the shoes, the inheritance, whatever—because there was *nothing* about Harrie that would escape the rigorous scrutiny of his family. And telling her that the corsage was silly would've made her ask questions, the answers to which would've revealed to her the infinitesimal odds of her escaping this horror-show-to-be unscathed. And then she'd become panicky and his family would smell blood, and so *that,* instead of the corsage, or the dress, or the shoes, or the new money, would be her downfall. And so, since Harrie's only chance was to be so confident that she'd sail through on her innocence, he'd decided to forgo an apparel critique and summary of WASP holiday customs and concentrate instead on Isletrek. He cleared his throat and spoke. "Now. Back to Isletrek. The partners want to sell shares in the company, so that they can raise capital to be used for expansion, which in turn will earn money for them and their shareholders. When a company puts its stock up for sale to the public, it's called a public offering."

"I got it, I got it," Harrie said, cranking back her seat and closing her eyes. The older brother was Robertson junior, called Rob, and his wife was B.Z., sometimes called Beez or Beezy. B.Z. was a gardener, so Harrie had gotten her a pair of rubber pads for her knees and a stainless-steel, red-handled combination trowel and rake from a fancy mail order catalog. She'd gotten Rob, because he was a businessman, a slim leather pocket diary with his initials embossed in gold.

"Good," said Dean, genuinely pleased. "Now. In order to offer up the stock for sale, proof has to be established that the company is worth what it's being sold for, so the first thing that happens is, our people go over the financials and ascertain the worth of the firm. That's what they've been doing. You remember, I told you about that."

"Uh-huh." And Henry was the middle brother, Harrie recalled, the artist, and she'd gotten him a book on Impressionism from the Museum of Modern Art gift shop and you could hardly go wrong with a book. His wife, Topper, rode horses and Harrie had found a small porcelain figurine of a horse with a hunter in a red jacket. She crossed her fingers over this gift. The biggest problem had been what to get Robertson Carrothers, Sr.

"And according to us, Isletrek is A-OK," said Dean.

"Well, that's good," Harrie said.

"And so now we have to get approval in each of the fifty states. It's called getting blue-skyed."

"Hmmm. That sounds nice. And so is Isletrek getting blue-skyed?"

"Yes, it is."

"Great. So now what?" So she'd gone to Brooks Brothers and bought him a pair of slippers, and Dean had said they were the right size and kind—well, Dean had said to get scarves and gloves for everyone, but how could she do that? That would be so boring and impersonal. So she'd gotten the slippers and written "Love from Dean and Harrie" on all the gift cards, and now all she could do was hope for the best. They wouldn't be able to say she hadn't tried.

"So now we, me, I. I call around and see how much interest we get from our other offices so we can determine how many shares we're

going to offer and how we're going to allocate the shares geograph-
ically."

"Uh-huh," Harrie said, not truly getting that last bit, and not
truly caring, either. She hoped Dean was going to like *his* Christmas
present. The overcoat was in a box in the trunk with all the other
presents. The coat was by Armani, Dean's favorite menswear designer.
It was a deep charcoal-gray cashmere blend, and it looked so right
for Dean, she just knew he'd love it. She'd gotten him other presents
of course—stocking stuffers, which he'd opened this morning in bed:
a marquetry box for his cuff links, a picture of them together at her
party in a small, silver Tiffany frame, a nifty pen with a calculator in
its cap. And a bottle of Rémy Martin. She had to admire her own
restraint. If they were married, she would've gotten him the damned
car whether he liked the idea or not. Well, there was always next
year . . . Dean's presents to her had been very sweet: a wonderful
leather photo album for new pictures of Blackfern, an ancient gardening book, an old brass soap holder for her cottage bathtub, and
a basket of sweet-smelling things for the bath. But he'd reserved her
big present—big in importance, that is, not size—as she'd reserved
his, for later in the day. And her present was in his jacket pocket.

"And at the same time I reserve a block of stock for you."

"Aha," she said. "So this is where I come in."

"Right you are," Dean said. He pulled into the passing lane and
zipped past four cars in a row before he pulled back to the right.

"You're not going too fast, are you, hon?"

"Don't worry. I've got my radar detector on."

"You're illegal. You can't use that in Connecticut."

Dean ignored Harrie's comment, but looked into his rearview
mirror anyway. "As I was starting to say, the hope here is that we
bring out, say, a million and a half shares at twenty dollars a share.
I try to get you maybe one hundred and twenty-five thousand shares,
which costs you two and a half million dollars. I'd try to get you in
for more, but first, there's no guarantee I can get that many shares,
and second, a hundred and twenty-five thousand shares is a big slice
of the company. The SEC has to be satisfied that you aren't going to
try to take over the company."

"Hah. But I guess that means I'll be a part owner of Isletrek,
right? If I'm buying all that stock."

"For a while. For a while. We're not looking for a permanent association here, Harrie. We're hoping that if the stock comes out at twenty dollars, once it starts trading, the price will move up. Twenty-one, twenty-two. At some point, we sell. Every point the stock goes up is a hundred and twenty-five thousand dollars for Harriet Braintree, which she is going to need, given that's what she's been spending every week for the last couple of months."

"A hundred and twenty-five thousand a week? Come on."

"Harrie. You spent over nine hundred thousand dollars from November one to present. You only spent a quarter of that in October, but you were just warming up in October."

"I don't believe it!"

"You can believe it, all right. At half a million a month, by this time next year, if we don't put some dollar signs in the plus column, you're going to be looking at a big fat goose egg in your checking account."

"Well, I'd always planned to spend it all," she said thoughtfully.

"You're a good planner. You planned it down to the nickel. A year of two-fisted spending, then back to the real world. I wonder if you've really considered what that's going to be like."

"Wait. You put some money away for me in those treasury bills."

"Right, Harrie. But that money is locked up until the year 2016."

"But if I need it . . ."

"That money is supposed to be for your retirement."

"Half a million a month? Are you sure? You're making me nervous."

"Finally. A victory."

"I'm serious. Am I really going to be flat broke in a year?"

"I'm trying to prevent it, hon. I'm doing the best I can. I'm trying to make what money you've got grow for you before you use up the principal. You and Roger."

Harrie chewed at her thumbnail. Between the Blackfern renovation, various charitable donations, and some miscellaneous shopping, she'd gone through over a million dollars, and it had been easy. Writing checks and plunking down gold cards had become natural to her. Too natural. Dean was right. Time to get a grip.

"Now, I've been thinking about this," Dean said, "and I think you ought to take out a construction loan. Between what I've already got invested for you and the two point five we're going to try to put into Isletrek, you're going to come up short of cash in a couple of months."

"Couldn't we just liquidate some of my holdings when I need the money?"

"We could, Harrie, but it doesn't make much sense to do that. You've got about half your money in CDs and in corporate paper, which means there are maturity dates attached. If we liquidate before the notes mature, you're going to lose money, given the current market conditions. If we sell off your Isletrek stock, you could lose the value of doing the deal to begin with. If you're making a good profit on the stock, we want to run with it, not sell it off."

"Uh-huh," said Harrie. "And if I borrow money . . ."

"If you borrow it, you'll be paying interest which is constant, and it's also tax deductible when we convert the loan to a mortgage. I think you ought to at least apply for a loan, get things moving, so if we need to move on this, we can do it."

"About Roger . . ."

"What about him?"

"Dean, will you go over the work orders with me tonight? And review the contract with me again? And see what I'm going to need to lay out for the next couple of months?"

"Of course. I don't mind working on Christmas for my biggest client."

"Your biggest client, who loves you."

"My only client who loves me."

"Your father loves you."

"He does, huh? Don't bet your last millions on it, okay?" Dean signaled for a turn and took the exit ramp off the highway toward the town of Litchfield, Connecticut.

·

The thing Harrie noticed as the car approached the house was how much it was exactly the house she'd imagined. It was a white Federal with two chimneys and black shutters, and it sat on a knoll where it had been built in the mid-1700s. The drive that curved from the road to the house had been blacktopped and edged with small evergreen shrubs. Two gigantic firs flanked the entranceway.

Dean parked his car in the porte cochere, behind his father's Bentley, behind Rob's Mercedes, beside Henry's BMW. He turned off the engine and stared through the windshield. It was only noon. They'd been expected at eleven, but they wouldn't eat until one. So a good way of looking at this was, arriving at noon meant one hour less they'd have to spend with his family. "Home Sweet Home," he said.

Harrie put her hand on his arm. "We'll have fun," she said. "It's Christmas."

Dean nodded, sighed, opened his door. He went around to the back of the car and opened the trunk. The pile of wrapped packages had slid around, and he was gathering them as Harrie joined him at the rear. Maybe this wouldn't be too bad. Eggnog, dinner, presents, then out. Possibly, with a little luck, they'd be out by three. Three hours might be bearable.

"I can't wait to see how they like the presents," Harrie said, stacking packages in Dean's arms.

"Harrie, don't expect too much."

"But—"

"You did very well. You chose wonderful gifts. It's just that my family isn't very open. They don't gush."

"Okay, okay. Dean, what should I call your father?"

"Shithead?"

"Dean? Try to have fun, okay? I'm a little nervous. I want to be able to look at you and think, what fun it is to be at Dean's house for Christmas dinner."

The chances of that wish coming true were only slightly better than the chances of a snowball in hell, Dean thought, taking Harrie's hand and squeezing it. "I'll do my best," he said.

Together, they walked up the granite stairs to the house.

·

Harrie thought, as she shook Mr. Carrothers's hand, that he was smaller than she had imagined. From the way Dean had described him, he should've been twice as big, and fanged. Instead, he was wearing a nice gray sports jacket and a yellow polo shirt and looked like a businessman on his day off, which was what he was. His eyes were steel gray, and so was his hair, and his skin was bright pink, which made a nice contrast. At first glance, she didn't see any of Dean in his face, but maybe Dean looked like his mother. "Nice to meet you, too," she said, stepping inside the foyer, then walking between the two men to the living room.

Harrie took note that she was walking on old Oriental carpets, that the living room was white and had three little seating areas furnished with antiques and upholstered armchairs and sofas, but her attention was actually focused on the cluster of people in front of the fireplace. Two men stood as she entered, and two women—one a flat-faced blonde, about Harrie's age, wearing a velvet frock with a lace collar; the other an elegant redhead, maybe five years older, in a long white cardigan and a slim, suede skirt—turned their faces toward her.

"This is my brother Henry," Dean said.

"Pleased to meet you."

"And his wife, Topper."

"Hello," Harrie said, taking the red-haired woman's cool, thin hand in hers. Close up, Harrie could see that the sweater was hand-made, swarming with cable stitches, fastened with leather buttons. A ruffled silk collar foamed out of the neckline, and a triple strand of pearls hung in staggered lengths from collarbone to waist. The brown suede skirt skimmed narrow hips and fell to midcalf, inviting a look at trim ankles and suede shoes. Henry was balding, and pleasant to look at. He wore slacks, a corduroy jacket, and a blue tie with nervous little squiggles on it in neon colors. Maybe, Harrie thought, he wasn't into Impressionism. And what would Topper think of the porcelain horse? Oh, it was too silly, she was sure.

"And this is B.Z."

"How do you do?" Harrie said to the blond woman in the blue velvet dress. A hand laden with sapphire and diamond rings came forward hesitatingly. Lips parted into a gummy smile. Pale blue eyes remained fixed in an appraising stare.

"And my brother Rob."

"Nice to meet you," she said to the barrel-chested man who looked a lot like Dean. In fact, if people came in sizes, Dean would be a medium and Rob would be an extra large. In a strange way, Rob looked more like Dean than Dean did.

"Have some eggnog," Dean's father said, pressing a punch glass into Harrie's hand. She thanked him, found a place on a small love seat covered with roses, and anxiously followed Dean's trip to the punch bowl with her eyes. He would sit beside her, wouldn't he?

"Cute whatjamajiggy," said Topper from the wing chair to Harrie's right. "Corsage. Haven't seen one of those in years."

"Thank you," Harrie said. "It's my mother's. She never throws anything out."

"Ah," said Topper, tossing the flaming mass of hair away from her forehead. "A keepsake."

"My mother was the same way," said Robertson senior, sitting on the couch beside Harrie. "She used to save cans, and old envelopes. Did you have any trouble on the road this morning?"

"We got a late start," Dean said, breaking in from across the room. "I had a little engine trouble."

"You really ought to get a Mercedes, Dean," Rob junior boomed. "Trouble-free. I've had five, you know. All ran perfectly. Never had a single problem."

Like everything else in your life, Dean thought but didn't say.

"We were just talking about our winter plans," Henry said, and Harrie's attention shifted to him as he addressed Dean with a description of the ski trip he had planned with Topper. Then Topper joined in with her views of the snow situation out west, and inevitably, someone asked Harrie where she liked to ski and she mentioned a slope in upstate New York that no one in the room had heard of, let alone skied. And then Rob described an accident he'd witnessed on a chair lift, and while he was describing this, punctuating his story with snorts and barks of laughter, Harrie admired Topper's incredible shape, outlined by the suede, finished by the soft wool. She could just imagine her in ski clothes.

"We're going to be too busy to get away this year," Harrie heard Dean say, as if they'd gone away last year. Then the talk turned to the last Christmas they'd all spent together, and B.Z. told what seemed to be a hilarious story about the minister of their church and how well he was looking considering a certain suspected piece of cosmetic surgery, and when she finished, Rob talked about the gun club of which everyone present except herself and Dean seemed to be members, and the amount of money that would be required to reseed the polo field. And from this she gathered that both Robs, junior and senior, played polo, but that Henry preferred water sports and so he and Topper would be off to a friend's private atoll in the Caribbean after their two weeks in Deer Valley. And so it went.

"So you won't be going away at all?" Dean's father mused at Harrie's side. He wasn't drinking eggnog, Harrie noticed. His punch glass had been replaced while she wasn't looking with a cut-crystal glass filled with scotch or something else that was a whiskey color. "And what's keeping you so busy?" he asked Harrie, not unkindly.

"Well, I'm working on my house," she said softly. What would that sound like to the others?

"House?" asked B.Z. "What's this about a house?" She took a cracker from a tray offered by her husband, who continued offering it around the small group of people at the center of the room.

"I'm sure I told you," Rob said to his wife. "Harrie was left a house."

"Oh," said B.Z. "And who are your people, dear? Are you the Philadelphia Braintrees?"

"No," said Harrie. "I don't think so, although we might have some relatives . . . My parents live in Long Island."

"And where in Long Island would that be?"

"It's a little town," Harrie said. "I'm sure you've never heard of it. Spode?"

"No—"

"Harrie's new house is between Cold Spring Harbor and Oyster Bay," Dean offered. He was standing by the fireplace—a neutral spot, a spot where he could watch the action and intercede, he thought, should there be trouble. Yes, he was a referee, or a linesman.

"I know Oyster Bay," Dean's father said. "Quite nice too."

"I like it," Harrie said.

"I think Rodney Bartholomew still lives in Oyster Bay. Do you know him?"

"No, I'm afraid I don't."

"And Walter and Margaret Wainwright own a summer place either in Oyster Bay or Cold Spring Harbor . . . I can't remember which. Are you familiar with them?"

Harrie shook her head.

"Well, I must look them up for you. The Wainwrights. I wonder what happened to them. I didn't get a card from them this year. I wonder if they moved to Ireland. They were always threatening to move to Ireland. They have horses, you know."

"So you're working on your house?" asked Topper. "Are you working with a designer?"

Harrie felt pinned by cold blue eyes. "We're still doing the construction. I have quite a good architect," she said.

"Would I know him?"

"Maybe. One of his projects was featured in *Metropolitan Home* . . . Roger Mayhew?"

"Doesn't ring a bell," Topper said dismissively.

"I'm starved," Dean announced suddenly. "I only had a cup of coffee for breakfast."

Harrie shot him a questioning look. He'd had oatmeal for breakfast and three strips of bacon, two English muffins with butter and jam, and juice. She'd fixed breakfast for him herself.

"Then why don't you go see how Sully is doing," the senior Carrothers mumbled, referring to the cook.

"I think I'll go see how Sully is doing," Dean answered.

"Would you like to freshen up?" Topper asked Harrie.

Harrie nodded and, feeling every one of her hundred and thirty-five pounds, followed the willowy beauty to the washroom.

·

Dinner reminded Dean of a glacier's course: slow, cold, scraping away the terrain as it went. He had endured the semipolite questioning about his business affairs by his brothers. He'd accepted Beezy's condescension, and Topper's piercing sarcasm, and his father's boozy inattention, but he found it hard to swallow the same treatment when leveled at Harrie.

It was funny how unless you were attuned, you might not notice what was going on until it was all over. It reminded him of a time when he'd been small, when he'd stepped on a nail beside a trailer at the polo grounds and the nail had gone through his shoe and into his foot. The family physician, now long dead, had shown him the capped syringe (which he now knew had been filled with tetanus antibodies) and said, "See, it's a rubber needle." And Dean had trustingly exposed his hip, and the needle had gone in, and it hadn't been rubber at all. That's what was happening with Harrie. She was trustingly exposing herself, and the needle wasn't rubber at all. The difference was, Harrie didn't need a tetanus shot. This whole exercise was completely unnecessary. "Romance novels," Rob had said, inquiring ever so sincerely as he passed the mint jelly. "How very interesting." "They own a nursery? How charming to grow up around horticulture," Topper had commented. "Won't you have some more lamb?" See? It was a rubber needle.

And then they'd once again gone to the living room, for coffee and the trial by Christmas presents. Dean had accepted the scarves and gloves and books and ties before he'd even seen them, but hadn't Harrie winced as the pile of impersonal items grew and as each of her carefully selected gifts was opened? Could she fail to feel that this event and these people were more important to her than it and she were to them? And if she figured that out, would she understand that it had nothing to do with her—nothing to do with the corsage or the figurine or the fruitcake that was passed around every year but only she had eaten? That it all had to do with him?

Dean stared up at the family portrait that was hanging over the fireplace. He had never loved this portrait, because it was painted before he was born. The background was a neutral blue gray. His father stood slightly behind his mother, who was wearing a brown dress and holding the baby who was his brother Rob. Apart from the fact that she seemed a little too happy with Rob, the picture seemed to be a good likeness of Sarajane W. Carrothers. Her skin was pale, her hair was tidy, her hands were slender, and her nails were perfect, unbitten ovals. If there could be a woman more his mother's opposite than Harrie, he couldn't imagine her. He swallowed a sigh as he glanced at fluffy, frizzy Harrie, a crumpled yellow dandelion on the antique crewelwork-covered chair. The truth was, it was a little too easy for them, a little too easy for these snipers to get to him through Harrie. "I'm ready to leave soon," he said, bending down to pick up a stray ribbon, speaking softly as he did so.

"But aren't you going to open your big present?"

"Not here. I've got your big present in my pocket. Why don't we open them when we're alone?"

"Okay," said Harrie. "A few minutes, okay? I want to finish my coffee." She needed a few more minutes to gather her thoughts. Dean's family had been very nice to her, but something was wrong. Was it just what Dean had said: his family didn't gush? Or was it that anyone would feel out of it in a room full of strangers? On the other hand, Dean wouldn't have felt like this at her house on Christmas, she felt sure of it, and suddenly she wished herself out to Spode.

Their tree, set up every year in the bay window in the small parlor, wouldn't have been decked with cold blue lights and crystal ornaments from Steuben. It would have had popcorn and cranberry chains, and shiny red and silver globes, and maybe a couple of starfish she had sprayed with gold paint when she was about seven. And an angel on top of the tree made from a toilet tissue tube, decorated with cotton and fabric and glitter. It would have been a louder kind of gathering too: everyone talking at once, Christmas carols blaring from the stereo, and the tiny house would have even smelled loud— of cinnamon and pipe smoke, and her mother's rare indulgence in Eau de Joie.

But to be scrupulously fair, even though the very temperature would've been higher in Spode, wouldn't she still have had to work very hard? Like sparks flying from a sparkler, she could see her family brightly pulling apart as they had just this Thanksgiving Day past. Her father had gone to the fields ("I'll be right back," but not returning until dark), her mother to the kitchen ("I just have to check on the gravy," then the pie, then the coffee). Doug had turned on the ball game, and Julie had invited Paula over and the two had been like Siamese twins. And Ivy, her dark, withdrawn sister—Ivy had put on her Walkman and, except for partaking in the meal and one conversation with Dean, had sat alone.

Was it all an illusion, this idea she had that a family was where you were all turned *toward* each other? It couldn't have been something she made up. This turned-toward-each-other family was obviously not something she would simply inherit, it was something she would have to create. And she *would* do it. It would be her only goal. She looked up at the portrait above the mantel and met Sarajane Carrothers's eyes. Help me, she implored the painting. And then she turned to Dean. He looked so handsome and yet so sad. In her family, the neglect had been at worst benign. In his, the neglect was so purposeful, so cold. And why? Was it because, as he said, he was less successful than his brothers? How could that be so important to them? Because his mother loved him the best? Could that grudge be held so long after his mother's death? Was it truly because his father saw him as defective? Shouldn't that make his father love him more? And yet she felt their distance from him, so maybe it was all true. She longed to put her arms around Dean, to warm him with her own heat, to comfort him and reassure him, and give him more than he'd ever had.

"Ready?" he asked.

She nodded, put her coffee cup down in its saucer.

The goodbyes began, handshakes and thank-yous and cheek kisses all around. And then they were out in the open air, which was somewhat warmer than the atmosphere of the house itself.

"I want to shake myself. Like a dog," Dean said, opening the door for Harrie. And then he did shake himself. And Harrie laughed for the first time in three hours.

"See," Dean said as he started the engine. "A fun group."

"Your father's nice."

"To you," he admitted.

"Henry seemed nice enough," Harrie added. "I liked that story he told about the scuba gear shop."

"He's not going to open a shop. Can you imagine Topper on a little pat of sand somewhere in the Caribbean? For real?"

"I guess not."

Dean sighed. "The best thing about this is, it's a year before we have to do it again."

We? Harrie thought, brightening. What difference did it really make if his family was tough? Given a few years, she would warm up the Carrothers clan. She didn't doubt it for a minute. The thought of the package in Dean's pocket tugged at her. It was as though it had a little beacon attached and it was calling her. She wondered whether, instead of driving all the way home to give her her present, Dean couldn't just pull off the road and let her open it now. "I'm dying to give you your present," she said.

"I'm dying to give you yours," he said with a smile. Harrie had been so brave. She shouldn't have to wait for her gift any longer. "There's a little park not far from here. We can open our presents there."

Minutes later the car was parked on the grass, and Harrie and Dean had walked to the gazebo. The park was empty except for some children skating on a pond beyond.

"I hope you'll like this," Harrie said, putting the box on Dean's lap. "Open it."

Silver paper and red ribbons flew, the box split open like an enormous bivalve, and then Dean unfolded the luxurious gray coat. "I love it!" he said. He stood, removed his old coat, and put the new one on. "How do I look?"

"You're the handsomest man I've ever seen," Harrie said gravely. And she meant it. Dean looked like a model, only better. The thought that he belonged to her thrilled her.

"This is for you, Beauty," he said, taking the gift out of his jacket pocket. It was a small package and under the paper the box was velvet, so it was sheer surprise and happiness that opened Harrie's eyes wide, then closed them and caused the tears to pour down her cheeks. What else could it be? Inside the velvet box was an absolutely precious little wristwatch.

21

---□---

HARRIE EMPTIED the silverware drawer into a shoe box. "I really don't want to keep this stuff, Mom. I'll get some silver I'll like better."

"Well, Cakes, it's perfectly good stainless. Can't you use it in the cottage?"

"I suppose so." She dropped the lid onto the box and added it to the stack of larger boxes she was going to have shipped out to Blackfern. She hadn't been in her apartment on Chester Street in months; the last time, it had been to grab a bag of woollies from the armoire, and she'd left so quickly she'd been a blur in the static atmosphere of the darkened room. Why had she kept the apartment for so long? What part of her still wanted to live in a room so small and dark? She took a garbage bag out from under the sink, walked the few paces to the bed, and stuffed pillows into resistant black plastic.

"Do you need help, dear?" Dottie asked. She was seated comfortably in the armchair, her feet up on a carton, a back issue of a garden magazine in her lap. She was looking at the pictures, making mental notes: Put some cleome in with the hollyhocks next year. Good idea.

"I hope they come soon," Harrie said, referring to the people from the Salvation Army. "It's too depressing here. How did I stand it?"

Dottie yawned. She lifted another magazine from the stack by the chair. She turned to the table of contents, then flipped pages. "Fuss, fuss, fuss," she said. "You're just fussing your little heart out today."

"I can't believe I'm saving pillows, for God's sake."

"Well, they're—"

"—perfectly good pillows," Harrie joined her mother in saying. "But I can get *new* pillows, Mom. I'll take the books. That's all. And don't argue with me. If you want anything for yourself, speak now or forever hold your peace."

"I thought so."

"What? What did you think?"

"That expression. 'Forever hold your peace.' "

"Don't start."

"You're thinking about Dean, and that's why you're fussing so much. Blaming it on these innocent pillows. The way things are going, you won't even be able to get real feather pillows in a few years. You'll be sorry you threw these out."

"Mother! Moving is stressful. Everyone says so." Harrie dropped the bag on the floor and flung herself onto the bed. It creaked familiarly. The first time she and Dean had spent the night in this bed, the metal frame had protested so much she'd thought it was going to disassemble itself on the spot.

Dottie sipped her tea. Why was it that things seemed so hard for Harrie? "If you'd gone through the Depression, like I did . . ."

Harrie groaned. She stared up at the ceiling, which was beginning to peel; a crack had started at the light fixture and was bubbling out toward the window. The only sound in the room was the soft slapping of pages, and Harrie found her thoughts heading out to Long Island, to Blackfern—yet when her thoughts arrived, they didn't know where to go. Or rather, they went to Dean. Then they hit a wall. Harrie punched the lone pillow remaining on the bed, and sighed unconsciously.

"I was telling your father the other night, we ought to take a cruise," Dottie said.

"Oh?"

"Take one of those ocean liners down to the Caribbean. It'll cost about four thousand dollars, but we've got a little put away, since Ivy won't go off to school, and we—"

"Mother, save that money. I can afford to send you on a cruise."

"Thank you, honey, but you've done enough. Do you remember Candice Brunner? Who runs the Women's Workshop over on Fishtail?"

"Uh-huh," Harrie answered distractedly. She could go to sleep about now. She was feeling more and more like doing that these days—just falling asleep, although she usually wanted to do it after lunch, not before. She was getting fatter and she was sleeping more. You didn't have to be a genius to figure out what was going on here. She didn't have enough to do. And she was getting depressed. She tuned in to her mother's monologue for a moment, ascertained the content—Candice Brunner's trip to the Bahamas—and tuned out again. According to the electric clock beside the bed, running faithfully in her absence, it was ten-thirty. Only nine hours before she'd be having dinner with Dean. She sent her thumb to the waistband of her skirt and tugged at it. Tighter, that was for sure. She was fat, all right. Funny thing was, Dean hadn't noticed. Or if he had, he hadn't said anything, and while she kind of liked that, it also made her nervous.

Dean was really full of himself these days. Talking constantly, buying new clothes, wearing a kind of glow when he arrived for the weekends. She'd never before seen him happy for such a long period of time. . . . But he deserved to be happy. He'd earned the right to wallow around in his accomplishment. Some brokers never brought a company public in their lives, and so Dean had pulled off a coup. On top of that, he'd earned three hundred thousand dollars and they'd handed him the check the minute the deal was consummated. And on top of *that,* he'd made a commission on the two and a half million dollars' worth of Isletrek she now owned and whatever he'd gotten for his father and for his other clients. So Dean had real money now, and he had respect from the guys at the office, and even his father had offered a couple of kind words. All of this was terrific. So why was she bothered? Was it the idea that Dean's happiness was all about Isletrek that made her uneasy? No, that wasn't it. It was his happy, isolated, distance that made her uneasy—like he was wearing a shiny, new layer of lacquer.

She could trace her uneasiness straight to its beginnings. Christmas Day. The gazebo. Frosted grass. Dean in his new coat, and metallic wrapping paper strewn all around. And a small antique watch on a grosgrain strap, its face encrusted with rubies which would not become diamonds any more than the watch itself would become a ring.

"Why the tears, Beauty," he'd asked.

So she'd told him. "I was hoping it would be an engagement ring," she said. And he pressed his lips together and got a hurt look on his face as though *he* were the injured party, not she. "I knew this would happen," he muttered to the steering wheel, and she, feeling on one level very ungracious and on another frustrated and hurt, said, "I want to talk about this," and Dean said, "Go ahead," which meant, I'm not talking. So she turned her head to the side window and in a while became mesmerized by the passing landscape and fell asleep. And she stayed asleep during the ride out of Connecticut and into New York, and nearly all the way out to Blackfern.

"I wonder what's going to become of us," she said later, when they were in bed.

"What do you mean?" he asked, irritability icing his words.

She shrugged under the duvet.

"Oh, shit," he said softly, the words of an unarmed man who has heard a noise downstairs in the middle of the night and, hoping it was the cat, now hears footsteps coming up the stairs.

"Don't say that!" she said, snapping the comforter down with her arms, turning to him. "Every time I even think about talking about our future, you shut me down. We've been together for two and a half years. I love you. I want to know if I can count on being with you."

"Harrie. Here I am. Didn't we go to my father's house for Christmas? Don't I drive out here every weekend? What more do you want from me?"

"I want to know if we're getting married." There. She'd said it.

Dean opened his mouth. Shut it. Then he sighed. He ruffled up his hair with both hands as if by moving his scalp he could move the problem. "I'm not ready, yet," he said at last. "I'm just not ready."

"But what does it take to be ready? Do you mean your career? Or do you mean me? Or what?"

"It's me, Harrie. Pressuring me isn't going to help. *I'm* not ready. I'm just not ready to move forward with us. This is as much as I can do right now."

"Dean. I'm not getting this. You're not a soufflé. Or a roast. Give me a clue. What's supposed to happen in order for you to be ready?"

"I don't know," he said. "I know I love you."

Harrie heard the "but" that Dean didn't say but was there any-way, larger with its three small letters than love itself. Then Dean turned off the light, kissed her, settled into the bedclothes and into sleep, but as she'd slept for three hours in the car, she was left alone to stare into the dark. And so, alone, she had conversations with herself about what she'd said, and what she should have said, and what she would say in the future, until she was rigid with anger. And fear. And the reason she felt angry and afraid was no longer the ring she hadn't gotten. It was because she couldn't imagine an occasion or an event that would make Dean be ready if nothing had made him be ready yet. This was a shocking revelation, a notion so notable she marked this night as surely as if she'd turned down a page in the chronicle of her relationship with Dean. And apparently, their con-versation had had a similar effect on Dean, because it seemed that along with a ruby-encrusted watch, Dean had given her another gift for Christmas: a newly lacquered Dean, a person she was able to see but not really touch. And now she was getting fat, and he wasn't noticing, and her mother wanted her to talk about it, but she couldn't. And wouldn't. Because her mother would pacify her, tell her every-thing would be all right. While her true self believed something else entirely.

⊡

Dottie watched her daughter sleep. Her girls were so different from each other. It was a mystery to her how that could be. Julie was stiff—afraid to wish upon a star or believe in happiness—and Harrie was the complete opposite. It seemed sometimes as if Harrie just spent her whole day, every day, wishing on stars and cars and tabby cats and whatever. Dottie thought she herself was probably to blame for that. She knew she was the original cockeyed optimist. But she'd never dreamed on Harrie's kind of scale. It was impressive, it really was, how *fearless* her Harrie was. And how *committed* she became when she made up her mind about something. This commitment to the house and Harrie's plans for it was as predictable, when you thought about it, as a full moon every month.

She would never forget the time when Harrie was only eight, she'd climbed into a messy old box elder Bill needed to cut down because it was growing in a bad place in the field, and Harrie had stayed in that tree a whole day and a night and part of the next day until Bill promised he wouldn't chop it down, no matter what. And the way Harrie had nursed that nest of field mice she had accidentally tumbled out of a pile of mulch, feeding the small doomed things with an eyedropper every hour until each had died. And Harrie had mourned each, buried each, mindless of the fact that they had cats around the place for the sole purpose of killing mice.

Or the way Harrie had stuck by that Weybourne boy even though he was not nearly bright enough for her, or attractive at all. But Harrie had called him her boyfriend up until the time she'd gone away to college. Mark had been the one to break it off—he'd told her she should be free to have a good time at school, and Harrie had protested and cried. At the same time, Dottie just knew that Harrie had felt relieved when she kissed Mark goodbye for the last time. So what had kept her with him? Pity was too easy a guess and it was wrong. She imagined Harrie had made a commitment to the boy with the thick glasses and the front teeth that stuck out over his lower lip, but why she had made the commitment, Dottie could only wonder. And now there was this poor distressed house, so of course Harrie would clasp it to her and never let it go. And that same maternal instinct, or whatever it was, was probably why she felt what she felt for Dean.

Of course, Dean was a different story than Mark. He was handsome anyway, and bright, and he seemed to care a great deal about Harrie. But there was a blockage somewhere, something stopping the natural way things were supposed to go. And Harrie was acting as though she was the impediment when anyone could look at that expression on Dean's face and see that the impediment was inside of him. Something was not quite right and the funny thing was, she had a feeling that whatever was causing that crimp in Dean was attracting Harrie. Like Dean was related to the box elder and the abandoned mice and the boy with the buck teeth . . . And continuing this very same thought, the house fell right in line. Dottie sighed. The tree had lived. The mice had died. The Weybourne boy had gotten his degree at Cornell and gone on to get married and open his little business, and maybe Harrie's sticking by him had given him the confidence to do those things.

But had Harrie gotten as much out of these commitments as she'd put in? That thought made her wonder again about how it would turn out for Harrie with this big house she owned, and with this boy she loved. Well, it would turn out all right, no matter how it turned out. Dean would love Harrie. Or someone else would love Harrie. Just as there'd be someone for Julie.

Dottie put the magazine carefully on the floor. Her girls were like primary colors. Harrie was red. Julie was blue. And Ivy was yellow. Would there be someone to love Ivy? Ivy was as resentful as a wet cat. And sad. And so there was Harrie again. Trying to take care of Ivy. She wondered why it was that her son was as solid as a stone, while her girls were so fragile and tissuey. Could it be because she named them after flowers? Juliana Moonflower. Harriet Periwinkle. And plain-named Ivy. Ivy Jane. She hadn't felt so imaginative by the time she gave birth to Ivy.

Dottie folded her hands in her lap and leaned back her head. She saw colors in her mind, spinning like a color wheel, and then they blended to white. She was planting the cleome among the hollyhocks when the phone rang.

Harrie bolted awake, picked up the receiver. "Hello."

"Harriet Braintree?" said an unfamiliar voice, a voice both sour and sweet.

"Yes," she said.

"My name is Avis Murphy."

"Hello," Harrie said warily to the owner of the peach yogurt kind of voice.

"Is it the Salvation Army?" Dottie asked. "Are they coming?"

"I got your number from someone at the house on Long Island."

"Yes?" Harrie said. Would Avis Murphy be a fund-raiser. A stockbroker? A real estate broker? "What can I do for you?" she asked. She twisted the telephone cord around her finger.

"A great deal," said Avis Murphy. "You see, Harriet—if I may call you Harriet. I'm David Tuckman's daughter."

⊡

Avis Murphy and her small, shivering dog sat on the bench opposite Harrie.

"My mother was David's lover," Avis Murphy said. She offered her thermos bottle to Harrie, who declined. They were sitting at a concrete checkerboard table under one of a dozen leafless linden trees in a small park two blocks from 111 Chester Street. The site had been picked by Ms. Murphy, ostensibly because she could not take Sir Lawrence into a restaurant, but having been offered the hot rum in the thermos, Harrie suspected the reason had more to do with bars and what time they opened. After trying desperately and without success to get Mr. Schoonmaker's home number from his answering service, she'd left her mother alone in the apartment to wait. And now here she was, sitting outside in the cold January morning, listening to a woman who looked like a poodle tell her that Mr. Tuckman had cheated on his wife and had sired *her*!

"I don't mean to be rude, but I know Mr. Tuckman loved his wife and I have a lot of trouble believing your story."

"Why would I make it up? Do you think I like having to admit to you that I'm illegitimate?"

Harrie shrugged and looked away. "I think it's obvious."

"What? That I made this up? You modern girls think nothing of illegitimacy these days. I suppose today my mother would have been called a single mother or some such thing." The woman unscrewed her thermos bottle and took a deep drink. She capped the lid. "She doesn't believe me," she said to the dog. "No, she doesn't." She looked up at Harrie and smiled. Her small brown eyes were smudged around with sooty makeup. Her lipstick was a soft carmine smear. "Well, think what you like," she said to Harrie. "I'm David Tuckman's daughter and I can prove it. And that makes me his lawful heir, not you."

Harrie pulled the collar of her coat more tightly around her neck. She was scared, but she didn't have to admit it. Surely, if this frizzy-white-haired woman were genuine, Mr. Schoonmaker would have known about her. Wouldn't he? If she were for real, wouldn't she have hired a lawyer and had her lawyer take the necessary steps instead of lying in wait for a chance to ambush her? Well, Monday was around the corner. This biddy wasn't going to be a problem for long. "You have a birth certificate showing David Tuckman as your father, I suppose."

"I have letters," the woman said smugly. "Letters from him to her. And I have pictures of all of us together. Here." She opened a large handbag, rummaged around in its interior, and pulled out a curled black-and-white photograph. She handed it to Harrie.

Harrie took the picture. It was shot from a distance on a hazy day, and it showed a group of three leaning against a railing. There was a dark-haired woman in a dark coat and sunglasses, a girl of about six standing in front of the woman, and a man, dark-haired and smiling, with his arm linked through the arm of the woman.

Avis Murphy leaned across the small table and pointed her wool-gloved fingers at the figures in the photograph. "This was taken in Coney Island in 1941. This was my mother, Maeve. And my father. But you recognize him, don't you?"

Harrie did recognize him. The thick hair, the wide grin. It was Mr. Tuckman, all right. But what did that prove? She handed back the picture. Could this Avis be sincere? If so, why wasn't she feeling the sincerity? The only thing she felt was threatened. "What exactly do you want from me?"

The woman smiled her smeary smile and put the photograph back in her handbag. "I want half," she said. "In exchange for not taking this to court and having to spend all that time and money, I'm willing to make a deal right now. And I think half is fair."

Harrie looked at the woman. Half? She didn't even have half to give her if she wanted to. She'd spent some, committed some, invested the rest, borrowed against the house. She hoped her monthly budget would keep her in food and electric heat. Giving back half the inheritance would mean that she'd have to sell the house, and everything she'd put into it would be forfeited. She rubbed her arms and stared at the person who claimed to be the daughter of her friend. It wasn't believable. He would have told her, told someone. There wasn't even a resemblance that she could see. Except maybe the shape of the face. And under that lipstick, the mouth . . . But no! The idea was crazy. Pure logic told her that if this woman was really David Tuckman's daughter, she would try to get it all. "Okay, that's it," she said. "Take me to court. I don't believe a word of this story." She stood, slung her handbag over her shoulder.

"She'll be sorry. Won't she, Larry?" Harrie heard the woman say to her dog.

22

---◻---

*I*VY SHOVED OPEN the front door so that it banged against the wall. She hoisted her handbag heavily onto her shoulder, then kicked the door shut with a pointed boot. "Hi," she said without looking at Harrie and Roger, who were sitting at the oak table. She ran her car keys across the bars of the cockatoos' cage, causing them to shrink to the far side, went through the bedroom and bolted up the stairs.

"Ivy? Do you want coffee?" Harrie called out.

"No," Ivy shouted down.

Harrie looked at Roger, who looked at her. He shrugged. She cleared her throat, then cleared newspapers from the table.

"About the tilework in the kitchen," Roger said. "I think we should buy everything we're going to need directly from this tilemaker I know in Milan. Giacomo's a perfectionist."

"Like you?"

Roger smiled. "Yeah. Like me."

"Well, that's good." Harrie measured coffee into the filter and turned the gas up under the kettle.

"I've been fooling around with that little crest idea as kind of a signature. We can have the crest done in cobalt blue and lay the tiles in a four-tile pattern, the crest in the top left quad. Here. Like this." He pulled his leather book out of a bag on the floor, turned to a page of grid paper, and sketched.

"Mmmm," said Harrie, looking over his shoulder. "I don't know, Roger." She poured water over the coffee grinds, turned off the stove. "It may be a little precious to have the crest everywhere."

"You think so?"

"Yeah. Crests, you know, unless it's your own, just scream nouveau riche. Like buying a title."

"Okay. So what do you say to white tiles with solid-color borders?"

Harrie brought the coffeepot to the table, filled her mug and Roger's. "Is that the catalog?"

He nodded. "I checked off the colors I like."

"Good. I'll look at it later." Harrie sat in the chair, put her fist under her chin and stared past Roger to the birds, now preening themselves and twittering happily.

"Want to tell me about it?" Roger asked.

"Yes. No."

"There's a woman who knows her own mind."

Harrie gave Roger a half smile. His hair was hanging down to his shoulders, his skin was ruddy from the fire, and the ragged sweater he was wearing, which would look like something from the shoeshine box on most men, looked disconcertingly sexy on him.

"You know," Roger said carefully. He spread his hands out on the table. Then he began to trace a crack in a board with one of his fingers. "You know, some people would have fired me." He glanced up at Harrie, gave her a quick look, took in her startled expression, dropped his gaze again to the table. "I'm glad you didn't."

"Well, don't think I didn't consider it."

"I'm sure you did."

"But I haven't even thought about it in a long time. So don't worry about it."

"Thanks, Harrie," Roger said, his gaze still fixed on the table. "I really love this place. I feel as much a part of it as if it were mine. I thought at first it was going to be a portfolio piece, just that, you know? But these days . . . I think about the house at night. I wake up and I'm thinking about the house. Every piece of hardware, every photograph I see, every color, I think about in terms of how it could be applied to this house."

"Oh, God." Harrie slumped in her chair, put her hand over her eyes.

"What did I say? What's the matter?"

"This horrible woman. She says she's going to sue me. She just showed up out of nowhere. Says she's David Tuckman's illegitimate daughter and legal heir and she wants half of what I was left or she's going to sue me for the entire thing."

"Half the house? Half the money? Did you believe her? Do you think she's telling the truth?"

"Who knows? She's a crackpot type, but just because she looks eccentric doesn't mean she's a liar. Look at me," Harrie said, stretching the sleeves of David Tuckman's sweater long past her fingers and pulling a comical face. "I'm eccentric and I haven't told a lie since I was in the third grade."

Roger laughed. "Well, you're not the ordinary eccentric. Let's say this babe is a liar and forget about her."

Harrie smiled. "Want some toast?"

"If you're having some."

Harrie nodded, pushed her sleeves back over her elbows, and went to the butcher block table. She sliced some bread, dropped the thick slices into the toaster, then returned to the table with pots of jam, small flowered plates, butter knives. And she looked at Roger. Since the time she'd caught him with Ivy, Roger seemed younger to her. Before she'd blundered into his indiscretion, she'd accorded him extra stature. His height, his attitude, his credentials, had all contributed to his air of authority. Now when she looked at his unlined face, she saw him as talented, approachable, flawed, and, most of all, a young thirty-two. "I called my lawyer."

"Good. What did he have to say?"

"You mean after he bawled me out for talking to the old bitch?"

"Yeah. After that."

"He said he found it hard to believe that David had a secret life. My lawyer and David were very good friends, you know."

"So he thinks it's a hoax?"

"I get that feeling." Harrie wished the lawyer had said she had nothing to worry about. But instead, he'd told her that he would have Avis and Maeve Murphy investigated and that until they were served with papers, there was nothing they could or should do.

The toaster popped. Harrie went to it, placed steaming slices of the warm, fragrant bread on a platter. Avis Murphy's poodle face jumped into her mind and leered at her. If that woman was genuine, all of this could simply disappear: the nutty bread, the toaster, the countertop in this little cottage on her wonderful estate. Oh, God. She was getting sentimental about nut bread. She sank down again on the kitchen chair.

Roger felt his insides shrinking with anxiety. He hadn't been exaggerating his attachment to this project. He loved the place. Being cut off from the completion of his plans would be like losing an arm. But how could he say anything to Harrie about his fears when all he would lose was a job? Harrie must be hysterical. No wonder she looked so tired, so worn. He'd spent so much time with her these last few months, he felt a closeness to her that was part of his feeling about the house. But with the house, he could touch it, shape it, and it would conform to his will. With Harrie—although his desire to touch her was getting stronger every day—he was blocked by two enormous obstacles.

First there was Ivy. He'd been seduced, no question about that, but he had to take responsibility for his actions even though Ivy had pulled down his zipper and just about thrown him to the floor. Anyway, he never wanted to go near Ivy again, but the fact that he'd been with her at all had damaged him in Harrie's eyes, so that any sincere movement toward Harrie had to get past this picture she had of him standing naked in the north wing. Still, and he'd replayed those startling moments many times, he couldn't have handled it differently. Having been with Ivy, he couldn't have apologized without making Ivy seem like a slut, and that would have been a shitty thing to do. So now all he could do was hope that Harrie would eventually see that a onetime tryst with her sister didn't define his entire character.

And then there was Dean. The few times he'd been in the same room with the guy had been trying. On both occasions Dean had shown polite interest in the project, asked a few questions, but he'd never gotten what you could call excited about it. And guess what? The guy acted the same way when it came to Harrie. He was attentive but a hell of a long way from passionate, while Harrie's very heartbeat seemed to boom out loud when he was around. It almost hurt to watch how she tilted that angelic face of hers toward Dean when he spoke.

But Dean seemed to be only half with her: one leg in, one leg out. And actually, he knew that feeling. He couldn't count the times he'd tried to explain to a woman he cared for that his work was the most important thing to him—even though he might love her. And yet, having seen so much of Harrie in this close-but-not-close way, he could see the woman's side of the issue. He could understand why a divided commitment was not enough. Harrie needed to be with someone who was excited about the things that excited her, and Dean was starving her by withholding his enthusiasm.

Harrie said, "It just doesn't make sense. I knew Mr. Tuckman so well. If he'd had a daughter, she would have been in his life. He wouldn't have cared that she was illegitimate. His wife died in 1963, for God's sake."

"So what's your plan?"

"I can't stop the restoration because of a threat. There's too much at stake here to stop. Avis Murphy is probably just an evil old grave robber."

Roger exhaled with relief. "You'll let me know if there's anything I can do?"

Harrie hesitated, sat up straight in her chair. "Can you get Ivy a job?"

Roger nodded, not looking at Harrie, looking at the damned crack in the table. "I'll talk to her," he said. "I'll try."

"Good," said Harrie. "Thanks." Then she stood. She collected the dirty dishes and, turning her back to Roger, took them to the sink for washing.

⊡

Laura shook honeyed cashew nuts into a silver bowl. She heard Dean's and Scott's voices in the next room and she liked the sound. She'd done a good thing bringing these two together. Scott had his capital, Dean had a feather in his cap, and she'd done an extremely good deed. Something good was sure to come from her generosity, and if she could choose her own reward, she'd know what to ask for. She capped the jar of nuts and, taking the dish in hand, walked into the next room.

"Dede and I are having a few people over next Thursday," Scott said, putting his glass down on the coffee table. "How about you and Harrie joining us for dinner?"

"That'll be fine," said Dean. "I'll have to check with Harrie. Make sure she doesn't have any other plans."

"And you too, Laura. And bring someone. Otherwise you know Dede's going to lasso some desperado for you."

"Ask her not to, okay, Scott? It's embarrassing." Laura straightened her skirt and sat in the wing chair. She crossed her very good legs. She tossed her hair and tried not to look at Dean. That she was single was grotesque. That Scott had to spotlight this grotesque condition—at a moment that should be hers—was cruel. "If I come by myself, it's because I want to come by myself."

"I'll tell her. Again." Slapping his knees, Laura's brother prepared to stand. "Let me know," he said to Dean, "and thanks once again."

"My pleasure. Sincerely," Dean said with a smile. All three stood, the men shook hands, and Laura walked Scott to the door. She gave him a cool kiss, then closed and chained the door. Immediately, she forgot that her brother had even been in the room. Dean was in her living room, sitting on the couch, and in a little while he, too, would want to leave. It was after seven and cashew nuts weren't a meal. What should she do? Propose going out to dinner? Ask him his plans for the evening? Sit there like a lump and see what he did? She strolled back into the room with forced nonchalance. Collecting her glass of wine from the table by the wing chair, she joined Dean on the couch. She kicked off her shoes, curled her feet under her, and scooped some nuts out of the bowl. Good move, she thought. This should hold him for fifteen minutes or so.

Dean was aware of a trace of Laura's cologne in the air. The room was softly lit and the woman beside him had arranged herself seductively. All he had to say was "Come here," and she would put down her glass and slide over to him. He had minded Laura's interest in him once. Why? He couldn't remember. She looked so kittenish now, so touchable. She'd tucked her feet under her, and that made her back arch, and that made her breasts poke at the fine knit of her sweater. What a beautiful chain reaction. Dean felt a pull in his groin. He cleared his throat loudly, shifted his position on the sofa. The words "Come here" were in his mind and in his throat, and he knew they should be stifled or in about two minutes he'd be fucking Laura right here on her camel-hump sofa. And then what would he do? "So you don't get along with your sister-in-law," he said, grabbing at the second sentence that came to mind.

"It'll be good to see Harrie again," Laura said, her words crashing head-on into his. The two laughed nervously. Rather than repeat her blatant white lie, Laura responded to Dean's remark. "Oh. Dede's all right," she said. But what she thought was, Dean is unnerved! And he wasn't acting like he was going to leave. She was getting to him. Would he make a move? Could he? He'd had three glasses of champagne on an empty stomach. She said, "It just bothers her sense of order to have single people around. Scott's her third husband, you know." Laura captured a diamond pendant that was hanging from a chain around her neck, and slid it back and forth. "And she's only thirty-two," she finished rather wistfully.

Dean nodded. "I don't know if I want to bring Harrie to your brother's next week. It hardly seems worth the hassle."

"Hassle?"

"The commute in from the Island."

"Oh. Is Harrie living out there, then?"

"Mmm."

Laura gingerly moved her hair away from her face. The air seemed so different since Scott had left, charged with a kind of tension that she knew she hadn't created alone. Could she trust it? Or would any loud noise, any sudden motion dispel the magic? "How's that working out?" she asked softly.

Dean sighed. Things had been so strained between them since Christmas. He was afraid to say anything to Harrie anymore. A simple, semiautomatic "I love you" was received with a challenging stare, an unspoken "Oh yeah? Then prove it." How long before she gave him the ultimatum he'd been expecting for the last year? "Marry me or let's stop." Maybe he'd been wrong to float the relationship when he'd known all along that Harrie was wrong for him. But he hadn't been playing with her. He'd been hoping that something would change for him, and now he was wondering if something had. He was feeling glassy around her, less accommodating. And something else was changing. He was warming to Laura. "Not so well," he said. "It's not working out so well."

"What seems to be wrong?"

"I don't know. It's just not working. I just don't seem to want to move forward. I don't know. I love her. I just want . . . more." He looked at Laura, then drained his glass. What *did* he want? To feel really great about himself, finally. He wanted the life he was supposed to have, not the weird life he was having with Harrie. He wanted to be a success on his own. And he wanted to be in love with a woman like Laura.

Laura took the bottle out of the ice bucket and poured the remains into Dean's glass. Funny, but she'd just had the most sudden shift in her feelings. One minute she was hoping Dean would say that his relationship with Harrie was fraying, and then when he did, she felt only sympathy for Harrie. How many times had she heard what Dean had said to Harrie? "I love you, but . . ." But what? What did men want, anyway? If she and Dean were together, would he be telling some other woman that he loved Laura, but?

It was while Laura was feeling this somewhat temporary kinship with Harrie that Dean set down his glass and fastened her with a blurry gaze.

"Come here," he said. He liked the way his voice sounded: kind of like Sean Connery with a hint of Charles Boyer.

"I think it's time to go out and get something to eat," Laura replied. She put on her shoes and stood patiently as Dean got to his feet.

23

———□———

*I*T WAS EARLY MORNING and Dean felt good. He was standing in his new but empty office, coffee cup in hand, staring out of his own, quite large window, watching snowflakes drift gently down to the street. Right now the maintenance crew was on their way up from storage with a new desk for him, and Elise was boxing his files. His computer was nestled in the lap of his desk chair, its screen flashing up the day's news, as it did continuously even before the market opened, and the flat, black telephone was beside him on the window ledge. For the moment, there was nothing to do but sip his coffee and watch the snowflakes.

So entranced, his mind drifted to a place it liked to go.

Across the street and two blocks to the west was the building where Laura worked. Once, not long ago, she had said, "I'll be just down the street. We can wave hello." And he'd thought, she likes me. How strange that I'm not attracted to her. Now he was attracted in a big, bad way, and he wasn't sure how it had happened. Or maybe this was the way things were supposed to happen. First they'd had the business in common; then they'd gotten closer after she left the firm. Then she'd handed him this incredible deal which by itself would have been fantastic, but the way things turned out, the opportunity had doubled, then tripled itself, and he owed it all to her.

Thanks to Laura, he'd made more money for himself in the last three weeks than he'd made in the past three years. And so his confidence was up. Maybe before this Isletrek thing, he hadn't felt good enough about himself to feel he was good enough for a woman like Laura. Now everyone seemed to be responding to the new and improved Dean. He'd been making better calls lately, and his clients were referring their friends. And people around the office were just plain treating him better—like a thousand percent: What do you think of USX, Dean? Where do you think gold is going? And Wales had invited him to lunch next week, the first time ever. And there was this office.

Even his father was starting to be a human being. Only that was the weird thing. His father seemed to be responding not so much to the recent up-tick in his career as to the damned Christmas dinner. He'd actually asked about Harrie. "How is that terrific girlfriend of yours?" he'd said with a warm little chuckle. Dean couldn't remember his dad's warm little chuckle being directed at him since he'd banged a drum in the Fourth of July parade in maybe the third grade. So what was this paternal approval all about? And why did he find it so irritating?

Dean shook his head, a gesture that was reflected back at him in the pearly glass of the window. Harrie. How had he gotten in so deep with Harrie? Who'd he been with at that party where he first met her? He could never remember. He'd gone out with so many different women that year. Anyway, it didn't matter. He'd seen her twinkling away by the guacamole, and maybe because he was drawn to her, and maybe because she was so not-his-type, he felt safe getting close to a person who was, after all, a wonderful woman. But he'd always thought he had an escape hatch. She was wonderful, but she was wrong. And then, wrong or not, he'd found himself loving her. Now things were good and complicated. The money. The damned house. His father's perverse approval out of nowhere. He was in a trap, trap, trap, and he'd closed it on himself. But maybe, if he could get an arm free . . .

He picked up the phone. He punched out a number. "It's Dean," he said when she answered.

"Well, hello," said Laura.

He could imagine her twirling her chair around to the window, plucking at the telephone cord with her tapered fingers, watching the snow, which was falling more swiftly now.

"Do you think this stuff will stick?" she asked. "I didn't catch the forecast this moring."

"It's going up to the high forties," he said. "Are you free for lunch?"

"No, sorry. I've got a lunch date way the hell uptown. You say this is going to stop? I left my boots at home."

"Yeah. That's too bad," he said, meaning Laura's luncheon plans.

"I guess I'll call a car if it doesn't let up," she said.

"So when am I going to see you again?" Dean asked abruptly. That seesaw action. It made him dizzy. First you didn't like someone and that someone was shaking in your presence. In public. Then you liked the person and when you called, they got fascinated by whether or not the snow would stick and ruin their goddamn shoes. Picking up the phone and stretching the cord to its limit, Dean kicked the door closed. He wouldn't appreciate a couple of moving men coming in at this particular moment. He returned his attention to Laura, who seemed to be flipping through her datebook.

"The twelfth? I'm free for lunch on the twelfth."

"Okay," Dean said without checking his own datebook, which was in a carton across the room. "Okay, the twelfth is fine for lunch, but I'd like to see you for dinner before then." There was a knock at the door. Dean ignored it. Elise had a key; everyone else could wait. He paced the length of his office, whipping the telephone line behind him like a stage performer handling the microphone.

"Well, uh, when did you have in mind?"

Good. She sounded nervous again, which for the moment suited him. The seesaw was sawing back. There was another knock at the door. Inspiration struck. "How's Thursday? This Thursday."

"Okay," she said, not exactly overpowering him with her enthusiasm.

There was a beat, silence while Dean wrinkled his brow and tightened his grip on the phone. Had Laura lost interest in him? Just because he fumbled the pass he'd made in her apartment? Surely everyone was entitled to be clumsy once in a while, especially if they'd been drinking. "Something wrong?" he asked.

There was another pause while Laura stared at her datebook, which had suddenly become a book of unlined, very blank sheets. "Not at all," she lied. "Dean, can you hang on a second? I've got another call."

Without waiting to hear his response, Laura put the line on hold. She had to get a handle on what she was feeling, what she wanted to do. Dinner with Dean was not business and it was not friendship. His voice had sounded urgent: the voice of a man with a hard-on. And although she'd longed to hear that sound in his voice for years, she felt stopped by it now. His voice was hungry, not tender. He wanted to sleep with her, not make love to her, and maybe that would be okay under some circumstances, but currently at least, Dean wasn't free. He said he loved Harrie and he hadn't broken up with her, so this dinner would be illicit, with perhaps a cover of friendship.

And she knew what dinner would be like. Clandestine. Atmospheric. White tablecloths. A maître d' who knew Dean by name. Good wine. And Dean would tell her again how he couldn't go farther with Harrie. Then he'd try to take her home. All of this added up to an invitation to get naked in every way and then be by herself, alone. No long weekends together, no going out with friends, no chance for the lust to turn into something real. And this was not a good deal for her. It was anything but a good deal.

It was funny how quickly things could change. A week ago she'd prayed for Dean to come on to her, but she'd never even considered the fact that she would be dating Dean while he was involved with Harrie. But maybe Dean *was* breaking up with Harrie. Maybe that was precisely what he was going to tell her. She should at least give him the benefit of the doubt one time. She wasn't committed to anything yet, and if she didn't like his manner, she was certainly capable of shaking his hand good night and going home.

Laura pushed at the blinking button. "I'm back," she said. Lines and dates reappeared in her Filofax. She studied the entries she had made for the week. Thursday, he'd said. "Wait a second. We're supposed to go to Scott's on Thursday."

"I know," said Dean. "You didn't want to bring a date, right?"

"Right."

"So. Why don't we go together?"

"Oh," she said, raising her eyebrows. What an interesting idea. Dinner with her brother. What could be more respectable than that? "Okay," she said. "Shall I call Scott or will you?"

"I'll do it," Dean said, smiling. This was going to be all right. A completely innocent dinner. No need for anybody to feel guilty about anything. No need to make excuses to anyone. Still, he would be trying it on—the idea of being with her. And she would be trying on the idea of him too. "I was going to call him anyway."

"Okay. Listen, I've got to go."

Dean glanced at his watch. The market would be open in minutes. He'd better let that desk in now. "Me too. I'll talk to you Thursday morning."

"Okay, 'bye."

"Goodbye," he said. Dean put the receiver on the hook, held the phone for a minute, then replaced it on the window ledge.

When he opened the door, he found himself face-to-face with Chip, who was looking at him as though he was a dead man.

"Are you watching your screen?" Chip asked without preamble.

"No, what?" Chip's alarmed expression caused a river of fear to flood his body. Crash, he thought. Another crash.

"Wildcat strike at SouthEast Airlines. I can't believe you didn't see the bulletin."

Dean turned and squatted beside the chair that held his computer. He tried to focus. The symbols for the forty stocks he considered the most important to him were shown in the top three quarters of his screen along with the fluctuating price of each stock. The bottom quarter of the screen was constantly alive with bulletins, reports of special interest, and general news that in some way affected the market. When a piece of news that affected one of Dean's top forty stocks came in, the stock's symbol was marked with an asterisk. Even as the numbers beside the stock wavered, even as the symbols blurred, Dean could hardly ignore the bleakly staring star beside the first symbol in the first column, which stood for Isletrek. Dean felt sweat gathering on his upper lip. "What's happening?" he asked as calmly as he could.

"Shit, man, I banged on your door. Didn't you hear me?" Chip swore from behind Dean's chair.

"Chip, what's happening?"

"The whole damned company walked out. Engineers, flight crew, ground crew, everyone."

"What's the beef?"

"The whole deal. Wages. Working conditions. The flight crew says the planes are unsafe."

"Oh my God," Dean said softly. The market was open, but

Isletrek wasn't trading. That meant the SEC wasn't going to let anyone buy or sell until they balanced out the accumulated orders that had come in since the news broke. It was a crash, all right. His own personal crash. A crash with his name in big black letters burned into it. He pressed a computer key, called up a news story about the strike, read the first headline announcing the grounding of all the flights in the northeastern corridor. "It's too late," he said in a whisper. "It's too late already."

"I would have taken the fucking door down if I'd known you were in here," Chip said. "I thought you were in the can. I looked. Elise thought you might have gone out for a paper. Why didn't you open the door?"

"I'm fucked." Dean stood and turned to his friend. "Did you get a sell order in?"

"Sure. But I've got nothing. A few thousand shares."

Dean's phone tootled. A button was lit, answered, put on hold. Another lit up, then another. Back at her old workstation, Elise was taking his calls. Dean looked dismally at the flat surface of an instrument he'd regarded so fondly ten minutes before.

"You would have had to hold on anyway," Chip said quietly. "You couldn't have dumped Harrie's stock unless you'd known last night."

Dean nodded, a condemned man acknowledging the priest who has come to pray with him in his last hours.

"You're just going to have to ride it out. The strike'll be settled. Maybe before you know it."

Dean nodded again. Sure. But first Isletrek was going to plummet; the only question was how far. Snapping out of his stupor, Dean snatched the receiver from its hook and stabbed the buttons that would get Sol Harris, the researcher, on the phone—the man who knew what the real situation would be at SouthEast. The line was busy, which meant every line in the research department was busy. "I'm getting sick," Dean said to Chip. He stabbed the buttons again. Another busy signal. "Oh, man," he moaned. "You can just feel those stop orders cutting in."

Chip groaned sympathetically.

"If I don't get a line in the next thirty seconds, I'm going to take to the stairs."

Elise appeared in the doorway, silken, unfrayed, doe eyes cast
down. She held a sheaf of message slips. "Your father called," she
said. "And Scott Taft called twice from his car. He said please don't
panic. I promised I would tell you that. And Laura Taft also called,
and Sol Harris, and the rest are clients."

"Thanks," Dean said dully. His father. He had his father in up
to his dentures in SouthEast. How was he going to tell him to double
up this time? And yet . . . And yet if this was all smoke, if Isletrek
dropped and the strike was settled fast, this could be a hell of a buying
opportunity. If, on the other filthy hand, this walkout lasted anything
longer than, say, a week, disaster would surely follow. It was the
worst possible time for the airline to strike. January. The Caribbean
was booked solid for the next three months. Other airlines might
make good on some of the SouthEast tickets when they could, but
the ugly possibilities were that the clients who had booked airfare
through SouthEast would never be able to get to the hotels booked
by Isletrek. If Isletrek had to make good on three months of hotel
bookings, they were going to be ruined. Don't panic, Scott had said?
Scott was probably shitting in his pants, praying Isletrek stock wasn't
being dumped all across the country.

"Mike, you can bring that in now," Elise said to one of two men
who began to roll a dolly loaded with a hardwood desk into the room.

"Wait," said Chip, squeezing through the narrowing gap between
the desk and the door. "Will you be okay?" he called out to Dean.

Dean looked at his friend's face. "Sure," he said, locked helplessly
between the moving men and his door. He watched as Elise directed
the moving men, as the desk was lifted from the dolly and eased to
the carpet. He grabbed the phone to his chest and called the research
department again. The line was ringing. Good. In a minute he'd have
answers. "Sol, please. It's Dean Carrothers." He listened as the secretary told him that Sol would call him back in a minute. He thanked
her and hung up. He held the phone under his arm. "Elise, screen my
calls outside, okay? I want Sol Harris only. Everyone else has to wait."

Elise nodded and disappeared outside the door. Dean chewed his
lip. What could he have done differently? If he'd been watching the
screen, maybe he could've fired off a sell order. The stock had risen
above the original twenty-dollar starting price. Maybe he could've
gotten in somewhere between last night's healthy twenty-one and a

half and the original twenty. Still made a profit. Still been a hero.

"Is this good, Mr. Carrothers?" Mike asked. "Do you want it here?"

"That's fine. Thanks." The desk. The most irrelevant object in the world. Dean lifted the computer, placed it carefully on the desktop.

"Let me do that," Mike said.

Dean ignored him. He got behind the desk chair and wheeled it into its new, surely temporary, position. He straightened out the telephone cords, then put the phone in front of the computer.

"I'll be back in a second," Elise called out. "I've forwarded the phones."

"No," Dean called back. Didn't she get it? This was life and death. Who cared who was out in the reception area? A million bucks said it was Scott Taft, who could damned well wait with whatever Band-Aid he had brought to patch the gaping wound in his company. But it was too late to catch Elise. She was a silken blur. Then she was gone. The phone lines were blinking, every last one of them. Some calls were being picked up at the reception area, some were going into outer space. Dead man, Dean thought to himself. He was truly a dead man. The office would go. The life with Laura would never come true. The "What do you think of USX, Dean?" would stop cold. The lunch with Wales would probably be kept, but its content would be changed. And as for the money, he'd parked most of his commissions in Isletrek. Yesterday his investment had been up seven and a half percent. By closing today, what would be left? Enough to take a plane to Marrakesh and lose himself for a few years? The phone tootled. Please be Sol Harris, he prayed. Dean grabbed the receiver.

"Hello?" he yelled.

⊡

Harrie took her handbag and dumped it out on the table. She pawed through the contents, refusing to believe what she knew to be true. Carefully, she opened each of the dozen envelopes she had been inadvertently collecting in her handbag. The money wasn't in with the telephone bill or the dentist's bill, or with the letter from the out-of-work aerospace engineer. It wasn't lodged in with the flier announcing the gallery opening or the car wash discount coupons. There were two tens and a five in her wallet, but yesterday there had also been three hundred-dollar bills and now they were gone. The money had been stolen and this wasn't the first time.

Did Ivy really think she wouldn't notice? Did she think it was her right to take the money if Harrie was dumb enough to leave her purse around? What was she spending the money on? All of her clothes looked the same. Maybe there were some new things. Maybe that black leather jacket she'd been wearing was new. It was hard to tell.

Slowly, Harrie put her things away. Ivy was still sleeping. When she got up, there would have to be a confrontation, and Harrie dreaded it. She didn't have any experience with this kind of thing. What if Ivy said she hadn't taken the money? What would Harrie say after that? If she called her mother, it would only alarm her, and there was no point doing that until she had something to tell her. Maybe Des could advise her.

Harrie punched out the numbers she thought were Desiree's, apologized to the person she reached by mistake, and concentrated before trying her call again. Hadn't she once known Desiree's number by heart? She listened as the phone rang, then asked for Desiree when it was answered.

Elevator music came through the earpiece as she was put on hold. It had occurred to her lately that she hadn't made any new friends in a long time. Well, there was Roger, of course, but he wasn't the kind of friend she would ever see again once this project was over. And there was a whole gang of men banging away with their sledge-hammers, carting and wiring and plumbing, and she'd had small friendly encounters with them, but there was a decided lack where Luna and Raoul and Jan used to be. Even Desiree had become an occasional phone pal instead of someone she saw several times a week and spoke with every day. The result of this lack of daily friendship was that she was becoming closer to her mother, which was okay she supposed, closer to her sister, which was less okay apparently, and more dependent on Dean, which was probably very, very bad. She sighed as "The Girl from Ipanema" went walking, then brightened as Des came on the line.

"Hey, Har."

"Hey, Des. Listen, I want to ask you something—"

"I've only got a couple of seconds, Har. An airlines has gone out on strike and I've got two million people calling."

"Oh. Well, this won't take long. I just want your advice on something before Ivy wakes up."

"Uh-huh," Des said impatiently.

"You see, I had three hundred dollars in my wallet. I was going to go to a tag sale—"

"Har. Can I call you back? I mean, I can't do this right now."

"Sure. Sure. I understand." Harrie said goodbye to her friend, who had probably already forgotten they'd even been speaking. So it was going to be Dean she'd be asking after all. She palmed the receiver, tapped out Dean's office number quickly and without hesitation. She was imagining the face of Dean's secretary, when Dean answered his own line.

"Hello," he yelled.

"Honey? It's me."

"Oh. Harrie. It's insanity down here."

"I won't keep you long. I just wanted to know . . . Dean. Ivy's taken some money out of my wallet."

"What?" Dean said, his voice infused with rage.

"I know, I know. I'm not sure what to do. She'll be coming downstairs—"

"Harrie, I don't have time for this."

Again! Was there no one who had time for her? "But it's important, Dean. I can't pretend I don't know I've got three hundred dollars missing and if—"

"Three hundred? What a laugh! Listen. The best guess is Isletrek's down four points. There's been a walkout at SouthEast."

"Oh, so that's . . . but we've got a contract."

"Don't you get it? The contract is irrelevant. No flights means canceled bookings, means refunds, means disaster."

"Dean, stop yelling at me." Harrie squeezed the phone with both hands. She felt her knees begin to buckle as her blood pressure dropped. "This can't be irretrievable."

"I don't know yet. I'll call you later," he said. And then he hung up.

Harrie put the phone down on its base. She had a sudden vision of a woman in a shoe store, a white-haired woman smoking a brown cigarette, smiling a benign smile, telling her that all of her visualizations would start realizing themselves. Had she visualized this? Her luck was turning out like one of those three-wishes fairy tales where the wishes turn to ashes in the end. Nothing about her life seemed safe anymore. She couldn't hold on to money. And she couldn't hold on to love. The little room seemed to shrink and spin around her. She had to get out of here. She had to get down to the water. Blindly, she groped for her coat, turned the doorknob, and walked straight into a startled Roger's duffle-coated chest. He grabbed her arms to steady her, and Harrie, reflexively, pushed him away.

"Are you okay?" he asked.

She nodded her head.

"Are you sure?"

As though a thread had been pulled, Harrie felt herself begin to unravel. She put her hands to her face and began to cry.

Gently taking first one hand, then the other away from her eyes, Roger put his arms around Harrie. Then he kissed her.

24

*H*ARRIE SAT in the wing chair in Schoonmaker and Schoonmaker's reception room. Her spine was firmly pressed against the back of the chair, her feet were flat on the floor, and her arms rested on the chair's arms. Braced this way, because all of her energy was being used by her brain, she processed five thoughts at once. One of her thoughts predominated, and that thought was not about Avis Murphy—the reason she was visiting Mr. Schoonmaker today. That predominating thought concerned a kiss, and since the thought was one she'd already had many times, she forced herself to think about other things.

For instance, Harrie wondered where Becky was; the little old woman who used to sit at the large desk under the gilded mirror had been replaced by a glossy brunette with red fingernails and a modern intercom. And Harrie thought about Ivy, who'd become a thief and had not been confronted. She speculated about the news Mr. Schoonmaker said he would give her about Avis Murphy. She worried about what new depths her Isletrek stock would plumb today. And, unavoidably, she returned to the kiss that had dashed to death her guarded feelings about Roger—a man she found so handsome that looking at him could restrict her breathing, a man whose naked image was still burned into her vision, a man whose eyes had been filled with concern for her and whose mouth she'd never imagined kissing, and now . . .

Harrie shook her head. She was becoming obsessed by a kiss. Days after it had happened, she could still feel the pressure and the warmth of that kiss and the depth and the breadth and the pull of it, and the way that kiss had seemed to be the answer to the question "What is the meaning of life?" And all of that, combined with the

fact that it had *happened,* had shaken her so much that she'd pushed
Roger away and run to the seawall, there to sit on the cold ground
until she'd been calmed by the rhythm of the rolling waves.

How could one kiss undo her so? And a kiss from a man who'd
made love to her sister! Maybe Roger would kiss anyone. Julie was
coming out for a visit next week. Maybe Roger would seduce Julie.
Yet even as she thought this, hurled the thought as though it were
an accusation, Harrie knew that Roger wouldn't seduce Julie. She
even felt safe supposing the kisses he'd given to Ivy had been of a
different kind than the one he'd given her. There had been so much
tenderness in that kiss, it seemed he'd shaped it just for her. And the
problem wasn't that she hadn't wanted that one kiss, it was that she
wanted more than one. She wanted to get to know Roger's kisses, to
experiment with them, to luxuriate in them, and since these new,
unasked-for feelings were not about Roger but about his kisses, she
had to acknowledge something. She hadn't felt this way about Dean's
kisses in so long she could hardly remember if she'd ever had those
feelings before.

But surely she had. Surely she'd been made faint in Dean's arms
once upon a time. Harrie squinted her eyes and tried to remember,
and pictures of herself breathless in Dean's embrace *did* come, but
the pictures were old and they were fading. Of course, the comparison
was unfair. She and Dean had reached that stage where sexual tension
was replaced by something richer, or so it was said. But Dean's love
didn't feel rich. It felt thin and pale. And that realization made her
announce his name so as to make him tangible, real, someone she
could shake.

"Dean," she said out loud in the empty room. Startled by the
sound of her voice, Harrie glanced nervously at the receptionist, who,
remarkably, seemed not to have heard her. If you said someone's
name out loud and no one heard it, did that mean you hadn't said
it? Was it like a tree falling in the forest with no one around to hear
it? Or was she like a dog barking in an empty house on a country
road? She was. And Dean had stopped listening. They were having
dinner tonight. Would they talk? Would they make love? Would an
electric kiss from a man she didn't love be blown out of her mind?
She hated to think it, but maybe their problem was this simple: One
day Dean had been involved with a woman who was earning less

money than he. Then, without warning, he was involved with a woman who had millions. He'd never once seemed happy about that fact. Maybe he just couldn't accept the change.

Well, what was she supposed to do about that? *She* hadn't changed. Really, Dean was being a jerk. Mr. Tuckman hadn't had any problem with Jazz's fortune. He'd enjoyed their way of life when Jazz was living, and had no interest in her money after she had died. Or was there more to it? Had Jasmine's money pushed him into an affair with Maeve Murphy? Harrie winced at the thought. People weren't perfect, although Mr. Tuckman had seemed that way to her. He really had.

She remembered a story he'd told her of a time when Jazz had broken her hip in a riding accident. Mr. Tuckman had brought together a group of actors and they'd had a reading right in her bedroom. And there were the simpler acts of devotion: He brushed her hair every night before they went to bed. She knit sweaters for him, funny-looking sweaters, and he wore them all. And if she'd never heard the stories, she would have been convinced of their love by the look of radiant happiness in the pictures of Jazz Defoe and her devoted husband. Harrie had felt a shade of that devotion directed from her friend toward herself: the way he'd listened to her, accepted her, cared about her, and ultimately given her the things he'd treasured most. God. This was the very devotion she wanted from Dean.

Harrie felt a sudden wave of sadness as she thought of her lost friend. She could visualize him so easily—the way he walked, the generous smile. And she tried to let the image speak to her, but she could recall only the lilt in his voice, not the words he had used. Mr. Tuckman had died in September, and already his memory was leaving her. If she could trade Blackfern and the money and everything that had come to her as the result of his death and have back his friendship and her formerly simple life, she would do it without hesitation. Or could she? In a way, her new life had stripped her of a kind of innocence. She was no longer a person who wanted; she was a person who had. How could she go back to a small, dark room on Chester Street and to a job where she answered to other people after owning herself as she felt she did now? Was there an equation between innocence and happiness?

Harrie gripped the arms of the chair. In a little while she'd be having lunch with Luna. Luna had insight enough for a dozen people, and after talking with her, Harrie would have a new outlook—that was practically guaranteed. She stood as her name was called, and walked down the corridor to Mr. Schoonmaker's office.

⊡

Harrie stared at Mr. Schoonmaker's polished scalp and winglike eyebrows. He'd welcomed her enthusiastically, told her about Becky, who had agreed to move to Florida and was now living in a ground-floor, ocean-facing, two-bedroom Vero Beach condo, with a companion to work all the electrical appliances. He'd asked her how the renovation at Blackfern was coming, and she'd told him that the roof was now sound and so were the staircases, and that the restoration was progressing well. Then Mr. Schoonmaker revealed the purpose of their meeting.

"I have to tell you the truth now, Harrie," he said. "I knew about Maeve Murphy. She and David were lovers for a few years, and I knew about the child called Avis."

Harrie heard this pronouncement in two distinct pieces. Maeve and David had been lovers. Not maybe. Truly. And there was a child. She felt a prickling sensation across her cheekbones and around her nostrils and in the tips of her fingers, and then she exploded: *"You knew? You knew and you didn't tell me?"*

"Now, Harrie, give me a chance to ex—"

"No, Mr. Schoonmaker. You can't do that! You can't be my lawyer and keep things from me."

"If you'll give me a minute, you can continue shouting at me when I'm done. All right?"

"Fine," Harrie said indignantly, fully planning to take him up on his offer.

"I don't think Avis was David's kid. I do think her mother might've told her that David was her father. Some people, especially back then, would have done such a thing."

"Now you're talking in circles. What are you saying? Is this woman a threat, or isn't she?"

"Harrie, Harrie, please calm down. And call me Eugene if you don't mind." The lawyer patted his littered desk with a spotted hand, gnarled at the joints—an exotic spider looking for cigarettes. He found the pack, shook out a cigarette and lit it. "I wanted to get some facts before I said anything. I didn't mean to keep anything from you, I just didn't want you to be unduly alarmed. As you are now. I'm sorry. Please forgive me."

Harrie's arms were wrapped around herself like a pair of boa constrictors.

"Now then," the attorney said in his raspy voice. He pulled at the knot of his tie—a yellow one with small gray elephants dotted randomly upon it—and cleared his throat. "Let me explain the situation in full. Maeve Murphy was a very pretty girl, ran a hatcheck concession at the Frangipani. A nightclub in the theater district. It's been closed now for many years. Uh, she had a few boyfriends. David was one of them."

"So then Avis *could* be his daughter?"

"Could be, but I don't think she is. What David told me—this is going back before the war, you understand—was that his girlfriend had a baby. He never said *he* had a baby and I'm sure he would have. Just as you're sure that if he'd had a daughter, he would've taken care of her. But listen, Harrie, if Avis Murphy is his daughter or not doesn't really matter. Under New York State law, you don't have to leave a dime to your kids."

"So does this mean I don't have to worry?"

"Normally, I would say you don't have to worry. Here's what our problem is. Her attorney is talking about making a case that you used 'undue influence'—that is, coerced David when he was not of sound mind. If you used undue influence, the will is null and void. If there's no will, then his estate passes to his heirs. Do you follow me?"

Harrie nodded dully.

"Now. First, they have to prove the will is null and void, therefore there is no will. Second, they have to prove that Avis Murphy is David Tuckman's daughter. And by prove I mean they have to convince the jury that it's more likely she is his daughter than not."

"Doesn't she have to have a birth certificate?"

"No. All she has to show is a likelihood that she's David's daughter. For instance, if David's blood type was O and hers is O—"

"Type O! Everyone has type O. *I* have type O." Smoke unfurled into the air. Harrie waved it away. She remembered sitting at the little concrete table across from the woman and a small, trembling dog.

"She'll be sorry" Avis had said. Harrie told Mr. Schoonmaker, "She said she had letters."

"I know. Her lawyer told me. As far as I can make out, they've got a few love notes. 'My dearest. Your eyes, your hair,' that sort of thing. And they've got some birthday cards to the baby girl, and some photos of what they're calling 'the family' at visits to the zoo, et cetera. Keep in mind what I said. This is by no means a piece of cake. First they've got to prove undue influence. Then they've got to prove blood relationship. I think if they could prove either of these things, we would've been served already and we'd have a court date. The fact that they're negotiating at all leads me to believe their case is a big bag of air. What I'd like to do is show up Avis Murphy as a fraud before an action is filed. We don't really want them to sue. We don't need the aggravation."

"Tell me again about this undue influence."

"It means they're suggesting you manipulated David, that you seduced him somehow and that he couldn't resist you, and so he made over his estate to you."

"Aw, jeez. That's disgusting. He was my friend."

Mr. Schoonmaker sighed. "I know." He pulled a wooden writing surface out from its sleeve in his desk, then swiveled his chair and put his feet on the little shelf. He was wearing golf shoes. With cleats.

"How could they prove that anyway? It's so ridiculous. In ten years we never did more than kiss hello and goodbye on the cheek."

"The seduction doesn't have to be sexual. You befriended David. You spent time with him. Suddenly, you show up in his will."

"His mind was absolutely sound. You know that."

"I know."

"I guess he forgot things once in a while. He lost his keys fairly regularly, but everyone's got some little mental kink, don't they? You're wearing golf shoes! Does that make you crazy?"

"If I wore them to bed . . ."

"Isn't the man allowed to have friends? We used to have dinner together and talk. Listen to music."

"I don't think they stand a chance, Harrie, but I'd like to nip this thing in the bud. It's got kind of an ugly feel about it."

"So what are we going to do?"

"I've already started. I put some detectives on this. If we can find out who the woman's real father was, their case will blow apart."

"I'm stunned."

"I know this is unpleasant but—"

"I'm stunned that Mr. Tuckman had a mistress. I'm stunned that there's any truth to this story at all." Harrie pushed off from the desk, threw herself back into the chair. Her whole defense to the scruffy woman in the park had been that David Tuckman had been faithful to his wife, and even if Avis Murphy turned out to be someone else's daughter, she'd been more right than Harrie had been.

Schoonmaker took off his glasses, tossed them to the desk, leaned back and took a long drag on his cigarette. He tapped ashes into a large green dish, dragged again, then put out the butt. He seemed to Harrie to be thinking, perhaps about mistresses of his own. "It could happen to anyone, Harrie. Try not to be too hard on him. I'm a bachelor, you know. I could never quite go along with the idea of being with one woman for the whole of my life. There are some who'd say men aren't meant to be true to one woman."

Harrie clucked her tongue dismissively. There were men of an ordinary kind, and there was Mr. Tuckman. "But they were *mated*. If you push me, maybe I can understand how he might've had a fling once over the course of their marriage. But you're telling me he had a whole other *life*."

Harrie listened with dismay to the sound of her own voice. She was screeching. What was the matter with her? Why was she so outraged? She knew people had affairs, had them all the time. It was just that this particular couple had been so wrapped in love they'd seemed exempt from anything as mortal as cheating. She couldn't be more shocked if she'd been told this story about her own father. The notion was disorienting—sickening, actually. Mr. Tuckman's fall from grace. The destruction of her belief in a perfect marriage that had been set in a place where she'd hoped to have a perfect marriage of her own. That was it. If Mr. Tuckman could deceive his beloved Jazz, then Dean could do the same. Somehow, without knowing it, she had determined that what was true about Mr. Tuckman would be true about Dean, that they were the same men at different stages of their lives.

"Thinking about it now, I wonder if it wasn't the baby girl that was the draw for David," Schoonmaker said, running a hand over his shiny head. "If the woman was pregnant, and he knew it wasn't his, but the woman was a damsel in distress . . ."

Harrie blinked. Was there some heroism here? An explanation? "You mean he might have started off by being kind, then he got involved?"

"Yeah. Something like that. And then the baby came, let's say. And the woman was earning five dollars a week in tips from the hatcheck and David had a little money. More than a little, you know? And his first instincts were always generous ones."

Harrie nodded.

"And David liked children. And he had none. I'm making this up, Harrie. I'm making it up because I know what you mean about David and Jazz. They doted on each other. It was a true love match. But Jazz was quite a bit older than David, you remember. Not that her age was the thing, but that and her wealth, and her enormous need for attention. I can imagine a pregnant hatcheck girl could bring out something David was missing with Jazz. Maybe he had to be the star in a household. Maybe that's what he was with Maeve. He was an actor. He had love and money to spare. I can see it."

Schoonmaker lit another cigarette, took his first deep breath and exhaled it before speaking. "However, all of that may be fiction. All David ever told me was that Maeve was his girlfriend and, later, that she had a little girl. He told me because you could see she had a thing for him—and the pregnancy wasn't much of a secret either. But as I said, when I asked him back in 1935, he said his girlfriend had a kid."

Harrie nodded again as Mr. Schoonmaker concluded his made-up story that didn't seem fantastic at all. "So this weird lady could be feeling she was abandoned by her own father," she suggested. "Or could be she's David Tuckman's long-lost flesh and blood."

"Could be," Mr. Schoonmaker admitted. "Or could be she saw an opportunity and thought she could get away with something. Now, first thing tomorrow there's going to be a bunch of detectives going over photographs taken in the Frangipani in 1935. And then there's going to be an investigation. And until these people know something, all we can do is . . ."

"Wait and see?"

"Exactly. Let us wait and see."

"Okay," Harrie said with a weak smile. She pictured her plummeting stock, her monthly bill from the bank for the construction loan, the generous checks she signed weekly for things like custommade Italian tiles. "Okay. And thanks." Then she stood tiredly, gathered her coat under her arm, and walked with a lanky, loping Eugene Schoonmaker out of his office and down the hall.

⊡

"I hope you don't mind. I ordered Chinese," Dean said when he opened the door.

"Hi." Harrie leaned forward to kiss him. Dean looked disheveled. His hair was uncombed and he was wearing a paint-spattered sweatshirt and a pair of old jeans. And while there was nothing strange about dressing down in your own apartment when you were having order-in Chinese food, Harrie, having worn some of her new clothes at last, felt overdressed.

"Give me your coat," Dean said, taking it from Harrie and locking the door. "I took a headache pill. I might be getting one of my killers, or I would have taken you out. I just didn't want to take a chance."

"It's okay." Harrie drifted through the living area. "I'll put on something of yours."

"I hope there's no MSG in the food. I told them no MSG and they seemed to understand, but how can you know? I ordered wonton soup, cashew chicken, spare ribs, string beans and diet Coke. Okay?"

"Be back in a second," she said. She went to Dean's bedroom, opened his closet and took out his robe. This morning when she'd dressed, she'd thought about how she would slowly unbutton her wonderful brown jumper, then undo the creamy cashmere sweater until she was standing in her camisole, leggings, and short wing-tipped boots. She'd thought how sexy she'd look. Now she held up Dean's robe, which did not flatter her, and decided the boots would look dumb sticking out from under it and kicked them off. Here she was again, she thought soberly, working herself around Dean.

Dean pushed the remote-control buttons until he found the news program he liked best. There'd been a hint of good news today. A rumor that a Texas millionaire named Halsey might buy SouthEast caused Isletrek to jump up two points, and while it dropped before the market closed, net net they were up a point, thank God. If only the rumor would pick up steam. Man, he hated this desperate feeling. It hurt to be so dependent on the rise and fall of one stock. It made you weak and stupid. You couldn't really act with guts when you were too involved. But how could he be otherwise? Half the people in the company from coast to coast were into Isletrek because of him. Not only was he in personally up to his armpits, but he had Harrie in up to hers, and he had his father in Isletrek *and* SouthEast. Then there was the extra complication of Scott and Laura, two people he didn't really want to be with right now.

Correction. He wouldn't mind being with Laura. Scott was a different story. Talk about desperate. Scott was scrambling to make deals with charter planes to fly vacationers down to the islands so that the hotel bookings wouldn't be lost. Only one problem. His customers were scattered like grains of salt across the whole damned United States. By the time Isletrek picked up the charter fares two and three at a time, it might as well absorb the loss on the hotel bookings. So Scott's company was losing money, the stock was going through the floor, and Scott saw Dean as the guy who could stave off the inevitable. How was he supposed to stop people from ditching Isletrek stock? By force?

The intercom buzzed. Dean told the doorman to send up the delivery, then went barefoot to the front door. He signed a credit card slip, took the brown bags to the kitchen and was dishing out cashew chicken, when he felt arms around his waist.

"Oh, here, take this," he said, turning and handing Harrie a plate. "I've set us up in front of the TV."

"Dean, I've got tons of stuff to tell you," Harrie said.

"Here's your Coke."

"Thanks."

"Your stock's up, did you know?"

"Yeah. A point. Thank God. The paper said there's a takeover rumor."

"Let's hope and pray it's not just a rumor. I've got you, me, and everyone I know in that stock." And then Dean told Harrie every nuance of their position until his words ran together. Finally, they were seated in the living area.

"I saw Mr. Schoonmaker this morning," Harrie began.

"Everything okay?" Dean asked as he turned up the volume on the television.

"Do we have to watch television?"

"I guess not," Dean said reluctantly. "But do you mind if I just watch this? I want to see *The Wall Street Report*."

"Go ahead."

Harrie crossed her legs Indian-style and gnawed spare ribs. Together, they watched *The Wall Street Report*; and afterwards they watched Dan Rather. Then Dean told Harrie that after the day he'd had, he really needed a hot bath. So Harrie cleaned up the dirty dishes and thought about her lunch with Luna, who'd looked lovely and in love, and about how Luna had begged her to read the manuscript of one of Harrie's favorite clients who was proving hard for Luna to handle. And how she'd said she would love to. After a while Dean reappeared in his sweat clothes and they watched the ten o'clock news together. Following the news, they went to bed.

·

Harrie stared up at the ceiling. An occasional flash of light from the reflection of car headlights appeared, then disappeared. She could feel a small margin of heat where Dean's side touched hers but in terms of connection with him, that was all she felt. He hadn't asked her about her meeting with Eugene Schoonmaker. He'd barely asked about Luna, although at this late hour, she could scarcely force herself to raise either subject. And pretty soon they'd both be asleep. And in the morning, Dean would leap out of bed and go for his run and she'd go back to Blackfern, and this simmering feeling that their relationship was in trouble would not be addressed and would continue to simmer.

So Harrie, hoping for something sweet and connecting, rolled onto her side and kissed Dean's neck. Then she ran her hand across his chest and slowly downward until she touched a place she hoped would be transformed from a soft lump of flesh to an object of a completely different size and shape that was capable of making her feel loved and maybe more. And this transformation did take place, so that she was shocked out of her pleasurable anticipation when Dean's hand covered hers and moved it firmly away.

"I'm sorry, hon," he said. "I just don't feel like fooling around."

·

Dean watched the reflection of car lights on the ceiling. Alone with Harrie, without the welcome distraction of the television, he realized how trapped he felt when he was with her. Harrie was too dependent on him. He was the authority, he was the source of affection, he was the future Mr. Braintree, and he'd caused Harrie to see him this way because of his purposeless love for her. If he hadn't been so weak, he would never have let this relationship go on for so long. Although it hadn't been his intention, Harrie must notice how cool he'd become. Tonight his mind kept going to his job and his standing there and whether the damned airline strike was going to be settled, or Halsey was going to bail them out, or SouthEast Airlines was going to continue its tailspin and go splat all over Wall Street. And he thought about how, his relationship with Scott Taft notwithstanding, if the rumor pushed the stock up even another notch tomorrow, he might get Harrie out. A two-point loss could be survived, and if he got Harrie out of Isletrek, that would be one less reason to feel guilty, as he did much of the time when he thought about her.

He knew guilt was a useless emotion. And it was especially useless when he couldn't apologize and make things better. What seemed to be happening was that the cumulative load of unrelieved guilt had produced a kind of physical numbness toward Harrie which she seemed to ignore. If he touched her, she leaned into his touch. If he kissed her, she parted her lips and threw her arms around his neck. If he were to put his arm around her now, she would put her hands over his body. And all of these attempts at more intimacy on her part only made him want to flee.

It was getting to be about that time when he would have to say, "I'm sorry, but this isn't going to work out." He'd rehearsed some version of this separation speech many times before, but no matter how many times he thought he was up to it, he found that making a small adjustment, giving Harrie what she wanted, was easier than breaking up. But now his adjustment machine had been cranked to the max. He couldn't give any more. And as Dean was having this thought Harrie kissed his neck, ran her hand over his chest and down into his shorts, and the only thing he could reasonably do was move her hand away. "I'm sorry, hon," he said. "I just don't feel like fooling around."

There was silence for the moment it took Harrie to register the blow. Then she said, "Then why don't you go fuck yourself?" She boiled out of the bed, grabbed her underwear from the chair and viciously yanked it on.

"What are you doing?" Dean asked, somewhat alarmed.

Harrie didn't answer. She was jamming her legs into leggings, shrugging on the camisole—items she had put on with pleasure that morning, now being put back on with fury. It was the second time today that she'd exploded with anger, only this time her anger was so great she was afraid to have it. Not that she was wrong to have it, not that Dean didn't deserve it; it was only that if she let go, something was sure to break, and that thing would be them.

"Where are you going?"

"Where do you think?" Harrie pulled the jumper off a hanger, which twanged as it shot back into the closet.

"It's midnight. You can't go home now," Dean said, the alarm more evident now.

"I'm not going to stand for this anymore," she said. "You are *pitiful* and *small* and I deserve *better*." With that, Harrie stormed into the living room and got her coat out of the closet. When she turned toward the front door, she found that Dean had planted himself between her and it.

"You can't leave like this. I was just tired, that's all. You're taking this too hard."

"Get out of my way," she snarled. She could pick him up. She could hurl him out the window. And she would do it if he didn't move from the door.

"No," he said.

So she shoved him. But he had turned to rock and couldn't be budged. "I hate you!" she shouted in his face.

Dean took Harrie's flailing arms down to her sides, then wrapped his arms around her. As she struggled and grunted and shouted, "No, no, no," he held her tightly and he kissed her hair. And then Harrie found herself sobbing, more from frustration and anger than from sadness. "Get out of my way," she said, through her tears.

"No. I can't do that."

"You're a prick, you know that?"

"I know."

"You're a bastard," she said, running down her list of invectives and coming up with only those.

"I'm sorry," Dean said—an apology with no reason attached—and when he felt Harrie would stop fighting him, he released her arms, hugged her even though she would not hug him back, then led her back to bed.

"What's the matter with you anyway?" Harrie asked, still partially dressed, lying in the dark, letting her hand be held lightly by Dean. "You used to tell me you loved me, you used to want to make love to me, you used to want to *talk* to me."

"It's gotten harder to do all those things."

"But why? What is it? Was it my asking if we were going to get married?"

"No. That wasn't it."

"Is it because I have more money than you or because I spend so much time at Blackfern—?"

"Har. It's nothing you did or didn't do. I don't want you to change anything about yourself for me."

The weight of this statement struck Harrie dumb. If she couldn't do anything, how could she make things work?

There was a heavy and interminable silence, broken at last by Dean. "I love you, Harrie. I'm just afraid that love may not be enough."

"What do you mean, not enough? Love is everything."

"In fairy tales. We should have talked sooner, Harrie. I was just afraid that if we talked, we would reach some critical point"—Dean swallowed—"that I wanted to avoid."

"Oh, God," Harrie said. Make this stop, she thought.

Dean sensed that things were going too fast, but at the same time he couldn't hold back his feelings any longer. "I'm just feeling that I'm in someone else's life," he said, hoping Harrie would somehow understand and agree. He squeezed her hand. "And it doesn't feel right to me."

Harrie could hear some sort of music. It was as if the electricity in the wires and the whirring of particles in the air and the sound of her very breath had combined in this one sad chord. She could hear everything now. Nothing would be missed. "What is this *it* that doesn't feel right?" she asked, and then she waited for an answer in the musical silence.

"Oh, Har," he said sadly.

"You don't feel right with me?"

Dean nodded once, shamefully, guiltily.

Harrie's fear cracked open and inside was a pure, almost beautiful anger. She snatched her hand away from Dean's. Her voice when she spoke was low and dangerous. "What a miserable son of a bitch you are. I'm not good enough for you? Not smart enough? Not pretty enough? Is that what you're saying?"

"No," Dean said, and his look was genuinely quizzical. "It's none of those things."

"What then?"

"It's hard to describe. It's just a feeling that if you were the right person for me, I wouldn't be afraid to go forward. But when I try to, I think, I love her, but she's not the person I . . . she's not right."

"So all this 'not ready' crap you've been telling me was really that I'm not right?"

"I guess."

"You love me, but I'm not right? Do you have any idea how stupid that sounds?"

"Yes. I know. I know it sounds stupid. It's been sounding stupid to me for so long and I've been trying to get over it, but it won't go away." Dean stared at his hands in the pale glow of the light coming in through the window. Now that the thing he feared had arrived, he wanted it to disappear.

"So, fine. I get it. Thanks for telling me," Harrie said, every word a lie. It wasn't fine. She didn't get it. And she didn't feel grateful at all. She felt like putting miles between herself and a man who loved her but didn't find her—what else?—good enough. "I'm going out to the couch," she said, putting pillows under her arm, dragging blankets from the bed.

"Don't do that."

"It'll be easier to say goodbye to you tomorrow if we don't sleep together tonight." It was remarkable how calmly these words came from her mouth, she thought. The anger had been released, the fear had become the truth, and the truth had been told. And she was feeling strong, almost like singing. She had loved Dean her very best and it hadn't been good enough. So it was finished and he could die before she'd give him any more of herself.

Dean stared at Harrie. The flatness of her statement derailed him. Had he wanted this? To tell Harrie goodbye for good, get out of here and take your toothbrush with you? If so, where was the feeling of imminent relief? Why, instead, had a chasm about a mile wide and bottomless opened up at the foot of the bed? What had he thought he was doing? Breaking out of a trap? Pursuing a dream? Clearing the decks for Laura? He peered over the footboard into the chasm and he was washed over with nausea.

Harrie, standing now, was feeling even better by the minute. Dean was an asshole and she didn't have to try to figure him out anymore. "Has it occurred to you that the relationship is great, but you're fucked up?"

"Harrie, I don't know if I mean let's break up forever. I've been under a lot of stress. You've been under a lot of stress. I think we just need some time off to get perspective."

"We do? I don't need time off. I need someone who is on my side a hundred percent. Someone who doesn't put the word 'but' after 'I love you.'" Harrie stalked from the room with an armful of bed-clothes and Dean trailed her. At the couch, she folded a blanket lengthwise, stuffed one side deep into the cushions.

"Hon," said Dean.

Harrie fluffed the pillow.

Dean sat down on the couch and pulled Harrie down beside him. Harrie pulled her arm away from him. "Hon." Dean tried again. He put his hand on Harrie's thigh and squeezed it gently. "Why don't we just separate for a little while? A month, say. Why don't we just take off the month of February . . ."

Sitting beside Dean, sensing the warmth of him and the plea in his voice, she felt her righteous anger start to fray. Was it possible Dean would find his sanity, realize how important she was to him, put them back together?

"Just take the one month," he said, "okay?"

"And do what? What are we supposed to do during that month?"

"Just be. Go about our individual lives."

She could almost make it out in the gloom, the small flame of hope. She'd heard that sometimes the only thing that could activate a stuck relationship was a breakup. If he missed her. If he realized. "You mean take off February and make a date for the first day in March?"

"Why not? Yes. Let's do that. We'll get together for dinner on the first day in March and see how things look then. How does that sound?"

"Some part of me thinks, okay, this is worth a try. Another part thinks this is loony. That this is a way to break up in stages." But even this conversation was encouraging, Harrie thought. They were communicating.

"Well, what do you want to do?" Dean asked.

"I want to wash your mouth out with soap. I want you to tell me you're sorry and if only I would lose five pounds, everything would be all right."

"Harrie." Dean couldn't help but smile. "Let's try this, okay? I've tried a lot of loony stuff for you."

"Like what?" Harrie asked, knowing full well what loony stuff Dean meant. And they laughed.

"Okay?" he asked, giving her shoulders a little shake.

"Okay," she agreed reluctantly. The deal was sealed. Tomorrow they would say goodbye for a month. Would they speak during the break? "What about my account? Are we going to still talk, or what?"

"Sure, we'll talk. I'll be your broker until this Isletrek mess is wrapped up one way or the other. After that, I want you to go with someone else. Whether we're together or not. Being your broker is too hard on me. I can't make good calls when I'm worried so much about what's going to happen to you. A client can curse me and fire me. I love you . . . ."

Harrie sighed and hugged Dean's chest. He had told her he loved her more often in the last twenty minutes than he had in the past three months.

"I love you and I feel sometimes like I'm a surgeon performing experimental surgery on my . . . I don't know . . . my own child. It's not a good thing." He looked down at Harrie. She was moist and warm and utterly his. With all he had said and done, she still loved him. She loved him. He put a hand to Harrie's cheek and looked into her eyes. He did love her. He hadn't lied.

Harrie felt Dean had returned to her. She hadn't fabricated this feeling out of wishfulness. It was real. He didn't want her to leave him. She was wishing Dean would kiss her, when he gently touched her lips with his.

As Dean kissed Harrie a flame shot into his groin, and the intensity of the charge was so unexpected he groaned. He took a breath and gripped her arms with his fingers and pulled her to him. And then Dean kissed Harrie again, a harder, more demanding kiss, and her mouth opened against his and he found he wanted to be in her mouth, be inside her body, be totally surrounded by her. They fell back together on the blanketed couch, and made sad, tender, ferocious love. The way lovers do when they know that in the morning one of them is going off to war.

25

────□────

$\mathcal{A}$LL OF THE BRAINTREE WOMEN were in the greenhouse boxing earthenware pots of paper-white narcissus. Julie, her glasses fogged, her hair resembling a dead asparagus fern, was making neat rows of pots in the cardboard boxes as Ivy mechanically brought the pots, two at a time, from the benches. Dottie sealed the cartons, affixed labels, and clucked over her brood as Harrie, wearing an air of inexplicable calm, clipped browned leaves and blossoms from the plants still to be packed.

Harrie took her emotional temperature again. She felt absolutely fine. Instead of enraged or numb or awash with pain as she had expected, she felt a sane ninety-eight point six. She was certain that the month would pass and then, on the first day of March, Dean would drive up to the cottage, shake the snow off his new coat, stoke the fire, and eat heartily before undressing and climbing into bed with her. His sweaters and underwear were still in her drawers. His razor and toothbrush were still in the bathroom. His battery charger and cables were in the trunk of her car. She wore the ruby-encrusted watch, even now under her gardening gloves, and she wore his Battery Park City Racquet Club T-shirt under her sweater. And all of these things added up to this one thing. Dean, the man she loved, was still as much a part of her as her own skin.

And that's why she'd been irritated by Desiree's flippant advice on the phone this morning— "There are thousands of men out there, Harrie." What was with her, anyway? Harrie wasn't going to be going out with any of the thousands of men. And she was just as irritated by her mother's hovering concern. Harrie *knew* things were going to be all right between her and Dean, she didn't need reassurance. And then there was Julie who seemed to be happily dating someone and not talking about it—as if in deference to her bereavement.

The only person around who was acting normal was Ivy, and by that she meant normal for Ivy. Ivy had worn her Walkman earphones clamped over her skull, going into her cloaked silence for the whole of the drive from Blackfern to Spode. If Harrie had wanted to talk to her sister about Dean, or about *their* relationship, she would've had to rip out her wiring.

Harrie swept a pile of plant clippings into her apron pocket, then advanced upon another tier of potted bulbs. Between precision clips, she wondered what Dean was doing. Were his questions about their relationship being answered? Was he lonely? Dean was lucky. His work could completely eat him up. She, on the other hand, had two dozen idle hours every day in which to think—and though she could be thinking about Avis, or about her finances, or about her sister, she thought only about Dean, winding thought upon thought. Right now, while she was snipping blasted narcissus blossoms and thinking about Dean, he was probably hooked to a video display terminal and ten telephones and the world. He might not be thinking about her at all.

The one phone call she'd had from Dean this week had been about business. He'd sounded happy, and with good reason. The SouthEast walkout had been settled, Isletrek was climbing, and while she'd been happy to hear the news, she'd been hoping for a tone, a hidden message in Dean's "How are you?" and she hadn't heard it. Happy at work. That was Dean. And maybe that wasn't so odd. Men were different from women. Less sentimental. And they'd only been separated for five days. Maybe he, too, was looking forward to the month's end. And since February was a short month, there were only twenty-three days to go. Harrie was double-checking her mathematics, when she heard Julie scream.

"Mother!"

"Oh my God!"

"Would you please cool it?" Ivy said, calmly clamping tissues to her nose. Blood stained her pallid complexion, spotted the green apron she wore over her black sweater and pants.

"Ice," Harrie said. "I'll get some ice." Her movements toward the greenhouse door were cut short by Ivy's contained, "I've had these before. It's nothing."

"You have?" Harrie asked. "At my house?"

Dottie took Ivy's thin wrist and pulled it away from her daughter's face. "What do you mean, you've had these before? You've never had nosebleeds."

"Have too."

"Harrie?"

Harrie shook her head dumbly. "This is news to me."

"Will you all just chill, please?" Ivy said, wrenching her arm away from her mother's grasp. "It's from the lifting."

"Lifting, my ass," said Julie. "It's coke, isn't it? You don't suddenly start getting nosebleeds from lifting five-pound clay pots."

"You're crazy," Ivy said flatly. She dabbed at her nose until the tissue was sodden, and still the blood came.

"If she said it's lifting, it's lifting," Dottie said. "Or maybe you're anemic, Ivy dear. Let me take you into the house and put your head back."

"I'm *fine*, Mother. Okay?" Another wad of tissue materialized in Ivy's hand.

"Harrie, have you been giving her money?" Julie asked. With her hands on her hips, her lips pursed, Julie looked like a cartoon of a spinster schoolteacher.

"What are you saying, Jules? That I gave her money for drugs?"

"I'm not invisible, you know?" Ivy said. "You're such a bitch, Julie."

"Did you ever find anything missing?" Julie persisted, ignoring her youngest sister.

"No, I—"

"Harrie, if you stick up for her, you're out of your mind. I caught her with that pendant Alan gave me as an engage— The one with the ruby and the diamonds . . ."

"I was just trying it on."

"My ass. You were going to sell it."

"Will you listen to how she talks to me?"

"Girls. Girls," Dottie admonished, waving her hands, trying to disperse the agitation. How had things gone so wrong? A half day together. The girls all together, crating pots like they used to do, and it was all out of control.

"Mother. Don't you *get* it? She's on drugs. She says herself she gets nosebleeds all the time. Take her to a doctor if you don't believe me. You don't fix a hamburger septum by putting ice behind her neck."

"A hamburger what?"

"You all *slay* me," Julie shouted, ripping the apron strings from her waist, pulling the ties from around her neck, and throwing the garment to the floor with a great deal of force and very little impact. "Don't you read the papers? Don't you watch television? Don't you live in the real world? Do you think the way she behaves is normal?"

"There *has* been money missing," Harrie said quietly, as if she were confessing.

"So now I'm stealing money?" Ivy asked incredulously. She righted her head, which she had tilted back at her mother's insistence. Her eyes, always large in her pale face, seemed larger and more animated—wild areas of movement on a static plane. "This is unbelievable. I get a little nosebleed and suddenly I'm accused of—"

"And you look like a wraith. Or a zombie. And no one ever knows where you are . . ."

"Now I'm a zombie. Thank you."

"What's going on here?" Bill Braintree asked from the entrance to the greenhouse, his sudden appearance jarring the women so that they all turned toward him together.

"Nothing," Ivy said.

"Ivy's had a little—"

"Your daughter's been doing—"

"*Nothing,* I said, you bitch."

"Is that blood?" Bill's voiced boomed. "Dot, what's going on?"

"Will everyone just leave me alone?" Ivy spat, white-faced. "God." She pushed past her mother, her sisters, and the wall of flesh that was her father.

"Wait a minute. Where are you going?" Harrie asked the air.

"I can tell you where she's not going," Dottie said quietly. "She's not going back with you, Cakes. Not until I find out from her what the problem is."

"This is my fault?"

"Of course not. I just don't like having that child out of my sight."

"But I can't give up on her like this," Harrie said. "We're trying to work out our relationship . . ." She *wanted* it to be a relationship, but Ivy was impossible to reach. They barely conversed. She never knew what Ivy was up to when she wasn't working in the antique shop. And she felt guilty most of the time for not knowing how to take care of the little—zombie. Ivy could be on drugs. It was possible. There was that time . . . with Roger. But as Dean had said, smoking a little grass didn't make you a drug addict.

"I haven't liked her staying with you from the start, if you remember. But you two wouldn't listen to me. I'm just a mother. She could be getting into any kind of trouble, and between here and there we'd never know."

"Mom. She wants to be with me. She's got that job that Roger found for her. Maybe we could go into some kind of therapy with her. Get some professional help."

"I guess no one's going to answer me," said Bill. "I guess I'll talk to Ivy myself."

"You go ahead, dear. I'll be right there," Dottie said, taking off her gloves.

"I'll come with you," Harrie offered. She untied her apron and set it down.

"Better not. Better let your dad and me handle it."

Harrie watched the greenhouse empty and her family head toward the house where she didn't live anymore. Where she no longer belonged. "I feel like I've failed her," she said, following behind her mother, walking with her out of the humid hothouse into the dry winter air. "I think I should have seen more. Maybe I should have been tougher on her."

"Cakes. You're her sister. Not her mother."

"No, I really blew it. I should have told you when I found that three hundred dollars missing. I told Dean," she remembered aloud.

"Three hundred dollars?"

"I was pissed off, but I thought she was buying clothes, not drugs."

"Well, maybe she was. Julie isn't right about everything."

Harrie's vision blurred in the cold. She buttoned her coat, replaced her gardening gloves with the fur-lined ones that were in her pockets. She clasped one hand over her watch and felt its face with her fingertips as though she were reading it in Braille. Beside her, an inch or two shorter than she, Dottie seemed gnomelike and old. Her nose was bright pink, and her blue eyes teared as she squinted against the hard, snow-reflected light. Her tiny mother hardly seemed a fair match for the fierce presence of Ivy. "You should go inside," Harrie said gently. "You're going to turn into a Momsicle. And I guess I'll go home."

"I'll give you a call after everyone's settled down."

"Okay," Harrie said, prickled by Dottie's tacit agreement that this house was no longer her home.

"You'll drive safely, won't you? Everything's going to be all right."

Harrie pulled her collar up around her neck and looked around the small compound composed of the house where she grew up, the outbuildings, the greenhouse, the symmetrical lines of evergreen trees, all coated with a fresh layer of snow. She was struck by how much she wanted to stay here, and by how much she wanted to leave. This place was where she used to live. Blackfern was where she wanted to live, but although she had marked the place as hers, she and it had no history together. And the future she was trying to project was not becoming concrete. It was sliding away.

Harrie heard the familiar squeal of kitchen door hinges, saw Julie and her father disappear behind it. She heard the door slam twice— once in reality and once again in her mind. Leaving Ivy behind hurt, not simply because she felt she'd failed, but because she knew Ivy would be in better hands with their parents.

"Tell Ivy . . . Tell everyone I said goodbye," she said, already feeling the loss of her sister's company. Now, without Dean and without Ivy, she would truly be alone.

"I'll call you tonight," Dottie said, rubbing her arms briskly. She hugged her middle daughter, then scurried toward the house.

⊡

The engine started easily and Harrie backed up carefully on the slippery ground. She honked the horn twice—good, bye—then eased the car out onto the service road. She slipped a tape into the tape deck— one of Dean's—and instantly the car was filled with Dean. She could nearly see him with her peripheral vision. It almost seemed as though she could put her hand out and touch his knee. But she knew the passenger seat, where only a few hours ago her sister had been sitting, was empty. And this emptiness stirred up a feeling she'd been denying and made her long fiercely for Dean.

The cellular car phone she hadn't needed but Dean had insisted she buy for road emergencies rested beside her. It was three o'clock in the afternoon, not a good time to call Dean at the office, she had learned, but she needed to hear the reassuring sound of his voice. They hadn't made rules regarding their separation, although there was an implied rule that casual phoning was out of bounds. So what if she just left a message on his answering machine at home? If she did that, she could hear his voice. And maybe when he got home and heard her message, he'd call her.

The light at Spode's only intersection turned yellow, then red. Harrie slowed her car carefully and came to a stop. She mentally rehearsed a few lines—*Hi. It's me. I'm just calling to say hello and that I miss you.* That sounded okay. Truthful. Not too needy. A return call would not be required, but it wouldn't be out of line if he decided to call her back. And it could provide an opening. If he called her, maybe he'd say, "Let's forget this separation nonsense. I miss you too."

Harrie lifted the receiver and pressed the buttons for the number that rang the phone by a platform bed in a room she could re-create in her mind down to the color of the stitching in the bedspread. She pressed the send button. It was like a prayer. Then she listened as Dean's voice told her he wasn't home. A beep tone followed his message and Harrie spoke the words she had practiced. And then, reluctantly, she hung up. She put the car into gear and waited for the light to change. She stared down at the phone. Now that she thought about it, her message was so short and so nondemanding that Dean might not call her back. And now that she'd committed herself to tape, she knew she really wanted to speak with him. Was dying to. How had she managed to fool herself into thinking that just hearing his voice would be enough?

The traffic light changed and Harrie drove through the small, aluminum-sided town. She passed the train station—an empty lean-to on a concrete platform between two tracks—then came to the ramp that would take her to the Expressway. At its entrance, Harrie stopped the car again. An idea presented itself. She knew the code that replayed the messages on Dean's answering machine. She could call again and this time listen to her own words. If they didn't sound compelling enough to provoke a return call, she could call again and leave another message. A better one. She looked in the rearview mirror. There was no one behind her. There was time. Harrie pressed the buttons on the car phone, savored Dean's voice once more, then pressed in the code that would play the message tape. At the signal, the tape rewound and began to play. But instead of hearing the words she had left, Harrie heard another voice, a female voice, and it sucked the warmth out of her body.

"It's Laura. I thought you'd be home by now . . ." Harrie's mouth fell open. She stared, eyes fixed on a dial in the dashboard. Who was this speaking? Laura who? Laura Taft! Harrie saw blond hair. Thin lips. Her own mouth was frozen open as the echoes of Laura's voice outraged and terrified her. Laura's tone was too familiar, too possessive. Didn't she know she was trespassing? Five days. Five days, and this woman had stepped in as naturally as if she'd been standing just outside the door waiting for Harrie to leave. "I thought you'd be home by now," she'd said. She knew Dean's movements that well!

But wait. She would miss what Laura was saying. Harrie tuned in. The confident voice left the time and date—yesterday evening. Quick. What did that mean? It meant that Dean hadn't picked up his messages from home since yesterday, or the tape would've been reset and Laura's message erased by her own. What were the implications of that? Dean hadn't gone home. Harrie's heart pounded hollow in her chest. *Boom. Boom.* A hard stick beating against an ice-cold drum. And the languid voice of the enemy rolled on. "I'll be home by eight, so why don't you come straight over? I hope you like veal. Will you bring the wine? Oh, heck. Maybe I can still catch you at the office. 'Bye."

And then there was a beep and Harrie heard her own sorry voice break the crackling silence that followed, telling Dean she missed him. How pathetic she sounded. How weak compared with the self-possessed Laura. The chill that had taken her over moments ago was replaced by an incandescent heat. She hated Laura. Hated her. Laura had slept with Dean—and that thought was so depleting and horrifying, Harrie blocked the temptation to imagine further. She slammed the phone down on its base. Terminate, she commanded herself. Halt.

Forget this. But the thoughts were there, of wine and a domestic cooking scene, and of blond hair— Stop! She should never have agreed to this break. Never. Half a loaf *was* better than none. She should have held on to what they had, been more patient. Been less demanding. Tried to work things out. But then, she'd never even considered that Dean would start seeing someone during their one-month break. Had she been stupid? A new, terrible thought occurred to her. Had Dean proposed this break *because* he wanted to see Laura?

A horn honked behind her. With an effort, Harrie dragged her eyes away from the tachometer and looked into the rearview mirror. There were two cars behind her and a clear road ahead. She put the car into gear and it lurched forward. Then she entered the stream of traffic in the outside lane and stayed in it, allowing all the cars around her to pass as she stared into a windshield that was nearly opaque from the blast of her hysterical thoughts. She had to get her mind organized; to think clearly and decide what to do. Should she call Dean? Confront him? She'd have to. She'd have to get to him before whatever was going on with Laura went any farther.

So decided, Harrie turned the car into the passing lane and sped toward home. She would call Dean when his workday was over at around five, and she would make a date with him. And if at all possible, she'd drive to New York tonight.

For the first time since she'd bought Blackfern, Harrie was oblivious to the splendors of the entrance drive to her house. She failed to salute the centaurs on the gateposts. She did not roll down the window so she could sniff the evergreens and hear the sound of the brook. She pulled into her parking spot so blindly that she only missed flattening the skeletal Mr. Schoonmaker by the skin of his down parka.

26

———□———

S
O HOW WAS IT?" Chip asked Dean. They were sitting together at the bar, drinking their beer from bottles as was more or less the custom at Nelson's.

Dean swallowed, set down the bottle, and was interrupted before he began to answer.

"Never mind. I didn't mean that. I really don't want to know."

"Jealous?" Dean asked with an irrepressible smirk.

"Not in the way you mean."

"We didn't do it," Dean said. He bit into a square of pizza. He was pretty sure they hadn't put any garlic in this stuff. He hoped not, anyway. He'd told Chip the truth but he also hoped if Chip asked him tomorrow, he could answer truthfully, "It was great."

"Huh," Chip said with apparent disinterest. He looked around the room. His eyes flickered over the two women he could see; one he knew and despised, the other one had the personality of a backhoe. He hadn't slept with anyone in so long he was starting to bird-dog again. He hated the feeling.

"She wanted to wait a little longer, you know?"

"That's all I hear these days. 'I want to get to know you better.' How can they get to know you when everything you do is based on your being sexually deprived?"

"It was nice. The cuddling and stuff." Especially the "stuff," he thought, a wave of arousal flowing over him. Little tiny bra. Little tiny panties. He could have ripped those silky scraps away with two fingers. Instead, he'd been a gentleman. He'd just taken off the bra. He shifted his weight on the barstool.

"So I guess it's over between you and Harrie."

"Not so fast, buddy."

263

"I didn't say anything. Although . . ."

"Not so fast."

"Don't worry. I'm not her type."

"I didn't say I was worried. You got a cigarette?"

Chip took a pack out of his pocket, laid it on the bar. Dean palmed the pack, shook out a cigarette, lit it with Chip's Zippo. "It's one of those things that you can't say no to," Dean said, inhaling the smoke. "It's better to be doing it in the open than sneaking around while I'm seeing Harrie."

"You don't mean Harrie knows about Laura?"

Dean gave Chip a look that said, "You must be kidding."

"So what do you mean 'in the open'? You're doing it in the park?"

"Give me a break."

"Well, I hope Laura's worth it. I hope either she's worth it or you get away with it. One or the other."

"Life is good," Dean said, exhaling pleasurably. "I just have the greatest feeling that this year has my name on it." He tapped his knuckles on the bar for luck, thought of Harrie tossing salt, wishing on stars, then guiltily flattened his hand. It wasn't that he felt completely clean about what he was about to do. It was more that he knew he was destined to be with Laura—maybe as a trial, maybe as more—and he just had to go with it. The pull was too strong. And what Harrie didn't know wouldn't hurt her. He cleared his throat. "Pretty fucking wonderful about the strike being settled. I feel like I've been given a new lease on life."

"Lucky son of a bitch. That's what you are," Chip said. "And more power to ya. Gotta say though, I'm glad those weren't my nuts in the wringer."

Dean nodded. "I deserved a break. I really did."

"So when are you seeing her again?" Chip asked morosely. Maybe he ought to get his hair cut. Maybe he ought to go to that AIDS benefit. There were always women at benefits. Maybe he ought to call Riva and see if she'd have breakfast with him. Maybe he ought to have a silicone implant put into his chin.

"She'll be here any time. Want to join us for dinner?"

"Yeah, sure."

Dean's face froze momentarily.

"Just kidding, Dean-o. Have a good time."

Dean thought about how he'd left his apartment the last time he'd been there. Seemed to him it was clean enough. He remembered loading the dishwasher and making the bed. He might not have put down the toilet seat lid. A little thing like that could bug a woman like Laura. She was a blue blood, all right. A little too much on the fastidious side, but that was a detail. Anyhow, he'd have time to whip into the bathroom real quick and make any minor adjustments. And he was glad he'd had a clean shirt at the office to change into. She'd be here soon. Maybe they'd have a drink first, then dinner in the Village—Pierre's on Waverly Place. With a little luck, she'd come home with him afterward. And they could pick up where they'd left off. In his mind, he tucked his hands into the back of Laura's small underpants. He'd cup her cool little ass; then, in one movement, those panties would be history.

⊡

Harrie braked the car with such force the seat belt across her chest threw her back against the seat.

"Eugene," she said, swinging open the door and unclasping herself from the harness. "Are you all right?"

The elderly man looked down at his feet dramatically. "No tire tracks. I'm fine."

"Thank God. What if I'd run you down?"

"You would have run down a damned fine lawyer."

"I'm awfully sorry," she said. She shut the door and looked up into the man's smiling face. He was wearing a sea captain's hat—an interesting accessory to the down coat, the too-short cuffed trousers, and the ever-present golf shoes. What was he doing here? She would've remembered if they'd made an appointment. People didn't drive out to see her every day, that was for certain. But what timing! Did he plan to stay long? She was going to be a wreck until she could call Dean. "I wasn't expecting to see anyone in my parking spot. I didn't know you were coming, did I?"

"No, no. I was in the neighborhood and I took a chance. I went up to the main house and took a stroll. Left my car over there," he said, pointing to a spot beside a giant rhododendron fifty feet away. "Nice young man's been showing me around."

"Uh-huh," Harrie said distractedly. It was just after five now. She could try Dean any time until six at the office. Sometimes he liked to play squash after six, which would work out fine with the plan she was making. While Dean played squash she could drive in to the city and meet him at his apartment by seven or seven-thirty. There they could talk. The results of this talk couldn't be calculated, but she had time to think about what she wanted to say. "Well, why don't you come in? Would you like some tea?"

"That would be wonderful," Mr. Schoonmaker said. "The place has really changed," he continued as they walked toward the cottage. "I can hardly believe how much progress you've made. And I looked at the plans. My, my. It's going to be grand."

"Well, with about twenty people working on it every day."

"So your architect says. What's his name again?"

"Roger Mayhew."

"Roger Mayhew. Seems like a very talented young man. And he's also your contractor."

"Right."

"He seems very capable."

Harrie opened the cottage door, took off her coat and helped her guest out of his.

"This is very nice. I don't believe I was ever actually in this building," he said, stooping slightly in the entranceway, then taking a few steps into the room. "Why, here are the famous Sidney and Angel—long time, no see." He made some kissing noises and touched a finger to the cage: a tasty invitation to a cockatoo. "Ouch, ya little stinker," he said in surprise.

"Sidney," Harrie admonished.

"I forgot these things were carnivores."

"We're a pretty dangerous crew," Harrie said. "First me with the car, then this bird."

"You know, it feels like England in here," Schoonmaker said. "All you need is a couple of corgi dogs. And a portrait of the queen."

"Come on in," Harrie said, switching on the lamp by the easy chair, moving quickly to the kitchen area and turning on the light over the stove. "And have a seat." She filled the kettle, lit the stove. How long would he want to stay? If she was to drive to New York, she was going to have to change her clothes. She stank of narcissus, her hair was dirty, and she'd really have to think about what she was going to wear. "What kind of tea would you like?" she asked, her voice rasping from her strained vocal cords. "The breakfast kind, or something herbal?"

"Whatever you're having, Harrie. I thought, as long as you're here, I might take you out to dinner. There's an old inn where we used to go for dinner, not too far from here . . ."

"Oh, I'm sorry, that just won't be possible tonight," Harrie said quickly. "In fact, I have to drive in to the city for dinner in just a little while."

"Could you use a lift in?"

"No, thanks. I'll need my car to get back."

"Maybe some other time," the lawyer said, leaning his head back in the chair.

"Maybe some other time," Harrie repeated nervously. "Would you like an ashtray?" Harrie found a glass condiment dish in the cupboard and brought it to her visitor. She returned to the kitchen and set two cups and saucers, milk and sugar, on a tray. She added loose tea to the flow-blue teapot Ivy had brought from the antique shop. The kettle whistled, and she quickly poured hot water into the teapot. She opened a box of cookies, spilled them out onto a plate, and took the loaded tray to the sitting area. Setting the tray down on the small coffee table, she unconsciously wiped her hands on the sides of her pants and gave Mr. Schoonmaker a look as if to say, "Will there be anything else?" She could have been a waitress wanting to go home after a long shift.

"Am I holding you up, Harrie?" the lawyer said in answer to her unspoken question.

"No, no. I'm sorry if I seem deranged . . . I'm kind of a wreck today, that's all. Family stuff," she added, putting a twisted smile on her face. Dean and Laura. Dean and Laura. Stop them. It was all she could think about.

"Don't apologize. I'm the one who should be sorry, bursting in on you without warning. Anyway, sit down. I won't keep you long. I've got good news for you."

"You do?" Harrie brought over an oak chair from the set of four at the table and positioned it across from the construction of long bones and knobby joints that made up Mr. Schoonmaker's frame.

She took her cup of tea from the tray and held it in her lap. She hadn't even thought about what Mr. Schoonmaker might want to tell her. She'd thought of him as an obstacle in her evening's plan from the moment she recovered from the near accident.

"I received a call this morning from Avis Murphy's lawyer."

"You did?"

"And he was very embarrassed."

"No kidding," Harrie said, letting out a sigh of relief. This *was* going to be good news. The part of her mind that had been worried about Avis Murphy but drowned out by her preoccupation with Dean moved to center stage.

"Uh-huh. In light of some hard evidence, Ms. Murphy broke down and confessed all: that David was not her real father, that she thought she could get away with her scheme because all of David's family were deceased."

"Wow," Harrie said automatically. As though she were watching a rerun of an old Perry Mason show, she listened while her lawyer told her about the work the detective agency had done, about the discovery of Avis's real father—a onetime bartender at the Frangipani who had moved to Key West shortly after Avis had been conceived— about the birth certificate that had been uncovered in the records department at City Hall. Harrie tried to match her expressions to Mr. Schoonmaker's, going so far as to drink her cold tea when he lifted his cup to his own mouth. Dean and Laura. Dean and Laura. Stop them.

"So your hearth and home are safe," Mr. Schoonmaker said, grandly stretching out his arms.

"I couldn't be happier," Harrie said, and stood up agitatedly. Her cup jiggled in its saucer. "You're really a lifesaver."

"Well, I guess I'll be going," the elderly gentleman said. He gave Harrie a curious look. "I hope whatever's worrying you turns out for the best."

"Thank you," she said, taking Mr. Schoonmaker's cup. She held his coat for him, handed him his hat, and, without putting on her own coat, walked him out to his car. She thanked him profusely for making his visit and said goodbye, waved briefly in the darkening end of day, then raced back to the cottage. There wasn't time anymore to take a bath, but at least she could shower. She discarded her clothes and, hobbled by her partially dropped jeans, hopped into the next room.

⊡

The light on Dean's answering machine was blinking in little sets of three. That meant three calls had been logged, and Dean couldn't imagine who they could be from. And he didn't have time to find out. He had hung up Laura's coat, left her with a stack of CDs to choose from, and was now doing a cursory cleanup job on his bed and bath.

That done, he returned to Laura. Amazing luck. He not only had a bottle of port but he had clean glasses in the bar. He opened the bottle, set up the glasses, and reflected approvingly on the last few hours. Dinner had been perfect. Pierre had made a fuss over them as he liked to do. The duck, the salad, the wine, the crème brûlée, the service, had all been just right. They had been wedged snugly into a corner of the small restaurant, their knees bumping, their legs finally fitting together, alternating, his, hers, his, hers, approximating a position he hoped they would be in, only lying down and without clothes, in the very near future. It was nine-thirty now, a little too early to be taking Laura off to bed, so he poured them each an inch or two of the ruby-colored wine, turned down the lighting so the lights from the World Trade Center would be that much more dramatic, and settled in with Laura. Then the phone rang.

Laura gave him a questioning look, but Dean let the phone ring the three rings until the answering machine picked up. He gave her a kiss.

When the phone rang again fifteen minutes later, he was ready to let the machine pick up once more, but Laura's expression indicated that she didn't understand why he wouldn't take his calls. Or rather, she understood that his not taking the calls meant something. Something she didn't like.

⊡

Harrie was still in her bathrobe. It had become clear, even to her manic self, that she wouldn't be driving into Manhattan tonight. What had started out as a risky-but-I-gotta-do-it idea had now become a better-to-die-than-do-it former idea. Still, she was loaded with emotion. Wherever Dean was, no matter how innocent he might be, the long hours of wanting to talk to him had built up a critical mass of fear and anger that seemed impossible to discharge without an explosion.

Her call to Dean at his office had been intercepted by Dean's secretary, who told her Dean had just left for the day. No, Elise said, she didn't know where he had gone. The call to Dean's squash club yielded her nothing. Mr. Carrothers had not booked a court. The call at 6:01 to Dean's apartment was received by his answering machine. She left a simple "It's Harrie. Please call me when you get in." She called at six-thirty and hung up when Dean's recorded voice came on. She hung up again at seven, seven-thirty, and eight. After that, she called information, got Laura Taft's number, called it just to see if Laura would answer, knowing she would hang up if Laura did answer, and the result of this reckless game was a lucky null score. Laura's machine answered, Harrie got to hear Laura's voice, and then, unwitnessed, unrecorded, she hung up.

At nine o'clock, Harrie took stock. What had actually happened? Dean had had dinner at Laura's last night. He hadn't picked up his messages, but maybe he'd gotten in late, forgotten to listen to his machine, gotten up early this morning and left for work without giving his machine a thought.

This was an improbable scenario, but it was possible.

Or . . . Dean had had dinner with Laura and spent the night. If that was true then nothing could change it. It was done. So, what else? Today she'd left two messages on his machine. One, that she missed him. Two, to please call her when he got in. The compulsive calls had gone unregistered, so as far as Dean knew, Harrie had just checked in a couple of times. She had not disgraced herself. She was in full, or mostly full, possession of her pride, and she also had over two years of history with Dean. All of that history could not be overturned by one night in bed with Laura. No matter how good she was. Sooner or later, Dean would get the messages she'd left and he would call her. He would not ignore her. So. What she should do is cool it. And wait for him to call.

Harrie took off her underwear and put on her pajamas, her robe, her fluffy slippers. She rearranged the chair by the fireplace, turned on the small television, poured herself a snifter of Rémy, and let the birds out. She put the cordless phone on the table beside the chair and tried to get interested in a sitcom she had never seen before.

Where was Dean? Why wasn't he home? Was he at Laura's again? Where *was* he? Sidney flapped around the room. He landed heavily on a curtain rod, chewed at a toenail for a minute, uttered a few sage cockatoo words, then took off again to touch down on the mantel clock. Angel walked across the back of Harrie's chair and climbed onto her head, whereupon the big bird began to nibble gently on Harrie's hair. Harrie thought she could be a statue. She sat as still as one, eyes fixed on the television, hands folded in her lap, letting the bird take whatever liberties it wanted to take. And still Harrie didn't move. If she moved, she was sure she would break into a million pieces. The phone rang.

Harrie grabbed at the receiver and a great flutter of peach-colored feathers flew up and away. "Hello," she said tentatively.

"Cakes, it's me," said Dottie. The letdown felt almost physical. Where was Dean? Harrie listened as her mother told her the aftermath of the afternoon. Futile conversations with Ivy had begun with pleading and had ended with recriminations on both sides. Denials by Ivy and a search by Bill of Ivy's bathroom that turned up glassine envelopes of white powder in the core of a roll of toilet tissue dressed with a toilet-tissue-roll doll Dottie had crocheted with her own hands.

Harrie listened to her mother's words, which layered pain on top of more pain, and she was powerless to do more than murmur "Oh, no" and "Poor Ivy." When her mother said good night at last, Harrie found she still held the phone in her hand, and if it was possible, she now wanted to talk with Dean even more. The cognac was gone, the birds were cuddling on the curtain rod.

She called him.

When the machine picked up, Harrie hung up.

She was still innocent, still where she had been at six o'clock. The bottle of cognac beckoned from the old art deco vitrine. She brought the bottle to the rickety little side table beside the easy chair. Thick amber liquid filled the bowl-shaped glass in her hand. Fifteen minutes went by and Harrie called Dean again.

⊡

He should've turned the ringer off when he had the chance, Dean thought. "Excuse me. I'll be right back," he said to Laura.

"I'd like to use the john," she said.

Dean pointed the way, went to the phone in his bedroom, sat down on the bed, and, with a foreboding he couldn't explain to himself, picked up the receiver.

"Hello," he said.

"It's me."

"Harrie." He was startled and he was not. The flashing light on his answering machine blinked malevolently at him. Harrie must have been the caller. Of course.

"Hi," he said, putting some enthusiasm into his greeting, praying all the while that Harrie wanted something short and sweet. Or something he could call her back about tomorrow. His hope disappeared as Harrie said, "Dean, I think we have to talk."

·

Harrie was so startled by the sound of Dean's actual voice, she almost dropped the phone. He sounded so natural. There was no pent-up anxiety in his voice. No guilt when he said "Hi." She was confused. What now? Pretend nothing was wrong? Make small talk with him for a few minutes? Make a dinner date for later in the week? Yes, that's what she should do. Make a dinner date with him. "Dean," she said, a seminormal beat returning to her stoked-up heart, "I think we have to talk."

·

Dean had been listening to the sound of water running. Now the bathroom door was opening. In seconds, Laura would be walking past his door. Anything louder than a whisper would be overheard, and unless he wanted to close his bedroom door, an act that would have to be explained, Laura would be able to hear every word as if he were sitting beside her. His loft was large, but the vast expanse of wooden floors carried every nuance of sound. He heard the bathroom door being closed again and the clacking of heels on the oak floor. "Okay," he said tersely. "But this isn't a good time."

Harrie clutched the phone. Her mouth fell open for the second time that day. She hadn't wanted to talk to him on the phone, she'd wanted to set up a date, and now, without warning, he'd thrown a lance into her belly. "This isn't a good time"—synonymous the world over with, there's semeone here. Someone who shouldn't hear us talking. Someone who counts more than you do.

"What do you mean?" she asked, pushing the small amount of air she had left in her lungs into her larynx. Let there be a pot on the stove. Let him say his boss is there. Anything but . . .

"I just can't talk right now," said Dean. This was cruel, but he felt helpless. Laura's shadow fell across the threshold to his bedroom before it moved on. He couldn't look up, afraid his guilty feelings would show on his face. This was so unfair. Didn't Harrie realize? He had to find out. She had to let him go so he could find out.

"Laura's there, isn't she?" Harrie heard her detached voice say to Dean. How little passion there was in her question. Perhaps she had died.

How did she know? How could she possibly know? Had Chip told her? No one else knew. Or was it her damned intuition? Or some weirdo in a shoe store? "Harrie," Dean said miserably.

"Yes," she replied calmly in someone else's voice. It was true. There was no way to avoid knowing what she knew. Laura was there. In Dean's apartment. Maybe at this minute lying in his bed.

"Harrie, let's get together for lunch this week. I'm not sure exactly what day I'm free . . ."

"Lunch?"

"Or dinner. I don't have my book with me. Can I call you to-morrow?"

The brew made up of one part fear, one part anger, and one part first-rate cognac exploded at last. *"Lunch? Your book? Who the hell do you think you're talking to?"*

"Harrie," Dean pleaded. "I said—"

"Forget it, Dean. Forget I called."

"Harrie."

"Go fuck yourself. Okay?" And Harrie slammed the phone down so hard on its base that the little table supporting it buckled at the knees and fell with the phone, the lamp, and the bottle of cognac into a satisfying heap of rubble onto Harrie's floor.

·

Laura set her glass of port down carefully on the table as Dean approached her. "That was Harrie?" she asked.

Dean nodded.

"I thought you told me the two of you had broken up."

"We did break up."

"Dean, I'm sorry, but I'm going to call a car now, if you don't mind."

"A car? Why?"

"It's been a lovely evening. Really. But I'd like to go home."

"Because of what just went on."

"Yes. I suppose. I didn't mean to eavesdrop but . . ."

She indicated the open space with a graceful flick of her hand.

Dean nodded again.

"Things are still a bit messy right now. You should probably be by yourself tonight."

"Actually, Laura . . ." Dean began to protest.

"I just wouldn't feel right," she said with finality. "It would be like dining on someone else's . . . I don't know . . . bones. I'll just be a minute."

Dean watched Laura's hips as she walked away from him. Then he sat down on the couch and leaned back heavily. He stared at the millions of lights he could see from his window and let his eyes go out of focus. He heard Laura calling the car service. Heard her hang up the phone. He heaved a sigh. She was smart. It would be hours before his head emptied of Harrie's anger. After Laura left, he should call Harrie back. He'd been miserable to her. He'd let the thrill of the hunt, or whatever it was that made men the slaves of their cocks, get the better of his humanity to a woman who'd been the best part of his life to date. "You're absolutely right," he said to Laura as she stepped around the glass coffee table. He reached up and took her hand and she sat down again beside him.

"The car will be here in twenty minutes or so."

He nodded. "Some more port?"

"No," she said. She put one hand to Dean's face. "I've had enough for one night."

Dean took her hand and kissed it. Then he held her in a delicate embrace.

·

Harrie stood still and listened to every molecule in the small space reverberate. The aftershock of the table crash seemed to echo around her. The birds, their irises contracting and expanding furiously, were shrieking their heads off, and the sitcom laugh track added an extra helping of dementia to the din. Harrie shut off the television. Then she collected the birds with a broomstick and nudged them into their cage. She mopped up the spill, put shards of glass in the trash. She righted the lamp and gathered up a heap of papers that had been scattered. When order was restored, the birds covered in their cage, the quiet of the night reestablished, Harrie sat down in her chair. The newborn silence was absolute. She could be in an isolation tank. Or an underground tomb. There wasn't a squeal of a brake or honk of a horn or a voice other than the repetitious one that circled inside her head querying madly, "Now what are you going to do? Now what are you going to do?" She was drunk, and alone, and as far as she knew, she hadn't a friend in the world. She was a statue again, and everyone knew that statues had no answers for stupid nagging voices.

A piece of paper beside Harrie's foot summoned her with the audacity of its brightness. Reluctantly, she picked it up. It was a sketch of a piece of molding annotated in a radically neat, draftsman's hand. A "very talented young man" had drawn this. He had been described as such by her adopted uncle, Eugene Schoonmaker, Esquire. What better reference could a person have? Say, hey. Roger was her friend. Maybe Roger was her only friend in the world. Actually, it made a lot of sense to pick up that phone once more and call him.

So that's what she did.

27

---◻---

WHEN HARRIE AWOKE, the sky was the plummy-black color of the inside of a mussel shell. She could see the barest outline of the branches of the crab apple tree outside her window. When she turned her head just slightly to the right, she could make out a large form on the bed beside her. The form was breathing heavily. It was Roger. She marveled at this fact for a moment; then before she had a chance to protect herself, the significance of Roger's being there struck with terrible force. Dean and Laura. They had been together. *Dean had slept with another woman.* She wanted to scream and would have, but Roger's presence stopped her. So she did the only other thing she could do. She disconnected her conscious thoughts as surely as if she had pulled a phone out of its jack.

◻

When Harrie awoke for the second time, the light was pearly gray. She could see the shriveled black fruit that clung tenaciously to the crab apple tree, and when she turned her head toward Roger, she could see that the T-shirt he wore was brown, and that the blankets were folded neatly under his arms. She took one of her own arms and placed it next to his. Objectively, she compared these two arms as though they were sculptures, not living limbs. His arm was bare, covered by a pale blond shimmer. Hers was covered by a blue pajama sleeve. Her hand was small, her fingers tapered, and Roger's hand had rivers of veins flowing across the surface. His knuckles were darker than the rest of his skin, and his fingernails were torn, as though he'd used them as screwdrivers.

Harrie had watched these hands a lot in the last four months. It had been much easier to look at Roger's hands, scribbling, hammering, holding a teacup, then it had been to look into his intense blue-green eyes. Last night, Roger had used his hands to stroke her back and to rub her neck, and she wanted to take one of these hands into her own, just to thank it. But she didn't. She turned her eyes upward and looked at the ceiling.

The ceiling was still tinted gray by the morning light but she knew its true color was creamy white. She'd mixed the color herself, had dribbled a little yellow paint into the white, once upon a time when she'd been a happier person. She'd also picked out the wallpaper and the border of vines that now wound around the room just under the molding. The vines and the north light and the low ceiling and the smallness of the room made it seem like a burrow just right for two. And this thought made her eyes burn, so she covered them quickly with her hand and pressed at them to make the tears go away. Why wasn't Dean beside her in this bed?

She could almost see him: spiky clumps of hair rearranged by sleep, the beginnings of beard shading his face, the white T-shirt and blue shorts he always slept in. Had he slept in his shorts with Laura? No. She would not picture that. She would not picture him in shorts because that thought made her think of him taking them off and she would *not* imagine Dean aroused. She would not! God. She bit the web of skin between her thumb and forefinger until it hurt. Maybe nothing had happened. Maybe she'd made it all up.

An image imposed itself: Dean in his wide bed, the lights sparkling pinpoints outside the wall of windows, and Laura in one of Dean's shirts. Unbuttoning it. Dean in his T-shirt, his erection straining against his blue cotton boxers—a part of him that she felt exclusively hers. The image overwhelmed her. Her body went hollow and cold and it filled with seawater. She tried to hold the water in but it seeped out through the slits in her eyes. She wrapped an arm across her eyes, then covered that arm with the other. She sobbed silently, trying hard not to shake the bed. And then she fell back asleep.

⊡

In her dream, Harrie was standing with Dean at the seawall. His hair was blond and his shirt, which was unbuttoned, was billowing around him. They were looking out across the water and Dean was pointing out the mountains he would cross. He was excited and happy and he

was including her in his happiness. But not in his plans. She wanted
to ask him about this omission, but she couldn't speak. She could
only look up at his face, which was limned with the blinding light of
the sun. Then he encircled her with his arms and pulled her to him.
Harrie snuggled in close. She felt safe now. This was where she belonged. "I'll always love you," he said.

·

When Harrie awoke, she was with Dean. Her arm was across his
chest and her hand gripped a thick fold of his T-shirt. But the color
was wrong. And the expanse of chest. She knew before she looked
at Roger's sleeping face that she'd made a mistake, that she wasn't
lying with her lover but with an impostor—albeit a friendly impostor.
One to whom she'd gone crying last night. One who had dropped
whatever plans he might've had and come to her aid. He had hugged
her, made tea, fetched tissues, listened to her, really listened to her
without giving her advice. And then he'd taken off her shoes and
made her step out of her jeans, which she'd worn over her pajamas,
and he'd tucked her into bed. She didn't remember him tucking himself
in afterward, but it was cold last night, and it was late, and he hadn't
made any sexual moves, so there was nothing wrong with his coming
into her bed fully clothed as he was.

Was this innocent sleeping together all that Dean had done with
Laura? Had she jumped on him too hard? Too fast? "I can't talk to
you right now," he'd said. If the phone rang right this minute and it
was Dean, she would talk to him. She would talk to him and wouldn't
worry about what Roger heard or thought. Dean had been guilty,
guilty, guilty. *Want to have lunch? Fuck you.* See him on the first day
of March? She'd see him in hell first. Harrie stroked the fabric under
her fingers, a very natural thing to do, except for one thing. She'd
never stroked Roger's anything before. She stopped her hand. It was
nice to lie in someone's arms, even if they were only the arms of a
friend.

Harrie sighed and separated herself from the warmth of Roger's
unconscious embrace. She turned toward the window, took a pillow
into her arms to hug, and tucked up her knees. Instinctively, Roger
followed Harrie, matching her curled position by coiling around her.

Harrie froze as Roger wrapped his arms around her and pressed hard against her. She felt a jolt of pure desire and her reaction was almost instantaneous. She straightened her body, turned back around to face him, and with both hands against his chest, she pushed Roger away.

⊡

When Roger woke up, the light in the room was pearly gray. Harrie was in his arms sleeping fitfully. She'd had a rough time, the kind of time you wouldn't wish on a dog. Not that the breakup had been a surprise to him. It had been fucking inevitable, although Harrie deserved a softer landing than she'd gotten. Dean had been sleeping with another woman, for Christ's sake. What a jerk he was to give up this woman who had everything. Smart, funny, beautiful. Triple threat. He'd had an aching hard-on all night, but he liked Harrie too much to take advantage, and besides, he knew bad timing when he saw it. With no other place to put it, Roger placed his free hand on Harrie's hip. His left arm had gone to sleep long ago, but he didn't know how to get it loose without waking her up. And he didn't want to do that. If he woke her up, she might get out of bed, and he wanted to lie with her for as long as he could.

⊡

When Roger woke again, he was curled up beside Harrie, who had half turned and was struggling against him. Her two small hands were pushing at his chest, and if he hadn't felt so aroused by this ineffectual motion, he would have laughed. Instead, he held on to her more tightly, bent his head, and kissed her.

⊡

The moment Roger's mouth touched hers, Harrie felt as though she had burst into flames. This kiss was more than lips and tongue and teeth; it was a torch to the inflammable stuff that had once been her body. She became keenly aware of the strength of his body, and the feel of his hair in her fingers, and the exquisite sensation of those hands of his sliding beneath the silk of her pajamas, pulling at them, making them disappear. And then she was fumbling with a zipper and with a particularly challenging T-shirt, and with socks that she toed off her feet. And then all of the clothing was gone and Harrie held him hard and naked against the entire length of her. She could hardly breathe.

"I'm dying for you," he said.

"I want you too," she said so softly she could hardly hear herself. *Dean,* she thought, but she didn't complete the unspoken sentence. The fragments were *stop me, don't let him, so there, take that, I still love you*—but all of these mental scraps were swept aside by the violence of her desire to have and be had by Roger.

If making love with Dean was so natural it felt as though she were making love to the other half of herself, making love with Roger was an experience so unique it felt as though she'd never made love before. To start with, he touched every part of her with his huge, rough hands, and the part that he'd most recently touched stayed hot and eager until he touched it again. The mouth that had kissed her so that she had obsessed about the kiss for days afterward loved kissing all of her, not just her mouth, but when it returned to her mouth, it took her on a journey to places she'd never imagined before. When Roger entered her, she climaxed, instantly. And she was so startled by this, she opened her eyes wide into the smiling face of the titan above her. "Come for me again, Harrie," she heard him say, and the words themselves caused her to make the climb again. And what she was thinking before she fell, as she was holding on to Roger for dear life, was that after this, nothing would ever be the same.

28

---□---

EAN STOOD at the bar and drank his Perrier while waiting for his father. He'd wanted Laura to join them, but Laura felt that he and his father ought to have dinner alone, and although he wasn't dying to be alone with his father for three hours, he'd agreed. Laura always seemed to know what people should do. It must be nice to always know what to do.

The bartender filled a dish and set it down beside Dean. Dean chewed an almond and looked at himself in the mirror behind the bar. He looked better than he'd ever hoped he would look. At Laura's suggestion, he'd let his hair grow out to all one length. And he'd replaced his horn-rims with FDR frames complete with sunglass attachment and its attendant roll bar. American classics made in Italy, also suggested by Laura. And since he'd begun running with Laura every morning, he could run six miles a day without breaking a sweat. Dean sighed. He looked great, he was in good shape, he had a gorgeous girlfriend, and he was making money.

So why, if he was so happy, was he sighing all the time?

"Dad," he said, sighting his father in the entranceway. His father lifted his hand in a wave, and checked his coat.

"Had to park the car on the other side of Fifth," Robertson Carrothers said, coming toward his son, touching him awkwardly on the shoulder. His short gray hair was windblown and his cheeks were pink from the long walk.

"How was the drive in?" Dean asked.

"Fine, fine."

The two followed the maître d' to their table and ordered drinks.

"You look good, son. Success agrees with you," said Carrothers, offering a sliver of smile. He lifted his glass.

Dean touched his glass to his father's and acknowledged the compliment. "I guess I was due for a hit."

"Nothing lucky about it, Dean." The older man drank thirstily from his glass, refilled it. "You took a risk. It got shaky for a while but you held firm when others would have bailed out. That took guts. I'm proud of you."

"Thanks, Dad," Dean said. He felt the blood move up past his collar and warm his ears. Well, here it was, the approval he'd waited his whole life to get, and all he could think to say was "Thanks, Dad." What else could he say? The truth? It was a fluke, Dad. My new girlfriend handed me the deal. I almost blew it because I was asleep at the controls. I didn't hold firm. I hung on for dear life, and no thanks to me the damned plane pulled out of its nosedive and flew straight.

"Very proud of you," his father said again.

"Look, Dad," Dean started.

"Hmm?"

The waiter came to the table and recited the daily specials. His father ordered a steak, and Dean, who would have liked to order the same, asked for grilled swordfish. He'd been recently reminded about the dangers of animal fat. Laura again.

"What were you about to say?" Robertson Carrothers asked his youngest son. He broke open a roll and buttered it lavishly.

"I don't— I'd like you to meet Laura sometime," he said, losing his nerve. "She's really something." He looked around the room. The restaurant was an archetypal New York steakhouse: no-frill interior decoration, white tablecloths, tan wallpaper, ceiling-mounted light fixtures, and late-middle-aged waiters who had worked in the restaurant forever. There were only three women in the whole place, and two of them were wearing suits. The rest of the restaurant's patrons were businessmen dining out on their expense accounts. Laura would have really stood out in here.

His father spoke. "Why'd you give Harrie up? I liked her. And she seemed to adore you."

"It's complicated," Dean said shortly. There was that weird acceptance from his father again. What exactly had he liked about Harrie? It was so typically perverse of his father to be asking about

Harrie when here he was, practically announcing that he'd finally found the right woman.

"Try me. I'm not a fossil, you know."

Dean blinked. He took off his glasses, polished the lenses on his napkin. He'd never talked about women with his father. In fact, he'd never been successful talking about anything personal with his father. So how was he going to discuss something he found hard to understand himself? "It's not that. It's hard to explain."

"Hmmm."

Was his father losing interest? Dean considered letting the subject drop. He considered picking a neutral topic from the day's news. He considered talking up a new issue of stock that he'd been thinking of buying for himself. But he found himself saying, "I loved Harrie, but she wasn't the right girl for me. I know how that sounds, but that's the best way to say it. She was just—even though I loved her—that house in the boondocks just tore it. Laura's much more . . . right."

"Right for what?"

The older man stared at Dean. His look implied that this was a serious question that demanded a serious answer. Dean stared back. He knew he was blathering, but why didn't his father understand? If he could look at Harrie and Laura in a side-by-side comparison, like in a TV-commercial product demo, the truth would be obvious. But his father had never met Laura. Dean pictured the horrible Christmas Day in Connecticut: Harrie in her yellow outfit with the holly corsage. His stiff-necked brothers. His tight-assed sisters-in-law. If he had brought Laura to Christmas dinner, the whole family would have fallen in love with her. "Just *right*," he said with exasperation. "Vassar, the Cosmopolitan Club. She's well connected. She works on the Street. Laura really adds to my life. We'd make a good team if we decide to get married." Dean looked at his father as if to say, "You know what I mean," but his look was met with a perplexed expression. "Like Mother was good for you," Dean explained patiently.

"Like *your* mother?" His father laughed, a raspy, snorty, unpleasant little chuckle.

Dean looked away. He tore off a bit of roll and chewed it. He hadn't meant to say what he'd said, but so what? Why was his father laughing?

"Your mother. You've really idealized the woman, you know that, Dean. You always did." A remnant of the original laugh returned for an encore.

"What are you talking about? What do you mean?"

Hot plates of food were delivered. On one was a bare piece of swordfish and a mound of something orange, pumpkin maybe, and next to the mound was a plop of something wet and green—spinach or escarole. The other plate was covered with a grill-branded steak that overlapped the sides, and a haystack of thin fried potatoes, salty and glistening with oil. Dean swallowed. He watched as his father turned the plate with his fingertips until his steak was facing just the right way.

"Want some of these fries?"

"No. Thanks."

"Huh." Carrothers asked the waiter for steak sauce and catsup, then applied the condiments liberally. "You idealized her," he said, thumping the catsup bottle. "You made her a saint. I guess it was natural. You were still practically a baby when she died." He delivered this statement with no sentiment. His eyes were focused on his food.

"But I *remember* her. She was wonderful." Couldn't his father see himself? He was so crude. Didn't he see how marrying Sarajane Winston had polished up his act, how the very fact of her lineage had positioned the family in a better way?

"Oh, she was wonderful, all right. But she wasn't a saint. She drank, you know." The senior Carrothers sliced into his steak. Blood flowed from the gash.

"Everyone drinks," Dean said pointedly. Shit. Couldn't he just go out with his father for a dinner and eat? Did it have to be a major high-blood-pressure event every time? Whatever glow he could have gotten from the praise his father had mistakenly awarded him had dissipated long ago. "She *helped* you. She helped you get where you are today."

The raspy chuckle returned. His father shook his head ruefully, stabbed a piece of meat and held it in the air. "I know you think Sarajane was this perfect wife, but you don't know. You don't know the times I had to carry her out of a dinner party over my shoulder like a sack of grain."

"Come on, Dad," Dean said, holding in his anger. "You're exaggerating."

"No, I'm not." He chewed on a mouthful of steak. "What do you think killed her?"

"She had cancer," Dean answered. What was his father doing? Playing with him? "She had cancer. That's what you told me."

"Yeah. Well. Let it be. Let it be."

Dean dropped his silver into the plate holding his untouched fish. His hands clenched the sides of the table. His anger was huge and unstoppable. He hissed at his father, "How dare you? How dare you patronize me about something like this?"

The older man looked startled. Then the muscles of his face lengthened; his eyelids drooped. "I'm sorry, Dean. I forget sometimes that you didn't know her."

"Stop saying that. I *knew* her. I *loved* her. If it hadn't been for her . . ." Dean stopped talking. How could he say what he meant? If it hadn't been for his mother, he wouldn't have felt loved by anyone. Until he met Harrie. His throat was swollen shut and his eyes felt gritty behind his glasses. He would not cry in this restaurant in front of his father, he would not. It was his own fault. This was entirely the wrong time and the wrong way to be talking to his father. The thing to do with him was to be very cool. Limit himself to topics that didn't matter. Do as his father did. What was wrong with him anyway? Why was he looking at him that way?

"I know I haven't been a very good father," he said quietly.

Dean rocked back in his chair. "What?" If his father had said he dressed in women's underwear, he could not have been more surprised.

"I've been meaning to . . . I'm not very good at this. I want you to understand the way it was. I had three little boys and a sick wife and I didn't know how to handle all of you."

"Dad," Dean said helplessly. His anger was suddenly gone, but his urge to cry nearly overwhelmed him.

"I hope you can understand what I'm trying to say," Dean's father said to the wineglass he was gripping. His voice fluctuated in his throat as though there were a flutter valve where his larynx used to be. "Men were men twenty years ago. We didn't wet-nurse our sons. Didn't talk to them like the fathers these days talk to their kids. 'What are you feeling?'—that kind of fairy shit. You played ball with your kids. And you taught them to box." He lifted the glass to his mouth and drank. Then set the empty glass down hard. He half turned to look at Dean. "You weren't so good at ball, so I gave you money."

"You played ball with me . . ."

Rob Senior waved away Dean's words. "You don't have to make it easy for me. I'm just sorry it's taken so long for me to, uh, apologize, son." He turned his eyes from Dean and moved his wine glass back and forth in a six-inch-long path.

Dean felt depleted and at the same time filled up. He had never seen his father vulnerable before. Even on the day of the funeral, the man had been calm. Dean stretched a hand out and touched his father's sleeve. He wanted to give something back. "It's okay, Dad. I'm okay."

"I know that," his father said gruffly. He straightened his jacket and appeared to regain his composure. "I'm glad things are working out for you."

Dean blurted, "I got lucky with that deal, Dad."

"What's that?"

"Isletrek. It could have gone either way. I got lucky."

"It doesn't matter."

"It does matter. It matters a lot. I don't think I'm very good at the brokerage business." Christ. Now what? Now what was going to happen? Dean felt his father's hand on his shoulder. He looked up.

"Luck is part of the game. And it's never really luck, anyway. It just seems like it. You'll be lucky again. You'll see."

Dean nodded. He picked up his fork and broke off an edge of his fish. If he'd been offered a million dollars to his one that he would have this conversation with his father, he wouldn't have taken the bet. He was still trying to assimilate this new sense of closeness to his father, when the older man spoke.

"So, tell me about this new girl."

Dean chewed, swallowed, then told his father about Laura. He talked about how they met, what she looked like, what he liked about her, and as he did he had to fight off the unwanted realization he was coming to—just by listening to the mechanical sound of his own voice—that the right girl was the wrong girl after all. He half listened as his father changed the subject to the trip he was taking to the West Coast in the next week, and he managed to nod in the right places and look interested while his father described his plans. But his mind was back to this morning.

Dean had been lying in bed beside Laura, when his watch alarm sounded. He'd pressed the little button to silence the beep and then turned to look at her. Her hair was fanned out across the pillow like a sheaf of gold. Gently, he reached out a finger and touched her hair, and then he stroked her temple. He saw her eyelids quiver. She was awake. He had a hard-on, but he was nervous. What if he touched her and she said no, as she often did? He made a decision. You couldn't have a relationship with someone and feel afraid to touch her, so he propped himself up on one arm and cupped her shoulder. Gray eyes looked at him lovingly, and he kissed her. She responded to his kiss—he heard the excited intake of her breath over the sound of his own—and he put his hand under the sheets and allowed his palm to graze her breasts. She put her arms around his neck and deepened the kiss, and so he ran his hand down her flank. "Stop," she said. And with a sickening sense of disappointment, he stopped.

Laura had clung to him then, kissed his neck, and halfheartedly, in response, he'd rubbed little calming circles with his hand to the small of her back. To his surprise, he heard her breathing accelerate. She moaned weakly and fitted herself to him, and as he pressed himself against her warmth he heard her say, "I can't. It feels . . ."

"It feels what?" he asked. His erection had already begun to flag. "It feels . . ."

"Too good," he finished for her.

"I'm sorry," she said into his shoulder. "I just get frightened when I feel myself going out of . . . Let me try again."

And she'd obediently opened her legs to him, and even if he could have entered her, he didn't want to anymore. All he could do was take her into his arms, so he did that. She relaxed while he stroked her beautiful hair, and as he lay there in Laura's bed he thought about Harrie. He thought about how their lovemaking had been wild and free and how Harrie had always been eager for him. If anything, he'd held himself back with her. He'd had a reason. He hadn't wanted to really give himself until he felt he could commit. How controlling he'd been, he realized now. How sickening. Harrie had been right when she said she deserved better, and she was right to hate him. When he called her these days, she was all business and very cool. It killed him not to be able to do the simplest thing with Harrie, see her, touch her arm or her cheek—simple pleasures he'd taken far too much for granted.

"What are you thinking about?" His father's words recalled him.

Dean collected himself, rearranged his expression into a smile. "I was thinking about Laura." *Your mother wasn't a saint,* he heard his father say. "Laura's really special." And as he said this he felt his heart revolt, and pull him toward Harrie.

29

---□---

*H*ARRIE. IT'S DEAN."

"Hi."

"Am I calling at a bad time? Because I'll—"

"No."

"Good . . . So, how are you?"

"Fine. How are you?"

"Okay. Not really. I miss you."

"Well, I miss you too."

"Um. I'd like to see you . . . Would you like to get together?"

"Dean. Are you seeing Laura? Because if you are, I want to know now."

"Harrie."

"I mean it, because I don't want to get all worked up to have lunch with you so you can tell me you're seeing Laura and you're sorry things turned out this way between us."

"Harrie."

"That's yes, I take it."

"Listen, just because I'm seeing her—"

"Doesn't mean what, Dean? That we can't be friends?"

"You're not giving me a chance."

"Oh, please . . . Okay, tell me what you want to tell me."

"I'm very confused."

"I'm not going to do this. I'm not going to compete for you . . . I'm furious with you, Dean. I really hate your guts right now."

"I know. I'm sorry."

"I've gotta go."
"I'll call you next week."
"I can't talk to you anymore."
"Okay, I'll call you—"
"Goodbye."
" 'Bye."

30

———□———

Harrie and Desiree were hunched over a little octagonal table at The Peacock Caffe, a coffeehouse in Greenwich Village. All of the tables were small and eccentric, and the seats were ice-cream-parlor chairs. Even though it was midday, the April sun barely bothered to look in the window at the front of the room, so the tone of the place was determined by the wooden walls and dark-stained floors. It was a brown kind of place. Like coffee.

"You don't get it, Harrie. You deserted me," Desiree said. She put down the dry anisette biscuit she'd been nibbling and wiped her fingers daintily with a napkin. Harrie could see that Des's hands were shaking.

"To be fair I didn't desert you. I just moved," Harrie said gently.

"You moved. *And* you deserted me. You only call me when you've got a problem. What about when I've got a problem? I've been seriously distressed for the last three months, not that you'd know it."

"But we've spoken during that time. Why didn't you say anything?"

"I didn't feel like it."

"Oh."

Desiree hoisted her cappuccino, which sloshed dangerously toward the edge of the cup.

"You wanted me to guess?"

"You used to know how I was feeling because we talked three times a day. You didn't have to guess, but if you'd had to, you could have."

"Aw, Des. I'm sorry." Harrie watched as Des set down her cup and dabbed at tears in the corners of her eyes. She did this in a very precise way, as though she were blotting dust specks, not the effects of anger and pain. Harrie reached out and touched her friend's arm. "Please tell me what's going on."

"What *was* going on."

"What *was* going on," Harrie said agreeably.

"How would you like to be on Nutrafast two meals a day for three months? And Smoke-stoppers?"

"Both at the same time? Are you crazy?"

"I guess so, thanks very much."

"Why'd you do it? You look great." And Des did look great. Despite the smudges under her eyes, her face glowed as though it were carved from a seashell. Her thick, tangled hair was glossy and full, and her red wool dress, a long sweater really, flattered her curves.

"Thanks."

"Des. What happened?"

"You mean, how did I come to put on twenty pounds? How come I started smoking again?"

"Do you want me to beg?"

"Yes, please."

"Okay. Woof." Harrie assumed the classic dog begging position.

Desiree laughed. "That's better." She wound a curl around her finger and tilted her heart-shaped face upward as she reflected. "It was Anthony," she said. "He cooked. Like all the time, and his favorite thing was to have me over and be his assistant while he whipped up things. And he didn't believe in using light-type ingredients. So it was all heavy cream and real mayonnaise and pan-fried this and deep-fried that, and it was awful. You know how I like to eat. I love to eat. But I can restrain myself, you know? Or do penance. If I'm a bad dog one day, I cut way back the next."

Harrie nodded. "Sure, I know."

"But with Anthony, there was no getting away from fat food. If I cooked, he hated what I made."

"He told you he hated your cooking? How charming."

"I know. He'd tell me how the fish would taste better if I'd sautéed it in butter. Or he'd ask for Roquefort dressing. And I just got so self-conscious I couldn't cook for him anymore. And he did the same thing in restaurants. Picky, picky. So we ate at his place, slept at his place. Pretty soon I'm eating every meal with him and I've become a hippo."

"And so you started to hate him after a while."

"No, I kept thinking, there are worse things than this. He's a bit of a nut about food, and he's a little old for me, but what the hell. He's Jewish. He's single. He's pretty decent in bed. He's got a good job. He likes me. And he wants to get married. I'm thirty-three point nine. I'm looking square in the face of thirty-four. What are my options?"

"So what happened?"

"What do you mean? I told you. I put on twenty pounds and I started smoking again."

"What happened with Anthony?"

"Oh. I went to see a shrink. Nice woman on Central Park West. Shelly, her name is. A hundred and fifty an hour, not that I can afford it, but she was worth it. She told me Anthony's behavior was very manipulative and that my body belonged to me and he was way out of line."

"So you broke up with him?"

"No. Of course not. I had it out with him. I told him no butter. No mayo. Dressing on the side only. And I told him there were going to be times when he was going to have lobster Newburg and I was going to have Lean Cuisine and that was that. Boy, did that feel great. I felt like I was having it out with my father or something, at long last. You know? I am me. I'm not part of you. I felt so strong."

"And Anthony said forget about it."

"No, Harrie. He said he was scared. He said he was only trying to show me he loved me. And you know what I said?"

Harrie shook her head.

"I said, 'Show me you love me by respecting me and what I want.' And then he started to cry."

"Actual tears?"

"Actual tears. And then he said the most amazing thing. That he thought I was so beautiful that he guessed, subconsciously, he wanted me to get fat so no one else would love me, and Har, that just went straight into my heart. I don't think anyone's ever loved me so much before." Desiree's features crumpled and she covered her mouth with her hand.

"My, my, my," Harrie said. "So why did you break up?"

"We didn't break up. Why'd you think that? Anthony's my sweetheart. I just felt so *bad* that I'd considered him a compromise. And Shelly says I was sending him signals that I didn't consider him very special, so that made him try to capture me."

" 'Peter, Peter, pumpkin eater, had a wife . . .' "

". . . 'And couldn't keep her.' That's really good, Har." Desiree sighed deeply. "So now I'm trying to deal with my fear of commitment—now that I've got a good man who loves me, how not to fuck it up. That, and I've had to be very strict with myself to get all that butter off my thighs. I'm down to one Nutrafast meal a day now. Breakfast. I eat only a very light lunch. And then some nights I let Anthony do his worst, but we joke about it now. And I guess you could say some part of me is happy to know that I'm lovable at a hundred and forty-five pounds."

Harrie grinned at her friend. Des was right. She'd been off in her own world for so long she'd lost track of what it means to be a girlfriend, a person who connects with another person who has heard, felt, borne witness to the sad and happy things that happened over the last ten years. "So are you making an announcement of some kind?" Harrie asked.

"Not that I want to jinx anything, but stay tuned," Desiree said, suddenly flustered. She brushed crumbs from the table with quick flicks of her hand, then looked up at her friend. "And so, what's with you? You've got good news just bursting out of you."

"Oh, yeah?"

"Oh, yeah. You look like you're getting laid."

"Stop," Harrie said, blushing but delighted. "What have I got? Whisker burn?" She touched her chin. She had a flash of memory: Roger standing before the bathroom mirror in his rented apartment in Oyster Bay, razor in hand, mug of tea on the ledge and a towel wrapped around his hips. She'd been sitting on the edge of the tub, dressed for work and ready to leave. "I don't want to take you to the train," he'd said. "No?" "No. I want to take you back to bed." She'd gotten up and hugged him around the waist.

"Something like that. You've got that sex glow."

"Maybe I'm just glad to see you. Ever think about that?"

"Oh, sure. The day I start bringing on a glow in women, I'm going to worry about myself."

"Okay, okay," Harrie said with a laugh, "but I've got a ton of other stuff to tell you first."

"Well, go *on*."

"Well, here's a headline. Luna and I've been talking and she really wants me back at the agency. I told you I've been handling a few clients lately?"

"Uh-huh."

"Well, I'm going back to work three days a week, the way I'd originally wanted to, but this time I'm really going to make it work."

"Yawn," said Des.

"No, I'm serious. My heart's really in it this time." She pictured what it had been like going into the office this morning. There'd been a bunch of jonquils from Luna waiting in a vase and the new secretary had brought Harrie her coffee. Raoul had moved another desk into the room and even *he'd* been glad to see her. She'd pounced on her message slips as if they were gold ingots and she'd actually been thrilled to talk with Jan. "I miss the people," she said to Desiree. "I miss being plugged into the business. It's hard to believe I couldn't see how bored I was going to get out on the Island after a while."

"Nyah. Who told you so?"

"I don't remember."

"You remember. Who?"

"Okay, so you were right."

"Thank you very much," said Des. "So nice of you to say so. But strangely enough, I can understand, Har. You probably needed the time with the house at the beginning. It was like having a new baby."

"Exactly. Exactly right. My baby, the castle. Oh, and—brace yourself—Julie's getting married."

"Not to the guy who stood her up at the church!"

"The same. They're really going to do it this time."

"You swear?"

"I swear. The church is booked. Again. The dress has been dry-cleaned. Everyone's been reinvited, and Alan's paying for the catering."

"What do you know? The worm turned," Desiree said wonderingly. "Now there's your basic made-for-TV movie."

"What? *As the Worm Turns?*"

"You got it," said Desiree. "But seriously. I'd be terrified to put on that dress again if I were Julie. What if he bolts again?"

"If he bolts this time, he'd better move to another continent. South America. Australia."

"But he wouldn't dare. Would he?"

"Nah. He won't. He loves Julie and he did the whole eat-crow deal. A man-to-man talk with my father. Took my mother to lunch at this nice little restaurant in Montauk. He even called Ivy and me and apologized. And Doug told me that he and Alan went out and 'knocked a few balls around.' "

The two laughed.

"So Julie must be over the moon."

"Completely. And Ivy's going to be in the wedding, of course. She's been in therapy, by the way, and you've got to be hopeful. She's making plans. She's got her job back and she's applying to some colleges."

"Whaddya know?"

"I know you don't like Ivy particularly—"

"It's not that—"

"No, I didn't mean to put you on the defensive. What I mean to say is that she's not been particularly likable."

"Uh-huh," Des said tentatively.

"But I didn't see it. I mean, I saw it but I thought I could change it—her—somehow. When she said she wanted to live with me, I had an idea that I could *bond* with my little sister. I thought we'd garden together, and talk about men and bake pies—and then one day, I'm talking to her on the phone—the real Ivy, the depressed, scared, angry one—and I realize how weird it was that I'd tried to make her into one of these storybook virgin sisters who lives in a gingerbread cottage in the woods. And how doubly weird it must have seemed to Ivy. I mean, Des, it wasn't what she wanted. What she wanted was to get away from home without doing anything for herself."

"Uh-huh."

"You think I'm nuts?"

"No."

"So why are you giving me that look? Told you so, again?"

"No," said Desiree. "I'm just wondering when you're going to tell me what's happening with you and Dean."

"Dean?" The sound of the simple, one-syllable name shattered her mood like a rock crashing through the window of The Peacock Caffe.

"The glow, you know."

"Dean's seeing someone," Harrie said slowly. The room seemed to have filled with water. "I told you. I remember telling you."

"I know, but that was a while ago. Things change."

"Not this."

"Oh, boy," Des said sadly. "I'm sorry I brought him up."

Harrie sighed. "It's okay. We talk about business but that's all. It's still too uncomfortable to get into anything else with him. And when he calls, even if he just leaves a message on my machine, it throws me off for hours. And Roger can always tell."

"Roger?"

"Uh-huh."

"Don't tell me Roger's the one who put the glow on your face?"

"Uh-huh."

Desiree's expression lightened and she whistled through her teeth. "Some booby prize," she said. "He's a walking, talking dream. I swear I dream about him sometimes."

Harrie found herself. The water receded. She smiled at Desiree.

"I'll never forget that scene as long as I live, speaking of Ivy." Des paused as if in a trance. "And you're doing it with him?"

The smile stayed on Harrie's face as she nodded.

"Forgive me, I just want to make sure I've got this right. You put your hands all over that godlike body? And he does the same to you? And then the scene respectfully fades to black?"

Harrie laughed and nodded again. "He's very nice."

"He's very nice," Desiree repeated.

"I can be with him all day and not be bored by him."

"Uh-huh."

"It's fun. Doing the house with Roger and then going home with him at night. Going to the movies during the week. We drive in to the city and hang with some of his friends once in a while. He really likes me. And I trust him. And that time with Ivy . . . I thought he was the kind of guy who'd sleep with anyone. Now I think it was just one of those things."

"Has he told you he loves you?"

"Yeah," Harrie said shyly. "He said it last night, as a matter of fact." She'd been nearly asleep. Maybe Roger even thought she was asleep. She was snug in his arms and her head was under his chin when she heard him say it. He'd murmured it very softly. "Love you, Harrie," he'd said. And she'd squeezed his chest and burrowed in even closer.

"And you? Did you tell him you love him too? Do you?"

Harry shrugged. "Maybe. I don't know yet. I sure do like him a lot." But how could she know if she loved him, Harrie wondered, when she still hurt so much from Dean?

"How long's this been going on?"

"A few weeks. A month."

"Don't *you* work fast! So, what's wrong with him?"

Harrie thought about the question for a moment before she shrugged again. "Nothing. Nothing's wrong with him."

"You're going to make me ask, aren't you?"

"Ask what?" Harrie sipped her mochaccino.

"How he is in bed."

Harrie set down her glass, then folded her hands, making a pedestal for her chin. She sighed contentedly. "Merely the best. Roger Mayhew's the best lover I ever had in my life."

□

Dean and Chip were walking up Madison Avenue at a goodly pace even though neither of them had any business uptown. It was just that uptown had the smartest and best-looking women, and sometimes Chip had better luck when he was with another man—it made his pickup attempts seem less dangerous to his targets—so occasionally Dean would accompany him on a foray. Dean looked cool and straight, which really helped the cause, although right now he was wild. If Dean were a cat, thought Chip, he'd be thrashing his tail back and forth.

"It's so weird, man," Dean was saying. "She wears all this Victoria's Secret underwear and then you have to pry her legs open with a crowbar. I don't even like that slinky stuff. Do you?"

"Look at that one," Chip said, pressing his arm against Dean's chest to slow his pace. "The brunette coming toward us. Wearing the storm coat. See her? Look at those legs. Look at that hair. I love hair like that. I love hair you can get lost in."

"Do *you*?" Dean asked again. "Those stupid garter belts and push-up corsets with ten million hooks." He groaned. "I think I just got it. Victoria didn't like sex, did she? That must be the secret."

"Excuse me," Chip said to the woman in the storm coat, who paused midstride and looked at Chip suspiciously. "My friend and I are looking for a nice place to eat around here. I wonder if you can recommend . . ."

"What kind of place did you have in mind?" the woman asked warily. Were these guys legitimate? Or was this a hustle?

"Oh, we're open." Chip looked at Dean for support. Dean smiled halfheartedly, then looked out toward the street.

"You could try Calio's up two blocks on this side of the street. Food's good. Not too expensive."

"You wouldn't be going to lunch, by chance? Possibly you could join us. I'm Chip Martin, by the way. This is Dean Carrothers."

Dean dipped his head. Boy, did he hate this. Chip was getting so desperate. Thank God he was working the good neighborhoods. Things could be worse. He could be cruising the Lower East Side. He could be picking up schoolgirls outside NYU. "And your name is . . . ?" he heard Chip ask.

"I'm sorry, I've got to go," the woman said.

"Well, so long," Chip said to the empty space on the sidewalk. "Adios. Sayonara. Win some, lose some. I think she's married," he said to Dean.

"Uh-huh."

"I think I saw a ring."

"Uh-huh."

"Where were we?"

"Laura."

"Laura. You don't like her taste in underwear."

Dean sighed. It wasn't the underwear. It was that she couldn't give up control for a minute, not even to allow herself pleasure. The underwear was just a fake-out. Not like she was pulling anything on *him*. More like she was trying to fake herself out.

"You want my advice? This girl is not for you. Get out now. Minimize the damage to you both. It's not meant to be, Dean. I've been telling you for months." Chip ran his hands through his thinning reddish hair. His camel's-hair coat flapped around him, and his eyes swept the sidewalk from left to right like radar. "Look at that," he said. "Other side of the street. Standing in front of the bookstore. Blondish hair, red coat. If she goes in, let's follow her. I love bookstores."

"I'm getting hungry," Dean complained mildly.

"Shit, there's her boyfriend," Chip said. "In the trench coat. With the hot dogs. Oh, well. Want to try that Calio's place?"

"Okay."

"Or we can keep walking. There's a place in the seventies I kinda like. A charcuterie. I can't remember the name."

"Whatever."

"Riva goes in there sometimes."

Riva, Riva, Riva. Over three years, and still Riva. "Chipper. What happened to that girl you were seeing? Carla something."

"Cara," Chip said sadly. "Sweet little Cara."

"Right. Cara." Dean stuck his hands deep into his pants pockets. He exhaled loudly. Chip was still following around after Riva. That was bad. It could indicate he'd be doing time for Harrie. As it was, he thought about Harrie constantly. At the beginning, when he was first obsessed with Laura, his thoughts about Harrie seemed to be nagging, unwelcome ones. Now he thought of her longingly and often. He thought he'd seen her several times in completely improbable places: a coffee shop on Broadway, outside Laura's apartment hailing a cab, at his gym. Each time the look-alike had turned out to be a stranger. When he talked to Harrie on the phone, it was like talking to someone he hardly knew. The same speech patterns were there, but the love was gone from her voice. Could she really have stopped loving him so soon? Probably a brutal shock could throw a switch in a person, and if that was true, that he'd gotten involved with Laura was shock enough.

"I'm actually in bed with her," Chip was saying. "The damned courtship has taken forever and I'm finally in bed with her. Keep in mind this is the first time I've had a totally naked woman in my bed in about nine months."

"Okay," Dean said. "I'll keep that in mind."

"And I tried something. I'll admit, it was a little tricky. Okay, I was showing off a little. And my leg cramped up."

"Huh."

"Cramped right up, the bastard. The pain was awful. And so I lost it."

"Oh, boy," said Dean. He put his hand on Chip's back.

"And you know what she says?"

"No."

"She says, 'You older guys are amazing.' "

"No."

"Older guys. Dean. I'm thirty-six."

"So what'd you do?"

"Spanked the little bitch."

"So what'd you do?"

"Laughed, of course. Told her to be a nice girl and massage my leg."

"And did she?"

"Yeah," Chip said morosely.

"Anything else?"

"Yeah. She got the message. She's young, but she's not stupid."

"And then what happened?"

The two men stopped at a traffic light. A bus rolled by ponderously. The sound of a siren parted the air and was gone.

"I redeemed myself, of course."

"Yeah?"

"Made her beg for mercy before the night was over."

"That many times, huh?"

"Yeah. Twice." Chip laughed. "But the second time was a record breaker. So she told me."

"Good for you. And you've seen her since?"

"Hell, no."

The light changed and Chip and Dean advanced toward the restaurant.

"Why not?"

"Her old boyfriend returned from the land of the dead."

"Christ."

"It's rough out here in Dateworld," Chip said. "Well, this is it."

He stopped in front of the window to the restaurant and peered in. "She's not in there."

"I'm still hungry."

"Okay," Chip agreed sadly. "Might as well eat."

There was a sprinkling of small Formica tables around the perimeter of the restaurant, and a counter at the center of the room. Beside the counter was a case filled with exotic salads, and on top of the counter were vats of soups and hot dishes. Chip and Dean ordered from the woman behind the counter, then found a table by the window. In moments, their soup was served.

"I don't get it," Dean said. "Are you in love with Riva in retrospect?"

"What do you mean?"

"Look. Here we are almost four years after you two broke up, and when you're not hurling yourself at moving targets, you're still looking for Riva. Like the Holy fucking Grail. If you loved her so much when you were with her, how come you didn't marry her?"

Chip stirred his soup tenderly, then lifted a spoonful to his mouth. "I wasn't ready when I was dating Riva. I jerked her around. Yes, no, yes, no. Until she was sick of me. I wasn't ready. And ripeness is all."

"Ripeness is all?"

"Shakespeare. *King Lear*."

Dean followed Chip's gaze as he looked out at the attractive women hurrying by, and he knew he wasn't interested in any of them. This was news. Once upon a time, not so long ago, the search for the right woman had seemed, if not sport, at least the way things were meant to be. Images presented themselves. Elizabeth: funny, athletic, but too old for him. Cory: pretty, refined, but not smart enough for him. Barbara: too intense. Sandy: Her legs were fat. Nadine: What was wrong with her? He couldn't remember. He'd been crazy about her for an entire year before he'd found the escape hatch. Harrie: Two and a half years, the whole time loving her and the whole time bitching that she wasn't right. Was that the truth? Or was it more like she was going to pin him down, and the only way he could escape was to tag her with the handy excuse that she wasn't "right"?

"So, I guess you're saying that now you're ripe?" Dean said to Chip's radar-eyed reflection in the mirror.

"I'm getting there. I'm either ripe or I'm getting ready to be ripe."

Dean laughed. So, what he was doing was ripening. Becoming more mature. Going from green to bright, golden yellow. Like a pineapple. It made sense. His reluctance to leave Laura had to do with a new feeling he was having, that when you were ready, the person you were with was the right person, whether or not she conformed to the specifications you created in the past. He was trying to love Laura in spite of what were clearly deep-seated problems that might never go away. And if he hadn't been able to commit to Harrie, maybe he could commit to Laura. "I think my father would really like Laura," he said out loud.

"Fuck your father," said Chip. "You love Harrie and you know it. What do you need your father's approval for? Dump Laura. Get Harrie back before it's too late. Stop being an asshole."

"Yes, sir."

"I'm serious. Full-court press. Surround her. Immobilize her. Make it a mission."

"Shut up and eat your soup," said Dean.

31

———◻———

I CAN'T GET OVER the marvelous job you've done on this old place," Ricky Boyd said. She tied her flowered scarf around the collar of her raincoat, shawl style, then pushed back the headband in her taupe-colored hair. She hooked her car keys out of her pocket and, with Harrie by her side, walked toward her car. "When I saw Black-fern a year ago, it was bulldozer meat. And now? Even in this market, we're going to have to fight off the offers."

"I'm glad you feel that way, Ricky." The rain was sprinkling now but it was already falling harder than it had been a moment ago when they'd left the conservatory. Harrie took the broker's card, stuck it in her pocket, and said goodbye. She watched as the station wagon lumbered down the main drive toward the gate; then she turned and ran back to the house.

Roger was in the Great Hall preparing to set stones in the hearth. A heater was blowing warm air a few yards from where he was kneeling; although it was the beginning of May, the air was always cold in this room.

"Tea?" she asked.

"Love some."

Harrie went to the kitchen. The old enamel stove was working now and the counters and cabinets were tiled in pristine white with a cobalt-blue border. The broker had been right. It was astonishing how much Roger and his crew had accomplished, even when you considered how much labor and how much money had been simply thrown at the house. But despite Ricky's enthusiasm, her appraisal of the property's value did not equal the money Harrie had spent on it.

Harrie filled a kettle, turned on a gas jet. She performed this act mechanically. It was odd how detached she felt from the house now that it was becoming livable. It was so big. And so cold. The temperature was one thing and that could be fixed. But the coldness, which had to do with the size and scale of the rooms, was a different problem. One could not simply stuff a room the size of a football field full of chintz and call it warm.

Last week she and Roger had pushed an enormous ten-foot-long sofa in front of the fireplace so they'd have some place to sit, and the room dwarfed the sofa down to a dark blue blot the size of a love seat. It would take half a dozen sofas to fill up this room to a comfort level that was consistent with her need to be surrounded by softness, and unless she was prepared to live in a furniture warehouse, she was going to have to get used to sparse furnishings, clean lines, and gigantic modern artwork. It was becoming clearer and clearer that her style and the style of Blackfern Castle were at odds. Of course, these days she was picturing herself in this house in a completely different way than she'd pictured herself last fall.

Back in October, she'd been with Dean. Within that context she'd fantasized a family of little Carrothers children and her own parents and siblings, all filling the rooms with pets and games and all kinds of activity. She'd wanted a concert grand, for God's sake—a notion that seemed as likely to her now as the possibility that she'd take up nude skydiving over the Canadian Rockies. She'd envisioned a long table and holiday dinners and children stuffing themselves noisily: the kitchen from the farmhouse in Spode, all dressed up. She'd seen her father puttering in the conservatory with a team of assistants, breeding orchids or something. Now all she could see was a room that would have to be filled with plants whether or not there was someone to enjoy them. She'd seen the bedrooms in the north wing filled with a living, breathing family. Now she saw a guest wing to be used for the occasional visits of friends.

And that was a very interesting thing. Change the key players and the whole picture changed. She was no longer wrapping her fantasy around a brooding lover and a family that had outgrown a dusty little farmhouse off a service road in a dying rural community. She was with a hip, Italian-speaking, Calvin Klein–bodied artist. When she imagined herself with Roger, or rather, when she tried to imagine herself with Roger, she got magazine images. She saw the two of them stalking the newly plastered and painted corridors, the sound of their footsteps ringing out and rebounding from the twenty-foot ceilings. Roger said he wasn't ready to have children, even the idea of marriage seemed premature, and so the noisy dinnertime image disappeared. It was replaced by a visualization of dinner parties for successful young painters and photographers, their well-toned bodies draped in Italian clothes, and she could see these people sipping champagne from Baccarat crystal, tossing lire into the reflecting pool. Instead of serious gardening in the conservatory, her serious dad and his intense, young staff from the horticultural society, she pictured a small table for two in the center of the immense glass room, and she saw herself and Roger drinking espresso from an antique coffee service, quietly reading the *London Observer*. And while these images were exceedingly stylish, they had nothing to do with who she really was. They had everything to do with Roger. It was equally true that her original fantasy had to do with changing other people. No wonder it hadn't become reality.

The kettle, a highly polished chrome cone with a blue rubber-coated handle and a small red bird at the end of its spout, whistled in E major. It was Roger's kettle, one of his gifts for the house, and though Harrie appreciated its modern lines, she liked her own dinged-up enamel kettle better. She poured hot water into two large white mugs, dropped in tea bags, added honey, and took the cups out to where Roger was working.

"Here you go," she said, handing the tea to Roger. She fluffed a pillow, then settled into the sofa.

"What'd she say?" Roger asked. He was mixing cement in a small bucket and feigning nonchalance at the same time.

"That there were going to be fistfights over this house. And she went on and on about your work. She was kind of in raptures about the place."

"Really?" Roger mixed, stirred, and poured cement into the bed he'd prepared for it. He was wearing a T-shirt and khakis and old running shoes, and his hair was in a ponytail. He looked like an ad for something. An ad for sex.

"She said this place used to be bulldozer meat." Harrie laughed. "Isn't that funny?"

"Very," Roger said, not laughing. He fitted a stone into place, tapped it with a rubber mallet. He hadn't looked at her once since she'd come into the room.

"And she said carving off the parcel with the cottage and the drive to it and the little woods behind it was very doable. She said it was an easy subdivision because there's more than the required fifty feet of road frontage at the entrance to the drive. So that means we can keep the cottage and I can still get a decent price for the house."

"Great." Roger hefted another stone into place, twisted it, swore at it.

"Roger."

"I said, great. I'm happy for you."

Harrie reached out a socked foot and touched Roger's back with a gentle toe. "Rog," she said, trying to diffuse his anger.

"Don't," he said, twitching the muscles in his back.

Harrie pulled in her foot, then crossed her legs. "You're not being fair."

"Okay, I'm not being fair." Still squatting, he whirled around, his eyes sending out neon-bright sparks. "I know that, but it doesn't change how I feel. I happen to have invested a lot of myself in this project. I've worked like a fucking slave, and now I'm supposed to be a good sport while it gets sold out from under me before I've even finished it."

"So tell me what you think I should do."

"It's not for me to say."

The whining sound of a table saw sang out in the north wing. A couple of workmen came to the entrance to the room and paused under the arched doorframe. One called out a question in thick Long Islandese to Roger, who called back his answer. Then he became silent again. Harrie watched as Roger repeated the motions: smooth the cement, butter the stones, fit them in place, tap, tap, tap, scrape the surface, start again.

Harrie wanted to reach out to him, but she felt exhausted by the conversation they'd had so many times. There was no right and wrong. There was just an enormous gap between what Roger wanted and what she wanted. He was in love with the house and had projected a life around it. And the house no longer made sense to her at all. She admired it. She appreciated it. She was laying out several hundred thousand dollars a month to support it, but she could no longer imagine living here. So unless she was prepared to give Blackfern to Roger, keeping the house was pointless.

What she wanted to do was get out as much of her money as possible, pay back her loan, tuck whatever moneys remained into a retirement fund for herself, keep the cottage as a weekend hideaway, as a memorial to her friendship with David Tuckman, then throw herself fully into her career. Working again with Luna was restoring her sense of self. She'd felt like a star at the Romance Fiction Book Club party last week. So many of her friends were there and happy to see her again. And this week she'd made a six-figure, two-book deal for Jan Nugent which had made it possible for Jan to have a full-time career as a writer. She felt better lately and looked better too. The only problems she had now concerned Roger.

Roger's fantasy was so elaborate: They would live at Blackfern, he would get new projects wherever (he'd been offered work on both coasts and in Europe), and Harrie would work when and where she felt like it. There were telephones and fax machines and overnight-delivery services all over the world, weren't there? Roger reasoned. And so she'd be free to travel with him, keep him company, and when she wanted to go home, she'd come home to Blackfern. When she said that she would do her best work as a literary agent in the city where the publishing business was conducted, where she could have lunch with people, have meetings, do the cocktail party circuit, he'd waved a hand in the air and all but said she was being obstinate. He didn't understand that her work was important to her again. He hadn't wanted to understand.

Last night while standing in the exact center of the Great Hall, Roger had actually said to her, "Why not try my plan for a while? Let's just see how it goes before you decide. Maybe you'll love this life once we move into the main house and start living it." His words had summoned up a sickening feeling of déjà vu. Only the roles had been changed. Instead of her selling a fantasy to Dean, Roger was trying to sell a fantasy to her. It was ironic. It was also too pointed to ignore. Dean had tried her fantasy and it hadn't worked for him. Her parents hadn't even tried. And unless it counted that Ivy's drug problem had been exposed and addressed, Ivy's performance in Harrie's play had been a gross failure. It seemed too obvious, finally, that trying to force another person into your dream was conceptually doomed. She'd tried endlessly to explain this to Roger, but he wouldn't listen. And how could she blame him for wanting to make her mistake all over again?

Unfortunately, what had become a power struggle between them was weighted in her favor. The house belonged to her. There really could be no "us" in the decision, and that was damaging the still-new net of tenderness and caring about each other's feelings. It seemed incredible to Harrie that once again this house was going to test a relationship. It almost seemed as though she and her house were a package deal to Roger. That without the house, he didn't want her so much after all.

"Roger, I'm not going to let anyone tear this house down. I want you to know that. Ricky said I'd get more money selling it to a condo developer than I can to someone who will want to live here, but I'm willing to make the sacrifice."

"I've got to get some air," Roger said, and without actually throwing down his trowel, he threw it down. He put his leather jacket over his wonderful-looking, T-shirted chest, and leaving Harrie sitting cross-legged on a sofa in front of the fireplace, he walked out of the cavernous stone room.

32

———□———

ONCE AGAIN, Harrie found that she'd stopped listening to what Ben was saying. She liked Ben and found him interesting, but sometimes when he was talking to her, she simply dialed to another station. For the last few moments, however long it had taken to park the car and walk up the block, Ben had been talking about an editorial stance his paper had taken and Harrie had just been caught out by the question mark at the end of his sentence. "I'm sorry," she said. "I was on Mars for a second."

"And what's the news from Mars?" he asked.

"I was thinking about one of my new authors. I found her at a writers' conference last month and she's given me her first novel. It's absolutely wonderful, and so is she. Allison's very bright, very perceptive, and very happy. Completely optimistic. The way one can be at twenty-three."

"And what made you think of her?"

Harrie turned to Ben as they mounted the stairs of the brownstone. He was a good-looking, homey sort of man. He looked his forty-five years in a way that many of his contemporaries did not. His hair was thick but going gray, and he was rounding out around his middle, suggesting that he was not going to fight the aging process. Harrie found his appearance, if not electrifying, comforting. "Well, I'm ten years older than she is, and I see a lot of myself at that age in her. I was just wondering how she's going to get from her age to mine without . . ."

"Without what?" he asked.

"Without getting whacked. You know, without sustaining the damage that comes with the loss of innocence."

"Hmmm," Ben said, fiddling with a slip of paper he had extracted from his jacket pocket. He held the paper at different distances from his eyes and was fishing for his glasses, when Harrie, taking the paper from him, said, "One-A."

"Right," Ben replied. He pressed a button on the intercom. "But if you're going to be a writer, you've got to take your whacks. It comes with the territory."

"I know, I know," Harrie said. "You've got to lose your innocence if you're going to grow up, no matter what you do. It's just too bad growing up hurts so much." A buzzer rang out before Ben could reply, and they were admitted to the building. They continued down a hallway, at the end of which was a door that opened as they approached it. Then they entered the large foyer of the apartment.

On a table in front of a long mirror stood an enormous vase of ruby-streaked and pure-white lilies. A chandelier glimmered overhead. Ben introduced Harrie to their hostess, a graceful woman with auburn hair, a wide smile, and glasses hanging from a chain around her neck. She chatted amiably with her guests as she led them into the living room. A table laden with delicacies and displaying another vase of beautiful autumn flowers dominated the room, and there were soft, white sofas lining two of the walls. A third wall was made up entirely of bookcases, and at the far end of the room a wide doorway led to another sumptuous room.

Clusters of people bunched up around the table, leaned against the bookcases, collected in knots on the sofas, and among the thirty or so people there, Harrie saw someone she knew—Margot, an editor from Heartbeat Press, whom she hadn't seen in a long while.

Margot spotted Harrie, immediately excused herself from the conversation she was having, and bounded over to Harrie and Ben. Harrie and Margot hugged and kissed and engaged in a duet of happy exclamations. Ben listened attentively as Margot brought Harrie up to date on her life since they'd last seen one another, but when Harrie began to fill Margot in on her own last year, Ben, having heard this all before, left the two women to their reunion.

"He's awfully nice," Margot said.

"Yes, he is. He says he's every mother's dream," Harrie said with a laugh.

"Does he say it seriously?"

"Semiseriously. He's got a great résumé, if you know what I

mean. Power job at Hearst, all kinds of Ivy League credentials, and no sexually communicable diseases."

"What you'd call a real catch, huh, Harrie? There's mine," Margot said, turning her head forty-five degrees to the left. "With the light brown hair, talking to the perfect ten in the leather dress. He's in real estate."

"The one in the brown jacket?"

"That's my man. A true sweetie pie. He's a little depressed lately. What with the housing market in such a slump."

"Isn't it, though? I know more about the real estate market than I ever wanted to know." Harrie's thoughts turned to Blackfern and how the seven-million-dollar windfall she'd had one year ago had been halved almost exactly. The money she'd spent on renovation had been virtually unrecoverable; a house on two and a half acres in that part of Long Island was worth only what it was worth, no matter how sound the roof was, no matter how many custom-made tiles were in the kitchen. The house had sold for three million after the cottage parcel had been subdivided, and with that money she'd paid off the construction loan. Then she'd converted her stock equity into long-term interest-bearing bonds and treasury bills. The net result: Harrie had a small cottage on an acre in Cold Spring Harbor, about two million dollars growing in her retirement fund, and a fantastic apartment overlooking Central Park and the reservoir.

Reducing the story down to its essence, Harrie told Margot about the sale of her house, and about her new partnership arrangement with Luna. "*Junior* partner," she said to Margot, but Harrie knew that this was a step in a plan Luna had told her she'd been wanting to put in place for some time. She'd only been waiting for Harrie to commit to the business wholeheartedly before she actualized this fantasy of her own—that Harrie would be a full partner one day and take over the business when Luna retired. Harrie accepted Margot's good wishes and the two planned a lunch date; then Margot was snatched away by an introduction to another guest and Harrie went to the bookshelves with her glass of wine and browsed.

The owners of the apartment had an interesting collection of books. The classics were well represented, as were current best-sellers, and there were a large number of books on architecture. One of the books was familiar to her; it was filled with photographs and descriptions of the grand houses on Long Island's Gold Coast, and although Blackfern was not one of the mansions pictured, there was a description of the house and Harrie turned to it.

The description was only a page long, but Harrie relished every word because each one called up a series of images, of overlapping views, of details old and new. The house she had re-created with Roger was different from the one Sanford Defoe had brought to life, but her vision was a complementary one—and in the process of embracing Blackfern, she had taken herself on a fantastic trip she was sure Mr. Tuckman would have appreciated.

Harrie remembered how her late friend had told her that she was a dreamer. And he'd been right, although many of the events of the last year were not ones she had dreamed of. The loss of Dean, for one, and the doomed, rhapsodic affair with Roger. But she'd dreamed and had seen her creative imaginings come to life, a rare and special gift. And because of Mr. Tuckman's generosity, she knew things about herself she would never have discovered had she not been brave enough to live her fantasies. Yet it seemed that the last lesson of her Blackfern year was the hardest one to accept, and that was that dreaming could effect change for the dreamer, but one could not dream into being happy endings for people who did not share the same dream.

Yesterday she and Luna had gone upstairs to see how the renovation was going on the floor that would be hers to use within the month. There was an office facing the garden, which she would share with her new assistant; the walls were being painted a lovely French blue. "It's ironic," she'd said to Luna. "Dean would've loved the life I have now. I can't help but wonder if things would've turned out better for us if—" And Luna, regal in white, seeming as always to embody the wisdom of a sage, had interrupted her. "Harrie dear, if it hadn't been the house, it would have been something else. It would have been your seven million dollars or the two pounds you say you've gained, or that you trusted him too much with your money. It would have been something, I assure you."

"Maybe," she'd conceded.

"Truly," Luna had insisted. "It doesn't matter how much you had together or how much you long for him. He wasn't ready to make a commitment. What is the expression? It was close, but no cigar. On the other hand, when someone is ready, they're ready," Luna reminded her. "If I were in your shoes, I'd give Ben Cohen a good run. That man is ready to become a husband and he'd make a jolly good one, if you ask me."

And Harrie knew that Luna was right about Dean and right about Ben. She'd given her best to Dean, and still, he'd pictured another woman in his life. Ben, on the other hand, had made it very clear to her that after twenty years of bachelorhood, he'd put the search for the nonexistent perfect woman behind him. He knew he could make Harrie happy—as happy as he knew she would make him. And he'd come to this decision within weeks of their meeting. Quite a change from two and a half years of Dean's ambivalence.

Harrie returned the book to the bookshelf and turned to face the room. She could understand the logic of Luna's argument and of Ben's, but something was missing. Surely there was some kind of middle ground between hoping for the impossible and giving herself over to a practical marriage. As a child, she'd wished for romance, rapture, and a little magic. As a child? Last year at the age of thirty-two, she'd believed her mother's promise that she would marry Dean in a flurry of white tulle. Also last year, she'd believed a white-haired, cigarillo-smoking shoe store psychic who had described a field of heather and told her of two cords entwined together. She shook her head as she remembered how Dean had laughed at her. He must have known. All the time he was saying he wasn't ready, he'd known that he wouldn't marry her, and she'd been too dumb and too in love to believe it.

Harrie looked around for Ben and saw him on the other side of the room talking with their hostess. What had Margot said about Ben? That he was a real catch. And Harrie guessed he *was* a real catch. But she didn't care about the qualities that made him every mother's dream. She liked Ben's company, but the man had never touched her emotionally, had never shown her that she was anything but a collection of qualities to him. And while there were some people who would be happy to conduct an affair or even a marriage based on these matching qualities, she was not one of those people. Roger, who had never even considered being married, had touched her more. And Dean, who had really loved her, and had failed her, had touched her most of all.

In the last few months her anger toward Dean had dissipated and a dull kind of longing remained. Would it ever disappear? Or would she continue to love him even if she married someone else? Harrie heard the sound of Ben's laughter, and as she turned to him she saw him signal to her to come to where he was standing. Harrie began to cross the room, but stopped at the prettily arranged table to refill her wineglass. How strange it all was. People looked at Dean and the way their relationship had ended and told her she was lucky to be free of him. People looked at Ben and told her what a catch he was. And yet it was Dean who had moved her, loved her, had connected with her soul.

⊡

Dean was hiding things from Bonnie. Not just where he was taking her for her birthday—that was a surprise more than an evasion—but he was hiding away anything that would give her a wedge into his emotions. Like the other women he'd dated since Laura, Bonnie wasn't a keeper. And since that was true, he didn't want to give her reason to hope there would be more to their relationship than casual dates. Dean put an arm around Bonnie's waist as they crossed the street, then dropped it when they were safely on the other side. Bonnie found his hand, took it, looked up at him winningly and gave him a smile. And that sequence of small and simple acts of affection set off in Dean an impulse to tell Bonnie the truth, warn her about himself, say to her, Don't get serious about me. I'm not for you. This relationship is at its peak right now. But instead of speaking, he extricated his hand and covered the action with some inconsequential necktie adjusting which was part of a series of distancing actions he'd cultivated to an art. He called, but not too often. He was affectionate, but not overwhelmingly so. Bonnie's birthday present would be a book she had noted in the book review section of the *Times*, because there was very little sentiment one could attach to a book.

"It's nice of you to run this errand with me," Bonnie said. "I don't know why Karen decided it was so important I pick up my gift this evening. I told her it could wait."

"Maybe it's perishable," Dean suggested. "Maybe it's alive."

"Alive," Bonnie repeated with a delighted laugh. "You mean like a puppy? Or a houseplant?"

Dean gave a half shrug and a half smile. Bonnie had a kind of ingenuousness that reminded him of Harrie and that had attracted him at first. Now, that same Harrie-like quality in a person who wasn't Harrie killed him. He was worried about himself. He wanted a good relationship with a woman so badly he positively ached, but it seemed to him that as far as actually finding a woman to have a relationship with was concerned, he'd lost whatever ground he'd gained through experience.

If he were asked to describe his pattern with women, it would be something like this: Pre-Harrie—no, to be honest he would have to include Harrie—he'd eliminated women because of "design flaws." Then there was Harrie and his belated realization of how deeply he loved her. Then there was the repentant attempt to make a relationship work with a woman who was clearly wrong for him. And now he was eliminating women because of design flaws again. But even though the effect was the same, it seemed that his reasons for shuffling women were different now. Instead of looking for a vaguely under-stood notion of the right woman, he was gripped with intense sadness when he was with a woman who was not Harrie. He had better luck dating women than Chip had, but the essential loneliness was the same. Being with a woman who didn't know him made him ache for the one woman who had known him and loved him anyway. He hadn't spoken with Harrie in months, not since she'd asked him to switch her account over to Chip, and Chip, for the sake of all con-cerned, never spoke to him about Harrie.

"Don't forget to say we've got reservations for dinner as soon as we arrive, Dean. Karen and Joe can really go on and on once they get started."

"Okay."

"Don't even accept a drink."

"Not even if I was dying of thirst and this was the last stop before the Sahara."

"Exactly," said Bonnie. She took his hand again and gave it a little squeeze, which hurt more than the actual pressure she exerted on his fingers.

Dean returned the squeeze halfheartedly. His lack of feelings for Bonnie reminded him of how things had ended with Laura. The same precursors were there. You could almost flip to the last page of the book and read the ending of the Story of Bonnie. Attractive woman, smart, right-girl material, and yet he felt nothing. Finis.

There'd been a similar setup with Laura. After the thoroughly misleading first flush of sexual frenzy, an emotional numbness had set in and confirmed his original take on Laura—namely, she was a good pal, too bad there's no chemistry here. Despite his lapse in judgment, once he was involved with her, he'd tried very hard to make a fairly decent relationship with a very decent woman turn into the real thing.

But Laura had been onto him and she hadn't liked what he was doing. Fairly decent hadn't been decent enough for Laura, and why should it have been? She was wonderful. Wonderful for someone else. He could easily call up that image of her in the shower beside him, arms folded across her boyish chest, the water pouring from her hair in sheets, obscuring the angry tears he could hear in her voice. "What are we doing?" she'd asked furiously. "You don't love me. Why are we faking this?" He had tried to protest, but it was futile. They *were* faking it, and he didn't want to be accused of faking it again. So that's why Bonnie was getting a version of him that he didn't like very much. But what were his options? He could refuse to date. Or he could go out with women carefully, holding his real self in reserve until he met someone he could love as much as he had loved Harrie.

"This is it," Bonnie said.

Dean followed her up the steps of the brownstone. She pressed an intercom button, a voice answered, and then a buzzer sounded. Together, Bonnie and Dean walked through the door and down the hallway to another door which was opened by a lovely auburn-haired woman.

"Karen, hi. This is my friend, Dean," Bonnie said.

Dean shook hands with the woman and stepped into a large foyer, the focal point of which was a huge vase of lilies on a table in front of a long mirror. A chandelier glimmered overhead.

"We have dinner reservations at eight," Bonnie said.

"It will just take a minute," Karen replied. "We're going out as well. Come with me. I can't wait till you see this."

And so Bonnie followed Karen, and Dean followed Bonnie, and when they got to the living room, the lights went on and about thirty voices yelled, "Surprise!"

·

Harrie had been standing midroom at the table when the shushing sounds and the excited, rustling chorus of "It's her" began. Then the lights went out. When they went on again, she wasn't merely surprised. She was stunned. Standing beside the petite, blond, thirty-something birthday girl was Dean. It took a moment for her brain to understand her physical reaction—Dean looked different—but when she was sure it was he, Harrie knew why her heart had stopped. She reached out to the table to support herself, knocked over something heavy that made a broken-glass sound when it fell to the floor, and then Harrie lost mental consciousness. If she could have fainted, she would have. Instead, she went blank. The next thing she knew, Ben was beside her, dabbing at her dress with a dish towel. "It's going to be fine," she heard him say. "Everything's going to be all right."

"No, it's not," she said.

"Of course it will. White wine doesn't stain," he said, blotting the rug.

Harrie didn't know what Ben was talking about.

·

Dean looked toward the sound of the crash and saw someone standing beside the table, looking at the floor in a stricken way. The someone looked like Harrie, but it was probably some other person. No, it really was Harrie. He felt his heart pitch and the blood drain to his feet. Perhaps he had died. Harrie was standing with a good-looking, middle-aged guy who was dabbing at the skirt of her dress. It was infuriating to see him handle her clothing in such a familiar way.

"Dean, I want you to meet my friend Alex and his sister Janette," Bonnie was saying, and pulling his gaze away from the woman he loved, he allowed himself to be introduced. Conversing with these strangers felt as comfortable to Dean as if he were standing in front of the refrigerator, looking for a container of milk while a conflagration raged at his back.

"Will you excuse me for a minute," Dean said to Bonnie. "I'll be . . . There's someone I've got to see." And without waiting for a reply, he headed straight for Harrie.

·

"Hi," Dean said. He was aware of the shadow Harrie's date was casting over his shoulder, but he didn't care who the man was and he didn't care what he thought. His decision had been made. His course had been set. He would say what he felt or he would die trying.

"Hi," Harrie replied. Dean looked stricken, and she knew his expression was a mirror of hers. She hoped she wouldn't have to say anything more than "Hi," because her brain and her mouth were clearly disengaged from one another. She wanted to throw her arms around Dean, but there were two things stopping her. One was her awareness of Ben standing beside her. The other was a desire to protect herself from the man she'd loved so much, who had hurt her more than she'd believed possible.

"I've been the biggest jerk in the world," Dean said. He felt a surge of adrenaline, and with it, the first real happiness he'd felt in years.

"Dean, I don't think this is the right time . . ." The struggle between her conflicting emotions made Harrie feel almost ill. Her vision was wavy and she'd lost sense of time. She heard Ben clear his throat loudly and felt him take her arm, and when she'd processed these signals, she mechanically introduced the two men to each other.

A wooden handshake ensued, and then Dean, returning his entire attention to Harrie, said, "I still love you. I've never stopped loving you."

"I beg your pardon," Ben said loudly. "What's going on here?"

Her approach unnoticed, Dean's date materialized at his side. She was wearing an innocent and disarming smile. Her lipstick was pale pink and so were her fingernails. "Hello," she said, taking Dean's arm. She stuck out her hand to Harrie "I'm Bonnie Glover."

Bonnie Lover? Harrie collected her scattered composure and prepared to return the handshake, but before their hands met, the lights dimmed, and Karen, bearing a brilliantly lit chocolate cake, sailed toward the table. And thirty guests burst into song.

33

---□---

*I*T WAS RAINING HARD. It was Saturday, eleven o'clock in the morning, but the rain made it seem like dusk. Harrie's hands were shaking as she scooped parrot food mixture into the food cup and wedged it back into the cage. The birds climbed beak over claw around the bars until they got to the perch beside the cup. Once there, they plundered it, spilling sunflower seeds as they searched for whole peanuts and chili peppers, which they cracked with their sharp beaks and tasted with their small black tongues. Harrie stroked their feathers and made clucking cockatoo sounds and generally fussed over the two large birds, who responded in kind by fussing over her.

The cage was by one of the living room windows, which usually offered a wide view of Central Park: a vista of hilly green treetops broken by a shining swath of the reservoir. Today the windows were mirrored by the dull gray light and she could see her reflection in the glass. She looked worried and with good reason, she thought. What was Dean going to say? What was she going to feel? Was she going to be in ribbons by the time he left? Or was she going to be in love with a man who loved her? She put a hand to the glass and peered out, but all she saw was herself.

Harrie sighed and plucked at the wisps of hair that had fallen from the knot she had made at the back of her head. She pulled loose a few strands, then a few more, and in another moment she had overdone what started to be a subtle softness and was now a mess. She looked like a Yorkshire terrier. And Dean would be here in minutes. She hoped. She ripped the band from her head, bent at the waist, and bunched her hair again. She stood and looked at her image. She looked good enough. She hadn't been trying to look devastating, to begin with. She'd been trying for, and thought she'd achieved, a look that was soft and approachable: a plaid shirt and corduroy skirt with an oversize cardigan. She'd worn flat shoes, minimal makeup, and after vacillating all morning, had put on the watch Dean gave her.

The watch still evoked mixed memories. When she wore it, she thought about Dean, and that reminded her of that frigid day in Connecticut . . . She hoped never to have such a jarring, disappointing moment again as long as she lived. Still, the watch was lovely. There'd been weeks when she hadn't worn it and she'd missed it. And there'd been weeks when she'd worn the watch just to prove to herself that it was a beautiful piece of jewelry that suited her, not a sick attachment to a dead love.

The party last night had been such an occasion. The watch had glinted prettily on her wrist, and not long after she'd pulled half the contents of the table onto the rug, she'd looked at the watch and said to Ben, "I think it's time to go. I've really had a long day." And Ben had said, "Cut the shit if you don't mind." His words had stung and sent her scrambling for something kind to say—but Ben left her with nothing to say but the truth.

"Okay," she said. "This isn't working for me, Ben." And he asked her why not, and she tried to find a good way to say "I'm not in love with you," and botched it probably, so in the end, Ben looked as if he'd been in a bar fight. In an attempt to maintain his dignity, he tossed out a generous but abrupt, "Call me if it doesn't work out," and instantly upon stepping out onto East Fifty-seventh Street, hailed a cab for Harrie and practically threw her inside.

In response to this exchange and the encounter with Dean that had preceded it, Harrie had begun to flail herself by reviewing her evening's performance. Okay, she knew it had been a party, not a performance. But if it *had* been a performance, she would've been panned in the *Times*. She hadn't been able to act at all. Not with Dean, not with Ben. If Dean had been wondering if she still cared for him, he now knew. Dean's face and that of the woman beside him flashed on and off in her mind like a strobe light, and the crash of the wine bottle cued the dialogue, hers and Ben's, hers and Dean's. *Out of control*, said the *Times* theater critic. *Harriet Braintree seemed to have wandered into the wrong production as a stunned audience watched her blunder through her lines—when she could remember them at all.* But there had been one positive note in this calamitous evening; a truth had made itself known. Seeing Ben and Dean together had forced her to act on what she knew in her heart. She wasn't in love with Ben and she never would be, and if that meant being alone until she fell in love again, she would be alone.

At the time she was curled up in the cab, Harrie figured Dean would call soon, and the idea of seeing him again scared her then and scared her now. She needed to protect herself from Dean, but given last evening's events, she doubted her ability to do so. And protecting herself was more important than ever. Nothing had really changed. Laura might have been exchanged for a different blonde whom Dean was sleeping with, but that was all. True, Dean had looked broken up and she could believe he still loved her, but it was also true that he'd been with a woman who had handled him in a proprietary way, and as far as she was concerned, she would not share Dean, not after what they'd been through together. Thinking about the things they'd been through together had caused her to look so stricken that the cabdriver last night, a wiry skinhead of about sixty, had understood all in a glance and had proceeded to tell her interminably and in graphic detail about the heartbreak he'd just experienced himself.

Having staggered dizzily into her apartment at last, Harrie had automatically checked her answering machine. The light was blinking dully. There'd been one call, and it was Dean. "Call me when you get in," he'd said. "I don't care what time it is." She released a breath she hadn't known she was holding and let in the hope she'd been resisting. *He still wanted her.* She lifted the receiver and started to call Dean and say "Come over right now and get into bed with me." But something stopped her, some wise voice that said, not so fast. A night together, by itself, would be worse than nothing. The question was, was Dean available to make a real commitment to her, or was he not? And the answer to this question could not be determined by a phone call in which she said, "Come over now and get into bed with me."

So Harrie had put down the receiver and very deliberately taken off her clothes and her makeup and put on her nightgown, and brushed her teeth and flossed, and watched the eleven o'clock news, including the sports and the weather. And when it was too late to call, she called.

Dean's voice was hollow and dull. "God, I'm glad to hear your voice," he'd said. He wanted to see her. He was going on a business trip the next day, and he wanted to see her before he left. "I have a busy day tomorrow," she lied, her heart palpitating. But Dean pressed her. His flight left at half past one, he said, and could he drop by for just a while so they could talk? Would she please see him at eleven? Even as she agreed to see him she worried. Would she be so vulnerable to him that she would give in to him no matter what the terms, just to be back in his arms?

It was ten after eleven when the intercom shrilled and the doorman announced that Dean was standing in the lobby. "Send him up," Harrie said.

⊡

Dean was wet and he was queasy. He was nervous enough without having a wild man cabdriver who drove with the vengeance of a teenager playing carnival bumper car. By mistake, he'd gotten out of the cab at a red light three blocks away from Harrie's building, and was now standing in the lobby of a lovely prewar building, cold, dripping wet, a suitcase under one arm, a bushel of roses in the other, undergoing the scrutiny of a former cop–type doorman. All the while, his mind was rehearsing abject apologies. *I've been a cretin. I'm the lowest of the low. I miss you so much that if you don't forgive me, I'm going straight from here to the river and jump in.* He could only come up with worn-out, comic book clichés. What if nothing he said got through to her?

"You can go up," the doorman said, watching Dean skeptically as though at any moment he might drop his suitcase, part the roses, and reveal an assault rifle. Dean approached the elevator, and with difficulty pressed the button that would take him to Harrie's floor.

⊡

Harrie opened the door. Dean was standing in the hallway, hair wet, coat wet, nearly hidden by roses. "Hi," he said, handing the entire bundle to her. There were red roses, and white ones, yellow, peach, and lavender ones. Harrie had never seen so many roses in one armload.

"They're beautiful," she said, her voice crimped by the vise around her throat. She stepped back into the room and let Dean into her apartment.

"I hoped you'd like them." She was beautiful, beautiful. Please, God, give me a hand.

"I love them. I wonder if I have a vase. I wonder if I have about a dozen vases." Harrie dipped her face into the intense floral mass, then blinked at Dean. "Come in," she said.

"I know they're a little excessive. Buy a hundred, get a hundred free. What the heck." Dean followed Harrie as she took the armload to the kitchen. She filled up the sink, stuck the flowers in, took a vase out of the overhead cabinet and put a double handful of flowers in it.

"I'll get to the rest of them after you leave."

"Uh-huh," Dean said, the idea of leaving causing his chest to constrict. Wait, he wanted to say. I haven't even taken off my coat. Give me a chance. "You look beautiful." The pronouncement was so heartfelt it sounded like a plea or a revelation.

"Thanks," said Harrie. "Give me your coat. You're soaking wet." Why was he so wet? She wanted to ask but her voice was shaking. And that simply would not do.

Dean shrugged off his coat and stood in the kitchen doorway where he could watch Harrie go back out to the foyer and get a hanger from the hallway closet. She hung the coat on the hanger and held it in front of her. "I'll hang this in the shower. Do you want a towel for your hair? Leave your shoes in the kitchen and I'll get you some clean socks."

"I don't need a towel," he said, his voice plumping up and rounding out. You didn't give clean socks to someone you hated. You didn't offer him a towel for his hair. She still cared. Dean kicked off his shoes and pushed them neatly against the wall under the window. He peeled off his socks and put them over the radiator. He made all of these things look very neat. Beyond reproach.

Harrie reappeared with a roll of socks which she handed to Dean. "How about some tea?"

"Okay. If you're having some." He sat on a kitchen chair and self-consciously put the socks on over his white and wrinkled feet.

Harrie turned her back. How polite, she thought. They could be strangers on a first date if it were not for the microscopic awareness she had of his every word and gesture. His dear wrinkled toes. The way he pointed them when he put on his socks. Those features, those gestures she knew so well. She wanted to stop everything, freeze the picture and stare at Dean. She wanted to get a good look at his hair, which was longer than it had been when they'd seen each other last. And she wanted to take off his glasses, which were the kind everyone was wearing now, and try them on herself. She wanted to absorb these new things and add them to her total knowledge of Dean. But Dean hadn't made these changes by himself. He'd gotten help from a woman. Had Laura redesigned his look? Or had it been someone else? She'd like to ask him. Put him on the spot. Instead, she put the kettle on the stove with a bang and turned on the gas.

Dean shifted his weight and leaned against the counter. He was entirely at a loss for words. Everything he said was so simpleminded and so trite. He wanted to ask questions he knew he had no right to ask. Like, who was the guy? Do you love him? Does he live here? He wished someone would step out of the closet and coach him, tell him how he was supposed to talk to Harrie when she was acting like he was a guy she'd just met and had found herself alone with by some quirky, and not altogether pleasant, accident.

"Do you have a car coming to pick you up?" Harrie asked.

Again she was talking about him leaving. Tell me to stay, he urged her silently. I'll cancel the whole fucking trip. "Uh-huh, but not for a while. God, it's great to see you," he blurted.

Harrie smiled. She was relaxing in direct proportion to how uncomfortable Dean seemed. "You look good too. I like your hair."

"Yeah. Thanks." He stroked it back. "I just can't seem to do a thing with it in this weather."

Harrie laughed. "Herbal or breakfast?"

"Hmm?"

"Herbal or breakfast tea. I've got the loose English kind." Harrie flipped off the gas and removed the kettle before it whistled.

"Anything'll be fine. How long have you been living here?"

"About four months. Since June."

"It's very nice. It's very you. D'you live here alone?"

"Want to get some cups out?"

"It killed me last night to see you with another guy."

"In the cabinet over your head."

"I thought he was going to kill me, but I didn't care." And he was bigger than me, did you notice? Are you in love with the guy, or what? He's too old for you, don't you think? He has to be fifty.

"Are you hungry? I've got some cookies."

"Okay. I don't know. No, I'll eat on the plane, I guess."

Harrie dropped tea bags into the hot water, waited a moment, then removed them. "Sugar or honey?"

"I like it when you call me honey."

Harrie didn't reply. She spooned honey into the mugs. She lifted the large vase of flowers. "I hope peppermint's okay. Let's go into the living room. Can you get the mugs?"

Dean looped forefingers into the mug handles and followed Harrie out of the room. Dork, dork, dork. He was blowing it. What if he took her into his arms and just kissed her? What if she rejected him if he did that? "I'm sorry if I put you on the spot like that last night, but I had to do what I had to do."

Harrie put the roses on the coffee table, let Dean choose to sit on the sofa, then settled herself into a chair next to him. "I already felt like an idiot without any help from you. I was standing ankle deep in white wine. I don't know if you noticed."

"Harrie. I miss you so much. I've been so miserable."

"I'm glad."

Dean nodded. What else could he expect? He looked down at his hands. Kissing her wouldn't have worked. She would have pushed him away, like a dinghy from the mother ship. It would have been ugly and he wouldn't have been able to recover. He imagined himself standing in the lobby with the sergeant, waiting for his car, his tail between his legs.

"I sold Blackfern, you know."

"I didn't know."

"I thought Chip would tell you."

"He doesn't tell me anything about you."

"Oh. That's probably a good idea."

"Did you do okay? On selling the house?"

"Not so well, but the funny thing is, I don't care. I've got more money than I ever expected to have. I kept the cottage and I have the house right here. In my head." Harrie sipped her tea. Dean had cost her more than anything she could lose on a real estate deal. What was money compared with losing the love of her life? Did she still feel that way about Dean?

Harrie kicked off her shoes and tucked her legs up until she was nestled into the down cushions of the big chair. She leaned her head back. Every part of this apartment pleased her. The high ceilings, the plaster walls, and the parquet floors. She loved the many windows that looked out onto the park, and the huge closets and the wonderful kitchen. She loved the furnishings, too. Roger wouldn't have gone along with the eclectic mix of styles she had arrived at: part stuff that had been ordered for Blackfern, part Tuckman heirlooms, part new things she'd bought whenever she saw something in a store that she liked. One of the new things was a long mahogany dining table, which fit like a dream in her dining room. Just like a dream. And she loved having three bedrooms—room enough for Julie and Alan to spend a weekend, or her mom and dad, or both couples at the same time.

When she bought the apartment, she'd considered the possibility she'd be married someday, and if so, this apartment would easily house a child, a husband, and a nanny. But it was a general kind of fantasy, the kind that could also accommodate selling the apartment, moving into a man's apartment, or living here and never having children at all. She'd planned this apartment, and in fact her future, without allowing for any part of Dean. Was that why she felt so removed from him right now? Had she healed up? Were her other disjointed emotions simply the nervous effect of what had happened the last times they'd seen each other? That made sense. Chicken with the head cut off. Looking at Dean now, she couldn't find anything to be afraid of. He looked smaller to her than he'd looked when she had been with him. And he seemed so indecisive. Why didn't he say something? Do something? She was beginning to find his presence intrusive. Or maybe she was starting to get mad.

Dean stirred in the sofa. "You must have quite a view."

"Dean, what is it you want to tell me?"

Dean looked across the short distance from the sofa to the chair. Harrie had bent to the coffee table to pick up her mug and his eyes followed the line from her nape to the crown of her head that he loved, that he once felt belonged to him. She was so close to him that he could, just by stretching out a finger, touch the soft curve of her cheek, yet she was as far away from him this minute as if she were on the moon. "Harrie," he said softly. "Would you look at me?"

"I *am* looking at you," she said. She flicked a glance at him, then turned her eyes to the mug she held in her lap.

Dean got up from the sofa and knelt beside Harrie's chair. "Give this to me," he said. He gently pried the mug out of her hands and set it safely aside. Then he took her two hands in his and held them. "Come sit with me."

Harrie balked as Dean stood and tugged at her hands. And then she stood, bowing to the scarcely acknowledged part of her that wanted him to take charge, take possession of her. Dean led her to the sofa and the two sat together stiffly. Harrie was pressed up against the arm of the sofa and Dean was sitting right beside her. He picked up one of her hands and held it in his. He said, "I know you still hate me, but please give me a chance to explain. I screwed up and I know it. Believe me, I know it. I don't even know what I was thinking back whenever. It seems like years ago."

"February," Harrie said.

Dean nodded.

"We were going to take a month off."

"Please, Harrie. If I could undo what I've done, I would, but maybe I had to make some mistakes so I could figure things out. And I have figured things out. I'm not quite the same asshole you used to know." Dean waited for a laugh, a smile, a small sign, but Harrie just looked at him warily. He sighed. "It all sounds so trite, goddamnit, but I can't make up better words. I was afraid of so many things. I can't even remember what they were now, and I'm truly, truly sorry for what I've said and done to you. I want you back. I really do, Harrie. All I want in the world is to be with you. I want to marry you."

Harrie thought for a moment as she savored the words she'd wanted so passionately to hear from this man. She called up a picture of a wedding, but she couldn't see the face of the bride— As if she'd heard a shot, Harrie straightened her back and snatched her hand away. It wasn't working for her. She wanted it to work, but Dean's words were calling up all the old pain, and with it, anger. Two and a half years of ambivalence couldn't be dispelled with an hour of damp pleading. Did he really think he could buy some roses and she'd drop everything and come back to him? "Where'd you tie up your stupid horse, huh?"

"What? What horse?"

"What makes you think you can charge in here, say you're sorry, and get me back? Why should I believe you? How do I know you're not going to change your mind again? I've got my life under control, you know. I'm taking good care of myself." Inexplicably, giving the lie to all she'd just said, her voice quavered.

"Harrie." Dean reached for her arm.

Harrie shook him off. Then she stared at Dean's bewildered expression. Of course he was bewildered. He'd just said the words she'd once been dying to hear, and instead of covering him with kisses, she'd barked at him. Her voice, when it came out, was raspy and dry. "It's been a hard seven months," she said. "I don't think I believe in fairy tales anymore."

Dean took Harrie's hand again and looked at the watch that hadn't been a ring, and then he pressed her hand gently between his two. "Maybe I do. Maybe I believe in them." Dean put his arm around Harrie and pulled her ever so gently toward him. "I love you," he said. "I know we could be happy together."

Harrie tried but couldn't relax against Dean. He felt more a stranger to her than a lover. She'd put so much of herself into getting over him, perhaps she'd succeeded. Did she still love him? Did getting over the pain necessarily mean she didn't love him anymore? She suspected that somewhere under her anger she did still love him, but her anger was churning. And her anger seemed crucial to her ability to stand, to walk a straight line, to hold on to herself. Harrie crossed her arms over her chest and pulled away so she could look at Dean. "I don't know how I feel about you anymore," she said.

Dean nodded. "I know. I'm just wondering how to let you know it's okay to trust me." He clasped his hands together and leaned over his knees. Constellations of words, all inadequate, formed and dissolved. Could he tell Harrie about Laura? Could he tell her how the right woman had turned out to be the wrong woman? Could he tell Harrie how he understood now that he'd wanted the woman in his life to make up for all the things he wasn't—and how crazy that all seemed to him now? Would she believe him if he told her how he'd grown through the experience of losing her, and that he never wanted to be without her again? Would she understand that he'd truly changed? Probably not. Harrie was right. It was too much to dump on her at once. How could she believe that he'd changed unless he could prove it to her? And he couldn't prove it to her unless he spent time with her, and he couldn't do that if he got on a plane and flew away.

A buzzer sounded. The intercom.

"Are you expecting someone?" Dean asked.

"No." She stood and went toward the foyer.

"Shit," he said softly, almost to himself. He looked at his watch. "Then it's my car."

"It's your car," she replied. "He'll be right down," she said into the instrument.

Dean went to the kitchen, put on his socks and shoes, then returned to the foyer where Harrie was standing, arms tightly crossing her chest. He wanted to unclasp her arms, put them around himself. "I don't want to leave like this," he said. He reached out a cautious arm and touched Harrie's shoulder. He felt her relax to his touch, and so he reached out the other arm and gently brought her to him.

Harrie looked up at Dean's face. Behind the trendy glasses, Dean's eyes were blue, plain blue, not sapphire, and she noticed another thing. His hair was thinning. She could see pink scalp showing below the comb marks in his slicked-back hair. And then there was his expression. Dean was . . . scared. He looked human size, and in that moment, something inside Harrie that had been unbalanced shifted and became level. For the first time since she and Dean had met, she felt free to join him—and just as free to let him go.

⊡

Dean pulled Harrie more tightly into his arms. He rubbed her back and pressed his face to her neck and felt the entire softness of her against him. She was warm and the scent of rose came to him and with it memories of watching Harrie bunch up her hair, spearing it in place with a chopstick, and wash her face with that fragrant English soap she used. And he could imagine her in a long white nightgown, rubbing his shoulders, taking the tension from him, somehow getting him to tell her all of the things that he wanted to keep from himself, and how telling her those painful things would make them lighter. He thought about how Harrie saw things just a little differently than other people did. And he thought about how having his life without Harrie was just having a life, and how when she had been in it, even when he'd been frightened of everything that had meant, she'd added a joyfulness, a brightness, that just wasn't there when he was without her. Dean held the woman he loved in his arms and wondered how he'd thought he would be able to leave her. He couldn't imagine it now.

·

As Dean held his body against hers Harrie felt something inside her let go. She touched his throat with her lips, and the feel of his skin called up a hundred nights when she'd lain beside him and felt nothing for him but love. She remembered him rubbing her toes, and pouring bubble bath into her tub, and sitting there in the bathroom with her while she bathed, telling her how much he loved to look at her. She remembered him cooking in her tiny kitchen, both of them, and eating salads because she thought he didn't eat enough vegetables. She remembered him sitting up half the night listening to her describe plots from romance novels, and she remembered him driving out on weekends to Blackfern when he didn't want to be there at all. She remembered him stuffing newspaper in her wet shoes, and she remembered him comforting her family when a wedding hadn't happened. And she remembered the fights, and the rosy rims of his ears, and the lovemaking, two halves of the same person becoming one.

And Harrie remembered the first time she'd met Dean; she'd been standing at a party, wolfing down taco chips, wondering if she'd ever be in love, when Dean had come straight through the crowd as though he'd been pulled to her by a cord. She remembered how he'd claimed her. And how he'd done the same last night even though Ben had been standing there, huge and angry. She thought of how he'd tried to protect her money and how she'd tried to change the course of his life, whether or not he'd wanted to change it. She remembered a promise her mother had made, and the prediction of a woman in a shoe store, and the anguish she'd felt at the knowledge that he had been with another woman. And now, despite all they'd been through in the last months, Dean was standing in her apartment, telling her he loved her, and that he wanted her to be his wife.

Harrie took slow breaths—she and Dean were breathing to the same rhythm—and she knew that her love for Dean was the sum of the ways they knew each other, was about how *well* they'd known each other. She longed to feel that well known, that well loved again. As long as she had the choice, then maybe she could choose to be with Dean. Was it possible that even without promises and prophecies and pots of money at the end of the rainbow, she and Dean could have ordinary human happiness?

⊡

The buzzer rang again and a rough voice said that the driver was concerned about the traffic to the airport. Tentatively, Dean touched a curl with his hand; then, fitting his hand around the curve of Harrie's head, he brought her face to his and he kissed her. The first kiss was warm and sweet. The second was dedicated to their memories. Harrie pulled back from the passion of the third. She felt suddenly skittish, a wild animal trapped in a room. What if she gave herself over to him and he left her again?

"I have an idea," said Dean. "Come with me."

"What did you say?" Harrie was panting. Everything was sensation: the sound of the rain, the buzzer, the blurred look on Dean's face, the heat that was suffusing hers.

"Come with me. I'm on my way to D.C. I'm giving a talk at Georgetown tonight. It's career week and I'll be meeting some kids on Monday, but we'll have plenty of time together over the weekend."

"Washington?"

"We'll get separate rooms. I don't want to rush you. I want to do the opposite of that. I want to prove myself to you. And to do that, I need to have time with you."

Harrie pressed her hands against Dean's chest. Her fingers stroked the stitching on his shirt as if those tiny broken lines were a coded message that held the answer to her question: Now that she could choose, could she take a chance? She took in a sharp breath. "Your raincoat," she said. "You almost forgot your raincoat." She broke away from Dean and headed down the hallway.

⊡

Dean stood and watched Harrie walk away from him. She wasn't going to do it, but she'd felt something, he was sure of it, and although he felt the certainty of loss, he also felt shining and clean. He'd fought for her. He'd fought hard. He stooped to heft his suitcase. He refused to feel dumb or defeated. He would try again. He would call her tonight from the hotel. And he would keep calling her. He heard Harrie's footsteps on the wood floor. He turned to face her.

Harrie was holding Dean's raincoat over her right arm and another over her left. A small, soft-sided carryall was slung over one shoulder. "I'll take the shuttle back tomorrow night," she said. "I've got a meeting on Monday morning, first thing."

"What? What did you say?" Dean burned with hope.

Harrie handed the raincoat to Dean, then opened the bolt to her front door. "I'm ready," she said.

"What a coincidence," he said, giving her a smile that could light a city. "I'm ready too."